SHADOW TREE

SHADOW TREE

THE THIRD BOOK OF DORMIA

JAKE HALPERN
AND
PETER KUJAWINSKI

[SHADOW TREE]
© 2013 Jake Halpern and Peter Kujawinski

Inquiries concerning rights should be addressed to:

William Morris Endeavor Entertainment, LLC
1325 Avenue of the Americas
New York, New York 10019
Attn: Kathleen Nishimoto

ISBN-13: 978-1492211204

Chapter One
World's End

Alfonso Perplexon opened his eyes and winced as criss-crossing beams of sunlight flashed across his face. His back and legs felt cold. It soon dawned on him that he was lying in the snow, on his back, looking directly up at a canopy of trees overhead. The trees were massive, sturdy, and ancient-looking. They were Great Obitteroos. There was no doubt about it. Alfonso exhaled deeply and, as he did, he let days, weeks, and months of tension seep out of his body. He had been picturing this moment for so long. At long last, he was home in Minnesota. Just then, Alfonso felt someone – or something – squeeze his fingers. He turned his head and saw a girl lying next to him in the snow; she had blonde hair, fine cheekbones, and two eyes that twinkled almost incandescently.

"Resuza?" asked Alfonso, half in disbelief.

"He speaks!" said Resuza giddily. She seemed unusually happy that Alfonso had spoken – so happy that she leaned over and energetically kissed his cheek. "I was beginning to wonder if you'd ever talk again," she said. "Your father said it would take time, and I've tried to be so patient, really I have."

"I am… I mean we are…" stammered Alfonso.

"Back home," said Resuza, as she sat up in the snow. "*Your* home. I never thought we'd get here – you really do live on the other side of the world, you know? No wonder you call this place World's End."

Resuza sprang to her feet in one fluid movement, and Alfonso was reminded of her grace. Other memories of Resuza flickered through his brain – Resuza hiding in the darkened alleyways of Brash-yin-Binder, Resuza swimming by moonlight in his uncle's pool in Somnos, and Resuza holding his hand at the Hub in the dank gloom of the Fault Roads. She always moved so swiftly and with such poise and, even in the darkest of situations, she would flash that quick, electrifying smile of hers. He had last seen her at the gate leading into the labyrinth, just outside of Jasber. *That was how long ago exactly?* He had no way of knowing. More disturbingly, he had no memory at all of how he had gotten home. The last thing he could recall was being inside the burning armory in Jasber, running for his life, with a bag of green ash tucked under his arm, and then falling to the ground.

"I was in some sort of coma, wasn't I?" asked Alfonso finally.

"No kidding," said Resuza as she stepped on his toes, reached down, grabbed his hands, and pulled him to his feet. And like that, he was standing so close to Resuza that their noses were practically touching. "It was scary," said Resuza quietly. "Everyone was awfully worried. But then you sat up and began walking around."

Alfonso nodded. He was about to ask another question, but a sudden uneasiness passed over him. Alfonso glanced around and saw that the floor of the forest was alive with movement. There were hundreds and perhaps thousands of small creatures – rabbits, squirrels, chipmunks, raccoons, opossums, mice, shrews, and even a few foxes – racing underfoot. Resuza screamed. The animals parted around them and then flowed past as if they were two rocks in the middle of a mighty river. When the wave of small animals had passed there was a brief moment of stillness; then, in the distance came the sound of branches snapping. A second wave of animals appeared to be headed their way.

"Come on," said Resuza. "We have to hurry."

Alfonso and Resuza ran quickly through the forest of the Great Obitteroos, weaving their way between the massive tree trunks. All the while, they could hear the sound of a stampede behind them. At some point, everything began to shake – several trees toppled, a giant boulder began to roll, and the earth dropped downward creating a sinkhole just to the left of where Alfonso and Resuza were running. Alfonso stopped for a moment and took a good, long look down into the sink hole. The shape of the hole looked weirdly familiar. It had six perfectly even sides, like a hexagon.

Where had he seen such a hole before?

"Come on!" yelled Resuza.

They sprinted onward, hand in hand. Eventually, they emerged from the forest and into a great open field that sloped down gently toward the icy expanse of Lake Witekkon. In the middle of the field was an old deer stand – a rickety tree-house on four stilts – which their neighbor, Old Man Edlund, sometimes used as a hunting perch. A hundred yards or so beyond this was Pappy's greenhouse and the small ramshackle cottage that was Alfonso's home. They ran for the cottage, but about halfway there, Alfonso stole a glance backwards and saw a blurry herd of animals closing in. They would never make it to the cottage, but they might make it to the deer stand.

Alfonso squeezed Resuza's hand and tugged her toward the deer stand. They arrived at the deer stand and scrambled up the rickety ladder just as the first wave of animals thundered past. There were deer, wolves, moose, and black bears. Alfonso and Resuza held onto one another in fright. The tree stand shook mightily and, on more than one occasion, Alfonso felt certain an animal would slam into one of the stand's rickety supports and topple the entire structure. Amazingly, this didn't happen. When the last animal sprinted past, there was a brief spell of calm, and Resuza spoke.

"It's like a forest fire," she said, "Only without the fire."

"Huh?"

"When I was a girl, growing up in the Urals, I went hunting with my father once and we saw a massive forest fire," she explained. "Before the flames arrived, all the animals poured out of the forest just like that..."

Their conversation was interrupted by the sound of someone shouting.

"ALFONSO! RESUZA!"

Alfonso and Resuza both turned and saw the figure of Judy Perplexon standing in the doorway of the cottage, motioning frantically for them to come inside.

"Come on," said Alfonso. "We better go."

They scurried down the ladder, ran across the field and bolted into the cottage. As soon as they entered the cottage, Judy closed the door and locked it securely. The first thing that Alfonso noticed was his father Leif, who was sitting at the kitchen table with his head in his hands. He looked very distraught. "I'm such a fool," he was mumbling to himself, as he raked his hands through his hair. "A blasted fool."

"*Dad!*" yelled Alfonso. Something about the way his father looked frightened him to the bone.

"I thought we'd be safe here," said Leif without even looking up. "I should have known – it was all written out so clearly."

"Safe from what?" asked Alfonso. "What is it?"

Before anyone could answer, however, the entire cottage started to shake. Judy began to scream. Leif remained at the kitchen table, muttering to himself. Alfonso looked around frantically and saw, to both his astonishment and relief, that Resuza looked perfectly calm. He walked over to her. His mother's favorite vase fell to the floor and exploded into a thousand pieces. Resuza grabbed him.

"Listen carefully," she said. She was speaking loudly. The cottage was collapsing from the inside. Everything not nailed down fell and burst like shattered windows.

"You'll need me, before it's all over. And Bilblox as well."

The ceiling began to cave in, starting with a shower of dust and fist-sized chunks of stone.

"But most of all, you'll need-"

She stopped and looked up.

"Who will I need most?" Alfonso asked. "Who? WHO?!"

Resuza screamed as a massive wooden timber dislodged from the ceiling and headed towards them.

"Wake up Alfonso!" she yelled. "Do it *now!*"

Alfonso was overcome by a feeling of weightlessness, as if he were rising upwards from a great depth. He felt disoriented and sick. Most of all, he was terrified of what he was about to see.

Chapter Two
Sunlight

The girl plodded up the side of a mountain. Her legs trembled with each step. A large backpack hung from her back, filled to overflowing with supplies for a long journey. She had been hiking for the better part of a week – eating dried fish and sleeping in snow caves – and she was exhausted. She did not look like a hero, even though that is exactly what everyone in her hometown of Jasber thought her to be.

Marta could have transformed herself physically into an adult. Despite the fact that she was just nine years old, Marta was a Seer of Jasber, which meant she had been allowed to rub some of the green ash into her eyes. Upon doing this, Marta entered a year-long coma. When she returned to consciousness, she emerged as an ageling, which meant she now had the ability to transform so that one minute she could be a toddler and the next she could be an old lady or an able-bodied young woman in her mid-twenties. Although Marta had gotten quite good at shifting, it was mentally trying to do so. That was too risky. She would need all her wits about her in the coming days.

The mountain that Marta was climbing was jagged and quite high and the peak disappeared into the clouds. Marta looked up at the sky and hoped for a small glint of sunlight. The sun rarely made an appearance at the Sea of Clouds or any of the mountains that surrounded it. The sea was aptly named, given that it was perpetually shrouded in fog and mist.

Marta's goal was to see the sun. This was slightly problematic because Marta had never actually seen the sun before and so she was afraid she'd miss it. Of course, she had seen pictures and drawings of the sun, but she had spent virtually her entire life in Jasber – a city that existed underground, beneath a lake – and so she never had an opportunity to see the sky let alone the sun. Her only hope of doing so was to press onward, ascending one of the nearby peeks, which pierced the clouds and presumably was exposed to the rays of the sun.

After climbing for several hours, Marta stopped to catch her breath. She placed her pack on the ground very gently, as if the contents were extraordinarily fragile. She reached into her coat pocket and took out a piece of dried fish which she nibbled on sparingly. A minute later, she reached into her other pocket and pulled out a tightly rolled piece of canvas that she proceeded to study closely. On the canvas was a painting of a woman, sleepwalking along a narrow ledge on the side of a magnificent stone building, the walls of which were painted iridescent silver. In the background were mountains and a darkened night sky.

The painting had been a gift. It was given to Marta by the Abbot of the monastery where she had lived after being selected as seer. The name of the painting was "Roya's Dream" and it had been painted by a Jasberinian seer named Roya. Roya was an extraordinary young woman – both a poet, a beauty, and an athlete – and the city rejoiced when she was chosen to become its seer. When it came time for Roya to assume her duties as seer, the abbot of the monastery gave her a pinch of green ash to rub into her eyes, as the ancient tradition required. The abbot, however, was quite old and almost blind as well – it was said the he could not recognize his own reflection in the mirror – and he inadvertently gave Roya too much ash. Roya went into a deep coma from which she never recovered; indeed, she spent the rest of her days sitting idly in a chair, staring off into space. From time to time, she would talk in her sleep and beg to be brought to the window at once. She was most passionate about this request and the monks would always carry her over to nearest window as quickly as they could. Once, just once, she asked for a canvass and brush and on this occasion she produced the painting that Marta was studying.

"What a fine image," remarked a monk, when Roya had completed it.

"It's all I ever dream of," replied Roya quietly.

The monk was startled to hear Roya speak. It had been years since she had last uttered a word.

"It's a… very… lovely…" stammered the monk. "What is it?"

"It's a doorway," hissed Roya, desperately.

"No my dear," replied the monk, trying very hard to keep his calm, "You've painted a window."

"No you fool!" screamed Roya, "This is a doorway!"

"Yes fine," said the monk, whose voice was now trembling. "As you say – it is a doorway."

"Please," begged Roya, "You must take me here or I shall never wake up. It is my *wyjście*."

This was all that Marta knew about the painting for, unfortunately, this was all the Abbot had been able to tell her. "The truth is," explained the Abbot sadly, "We know very little about what happens to people when they rub too much ash into their eyes. They need sunlight – that much is certain. The rays of the sun seem to draw the toxins from their blood. That is how they kept Roya alive. Once a year, they took her up to the surface. But we never managed to get her any direct sunlight. It is simply too overcast in the Sea of Clouds. To get proper sunlight you must go all the way to the foothills of the Urals." Marta asked the Abbot what the word *wyjście* meant. "It's an ancient word meaning an exit. It seems that Roya had it in her head that this place – from her painting – was her way out of her coma. Gibberish, most likely. The girl had plainly gone mad."

Marta studied the painting for some time. She wasn't exactly certain why she had bothered to take it with her; as it was, she had brought too much. It was the Abbot who had insisted that she bring it along. He didn't like the idea of her leaving Jasber. "The whole city of Jasber has nearly just burned to the ground and our vault has been robbed," lamented the Abbot. "This is no time for our seer to be traipsing off into the wilderness."

Truth be told, Marta wasn't even certain that she wanted to be a seer any longer. She missed her family – her parents and her two brothers, Lukos and Danyel. She pictured her younger brother, Danyel, whose hair always stood on-end like the fine quills of a porcupine. He used to catch baby toads, place them in his mouth, and then pretend to vomit them up at the dinner table. The toads would hop away in every which direction. It was disgusting, but less so through memory's haze.

Fortunately, her entire family had all survived the fire that destroyed their townhouse and which had ravaged much of Jasber. This was all thanks to Alfonso, who had levitated into the air, and rescued them one-by-one. But what would her mom and dad do now – with no home? Where would they live? What would they eat? Marta could have stayed and tried to help them, but she didn't. She had left them all to fend for themselves. The thought of this made her feel very low, but she had made up her mind, and no one – not even the Abbot of Jasber – could dissuade her.

After some time, Marta placed her pipe back into her pocket and then rolled up the painting and placed it back into her coat as well. She then turned her attention to her backpack. She opened the top flap of the pack and there, nestled safely inside amidst a profusion of downy blankets, was her most important cargo: a newborn baby.

"Don't worry baby Alfonso," said Marta softly, "We'll find you some sunlight soon enough." She smiled. "Now that we're above ground, you're looking better already."

The baby's eyelids fluttered and he yawned tiredly. Alfonso was waking up.

CHAPTER THREE
KIRIL'S DECISION

About a dozen miles away, an ordinary rowboat glided through the icy waters of the Sea of Clouds. Two men sat in the boat, but only one of them rowed. This man was blind, and the second man in the bow was staring at his blind companion with a mixture of concern and contemplation. Thanks to the blind man, the rowboat had become a vessel capable of speed and grace. The man's thickly muscled arms maneuvered the boat skillfully and the boat sang as it pushed through the water. Despite his obvious skill, however, the blind man's face was a mask of sullen resignation; clearly he was in the boat against his will.

Sitting at the rowboat's bow, Kiril stared at the blind man and wondered again why he had saved his life so impulsively. He could find only one reason: instinct. It was the instinct of someone who had lived many centuries, and who had seen all manner of what humans could do to each other, and this very instinct told him that Bilblox, the blind longshoreman, might be useful in the future. After all, wasn't he proving his worth at this very moment? They had made it across the terrifying Sea of Clouds in record time, and even though Kiril was at the peak of his strength and ability, there was no way he could have matched Bilblox's easy mastery of the rowboat.

Kiril glanced up and scanned the horizon. Land was close – just a few hundred yards off the starboard bow. Good. They were making excellent time. Kiril returned his attention to a scrap of paper on which he was currently scrawling a brief note. He wrote hastily. As soon as he finished writing, Kiril leaned forward and removed his right boot. He fidgeted with the heel of his boot for a moment, until it came loose, revealing a hollowed-out space that served as a secret compartment. From this compartment he pulled out a silver ring that bulged in the middle with a fat ruby. He squeezed the ruby on two sides and simultaneously pushed down on the face. The ruby turned out to be false – it opened to reveal a small opening, just big enough for the note that he had written. He placed the note inside, snapped the ruby closed and placed the ring deep in his inside coat pocket. Kiril then returned his gaze to the coast. There was a pebble beach just ahead; it was a perfect place to land.

Bilblox could feel the water change as they approached the shore. The waves rose up to engulf them and abruptly died away in the shallows. Then the hull of the boat grated against the bottom. He looked up.

"Excellent work," Kiril said in a conversational tone. "Rowing across the Sea of Clouds can be terrible, but it didn't seem to affect you. Of course, we didn't have much ice to contend with – that helped."

The rowboat came to rest in knee-high water. Kiril easily leapt out of the boat, gripped it from the bow, and pushed it high onto the pebbly, ice-encrusted beach. He looked around. It was absolute wilderness – a shoreline of rocks slick with ice, driftwood and pockets of tidal algae, stunted trees rising up from the sea, and everywhere a covering of gray-white snow.

Bilblox just sat there.

"Let's go," said Kiril, his tone more demanding than before. "We have a long journey ahead of us."

Us. Kiril's casual use of that word startled Bilblox and reminded him of the strange journey he had begun ever since Kiril had saved him in the river surrounding Jasber.

"You can go to whatever hell is drawing you, but you're going alone," replied Bilblox finally.

Kiril noiselessly drew a curved dagger from its scabbard around his waist. It was a masterpiece of metal-working. Ancient hieroglyphs ran up and down the blade, and the mother-of-pearl handle shone like bleached bone. Kiril had stolen it from the armory in Jasber. He had taken it from that monk, the one that pleaded with him to take anything – anything at all – as long as he left behind the Jasber ash.

"And you're just going to plod on by yourself – totally blind?" asked Kiril. "No, no, no, that won't do – and we both know it."

For a moment, Kiril grew silent. However, Bilblox's hearing was excellent and he could discern the sound of Kiril returning the knife to its scabbard, and then fidgeting with his belt, unfastening a hook on a pouch or a pocket, grabbing something with his fingers, rubbing his hands together and sighing deeply. This whole episode lasted no more than five or ten seconds. It was a ritual of sorts, one that Kiril had performed once before while they were out on the Sea of Clouds.

"Feel better?' asked Bilblox.

"Much better," said Kiril, though his voice revealed just the slightest hint of surprise – as if he hadn't thought Bilblox had any idea what he was up to. But Bilblox knew. He had guessed correctly that Kiril was using the legendary green ash from the Founding Tree of Jasber.

"I'm not going with you," Bilblox declared sullenly.

In three or four steps, Kiril was at Bilblox's side. The Jasberian dagger rested on Bilblox's neck.

"Just going to let me walk away then?" asked Kiril jauntily. "Strange. I never saw you as the sort of chap to give up and die alone in the wild – blind and bitter – but then again you aren't the same man you once were."

"You never knew me," growled Bilblox.

Kiril felt a sudden urge to slide the blade across Bilblox's throat and be done with it. After all, it made no sense to keep Bilblox around. It was like keeping a wild tiger chained to a tree in your backyard – sooner or later the tiger will attack.

Kiril pressed the point of the dagger at an area of Bilblox's cheek just below the ear, and paused. He stared at Bilblox's hands. They were trembling, and what's more, thick beads of sweat had begun to form on his neck. This wasn't fear of the blade. It was something much more powerful. Suddenly he realized the man was in the awful pain of withdrawal. His body was craving the Ash. Seeing this gave Kiril pause. Perhaps Bilblox could be broken. This thought appealed to Kiril for a number of reasons. Kiril slid the dagger back into its holder and began unloading the rowboat. Within minutes, he had built a small fire on the beach and had begun to make tea.

Just as the tea kettle had begun to whistle and Kiril searched for some wild mint, he saw something that caught his attention. It was a gray bird with three dark green feathers on its tail. Kiril did not recognize the breed. It wasn't ideal, a bit too small – an eagle would have been ideal – but this one would do. Kiril crept up to the bird from behind and in a blur of motion, grabbed it by clasping its wings together.

"Easy now my little friend," whispered Kiril. The bird was struggling mightily, using all of its strength to thrash about and peck at Kiril, but it could not escape his grip. Kiril used his other hand to reach into his coat pocket and pull out the silver ring with the false ruby. This time, he pressed directly on the ruby without squeezing the sides. The ring sprang open into two semi-circles. Kiril snapped the ring around the bird's foot. Still holding the bird securely, he took a small black handkerchief from his jacket pocket and placed it upon the bird's head. Instantly, the bird, which had been struggling, became calm and focused.

Kiril drew close and whispered, "To Dargora." His warm breath caused tiny water droplets to appear on the handkerchief. The bird trembled, but remained calm. Kiril opened his arm and removed the handkerchief. For a few seconds, the bird sat quietly on Kiril's open palm. When Kiril began lowering his arm, the bird flew up in a steep climb. Within a minute, it had disappeared from sight.

Kiril returned his attention to finding wild mint that he knew was growing nearby. He discovered it a few minutes later. This pleased him – it had been a very long day.

As he later sipped his tea, Kiril stared at Bilblox, who was sitting in the boat. The longshoreman had not moved since their arrival on shore.

"How bad is your headache?" Kiril asked.

"Bad enough," muttered Bilblox.

"You can stay shivering in that boat for as long as you'd like," Kiril said. "However, I'm not leaving quite yet and as you can tell, I've made a fire. Come closer and have some tea."

For several minutes, Bilblox sat in the boat. He began to rub his temples vigorously and every few seconds, he sucked in his breath.

Sitting on a piece of driftwood, Kiril stared at the blind longshoreman. He was experiencing yet another of his headaches, brought on by his refusal to take any of the ash he had first experienced on his maiden trip to Somnos. For non-Dormians, taking the ash was a remarkably intense experience, but thereafter, the non-Dormian was doomed to a lifetime of increasingly powerful headaches. It had likely been at least a year, maybe two, since Bilblox had last taken the powder, and his headaches would likely be quite powerful.

The shuddering in Bilblox's hands moved into the rest of his body, and he appeared to be having a seizure. Kiril walked to the boat and lifted Bilblox out with only a minimum of effort. He placed him on the pebbly shore beside the fire and held his head in his hands, like a concerned father with a sickly child. Feverish sweat trickled down from Bilblox's head. The man was in serious pain.

"It's all right," whispered Kiril. "I can help you. I have ash from Jasber. It's better than the kind you've had before. I took some myself and as you can tell, I've never felt stronger." He paused and drew nearer to Bilblox's ear. "You'll be in a better position to help everyone – especially yourself."

Bilblox shook his head and silently mouthed a determined "no."

Kiril tried another tactic. "Are you sure you don't want to know what happened to Alfonso? I'll tell you, once you've joined me in taking the ash." He could tell this had an effect, even though Bilblox tried to ignore him.

Kiril reached into his overcoat and withdrew a cut glass vial from an inner pocket. The Jasber Ash inside seemed to leap up as if alive. Kiril carefully pried open the glass stopper.

"Take the ash," he whispered again. "Take it, and the pain goes away."

Bilblox closed his eyes and clamped his mouth shut. He turned away from Kiril's voice and tried to remain motionless, but the tremors in his body continued.

"I won't force you," said Kiril at last. "If you wish to die here, blind and alone, I won't stop you. I'm giving you a chance for real life again – with vision. Nothing is predetermined; there is no rule that says we must be enemies forever." His voice was calm and friendly and despite his hatred of the man, Bilblox felt drawn to that voice. The old rasp of elderly vocal cords had disappeared after Kiril had ingested the powder. He was young again, and Bilblox knew it could be the same for him.

They faced each other in silence. The wind off the Sea of Clouds was louder and colder than Kiril remembered. He shivered and saw he had two, maybe three hours of daylight left. He sighed. So be it. If Bilblox wanted to stay here and die, that was his decision. Instinct would only carry Kiril so far, and then reason kicked in.

"I'm leaving," Kiril announced. "And if you don't want to die tonight, you'll come with me."

Bilblox slumped in a heap, his body trembling. He said nothing, but knew that if Kiril left him now he would die. However, what upset him more was the thought that, once again, Kiril was getting away. Bilblox knew that Kiril had plans for the ash that he was carrying. Prior to arriving in Jasber, Bilblox and Alfonso had painstakingly pieced together a number of clues and deciphered Kiril's plan. Kiril was, they believed, intent on bringing the ash back to Dargora to help grow a Coe-Nyetz Tree or a Shadow Tree as it was also known. According to legend, this was a powerful and deeply evil tree whose roots killed everything for thousands of miles in all directions. The other remarkable thing about this tree was that – unlike a Founding Tree – if burned, it would regenerate. This meant that it could, in theory, produce an endless supply of ash. This is why Kiril and the Dragoonya wanted it. Bilblox and Alfonso had tried to stop Kiril from getting his hands on it. They had chased him down the Fault Roads, across the Sea of Clouds, through a labyrinth, and into Jasber itself; but, in the end, they had failed.

Bilblox wished that he had his vision back. If he could see, even for a few minutes, then he might have a chance of fighting Kiril, besting him, and taking the ash. As a blind man, however, Bilblox didn't stand a chance. He had already lunged at Kiril several times in the boat and Kiril had easily eluded him and then wrestled him into submission. What else could he do? He had to do something.

"Wait," yelled Bilblox. "Wait!"

But it was too late. Kiril had already left. With a heaving sigh of exhaustion, Bilblox stumbled towards the rapidly dying fire. He groaned from the vise-like pain of his headache and stretched out next to the fire, hoping for unconsciousness. He had lost. It was over.

Several hours later, Kiril passed through a forest of spindly pine trees. Their brittle branches covered in snow, the trees looked gaunt and terrified, and many appeared dead. He was breathing hard, after climbing steadily up since leaving Bilblox behind on the shore of the Sea of Clouds. Kiril wondered whether the longshoreman was dead, and at that moment, he felt a sudden dizziness envelop him.

It was happening – again.

The dizziness grew worse. Ten seconds later, he was sprawled on the ground. He knew that he was about to have another series of hallucinations. This strange phenomenon had just started happening. As far as he could tell, these hallucinations always occurred within a few hours of him using the ash from Jasber. Some of the visions were from his childhood – images of himself sitting in his mother's lap or of splashing about in the water with his older brother; but sometimes, the images were of him sitting or walking in some unknown place, and Kiril suspected that these were glimpses of the future.

By now, Kiril knew better than to fight what was happening. Instead, he lay in the snow, staring at the tattered branches and one by one, visions invaded his mind.

"So beautiful," he rasped, as he saw an image of his mother's face basked in the warm light of a candle. Other visions soon followed – one of his father chopping wood, another of his grandmother playing chess, and yet another of himself digging a shelter in the snow. Where was that last one from? The past? The future? Impossible to say. All together, the visions were a collection of smeared snapshots, some bizarre, others quite normal. There was a tropical scene – perhaps in ancient Travancore or Tenochtitlan – filled with trees and wildlife and tangled creeper vines. Kiril also had a brief glimpse of Nartam, stroking his face affectionately.

The final vision was of a very slender, shy girl standing on the edge of an abyss. He recognized her at once. It was *the girl* – the one he had taken in and cared for. Kiril would not go so far as to say that she was *his child*. They were not related. Nothing connected them officially, although he quietly dreamt of a future where they would be reunited. Kiril had saved the girl, brought her in from the cold, much the way that Nartam had once done for him – the only difference being that Kiril wanted and expected nothing from the girl. He simply liked the way that she sighed after drinking a cup of warm milk. He liked the peaceful look on her face when she slept and a sliver of moonlight illuminated her face. The girl lived in Dargora, where Kiril lived, but he had not been home in years. Would she be waiting for him? Would she be angry with him for being away for so long? Had anyone looked out for her? Was she even still alive? In the vision, the girl looked older than he remember her. She must be alive, thought Kiril. This had to be a glimpse of the future. Kiril had no way of knowing this for sure, but he felt it must be true.

The vision of the girl lasted longer than the others; and the final sequence of the vision was electrifying. The girl was dressed in furs and standing on a snow-covered platform, which jutted out over the edge of an old wooden sailing ship. Snow swirled about in the wind. The girl ran forward. She appeared to be rushing to help a large man who was wounded and lay on his stomach. As the girl ran to help the wounded man, a hand reached out and shoved her. Kiril could not see whose hand this was. Whoever it was stayed hidden in the shadows. The hand itself had blood on it – and an open-wound along the wrist that was in the peculiar shape of a crescent moon. The girl lurched forward, toppling into the abyss. Yet at the very last moment, the large wounded man – who had been lying on the ground, on his stomach – grabbed the girl's ankle and tried to pull her back to safety. The dream ended before it became clear whether or not the large man succeeded in saving her. The large man never turned around and Kiril never saw his face; but it didn't matter. Kiril recognized the man at once by his shape and size.

It was Bilblox.

Kiril's eyes flickered open. His head ached, his limbs tingled, and a metallic taste lingered in his mouth. He sat up, fighting off a feeling of dizziness. He took a breath, gathered his focus, and rose to his feet. A minute later, he was running back through the snow, retracing his own footsteps, racing back to the Sea of Clouds. If he was lucky, he'd reach Bilblox before the longshoreman froze to death.

CHAPTER FOUR

SHIPWRECKED

Leif Perplexon arrived on the shores of the Sea of Clouds almost two weeks after Kiril and Bilblox. This particular morning, he awoke with an aching jaw from sleeping too long on a rock. It was just minutes after dawn and the world around him was bathed in a gentle, murky light. He stood up, blinked his eyes, and surveyed his surroundings. To his left and right was a rocky shore, occupied by a smoldering campfire and the remains of a badly damaged rowboat. Directly in front of Leif was a forest comprised of enormous trees whose bark was as black as coal and whose leaves – despite the fact that it was mid-winter – were a fiery red. And behind Leif, as far as the eye could see, was a vast expanse of freezing-cold water; this was the Sea of Clouds, a ferocious body of water, nestled high in the Ural Mountains. The sea's currents, fog, and ice were legendary for destroying boats and marooning sailors. In fact, this is precisely how Leif had ended up on this godforsaken beach. He had been shipwrecked here, almost two weeks ago, and once again he found himself in a dire situation – cold, starving, and alone.

Well, not entirely alone.

Just on the other side of the destroyed rowboat lay the crumpled figure of a man who was resting under his heavy, green wool cloak. Leif knew very little about the man because he had not yet introduced himself or spoken a word of conversation. Most hours of the day, the man tended to the campfire and mumbled to himself incomprehensibly as if perhaps he were mad. At times it sounded as if the man was reciting a stanza from a poem, or perhaps an old ballad. Again and again he repeated the words, "Oh what a day to behold, when the truth is finally told." Or at least, that's what it sounded like. The rest of the time, the man was buried under his cloak, lying perfectly still. Once or twice Leif thought that perhaps the man had died; and, on these occasions, ever so gently, Leif nudged the man's cloak to see if he was okay. Then the man would stir and begin again with his muttering.

Leif did have one dependable companion – a female companion – and currently she was bounding down the beach, in a blur of motion, howling with delight. "How can you be so happy?" asked Leif incredulously. She howled again and then nuzzled her nose into Leif's hands. "Come here Kõrgu," he said. "You truly are a crazy wolf." Leif regarded the wolf affectionately. She was enormous and her fur was brilliantly white. Leif felt very fond of her – not only because she had saved him from drowning – but also because each new day, no matter how grim the circumstances were, she played friskily in the surf, as if perhaps they were simply on an extended vacation at the beach.

Kõrgu nudged Leif behind the knees, as if to goad him forward, and then she tore off toward the woods. Leif followed wearily. When he caught up to Kõrgu, at the edge of the woods, he found her yelping excitedly. "What is it girl?" asked Leif, as he strained his eyes to look into the shadowy depths of the forest. Truth be told, something about the woods made him very uneasy. If pressed on the matter, he would be unable to say what *exactly* he found so unnerving. There were no signs of any animals or birds – in fact, it was the most silent woods he had ever seen – and this was part of what spooked Leif. The place was deathly still.

Kōrgu yelped again and, finally, Leif saw what had gotten her so excited. Just a short distance into the woods, no more than fifty yards away, a rich beam of sunlight illuminated a perfect cluster blackberry bushes.

"You want the berries?" inquired Leif. "Is that it?"

Kōrgu merely panted, tongue lolling out of her mouth.

"They would be tasty," admitted Leif.

He could think of no good reason why he shouldn't just dash into the woods and gather some berries. The last food he'd had, other than some seaweed, was a small crab that he had managed to catch and cook over the fire. That was almost two days ago. And there was another consideration as well. Initially, Leif's plan had been to repair the old rowboat and make his escape from this place by sea; but, within the last day or so, he had come to grips with the realization that the boat was damaged beyond repair. Leif would have to leave this place soon and, when he did, it would have to be through the forest.

Leif sighed, crammed his hands into his pockets, and took his first step into the forests.

"The third law," said a voice from behind him. "What about the third law?"

Leif was so surprised by the sound of the voice that he instantly leapt backwards out of the woods and spun around in one quick, fluid movement. What he saw was the man, standing just a few feet away, wrapped tightly in his heavy, green wool cloak.

"You best not enter the woods until I can remember what I have unfortunately forgotten," said the man. He had a small shriveled face, covered with white stubble, a bulbous nose, and a set of crooked yellowish teeth. "I've been racking my brain for days but, I can't remember the third law."

"The third law?" inquired Leif.

"Yes," replied the man matter-of-factly. "There are three laws governing Straszydlo Forest. We were told to memorize them in school, but I only remember two of them now."

"What are the two that you remember?"

"Well," said the man thoughtfully, "You must enter just one person per day and, of course, you mustn't enter at night. That much I am sure of. But there is something else, something about where to look or where not to look, but for the life of me, I can't remember the particulars."

"And what happens if you break the rules?" asked Leif.

The man shuddered involuntarily, but made no reply.

"Well it would be great if you could remember," said Leif hopefully. "I think sooner or later we will need to cross these woods."

"Yes, indeed," said the man, "Perhaps if I see that other fellow I will ask him and in the meantime I shall mull this over..." Then the man began to mumble to himself again.

"What did you just say?" asked Leif.

"Oh what a day to behold, when the truth is finally told," muttered the man.

"You just said something about the 'other fellow,'" said Leif with exasperation. "What did you mean?"

"I was talking about the other fellow that's here on the beach with us," snapped the man irritably. "The boy."

The mention of "the boy" briefly filled Leif was a soaring sense of hope. Leif pressed the man for almost an hour, begging and then demanding that the man tell him more. "What boy?" shouted Leif. "What did he look like? Where is he? Speak to me!" But the man he retreated inward and was again merely muttering and repeating the same cryptic piece of verse. Leif was filled with despair and finally, in frustration, he bellowed at the top of his lungs: "Alfonso! Alfonso! Alfonso! Are you here?"

But there was no reply. Throughout that day, and through much of the following night, Leif did his best to engage the man with the green cloak – to get him to say anything at all about who the boy was. Once the man looked and said sharply, "I will tell you what I know, but first I must remember the third law, so please be quiet now so I can think." The man said nothing else and Leif was left alone with his thoughts.

Leif ached for his son. He had spent years stranded in a cottage in the middle of a vast labyrinth, dreaming of his family, yearning for the day when he would be reunited with his only child. Then, miraculously, it had happened. Alfonso had shown up with his two friends – Bilblox and Marta – and their wolf, Kõrgu. Together they had all traveled down the darkened tunnel that led to Jasber only to discover that the city was in flames. After that, much of what happened was a blur. Leif and Alfonso were separated as the city descended into chaos. Buildings were on fire, children were screaming, smoke was everywhere. And there was a bridge. Yes, the bridge he remembered with vivid clarity! Leif, Bilblox, and Kõrgu had ended up on a bridge that had collapsed and fallen into the water.

Leif remembered thinking that he was going to drown. He was too weak to swim; his head slipped under the water; and that's when Kõrgu saved him for the first time. The wolf had used her teeth gently and taking hold of Leif's shirt collar, she swam with him until they were rescued by a man in a small rowboat, the same man who was now shipwrecked on the beach with them.

"Get in the boat before you drown!" the man had yelled. Leif and Kõrgu struggled into the boat and, moments later, the tiny vessel was whisked into a whirlpool that sucked them downward into a underground river and out into the Sea of Clouds.

Since all of this had transpired, Leif had done little else but think of his son. Was he still in Jasber, or elsewhere? How would Leif find him? Was he even alive? As the days passed, Leif felt increasingly desperate. Then the man with the green cloak had mentioned that there was a boy on the beach with them. Leif had seen no traces of anyone else, but deep down, he felt that this boy had to be Alfonso – that he too had been sucked down the whirlpool and out into the Sea of Clouds – and it was just a matter of time before he showed up.

The following morning, Leif awoke and found the man with the green cloak in high spirits. He stood by the edge of the woods, pacing back and forth muttering excitedly, "Yes, of course that's it, why did it elude me for so long?"

"Have you remembered the third law?" asked Leif.

"Yes, yes, yes, I have," replied the man giddily.

"What is it?"

"Just this morning it came to me," said the man. "It came to me and I said to myself, 'Yes, of course, it is: *You must never look backwards*. But then, thank heaven, I realized that was not quite right – not at all. The rule was, I am of certain of it now, as follows: *You must only look backwards*. A bizarre rule, it is, but one that must be followed zealously!"

"What is your plan?" asked Leif.

"I will leave through the woods tomorrow at dawn," said the man eagerly, "And then I will be done with this wretched beach. I cannot wait to be off of it."

"If you are so eager to depart," asked Leif, "Why leave tomorrow and not today?"

"Because only one person per day may enter the woods," said the man testily. "Have you learned nothing from me?"

"I don't understand," said Leif, "Who has entered today?"

"Why the boy has," replied the man matter-of-factly, "He departed at first light."

The man with the green cloak then pointed toward the edge of woods and there, in the moist topsoil, were a set of footsteps leading into the woods.

The following morning, shortly after dawn, the man with the green cloak set off into the woods by himself. He walked backwards, so that he never once looked forward, as he said he would do. The man seemed well - even merry - and he waved once at Leif before he disappeared from view.

CHAPTER FIVE
TO BE AN AGELING

Within a minute of waking up, Alfonso was in the middle of a panic attack. After his incredibly vivid dream, the blackness he had woken up to felt comforting. However, he soon realized that the blackness was not temporary and instead he was in a place without any light. He also felt stuck, as if his arms, legs and entire body were pinned. He struggled to move, but his muscles refused to obey his brain's instructions. He tried to cry out, but the blackness swallowed any sound. He struggled again and again, and wondered in despair whether he was having any effect.

And then a blinding cascade of sunlight poured upon him. A massive face peered down and a fat, enormous finger stroked his forehead. The person smiled, but Alfonso's vision was too blurry to notice any distinguishing features. Only that the person was a giant. Alfonso tried to release his arms but he still could not control his muscles. His arms squirmed and wiggled spastically. More disturbingly, Alfonso found that try as he might, he could only hold up his head for a minute. All of the muscles in his neck – and indeed his upper spine itself – seemed to have turned into jelly. Something was very wrong with his body. He tried furiously to remember what had happened.

"Come on little guy," said a voice from above. "I've managed to find exactly what you need – a bit of sunlight. Look at that! You're already out of the coma."

Alfonso recognized the voice, but he could not recall exactly whose it was. Moments later, two large hands reached down and picked him up, hoisting him out of the backpack – in which he had been sleeping – and up into the cool air of day. The sun was shining and it was very bright. Alfonso blinked furiously, but his vision remained blurry.

"I would say that you are about two months old," said the voice. "Gosh, I hate being that age. You can't see anything, you can't control your muscles, and you pee on yourself all the time. Still, its better than being a hundred and ten – I've done that too – and believe me it's not fun."

Marta.

It was Marta talking. Alfonso was certain of it; and she was talking about being an ageling. Suddenly everything was starting to make sense. This is precisely what Alfonso had become – an ageling. The last memory he could recall was of being in Jasber, running through the burning remains of the monastery, with a bag of green ash tucked under his arm. Then he had tripped, fallen, and gotten a great deal of that ash into his eyes. This must have transformed into an ageling and now, apparently, he was a newborn baby. This was, to say the very least, a serious downer. He'd have to relearn how to walk, talk, and use the bathroom.

Alfonso tried to talk, but instead he merely burped.

"Take it easy," said Marta. "First thing's first, you need sunlight - the Abbot says that's the only thing that will make you feel better." Very tenderly, Marta set baby Alfonso down on a blanket that she had laid across the ground. Alfonso squirmed for a moment and then he closed his eyes and relaxed.

As baby Alfonso rested on the blanket, Marta looked around with some small measure of satisfaction and admired what she had been able to do. She had made it to the foothills of the Urals – largely on her own. The Abbot had escorted Marta and Alfonso for part of the way. He and several of his monks led them out of Jasber, through the maze of razor hedges, and across the Sea of Clouds in a boat. Before they could all set out for the foothills of the Urals, however, the Abbot fell ill with a high fever and the other monks all agreed that he needed to be taken back to Jasber at once. Marta insisted on continuing onward by herself. Alfonso had taken on the form of a baby and Marta declared that she would simply carry him herself.

"You both may die," warned the Abbot weakly. He was covered with sweat and shaking. "You mustn't do this!" he warned. Marta didn't waver. She explained that Alfonso had saved her entire family and, at the very least, she owed it to him to try and get him better. "So be it," said the Abbot with a sigh of frustration, "You always were a stubborn child." He then removed a gold chain from his neck. It had a small, circular Pendant on it, embedded with several emeralds. He handed the chain and Pendant to Marta. "When you are ready to come home," said the monk, "Build a fire and place the Pendant in the coals. Within a few days time, we will find you."

Before parting ways, one of the monks grabbed her firmly by the shoulder. He was a big man and very muscular. His name was Michael Papa and, before serving as a monk, he had been one of the "sweepers" who patrolled the labyrinth that surrounded the entrance to Jasber. In fact, he had been one of the so-called "Rogue Sweepers" – one of the very few who were, occasionally, allowed to leave the labyrinth and roam the landscape beyond. It was Michael who had navigated their boat across the Sea of Clouds. "Listen to me and remember this," Michael said as he pulled Marta close. "Avoid anyone you see – especially the children."

"The children?"

"Yes," said Michael. "The slave traders have captured so many of the adults in this region that hoards of children roam the hills – and they are wild and as fierce as wolves. They may call for help, but ignore them, or they'll quickly tear you to pieces."

Marta blanched, but said nothing.

"Good luck," said Michael.

After parting with the Abbot and the monks, Marta had walked for several days through a pouring rain. Both she and Alfonso got drenched to the bone. Alfonso's health appeared to worsen by the hour. He grew pale and sickly looking. His soft, wet skin glimmered like the moon as Marta held him close to her chest. He shivered constantly. Marta knew she should've been holed up in a cave or even an overhang to keep them both dry, but she had a long ways to go and she didn't want to take too long to find sunlight. According to the Abbot and the monks, it would be seven or eight days of steady walking before they reached the foot-hills; and so Marta pressed on without resting and the days quickly blended together.

Marta got her first sense that she was being followed just after dawn one morning. She had been cutting across a steep slope, heading north towards what appeared to be a distant area of rolling hills. She had no idea who lived in these hills, but they were green and therefore, they almost certainly received some sunlight. Marta was traversing this steep slope when, some distance behind her, she heard the sound of someone losing their footing. She whirled around and saw someone hurtling down the mountain in a cloud of dirt and rocks. Whoever it was had been following in her footsteps. For several minutes, she stood and listened. Silence. Nothing more.

For several hours afterwards, Marta occasionally thought she heard something and, in each case, she whirled around but saw nothing. She hoped it was fatigue or weakness brought on by so many days of ceaseless walking. But deep down she knew there was something back there, just out of her line of sight. *Perhaps it's just an animal that is following me,* thought Marta. *Maybe a dog or perhaps a coyote.*

The following day she neared her destination. Marta knew she had entered the hill country because the ground had short stubbly grass that cut into her ankles. Just beyond this, Marta saw the beginning of scrubland; short bushes tightly bound together, made of gnarled wood and woven together with tiny branches. She pressed onward, slowly climbing upward, and after a few hours of climbing – rather miraculously – the clouds parted and sunlight poured down from the heavens. She almost wept with relief.

With the sun out and shining, Marta's fear retreated. What's more, she saw no signs of any living soul around her. Marta set Alfonso down on the blanket and rested. At some point, she even gathered up some small kindling and started a fire to cook some potatoes that the monks had given her. She knew it was probably unwise to build a fire, but the thought of cooked potatoes overrode her sense of caution. She built a fire and ate. Then she lay down. An hour passed and then two more. The sky became a spotless blue.

As baby Alfonso lay on his back, on the blanket, he began to feel better. The warm rays of the sun bathed his body in heat. It felt so good. He lay there for a very long while, though it was impossible to say exactly how long. Ever so slowly, the deep cold in his bones began to diminish. He started to feel sensations in his toes and fingertips. Even his vision became less blurry. He relaxed, drifting in and out of sleep. At some point, he woke to the sound of Marta's voice.

"Alfonso," she said. "Can you hear me? Wiggle your feet if you can hear me."

Alfonso mustered his concentration, willed his body to do as he told it, and succeeded in wiggling both of his feet at once.

"Good," she said. "You look much better and I want to see if you can morph. You're an ageling now. You're like me. And you've got learn how to morph. It's not easy. It took me a while to figure it out, but I will try to help you, okay?"

Alfonso wiggled his feet again.

"Okay, good," said Marta. "Let's start with morphing back into your true age because that's the easiest one to do. It's hard to explain, but it's kind of like your body actually wants to be it's true age, but when you are tired, or scared, or sick, you often end up becoming a baby or a really old person. So the trick is to picture the last memory of yourself right before you became an ageling. Can you do that?"

Again, baby Alfonso moved his toes and his feet to indicate yes.

"Okay, good," said Marta cheerfully. "Now your memory needs a cue for this to work properly. For me, smell usually works best – onions and garlic, actually. The Abbot had onions on his breath when he gave me the green ash. Anyway, for you – you were in that burning building just before you became an ageling, right? And there must have been an awful lot of smoke." Marta then scooped Alfonso up and moved him close to the remains of the campfire that she had built. A few of the coals were still smoking. "Use the smell of the smoke," said Marta. "Really breathe it in and focus on the smell."

"Come on," urged Marta, this time in a whisper. "Smell the smoke. You're in the burning building again, picture yourself running through it, you just tripped and scraped your hands – go back to that moment! You're not a baby, you're a..."

Suddenly Alfonso's body began to change – the baby fat shrunk from his legs and arms, his torso stretched like taffy, his legs grew long and muscular, his hair turned darker and thicker, and his face grew long and narrow. Marta gaped as she watched Alfonso's jawbone triple in size in the span of five seconds. It was incredible – and more than a little spooky. She herself had morphed countless times, but she'd never witnessed anyone else do it. Alfonso lay gasping and shivering on the ground, covered only by a thin blanket. Marta took Alfonso's jacket from the pack and threw it on him.

"Don't move," Marta whispered into his ear, "You must lie perfectly still or your body will morph back."

She leaned close to him and stared into his eyes to keep him centered. Alfonso looked confused and panicked. Marta felt the same way, and struggled to keep her emotions in check. *Please let this work, please let this work, please let this work,* she repeated over and over.

CHAPTER SIX
VISION RETURNS

At first, Bilblox was only aware of a deep ache in his back, as if someone had pounded on it many times. But that feeling quickly gave way to something much nicer, the feeling of sun on his face. He wondered whether he was dead, especially because when he opened his eyes, he could see the sparkling blue sky. If this was heaven, he was already enjoying it – after all, he could finally see again.

But if he was in heaven, why was he now staring at Kiril's face? Bilblox's head felt muddled and cobwebbed.

"Welcome back," Kiril said. At first his voice sounded distant but then it became stronger.

Bilblox said nothing. Gradually, he made out where he was: on a makeshift sled of lashed together pine branches and none other than Kiril was pulling him. They were in a snowy ravine surrounded by spindly pine trees, and the early morning sky shone a bluish-purple. Of course, all these details affected Bilblox in an intense way, because it was the first time he could see anything for over a year; and that meant, he realized, that Kiril had forced him to take the ash. A split-second later, he realized it meant he was strong again.

His initial impulse was to leap off the sled and attack Kiril but he knew he needed to get a better sense of his capabilities. Plus, Kiril was watching carefully. "Feeling a little better now?" Kiril inquired.

Bilblox peered at Kiril through half-opened sensitive eyes. His mind struggled to keep up with the enormous amount of information conveyed by being able to see. Despite his situation, Bilblox felt like leaping up from the sled and running around like a joy-filled child. It was one of the happiest moments of his life. He could *see*.

Although he tried to contain his happiness given how he had received his sight, it was all too obvious.

Kiril smiled at Bilblox. "I can't quite imagine how you feel, since I've never been blind," he said. "However, I can greatly sympathize, given how sick and old I had been feeling before taking the Jasber ash."

This also was quite obvious. Kiril's stature and appearance were that of a man in the prime of his life. He had the look of a panther coiled into the body of a man. Everything about him – the way he leaned over with his hand on Bilblox's shoulder, his easy stance in the snowdrift, and the way he effortlessly kept the sled moving – everything pointed to a man at the peak of his physical and mental skills. Even the scar that once marred his face – twisting along his jaw like a snake – had miraculously disappeared.

Kiril stopped pulling the sled and Bilblox slowly rose to his feet. The two adversaries stood facing each other in the ravine. The wind had died down and the forest was quiet. Bilblox took stock of his situation. Overall, he felt good. The ache in his hands and shoulders from rowing across the Sea of Clouds had disappeared, and there was no trace of the unbearable headaches. The skin on his face felt taut and smooth, and deep inside he sensed the presence of strength he thought he had lost decades ago. He realized that in his whole life, he had never felt better.

"Why did you give me the ash?" Bilblox rasped. His voice sounded hoarse and raw, as if worn out by screaming.

"You should be thanking me for saving your life," Kiril replied. "I found you unconscious at the beach, and your pulse was erratic. You had at most a half hour before you froze to death."

"Why?" Bilblox repeated, his elation giving way to anger. "Why did you save me?" He tensed his entire body, ready to leap at Kiril at a moment's notice.

"We can spend the next hour destroying each other," said Kiril in a conversational tone. "But I think you'll find we're evenly matched, given that we've both just taken the Ash. And in fact, I may be a little bit stronger, given that I'm of Dormian origin. Still, I won't stop you from trying to escape. Go ahead. You'll suffer and then starve to death in a few days."

Bilblox stared at Kiril. There was a reason his enemy had saved him, first in the waters near Jasber and then as he lay dying on the beach. But why?

"I won't betray anyone," said Bilblox. "You must've already figured that out."

Kiril nodded with his head to one side – calm, relaxed, unruffled by his wild surroundings – like an 18th century nobleman on a gentlemanly expedition.

Bilblox kept staring at Kiril. Finally, he broke the stare and looked into the forest. The image was so beautiful that tears filled his eyes and ran down his face.

"You should've let me die," Bilblox said. "I've never hated being able to see as much as I do at this moment."

"There's plenty of time to die," Kiril softly replied. "But let's get through this forest, and then we'll talk about what happens next."

Kiril picked up his carrying bag, dropped the reins of the makeshift sled and began walking up the path. Bilblox watched him. His brain ached from a swirl of confusion, shame and excitement. Obviously Kiril had plans for him, but after all, why did this have to be a one-way street? Bilblox was not passive, nor was he any longer blind. He was a Magrewski longshoreman at the peak of his strength, and he could have plans too. Perhaps that was the best option: go along and see where Kiril was taking them. And then strike at the right time. What was it that people always said about revenge – ah, yes, it was a dish best served cold.

Bilblox permitted himself a smile, his first in many days. He walked quickly to catch up to Kiril.

Although he walked quickly, almost a trot, it took Bilblox several minutes to reach Kiril. The Dragoonya leader walked effortlessly through the snow-filled forest, as if walking on a paved sidewalk. Kiril heard Bilblox pushing through the snowdrifts behind him, and he slowed down.

"Now you're being reasonable," said Kiril. "I won't deny we're enemies, but in these circumstances it just makes sense to work together, doesn't it?"

Bilblox said nothing, although Kiril took this as agreement.

"What happened to your scar?" asked Bilblox. "It's gone."

"Thanks to the green ash," replied Kiril. "I rubbed a little ash into the scar and it healed. You too will be healed my friend. Good things will happen if you only trust me." Kiril stopped suddenly and turned in his tracks and once again, they were face to face. He smiled – startling Bilblox – and stuck out his hand.

"We'll stick together," suggested Kiril, as he extended his hand. "At least until we make it through this forest."

Bilblox nodded slowly and extended his hand as well.

Several hours later, as afternoon swiftly turned to evening, Kiril and Bilblox sat around a lively fire. It dispelled the gloom surrounding them and its warmth loosened their tongues. Kiril spoke about his journey along the Fault Roads, as the prisoner of Colonel Treeknot and Josephus. Bilblox was wary, but it all seemed perfectly ordinary. Never once did Kiril ask about Alfonso or what happened in Jasber. But then, the conversation did turn and Bilblox found himself trapped, not knowing whether to speak or remain silent, whether to run or just bury his head in shame.

Kiril had been speaking about old times – his role leading the Dragoonya sneak attack on Somnos. And then he brought up Alfonso's name for the first time.

"It was quite a weapon your friend had," Kiril remarked. "That sphere turned the battle around."

Bilblox nodded, suddenly aware he was on dangerous ground.

"I've often wondered where he found it. You certainly can't find that type of thing in World's End, Minnesota. No – that was something he found closer to Somnos, right?"

Kiril looked at Bilblox and it was clear he was fishing for information. Bilblox grunted, but made no reply.

"We Dragoonya will have to keep a sharp eye out for him," said Kiril in a soft voice. "A Great Sleeper with that type of weapon is rare heaped upon rare. And he is by far the greatest threat we have." Kiril looked at Bilblox. "Of course you know that, and don't worry, I'm not expecting you to tell me where he is. But in fairness, you should realize it's rather important for me to find Alfonso's weapon. We'll hunt him down." Kiril paused, stoked the fire, and then added softly: "And I'll pry it from his cold, dead fingers, if necessary."

"You're fools then," said Bilblox angrily, "He doesn't-"

Bilblox stopped. His cheeks turned red. He had walked right into Kiril's trap.

"He doesn't…what?" asked Kiril. He stared deep into Bilblox's eyes.

"Ah, I see," said Kiril. "He doesn't have the sphere any more. Well, that's interesting indeed. I wonder who does?"

Bilblox bit his lower lip. Kiril was a snake, a master of seeing through people. He wished he were back in the boat, waiting to die, instead of sitting here next to the warm fire and feeling this man bore into his deepest thoughts.

"Who has it?" Kiril wondered. "He wouldn't give it to just anyone. Hill, of course, but that's not Hill's style." He stopped abruptly, stood up and looked into the inky darkness just beyond the fire.

When he turned back, Kiril was smiling. "Of course," he said. "Of course he gave it to the girl – that's precisely the sort of sentimental, ill-advised thing he would do." He glanced at Bilblox and knew the first battle was over and he had won.

"That's very interesting information you've given me," Kiril said. "Now I wonder where she is?"

CHAPTER SEVEN
STAYING ALIVE

For many months, Resuza had woken and gone to sleep in the same way: in the darkness, surrounded by the dank odors of her unwashed neighbors, to the sound of a bass drum being pounded. The sound never failed to startle her, especially because it was more of a physical kick than a noise. The Dragoonya would choose a slave at random for the task, and everyone knew that if the drumming wasn't fast or powerful enough, the slave would have to face the *Goon-ya-radt* – the guards who were once prisoners themselves. One might think that these guards would be friendlier or more sympathetic, because they understood what it meant to suffer as prisoners, but in fact the opposite was true; they tended to be crueler than the Dragoonya. This was, in part, because the Drangoonya picked the angriest, meanest, and most twisted prisoners to lead the *Goon-ya-radt.* The group's leader was a man named Ure, whose face was horribly disfigured by a severe case of frostbite, which had withered his nose and turned his skin into what resembled a rotting piece of fruit. If and when a slave failed to beat the drum properly, it was Ure who handled the matter. He liked to force slaves into the snow, until they either froze to death or returned to the barracks looking like Ure. Once, when a little girl was chosen to beat the drum – and failed – Ure punished her simply by making her kiss his face. In Resuza's opinion, this might have been the worst punishment at all.

The drums were played twice each day – once early each morning, to wake everyone, and again at midnight to signal the start of the five hours or so in which they were allowed to sleep. Tonight, thankfully, the drumming continued for a full minute. The slave was strong, aided in his task by the fear of death. When the drumming finally slowed down and stopped, Resuza could still feel her pulse racing. She folded her arms in between her legs and tried to steady the trembling in her limbs.

There was a violent cough from below her.

"Hill?" she whispered. "Are you okay?"

No answer.

"HILL?!" she whispered louder.

A low, weak groan floated up to her. "I'm okay," he mumbled softly. "I'm just a bit short of breath."

Hill coughed again. Resuza was terribly worried about him. He had been coughing more or less constantly for weeks now and she was worried that he had the sickness known as consumption, which had claimed the lives of so many slaves.

"I'm fine," wheezed Hill.

Resuza was lying on a tiny upper bunk in the Dargora slave quarters, right above Hill Persplexy – Alfonso's uncle and only a year ago, a member of Somnos high society as its newly-appointed Foreign Minister. All of that, especially the mansion where they lived, now seemed like a cruel dream. Sometimes it seemed like a miracle that they were even alive at all. After they were captured by the slave traders, the journey to Dargora took a month. The days blended together as their caravan trundled across the steppes and into "the land of frozen earth" – what the slave traders called the permafrost tundra. The slaves' cages were exposed to the wind, snow and rain. Several of the older and weaker ones died along the way, and Resuza often woke up yelling from nightmares. Strangely, the nightmares all focused on one simple fact – namely, that she couldn't remember the names of those who had died.

Resuza recalled very little of her arrival in Dargora. She was too exhausted and famished to think properly. One of her only memories of the city's landscape was of a series of giant pillars that rose up from the ground and disappeared into the clouds above. The pillars were gigantic – so wide across that if you chiseled a tunnel through the base of one of them, a large elephant could easily walk through the tunnel. At first, Resuza thought the pillars were made of rocks – like giant chimneys made of stone and mortar – but when she took a closer look she saw the pillars were actually made of bones and skulls. "Those are slaves' bones," one old slave woman told her, who was helping unload the slaves. "One day, they'll add yours to the collection." The woman said this as if it were an undisputable fact, as if there weren't even the faintest hope of escape, and her certainty was both terrifying and profoundly depressing.

As soon as they were unloaded from the cages, the slaves were brought to a vast series of underground cellars, carved from the frozen dirt and rock. These cellars, which were connected by a maze of tunnels, were known as the slave quarters and it was expected that all the slaves would live out the rest of their lives there. The slaves spent their time hauling coal and boiling whale blubber in giant copper vats and turning it into oil which the Dragoonya used to burn in their heaters and their lamps. Resuza tended to the vats of blubber, which was disgusting, but not too taxing physically. Hill had a much more punishing job. He worked with the ovens. His job was to unload carts filled with coal and shovel this fuel into a series of giant ovens. Each oven was situated at the base of one of the giant pillars. The pillars, as it happens, were hollowed out – and this allowed the heat from the coal-fires to rise up through them the way that smoke and heat rises up through a chimney. No one knew where the heat went, since no one was allowed out of the slave quarters to look. And new slaves were always brought in during the night.

Upon her arrival, Resuza was hopeful that she might find her long-lost younger sister, Naomi. She looked everywhere for Naomi, hoping against hope that she might have survived such a long captivity in Dargora; but she saw no one that even bore a resemblance to her younger sister. Dargora was a terrible place for children, and there were very few in the slave quarters. At a certain point several months in, Resuza realized that she had stopped looking. She had given up. Now, even to think of her sister put Resuza in a dark mood. Naomi had been captured many years ago and she would have arrived here as a child. The chances that she survived were very slim. Resuza had slowly accepted the fact that her sister was almost certainly dead. The only hope that remained was that, somehow, she and Hill could escape.

Despite their very bleak prospects, Resuza and Hill did occasionally discuss how they might make it out of Dargora. It wasn't just wishful thinking. They had one possession that gave them hope; it was the Foreseeing Pen, the five-inch metal cylinder they had found hidden inside Alfonso's sphere. Alfonso had pried the sphere from a statue within Straszydlo Forest, and the sphere had quickly become Alfonso's weapon of choice. In fact, it proved crucial in winning the battle of Somnos. Alfonso had given the sphere to

Resuza right before entering Jasber, so she could protect herself and Hill. It seemed like years had passed since that moment, but in reality it had only been a few months.

The Pen represented escape, but it also was a clear reminder that Alfonso and Bilblox would be on the hunt for them. And one way or the other – via the Pen or with the help of Alfonso and Bilblox – they'd escape. They clung to that hope.

As for the Pen itself, they knew very little about it. Hill had played with it just a few times. Once, shortly after they were captured, Hill had unscrewed the top of the Pen and lit the inside of the barrel with a flame – much the way one might light a gas burner with a match. On that occasion, he then pressed the emerald button on top of the Pen, which caused a stream of fire to shoot out of the Pen's tip. The Pen was, clearly, a potent weapon – if one knew how to wield it properly. The problem was that, despite a great deal of effort, Hill still didn't know how to use it to his advantage, and there was really no place where he could experiment with it. In fact, Hill worried constantly about being discovered with it and he was obsessed with hiding the Pen properly. Using scraps of discarded leather, Hill had fashioned a sheath to enclose the Pen and he kept it stuffed into the side of his left shoe.

Every evening, after dining on a hunk of moldy bread and thin soup, Hill and Resuza usually had an hour to themselves. Unfortunately, this was the most dangerous time of day because the Dragoonya had informers everywhere who were only too happy to report on any suspicious conversations or activities. Any accusation at all from another slave – whether it was true or not – would usually mean that the accused would be cast out into the snow. In any case, during this time of night, Resuza and Hill lay silently in their bunks. Only after the lights went out did they murmur to each other about their plans.

Tonight, as the other slaves slept like the dead, Hill and Resuza planned to have another such conversation.

"Hill," whispered Resuza again through the darkness. "Are you okay?"

Spurred into movement by Resuza's whisper, Hill sat up in bed and took the Pen out of its hiding place within the blanket. It was silver with a sparkling emerald embedded on top. He stared at the following diagram carved across the barrel:

Hill had managed to figure out or at least guess the meaning of the five symbols. The symbols represented the five classical elements: the top triangle represented fire and the bottom one was water; the triangle on the left was earth and the one on the right was air; the fifth symbol, the one in the center comprised of three dots, represented ether.

"What's it doing?" whispered Resuza through the darkness, "Is it happening again?"

They spoke in Dormian, which none of the other slaves understood – a precaution just in case someone overheard their whispers.

"Yes," said Hill. He then had another fit of coughing before he finally caught his breath. Hil was huddled beneath his blanket to conceal his movements. "It's happening again."

For the last several evenings, at exactly midnight, the emerald on top of the Pen began to glow. The glow lasted for five minutes or so. Tonight, Hill and Resuza had vowed to tinker with the Pen and decipher what – if anything – the glowing meant.

"Are you going to press it?" whispered Resuza.

"Quiet," said Hill.

Hill held his breath and then pushed the emerald button. CLICK. Nothing happened. He waited a moment, then pressed it again. Still nothing. Hill sighed disappointedly. Finally, he pressed it once more – this time holding the button for several seconds. Then something very strange happened. The tip of the Pen emitted an intense green light and projected a small three-dimensional image, which came in and out of focus, like a brightly lit sign on a foggy night. It was the image of a hand with several numbers etched on and in-between the fingers. There was also a series of circles at the point where the thumb joined to the hand. He couldn't make sense of it. It looked like this.

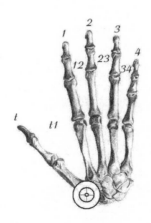

Hill stared at the mesmerizing, glowing three-dimensional image. His mind was racing with questions. *Why had the Pen started glowing in the last few days? What did this strange diagram mean? What was the Pen trying to tell him?* He played with the Pen for a while longer, but nothing else happened. Eventually, the three-dimensional image disappeared.

"That's puzzling," said Hill. "I'll need to think about this."

"I'm tired of thinking – I want to try what we discussed," said Resuza. "I want to go ahead with our plan."

"Now?" asked Hill.

"Yes."

"Do you really think that's wise?" asked Hill.

"I don't know," said Resuza. "But I can't just sit around here waiting to die."

Hill sighed.

"Please give me the Pen," said Resuza.

"Okay," said Hill finally, handing the Pen to Resuza. "But for goodness sake, please be careful."

Resuza crept out of bed with the Pen in hand. Resuza had rehearsed her movements and was fairly certain she could get to her destination without a noise. Whether she would go unnoticed was another matter. She tiptoed down a pitch-black hallway that was lined with slave bunk beds. At the very end of the hallway, on the left side, was an alcove that held a simple wooden table. In better times, several pitchers of water sat on the table; but even this small gesture of humanity had been discontinued as of late and now the slaves only received water at dinner. Those slaves who had been there the longest would often look longingly at the alcove, as if the days when water was once there had been the high point of their lives. Now, the table was bare and covered with a thick layer of dust. The alcove was only about

four feet high, but it was surprisingly deep, so much so that
Resuza was actually able to crawl under the table and hide
herself completely from view.

So far, she and Hill had only practiced using the Pen
with two of the elements: fire and air. Before coming to
Dargora, Hill had used then Pen to shoot a stream of fire.
On another occasion, in Dargora, Hill had blown into the
empty chamber and was then able to control a gust of wind
inside the slave quarters. This had occurred early in the
morning when everyone was still groggy from sleep, but
even then it had caused a great stir. People still spoke of the
day when a gust of wind had become trapped inside their
icy prison. Hill had been able to guide the wind in specific
directions – as if it were a gigantic fan of sorts – but he was
unable to dial up or down the strength of the wind. He
suspected this was possible, but they hadn't yet figured out
how to do it.

Resuza huddled under the table and listened quietly
for a full minute. She heard nothing aside from the usual
noises of slumber in the slave quarters – snores, mutters,
coughs, and – inevitably – the unnerving whimpers of people trapped in nightmares. Resuza pushed herself to the
back of the alcove and felt the wall. As she suspected, it was
made of dirt. The slave quarters were a mix of ice caves and
earthen cellars. In some places the walls were made of ice
and in other places they were made of rock and dirt. Here
the walls were dirt, which was a bit of good luck. She took a
pinch of the dirt and inserted into the lower chamber of the
Pen. She snapped the Pen back together, pointed it at the
wall in front of her, and pressed the emerald at the top of
the Pen. After a slight click, the Pen shot out a thin stream
of dirt, although it seemed to be lighter than the kind she
had initially inserted into the Pen. A cloud of dirt soon

engulfed her. Resuza clicked the emerald top again, and the stream of dirt disappeared. It took several minutes until the tiny particles settled on the ground and she could survey the Pen's effect.

The effect was disappointingly small. A shallow divot had been carved out of the wall, as if someone very strong had punched it. But that was it. Resuza thought back to the wind that Hill had been able to control, and looking back, even that wind seemed unimpressive. She wondered whether they had overestimated the Pen's powers. Resuza tried it again, pointing the tip of the Pen closer to the wall. The result was the same; however, this second time, she noticed something she hadn't before. When she pressed the emerald button, the metal area around the emerald became warm. Perhaps it meant something.

She tried a third time. While the Pen shot out its thin stream of dirt, she rubbed the area around the emerald. At first nothing happened, but then by chance she happened to rub in a clockwise direction around the emerald. The stream of dirt immediately died down to nothing. The Pen appeared to stop working. Resuza then rubbed in a counter clockwise direction, and the stream of dirt resumed and gathered force. For a moment, she panicked, fearing that she must be making a terrible racket, but she was both relieved and astounded to realize that the miniature tornado that she had created had been completely silent. She kept circling her thumb counter clockwise around the emerald until the cloud of dirt grew so thick that she began to choke. She clicked the emerald to stop, and then waited for the result. Finally, the dirt settled enough for her to see.

What she saw was incredible.

Instead of a small indentation in the wall, the Pen had carved a hole into the wall that was roughly two feet in diameter. She peered into the hole but could not find the end. Her pulse racing, she clicked the emerald again, turned up the Pen's potency, and widened the opening to the hole so that she could slip though it. She was getting the hang of how to use it. Resuza crawled into the opening, half-expecting to be met with resistance in the first few feet; but she kept crawling and, after about 20 feet, the tunnel stopped at a spot where the ground turned to ice. She stopped and gingerly pressed her hand to the newly carved ceiling above her. It was ice as well, which meant that the Pen had blown through the incredibly thick walls of the slave quarters, and had only stopped when it met a substance that was not dirt. And this meant that above her was ice and snow and – above that – freedom from her prison.

CHAPTER EIGHT
BACK TO REALITY

"I feel awful," muttered Alfonso.

"Shh," replied Marta. "You must whisper."

"Where are we?" asked Alfonso softly.

"Nowhere good I'm afraid," replied Marta with a weak smile. "I believe we're in the southern foothills of the Urals. Middle of nowhere really."

Alfonso sat up slowly. His entire body ached – his muscles, his bones, his joints, everything. He felt as if he'd been in a brawl with an angry mob.

"Do you feel like this every time you morph?" asked Alfonso. "Because if so, I don't know how I'm going to do it."

"Don't worry," said Marta, "It gets easier, but I won't lie to you, it never feels great."

"Okay," said Alfonso with a sigh. "Any good news?"

"I'm afraid not," said Marta. "I think we're being followed. It's probably been a few days."

"Who?"

"Not sure exactly," said Marta. "But there's more than one."

"Wonderful," said Alfonso and he managed a wry smile. He was nonetheless in a better mood. His vision had returned fully, and this gave him confidence. He glanced around, surveying his surroundings. They were well hidden in a thicket of shrubs and tall grasses; and they were situated halfway up a steep rise, which offered a sweeping view across a rocky plain below. In the distance, Alfonso could see a narrow vertical line that looked like it might be a tower. Judging by the scale of this tower – how tall it stood in relation to everything else – Alfonso knew that it had to be quite large. Something about the whole scene seemed familiar.

"Strange, I feel like I've been here before," said Alfonso. "But that's impossible, right?"

"Maybe you saw it in a dream," suggested Marta. "You know, when you were in your coma."

"Yeah, could be," replied Alfonso.

"That's kind of what happened to Roya."

"Who?"

"Roya," explained Marta, "She was this other seer from Jasber – a girl seer like me." Marta went on to explain how Roya had taken too much green ash and gone into a coma – after which, she did nothing and said nothing until, one day, she created a curious painting of a woman sleep-walking along the ledge of a building. "She begged to be taken to this place," explained Marta. "She was convinced this place was a doorway – you know, her way out of the coma."

"You think I needed to come to this exact spot to wake up?" asked Alfonso with a chortle. "Come on, really?"

"Didn't you say, 'I feel like I've been here before?'" asked Marta.

Alfonso looked off into the distance and stared again at the tower – or whatever it was. The sight of it gave him an uneasy feeling. He felt increasingly certain that he had dreamt of the place, but he couldn't recall any of the details of the dream.

"So what's the plan?" asked Alfonso.

Marta reached into her shirt and took a Pendant embedded with a number of emeralds. It was what the Abbot had given her.

"What's that?" asked Alfonso.

"Our way home," replied Marta.

"Home?"

"Back to Jasber," said Marta. "I got it from the Abbot. We just need to burn it and they'll come looking for us – the sweepers – they'll find us."

"No way," said Alfonso. "Forget it." That was the last thing that he wanted to do right now. "These are the same people who locked away my dad in the middle of a labyrinth for years – the same people who kept you locked up in a monastery where you had to sit in a chair all day and stare at a tree. Have you forgotten all that? You want to go back there? Are you crazy?"

"My mom and dad and brothers are there," said Marta. "Besides, I'm done being seer. I plan to quit."

"And you think they'll let you?" asked Alfonso. "Marta, be honest with yourself."

"I'm the seer," she said stubbornly. "They need me. We'll make a deal or something."

"Look," said Alfonso. "If that's what you want to do, I'm not going to stop you, but I'm not coming with you."

Marta studied her Pendant carefully. She appeared lost in thought, as if trying to make up her mind.

"You're not going to make it without me," she said finally.

"Look, I appreciate all that you've done for me, I really do," said Alfonso. "But I think I can survive without the help of a nine-year-old pipsqueak."

"Stand up!" said Marta. It wasn't a request – it was an order.

"What?"

"You heard me – stand up!"

"Fine," said Alfonso. With great effort, he rose to his feet. He felt weak and unsteady. "I'm standing," declared Alfonso. "Okay?"

"Walk forward ten paces," ordered Marta.

"Yes boss," said Alfonso. He took one step forward and then another. His legs ached and his balance was off, but he managed. He took three or four more steps and then, rather abruptly, he felt exhausted. He could go no farther. He dropped to one knee and, as he did, a spasm of pain shot up his leg. He grabbed his thigh and felt that his muscles had dissipated and his skin was soft and saggy. "My legs... I'm an..." He stopped mid-sentence – his voice sounded like the croak of a frog.

"A very old man," finished Marta. She couldn't suppress a hint of satisfaction in her voice. "Ninety five, maybe ninety-eight. You're a regular grandpa – probably even a great grandpa."

"What do I do?" croaked Alfonso and, as he spoke, he became aware of the fact that he no longer had any teeth in his mouth. "Tell me."

"That all depends," said Marta. "How old do you want to be?"

"My real age," croaked Alfonso.

"No," said Marta. "I've already shown you how to do that. Why don't you try for thirty-six?"

"Thirty-six?"

"Yes," said Marta with a smile. "It's a lucky number."

"Fine, thirty-six then, but how?"

"The trick is to picture people around you at that age, like your wife," said Marta. "Can you do that?"

"My wife," croaked Alfonso. "What are you talking about?"

"Your kids, too," added Marta. "You need to picture the whole scene – your wife, kids, dog, house – but start with your wife." She smiled. "It should be someone with a pretty name, like Hannah or Victoria. These are friends of mine from Jasber."

"How can I?" asked Alfonso with exasperation. "How can I picture someone I've never met?"

"Of course you've met her," said Marta with a smile. "You are a grandpa, you met her ages ago – you're an old man now – just look at yourself. You've lived a long life. And all your memories are locked away in your head. It's all there. You've just got to act your age."

"How do I..." began Alfonso. He was gasping for breath. All of this talking had exhausted him. "How do I do that?"

"Breathe – that's the key to everything," said Marta softly. "Just breathe."

"Breathe?"

"Yes," said Marta. "Concentrate on your breath. It places you in the moment – at least that's what the Abbot says. So you breathe in through the left nostril, hold it for four seconds, and breathe out through the right nostril. Then breathe in through your right nostril, hold it again – this time for eight seconds – and out through your left nostril. Repeat. Can you do that?"

Alfonso nodded. He concentrated intensely on his breathing. At first nothing happened. He just felt foolish. In fact, he nearly gave up, but he persisted for a few more minutes. Soon images started flickering through his brain – a boathouse on a misty river, a little blond girl in pigtails, a plate full of sushi at a fancy hotel, an old woman walking a poodle, children dressed as knights at a school play, and the images just kept coming. It was almost as if someone was pasting photographs into a giant album – at an astounding speed – and Alfonso suspected that the pictures were moments from his life. He came to understand that his brain was being filled with a lifetime of memories. After some time, the sound of Marta's voice brought him back to his senses.

"Look for your wife," said Marta. "It's confusing when you are so old – there are so many memories – but she is there. You probably want to remember her when she is a young mother. That'd probably be when you are around thirty-six. I don't know for sure. I'm just guessing. But when you see her, try to hold onto that image, and block out everything else."

Marta watched Alfonso closely. He appeared to be deep in thought. His breathing was rapid, and his sallow, hairless arms were trembling. He stayed like this for several more minutes – and then it happened. In the blink of an eye, he morphed into a tall, muscular man with a sun-tanned face, a mop of shaggy brown hair, and a thick beard. He looked a few years shy of forty.

"Keep breathing like I told you," said Marta. "In through the left nostril, hold, out through the right nostril. And keep at it – otherwise you'll go right back to being grandpa."

Alfonso nodded. He sat down, closed his eyes, crossed his legs, and continued with his breathing. "Good," said Marta. "You're holding your form. The longer you hold it, the easier it becomes to stay at that age. When you feel ready, I have some adult-size clothing that the monks from Jasber gave me. They should fit you more or less. But give yourself another few minutes to get used to being a tall guy with a beard."

She laughed. "You look like one of those scary guys who spends all of his time at the alehouse in Jasber. Do you like drinking ale?"

Alfonso shooed her away with his hand.

Roughly ten more minutes passed and then, finally, Alfonso opened his eyes. When he did, he found himself staring at a woman in her late twenties who bore a striking resemblances to Marta.

"You morphed," said Alfonso.

"I did," said Marta. "I figured we'd travel faster if we were both around this age."

Alfonso nodded.

"I think I figured something out," said Alfonso, as he rose to his feet. He looked strong, healthy, and determined. "I want to visit that tower – the one off in the distance."

"The one from your dream?"

"Yes," said Alfonso.

"Okay," said Marta, "I'll go with you to the tower, then I want to head back to Jasber."

Alfonso wiggled his fingers and moved his arms about – as if he were still getting used to feel of his own body.

"Weird isn't it?" asked Marta.

"Yeah," said Alfonso. "And by the way, I figured something else out."

"What?"

"You're not my wife," said Alfonso.

"Yeah, I know," said Marta with a smile. "You're not that lucky." She laughed merrily. "Come on, let's go."

Chapter Nine
Into the Forest

After the man from Jasber departed into the woods, Leif spent much of that day preparing for his own departure. He salvaged everything he could from the old rowboat including a pocket knife, a coil of rope, and an old leather flask. He spent several hours hunting for crabs and, with some luck, caught two. He hiked to a fresh-water spring at the far end of the beach where he bathed and drank until he could drink no more. Finally, he built a fire to stay warm and tried to sleep through some of the night.

Leif woke at dawn and promptly set off, walking backwards into the shadowy depth of Straszydlo Forest. Kõrgu followed Leif quite closely. At first, Leif had tried to discourage the wolf from coming, because he did not want her to break the rules unknowingly and suffer the consequences. But the wolf could not be dissuaded from tagging along. Leif hoped for the best; after all, Kõrgu usually seemed to manage.

As he walked, Leif kept his eyes trained on the ground. There were two sets of tracks: the first was fairly large and almost certainly belonged to the man with the green cloak; the second set was slightly smaller and Leif suspected that these tracks belonged to Alfonso. It wasn't easy to follow tracks while walking backwards – on numerous occasions, Leif tripped and fell over a log or large stone – but he persisted. As he went, he often called out to his son. Leif suspected it would do little good, but he couldn't help himself.

Leif walked for much of the day and, though he had no way of telling the time, it was late afternoon when he came upon the tattered remains of the green cloak. The cloak was shredded into hundreds of small pieces; and all around it were bones that had been picked so clean, it was almost as if they had been dipped in acid and bleached in the sun. The larger set of tracks stopped here and there could be little doubt that these bones belonged to the Jasberian who saved him. What had happened to him? Why had he been attacked in this manner?

Leif recalled his exchange with the man from the previous day. The man had said: "It came to me and I said to myself, 'Yes, of course, it is: *You must never look backwards.* But then, thank heaven, I realized that was not quite right – not at all. The rule was, I am of certain of it now, as follows: *You must only look backwards.*"

Perhaps the man with the green cloak had gotten it wrong. Perhaps the rule was, as the man had first suspected, that you must never look backwards. If that was the case, then Leif had been breaking the rule all day, and his best bet might be to spin around and face forward. He didn't know what to do – there was no way to know for certain which way he ought to face – but Leif felt that he had to do *something* and so, on an impulse, he spun around. As he did this, there was suddenly a great deal of movement in the forest – as if he were surrounded on all sides – and Leif waited in terror, expecting to be attacked at any moment. But the attack never came. Only silence. Without shifting his head in the slightest, Leif surveyed his surroundings, searching for a glimpse of whatever is was that was watching him. He could see nothing.

"Is this what I am meant to do?" he asked suddenly, his voice filled with fright. "Am I facing the right way?"

There was no reply.

Leif looked down at the ground and saw, to his relief, that the smaller set of tracks – Alfonso's, he hoped – continued deeper into the forest. Leif glanced upward at the sky. The light was fading quickly. He had an hour, perhaps a little more, until sundown. If he was still in the woods at that point, he would be in real trouble. Leif continued at a slow run. As he ran, he again called out the name of his son. "Alfonso, where are you?" he hollered. He was beginning to feel panicked. Around this time, Leif got the sense that he was being followed. Whatever it was, it moved very quickly and quietly, darting back and fourth among the trees, just outside his realm of vision. Leif also realized that Korgu, who had been bounding through the forest with joyous abandon, had returned to his side. She wasn't growling at all, even though by all rights this was the moment to do so. Instead, the wolf stood close to Leif, and leaned against his leg. A whimper came from deep within her throat. Just then, Leif heard the sound of a branch snapping. He looked up and saw, just a stone's throw away – right in front of him – the unmistakable figure of a teenage boy darting into the woods. *Had he been in these woods, wandering around, for the last two days? If so, how had he survived? Had he holed up somewhere? Was he lost?* Leif's mind raced with questions.

"Wait!" screamed Leif as loudly as he could.

The boy didn't stop. For a brief moment, Leif clung to the hope that he had found Alfonso, but there was something about the way he moved – and the figure that the boy cut against the dying light – that looked unfamiliar. Without looking back, the boy shouted back at him through the woods.

"Quit following me you fool," he screamed angrily, "I'm not your son!"

The boy darted deftly into the underbrush. Leif ran after him, but the boy was astoundingly quick and agile, and Leif could not keep up with him. Leif felt both exhausted and perplexed. He wondered to himself: *Why is the boy running away from me?* And then a thought occurred to him: perhaps the boy was not running away from Leif – but from something else – something just behind Leif. Leif panted heavily for another minute or so and then it happened. Suddenly, the creatures – the things that had been following him for much of the day – all charged at once. Leif knew instinctively he had to run and run faster than he ever had in his life.

Leif crashed through the forest wildly. Branches stung his face and whipped his body. His arms were soon wet with blood and sweat. He gasped for breath and pumped his legs as hard as he could. Behind him, he heard a chorus of voices. One voice was that of an old man, which kept asking: *Which way is it? I think we're lost. We never should have come into these woods.* Another was the voice of a younger man who kept shouting: *My wife! My children! Please don't!* Leif sprinted onward, all the while looking for the boy or Korgu, but they were gone.

He continued running through the woods until, in his fatigue, he tripped on a root and fell heavily to the ground with a thud. Leif stayed there motionless, waiting for the inevitable attack. The creatures surrounded him. Something like a claw or a beak meandered curiously down the back of his jacket. The smell of wet fur filled his nostrils. One of the creatures bent down so close that Leif could feel its hot steamy breath on his neck, and he heard it say, "Stand up slowly and keep your eyes closed." The voice sounded familiar. Leif had heard it before, perhaps in a dream. "Hurry now," said the voice, "On your feet."

Not knowing what else to do, Leif obeyed.

"You've broken our rules," said the voice.

"I know," said Leif. "I am sorry – I am just a father looking for…"

"Your son," finished the voice. "We know."

Several bodies moved behind him, there were snarls, and once again Leif waited for an attack; but it didn't come.

"I know *you*, don't I?" asked Leif finally.

"Yes," said the voice.

"Who are you?"

"Be quiet," said the voice. "Now listen carefully. I want you to reach backwards with your right hand, very slowly. I am going to give you something."

Once again, Leif did as he was told. He reached backwards tentatively and soon he felt someone – or something – press a smooth, flat, hard object into his hand.

"Hold it up to your face," said the voice. Leif obeyed. "Now open your eyes."

Leif blanched. *Was this a trick? Were they trying to make him break the rules? Were they looking for an excuse to kill him?* But surely, if they wanted to kill him, they already could have done so. He had little choice. He opened his eyes. It was dark in the forest, but the sky still glowed with the light of dusk, and Leif saw the face of a gaunt, haggard man, with a grizzly white beard. It took him a moment to realize that he was gazing into a mirror, at his own reflection. In all the years that had passed since he left World's End, Minnesota, he hadn't once had a chance to look at himself in the mirror. It was frightening to do so. It looked as if he had aged decades.

"Now turn the mirror slowly to the left so that you can see over your shoulder," said the voice. "And be careful. If you drop the mirror or turn around, my companions will feast on your flesh."

Leif took a deep breath and slowly tilted the mirror. As he did this, something clicked in his brain, and he suddenly recognized the creature's voice. It belonged to Imad, the Cyclops who had visited him in his dream; and as he continued to tilt the mirror, the image that came into view was Imad's broad face, with its single, bloodshot eyeball situated in the center of his forehead.

"You," stammered Leif. His hand trembled.

"Bloody hell – hold the mirror steady!" barked Imad. "You mustn't see the others."

"OK," said Leif. He tensed his wrist and fingers and held the mirror as tightly as he could. "But I don't understand… Are you a…"

"No," said Imad. "I am not. It is an illusion created by the mirror. The mirror allows you to see me as Imad. I do not exist. But let me assure you, the Straszydlo do exist. I can hold them at bay, for a while, but they will tear you to pieces if you do not do exactly as I say. Understand?"

"Yes," said Leif. "But what about the boy?"

"Forget about the boy," said Imad angrily. "He's not Alfonso. In fact he's not a boy at all."

"What?"

"Listen to me," said Imad. "Just a stone's throw off to your left, you'll find a faint animal trail. Follow it for a quarter mile or so – it'll take you where you want to go – to a great old tree."

"A great old tree," repeated Leif. "And is that where the boy went?"

"Yes," said Imad. "But the boy won't find what he's looking for."

"Why not?"

"Because I have hidden it," said Imad.

"In the tree?"

Leif heard more snarling and he struggled to keep his hand from shaking.

"Yes," Imad replied. "You will soon see. Now listen carefully because we are running out of time. Once you get inside, you'll need to retrieve something I've hidden there. It's what the boy was looking for. Go to my study and take the artwork. Do not leave without it."

"The artwork," repeated Leif, hesitantly. "What do I do with it?"

"Don't worry about that now," said Imad. "It will come to you at an appropriate time. You're not in the proper frame of mind."

"What?"

"You heard me," said Imad resolutely. "And one more thing. There is a parcel that you will find nearby – you need to burn it right away. There is a fireplace near my desk. Take the parcel and burn it there. Don't open it or... or I promise you – you'll regret it. Can you remember all that?"

"Yes," said Leif.

"Good," said Imad. "Now slowly put down the mirror and whistle."

"Whistle?"

"Yes," said Imad. "Whistle as loud as you can."

Leif put down the mirror and whistled as loudly as he could; then, in the distance, he heard something tearing through the underbrush, growling as it went. It was a ferocious growl, the kind that begins at the pit of an animal's throat and stays there, biding its time until the inevitable attack. At first, Leif thought this was yet another Straszydlo; but it was moving too quickly and too low to the ground. There was a great commotion directly behind him – it sounded as if the Straszydlo were fleeing – and then the growling newcomer emerged. It was an enormous wolf, fangs bared, the very picture of stark aggression. When the wolf saw Leif, it leaned forward, whimpered once and licked his hand. It was Korgu. Leif held up the mirror again. Imad was gone, but Leif heard him speak one last time, uttering three final words: "*Run, you fool!*"

Leif broke into a run. He headed to his left, until he found the animal's trail, and he followed it for a quarter of a mile or so. The whole time, he could hear a stampede of footsteps behind him. Finally, he saw it up ahead – a massive tree with deeply grooved bark and a thick trunk that shot upwards into the night sky as if it were propping up the heavens all by itself. This had to be it. Built into the base of the tree was a small, round door made of solid steel. It appeared bolted shut. Leif knew there would be no time to try to unlock it. The creatures were almost upon him. There was only one thing to do. He had only tried doing this once before – back when he was in the maze of razor hedges – but he had to give it a go.

Leif sprinted for the door and, as he did, he forced himself into hypnogogia – the narrow space between sleeping and waking that is the hallmark of Dormian Great Sleepers. He leaned forward and dove at the door. His head paused for a split-second when it hit the door and then his entire body transvaporated – passing through the steel barrier as if it were made of air. The rest of his body followed and he was conscious of falling through cold and damp air. When he finally hit the ground, his head was thrown back sharply. In the last seconds before he passed out, he was dimly aware of Korgu howling somewhere far above him.

CHAPTER TEN
THE JOURNEY TO DARGORA

After several days of traveling together, Kiril and Bilblox emerged from a forest of towering pine trees and reached a river cutting through a vast ice field. Both men paused to catch their breath. Bilblox blinked his eyes in the glare of the sun and drank in the sights around him – the pristine snow, the pale blue ice, and the crystal-clear water. The other thing that Bilblox eyed was the leather pouch on Kiril's belt – the pouch where Kiril stored his green ash. There it was, just waiting to be taken.

"I suppose it is pleasant to have your eyesight back," observed Kiril in a friendly tone. "I myself can't imagine being blind. Were you able to see any colors or was it just blackness all the time? It's the blackness that would get to me – like a never-ending night – dreadful, I imagine…"

Kiril waited for his companion to say something, but Bilblox made no reply.

"Come on then," said Kiril, "Help me cut down a tree so we can make a dugout canoe. It is two days of hard paddling and then, my friend, we're practically home."

"Dargora ain't my home," said Bilblox in what sounded like a growl.

"Don't be so disagreeable," chided Kiril. "No one is forcing you to do anything. You are a man of action, like myself, and I very much doubt that I could hold you against your will. If you want to escape, I suspect you will, but where will that leave you? Wandering in this desolate wilderness, searching aimlessly for food, shelter, and your friends? That won't do and we both know it. So why don't..."

Kiril never finished the sentence because, in the next instant, Bilblox lunged at him and, in one furious movement, raised his massive fist into the air and hit Kiril squarely in the jaw. Kiril flew backwards and landed with a thud on the ground. Kiril howled in pain and, for a brief moment, his jaw appeared mangled as if it had been broken in several places. Kiril spit out a tooth and some blood as well. Then something miraculous happened. The blood stopped flowing, a new tooth grew back, and Kiril's jaw realigned itself perfectly so that – in a matter of seconds – it appeared as if he had never been hit. Bilblox charged Kiril again, but this time Kiril was ready, and Kiril adroitly grabbed the longshoreman by the shoulder and threw him into a bank of snow.

"I broke your jaw," gasped Bilblox incredulously as he rose to his feet. "And now you're... you're fine."

"Indeed," said Kiril as he massaged his jaw gently. Even he seemed surprised by his near-instant recovery. "It hurt at the time," admitted Kiril, "But I feel fit to eat a steak now."

"And your tooth..." said Bilblox. "How did you do that?"

"And to think people pay so much money for dentists," said Kiril with a dark chuckle.

Bilblox frowned.

"Don't be discouraged," said Kiril, "You'll be able to do the same thing – so long as you keep taking the green ash. You see we are both, in a manner of speaking, invincible. It's a stalemate. Neither of us can beat the other."

"We'll see about that," muttered Bilblox.

"Here is what I propose," continued Kiril calmly, as if he were offering options on a dinner menu. "You come with me, and I will let you into Dargora – into my house. If you still feel that I am your enemy, then you will have ample opportunities to betray me or even kill me, assuming, of course, that I can be killed. And, on the other hand, if you change your mind about me – or simply want to buy some more time to think things over – then you can stick around and live a while without the nuisance of blindness or excruciating headaches."

He smiled at Bilblox, who had cringed noticeably when Kiril had said "Dargora."

"Come now, Bilblox. It's just a city. You probably heard some terrible rumors, of a city built on bones. Like most rumors, this one is largely false, with some truth at the core. I assure you – Dargora is a pleasant city. The views are quite spectacular."

Bilblox considered charging Kiril again, but then thought better of it. He had lost the element of surprise. Bilblox also considered simply walking away, back into the forest, but this didn't seem particularly sensible either. As much as he hated to admit it, Kiril was right. He had come this far; it would be pointless to stop now. But it seemed foolhardy to trust Kiril. Kiril was almost certainly luring Bilblox into a trap of one kind or another and his bait was the green ash. But what was Kiril's plan? Why was he going to such great lengths to keep Bilblox alive? *Maybe he wants me to be his trophy*, thought Bilblox. Bilblox could envision the whole scene: Kiril returning home to Dargora as a hero with the Great Sleeper's best friend in tow – not as a chained prisoner – but as a broken man who had become addicted to the green ash and who was now a convert to the Dragoonya. This would certainly be a feather in Kiril's cap. Bilblox suspected that there was more to it than this, and that Alfonso figured prominently.

What Bilblox needed now was a plan of his own. Bilblox knew that he was, in effect, playing a game of chess – and playing against a very skilled opponent. Bilblox had never been a chess player – he much preferred backgammon and any game involving dice – but he knew that the key to winning in chess was always to be thinking several moves ahead.

Kiril looked at him. "Well, are you going to help me make this canoe or not?" he asked.

"Yeah, I'm coming," said Bilblox.

"Good," said Kiril, "I always knew you were the sort of fellow who liked a challenge."

The two men quickly set to work preparing their canoe. They cut down a large fir tree, stripped off the bark, and then used a dagger to carve a large oval into the tree, marking the area that would have to be dugout. They then used axes and worked furiously to hack away and carve out all the wood then needed to be removed. Then they shaped the bow and stern of the boat into rough wedges so that the boat could cut its way through the water easily. Normally a project like this, requiring this much physical exertion, would take two grown men the better part of a week or even two. Kiril and Bilblox, whose bodies were brimming with vigor due to the power of the ash, finished their canoe in just under six hours. When this was done, they chopped a limb off a tree and used their axes to chisel away roughhewn paddles. By the time they finally stopped working, night had fallen.

"I think this little boat shall serve us well," said Kiril as he lay down his axe. He was drenched with sweat and appeared out of breath. "Shall we make camp and commence downstream at dawn?"

"No need to wait," replied Bilblox. The longshoreman suddenly appeared to be in much better spirits. "There

ought to be a near full moon tonight so I figure we can pad-
dle right through the night. I say we just start now, unless
you are too tired to continue."

Kiril glowered, but said nothing. "Fine," said Kiril irritably, still panting for breath, "I'll help you carry the boat
down to the river."

"No need," said Bilblox as he picked up the boat and
swung it over his shoulder. The canoe was bulky, and had to
weigh several hundred pounds, but Bilblox maneuvered it
with great ease. "You just take the paddles."

"The paddles," muttered Kiril.

"Yes," said Bilblox. "You look a bit tuckered out."

Kiril glowered at him but said nothing. The two men
went downstream, paddling more or less continuously,
throughout that night and all of the next day. When they
finally stopped to make camp, Bilblox hauled the boat
ashore while Kiril built a small fire. They wordlessly shared
some food, and then immediately went to sleep. It took
Bilblox a while to sleep, despite his exhaustion. His mind
whirred with ideas and plans.

When Bilblox woke, many hours later, he had a pounding headache. It felt as if someone were using a jackhammer
on his brain. He struggled to open his eyes, and when he
finally did so, the brightness of the snow was excruciatingly
painful.

Somewhere nearby, he heard a man talking to him, but
it was impossible to make out any words. The man was talking gently. Bilblox forced himself to focus on the words.
Slowly, he began to understand what the man was saying.

"What you're feeling is the first stage of withdrawal," said
the man. "The pain comes quickly. It's not like a migraine
headache – it doesn't build gradually – it ambushes you
suddenly."

Bilblox knew now that it was Kiril speaking and he lunged blindly at the sound of the man's voice, but it was no use. The physical exertion of moving only made his headache worse.

"Give me the ash!" demanded Bilblox.

"In a little bit," said Kiril. "But first there is something I must do." Bilblox heard the sound of footsteps trudging off into the snow, slowly growing fainter and more distant, until the only sound that remained was the deafening void of silence.

Chapter Eleven
The Pen's Reach

Resuza sat crossed-legged in the middle of an under-ground ice cave. The cave was spacious and comfort-able – just the way that Resuza wanted it – because she herself had carved it by using the Foreseeing Pen. On the floor of the cave were blankets, several half-frozen flasks of cider, a few knives with handles made of bone, and a large pile of biscuits. Resuza had stolen all of these things from a locked storage room within the slave quarters. By using the Pen, she had succeeded in burrowing into this storage room, getting what she needed, and then getting out – sealing the tunnel behind her, with the Pen, by forcing the walls of the tunnel to cave inward. Every night, for the past week or so, she had been using the Pen to lay the groundwork for their escape. The cave was her storage depot, where she was compiling all of the supplies that she and Hill would need to escape.

There were two tunnels leading into Resuza's storage depot. One tunnel led directly back to the slave quarters, which was only several hundred meters away. The other tun-nel went off in a southerly direction and continued for a very long way – perhaps as much as three miles – though it was impossible to tell. The prospect of building a tunnel that stretched for such a great distance would normally be inconceivable – especially for one person – but the Pen had made it possible. Once she had mastered it, Resuza simply flicked it on and walked forward very slowly and the Pen did the rest.

Resuza stood up and headed down the tunnel that went south, the one that would lead them to their escape. As she walked, the prospect of her escape seemed more and more real, and with this came another realization: she was officially giving up on finding her sister. Most likely, Naomi was dead – Resuza had come to accept this likelihood – but there was a small chance that she was alive, tucked away in some remote corner of Dargora. If this was the case, then this meant that Resuza was abandoning her sister – yet again. Resuza had abandoned Naomi for the first time when Dragoonya horsemen raided their village in the Urals. Resuza had begged her sister to run, but Naomi wouldn't budge, and so Resuza eventually fled without her. Afterwards, Resuza had vowed to herself that she would never rest or give up until she found her sister; and yet here she was, several years later, doing exactly that – giving up, running for it, trying to save her own skin – once again. The thought made Resuza feel disgusted with herself, but what choice did she have? If she stayed in Dargora much longer she would, in all likelihood, end up dead, and her bones would be yet more building blocks for the towers of the city.

No, thought Resuza. *No way.*

She walked for a long time, perhaps thirty minutes or so, until she reached the end of the tunnel. It wasn't really the end. It was just the spot where she had stopped drilling the previous evening. Once here, Resuza took out the Pen and opened it up so that she could see into its barrel. She then took an ice chip from the floor of the tunnel, loaded it into the Pen, aimed it at the wall in front of her, and clicked the emerald. A spray of water and powdery snow soaked her face. She squinted and pressed forward, continuing like this for two hours or so until she broke through and found herself staring into a gaping chasm. She peered into the darkness and saw that she was looking at a vast canyon made of ice. The bottom was hundreds of meters below. It made her nauseous just to look down into it. *Perhaps she could find a way to tunnel around this canyon – that was her only option.* But she would need to get her bearings, which meant getting up to the surface.

Resuza pointed the Pen to her right and began drilling a new tunnel that made its way, at a gradual angle, all the way to the surface. She drilled for twenty minutes until finally she broke through and saw the world above. The mere sight of it filled her with joy. The sky was cloudy and, hanging in a gap in the clouds, was the moon – shimmering in all its brightness. She scrambled up to the surface and quickly surveyed her surroundings. There was a large rock nearby, shaped like a giant egg, and she climbed up to the top of it so that she could have a better perspective.

What Resuza saw dashed all of her hopes. The canyon was not only deep and wide, but incredibly long. It stretched in either direction for as far as the eye could see, and it appeared to serve as a moat that protected Dargora. And beyond the canyon there was nothing but endless fields of snow. There was no way out and, more devastatingly, there was nowhere to go.

Escape seemed ridiculous. Perhaps it was, Resuza thought. But the thought that Alfonso and Bilblox were out there dampened her annoyance. She would need patience. Something would happen soon enough.

CHAPTER TWELVE

A VISION OF THE FUTURE

Alfonso and Marta scrambled down the rocky slope, heading east, toward the tall stone tower in the distance. They moved slowly at first because Alfonso kept tripping. "You're not used to your body," Marta told him. "It takes a while."

"Then why aren't you falling on your face like me?" he asked her.

"Because I know what I'm doing," she told him with a smile. "Just watch me. You won't believe how much you can learn from a nine-year-old girl."

Alfonso smiled. "Fair enough."

They walked for many hours – through the afternoon, through dusk, and into the evening. The night sky was clear, perfectly cloudless, but in the distance a storm was approaching. Brilliant flashes of lightning crackled across the sky and illuminated the landscape like flickering stadium lights. The tower was close now. It stood on the other side of a huge sprawling meadow, speckled with boulders, poplar trees, and tall, lush, green grass. In the moments when the sky lit up, Alfonso could see that it wasn't really a tower, but an obelisk – a massive stone pillar with a pyramid-like top. He recalled learning about obelisks in his world history class. The ancient Egyptians built them. In fact, on his brief trip to Alexandria, he recalled seeing one at the edge of the city. It was tall and thin, like a stone needle, and covered with hieroglyphs. This obelisk was bigger, much bigger. They were still half a mile away and yet it towered over them. It was very wide around the base – perhaps thirty feet by thirty feet – and as tall as a big city skyscraper.

"I was here with my dad," said Alfonso. "I'm certain of it now."

"Huh?"

"In my dream," said Alfonso. "I was at this obelisk with my dad."

"Oh," said Marta. "That's nice. Did the two of you have a good time? Was it a picnic?"

"I don't remember," said Alfonso. Then he laughed.

"What's so funny?"

"I was just thinking," said Alfonso. "If my dad saw me now – you know, with a beard and all – he'd freak out."

"You could shave the beard," said Marta.

"I don't know how to shave," admitted Alfonso. "I think I'll just morph back to being a teenager when the time comes."

Marta set down her pack and climbed up onto a nearby boulder. "I want to rest for a while," she said.

"What about the storm?" asked Alfonso.

"It's still far away," she said. "You can barely hear the thunder. Besides, before I head back to Jasber, I want to have a look at something." Marta crossed her legs, stared off into the distance, and sat perfectly still.

"What are you doing?" asked Alfonso.

"My job," said Marta.

"Your job?" asked Alfonso. "What's your job?"

"I'm a seer."

"I thought you were going to quit," said Alfonso teasingly.

"Please shut up," snapped Marta. "Go walk around and try to act your age – you're supposed to be a grown man for goodness sake."

Alfonso sighed, shrugged his shoulders, and wandered off into the tall grass. As he walked, he mulled over his situation. He had a strong sense that this was where he was supposed to be, at this obelisk, but he couldn't say why. In his dream, he and his father had been here together – at the very top of the obelisk – on a balcony, or a ledge, or something like that. He remembered the view: the green foothills and the snowcapped peaks in the distance. There was a woman there on the balcony too, a beautiful woman with a scar across her face, but the other details were hazy. It was a fragment of a dream. *Why couldn't he recall more of it?* He remembered the other dream from his coma with startling clarity – the one in which he and Resuza were in the woods in Minnesota, running from the oncoming tide of scurrying animals. All the details were still crisp: the trees shaking, the branches cracking, and the ground shifting. He thought back to the forest and recalled seeing the strange hexagonal hole in the ground.

Suddenly he knew where he'd seen something like this before: Paris.

The hole in the forest looked exactly like the one he had seen with Sophie, the wanderer, beneath the streets of Paris. These were "root holes" created by the deadly tentacles of the Shadow Tree. *Had it already been planted? Was it possible?* Alfonso recalled what his father had said in the dream: "I should have known – it was all written out so clearly." *What was his dad talking about?* Of course, maybe this was just a bunch of nonsense from a dream that meant nothing. This was the most likely explanation. But it was all so vivid – almost like it really happened.

More than anything else, he remembered Resuza's words before he woke up: *"You'll need me, before it's all over. And Bilblox as well."*

JAKE HALPERN AND PETER KUJAWINSKI

And then came those last, hurried words: *"But most of all, you'll need-"*

Alfonso felt like screaming. Who did he need? His father? There was no way to find out. Even if he found Resuza, she wouldn't be able to complete this sentence that occurred in *his* dream. He feared the worst. Perhaps he would need someone like Kiril or Nartam. This made no sense, but in the vacuum of his thoughts, Alfonso was without any guide.

Quite suddenly, Alfonso snapped to attention. Something was moving in the grass. There was a brilliant flash of lightning and, seconds later, an explosive clap of thunder. A gust of cool air rustled the grass. The storm was nearing. There was more movement in the grass. All around him, he could sense bodies – human, animals, impossible to say – closing in on him. Whatever had been following them for the past few days was finally here – and in full force. There was another flash of lightning and, ever so briefly, Alfonso saw the faces of almost a dozen children. They were dressed in rags, their faces were filthy, but their eyes appeared strangely alert. They were moving towards him slowly, but steadily. One thought leapt into Alfonso's mind: Marta. He spun and around and dashed back through the tall grass. He ran for ten minutes or so – Alfonso hadn't realized just how far he'd wandered while lost in thought – but eventually he came upon the rock where Marta was sitting.

"I just saw something pretty spooky," said Alfonso, panting for breath.

"So did I," replied Marta.

"Then you saw them too?" asked Alfonso. "The kids in the grass?"

"No," said Marta, "I had a vision of the future – you know, like the ones I used to have while sitting in my chair on Monastery Isle."

80

"What'd you see?"

"This field," said Marta. "A bunch of years from now."

"And?" asked Alfonso. "What else?"

"No," said Marta. "I'm not telling you – at least, not right now."

"What?" said Alfonso angrily. "You've got to be kidding. When will you tell me? Aren't you heading back to Jasber?"

"No," said Marta, "I've changed my mind about that. I'm coming with you."

"Coming with me?" asked Alfonso. "Fine, but we have to go – now!"

Alfonso and Marta ran toward the tower as quickly as they could, charging through the tall grass and leaping over rocks as they went. They had almost made it to the base of the tower when they realized that they were surrounded. It was a classic hunting scenario. One group of hunters chased its prey, driving them forward, and another group of hunters stayed up ahead – waiting patiently for the prey to arrive. Alfonso and Marta could both see that, around the base of the tower, there were two dozen or so figures crouching in the grass. It was very difficult to discern how big they were or how old, but they were clearly lying in wait.

"Who are they?" asked Alfonso in whisper.

"I'm not sure," said Marta. "But the monks warned me about them. They told me that the slave traders got so many of the adults around here that packs of kids now roamed the hills like wolves."

"You've got to be kidding," whispered Alfonso.

"How old do you think they are?" asked Marta. "I mean the ones you saw?"

"They were little," whispered Alfonso. "They couldn't have been much older than six or seven years old."

"Okay," said Marta. "You know what we've got to do right? It's our only chance."

Alfonso nodded.

"Can you do it?" asked Marta.

"I think so," said Alfonso.

"Okay," she said, "Let's do it – and remember to breathe."

CHAPTER THIRTEEN
THE LIBRARY

M any hours later, Leif stirred and began to wake up. For several minutes, he lay motionless on the dusty ground, trying to determine – without moving – whether he was badly hurt. He felt as if he were waking from the deepest sleep of his life. At some point, he began moving his fingers and then, at last, he opened his eyes. He remembered very well what had happened – the opening in the root of the tree, and then the long fall, so he was mildly surprised to see his arm intact and unbroken. He had a painful cut across his entire back, and while his shirt was soaked with blood, the wound seemed to be superficial and he was no longer bleeding.

So far, so good.

He stood up and looked around. He was in a long room with no sharp angles or corners. The walls, which were carved out of a finely-polished wood, flowed like a wave. A thick layer of dust lay over everything, and the room felt still in the same way that some caves do, as if no one had passed through here for centuries. Eventually, Leif found the rungs of a ladder inset into the wall. He looked up and became confused. Far above him – perhaps 200 feet or so – he saw, for the first time, a small patch of light. The light was so meager that it illuminated very little. Leif had no idea what this was, but he was intrigued.

He began climbing. It was steady work, climbing one step at a time, checking each rung first with his hand to confirm that it was steady. Leif assumed that no one had used this ladder in ages and, the higher he climbed, the more nervous he became. After ten minutes of climbing, he reached a wooden trapdoor with his fingertips. The trapdoor was made with several slats of wood, but there were spaces in between these slats, and through these slats light was pouring through. This was the source of light that he had seen from far below.

Leif pushed up on the trapdoor with gentle and then steady pressure. It creaked loudly, but was unlocked. Dust coated his head and shoulders. He emerged into a circular room lined with bookcases. A movable ladder rotated around the room on an iron rail. Leif looked up and stared in astonishment. The room's ceiling was several hundred feet overhead – so far above him that he could only barely make it out. Leif tried to grasp where he was. There was only one explanation. Initially, he had fallen into a hole in the ground and now he had climbed up into the trunk of a giant tree – the tree itself was hollowed out and its inner walls were lined with thousands of books.

As the book-lined walls continued upward, they were joined by what appeared to be light-filled tunnels. These tunnels concentrated light and formed them into rays. Upon closer inspection, Leif realized that the tunnels were actually hollowed-out branches that were channeling light into the main trunk of the tree via an elaborate system of small windows and mirrors. Looking upward, Leif could make out many rays of light crisscrossing the room.

There were several dozen books scattered across the floor. Some of the books were torn in half along the binding. There were also footprints in the thick dust that covered the floor. Someone had been here recently. This must have been the boy. *He was here, looking for something, but what?*

Uncertain of what else to do, Leif began climbing the moveable ladder, because there appeared nowhere to go but up. As he climbed, he read the binding of the books on the shelves: Bektair Aagar, Bo'orchu Cagar, Jamukha Gbosh, Chila'un Obzok... Each book appeared to bear a person's name. The lower bookcases were filled with identical handwritten books of varying thickness. Leif examined a few. Each book corresponded with the life of a person, although it was presented in a dreary manner. For example, on the spine of one book was written, *Jugal Patel.* Page after page was taken up intricate logical progressions and what-ifs. Each what-if, was proceeded by a complex notation of symbols and numbers, which Leif could not decipher.

(☼ ‰⅛๗†) If J.P. turns left down Folken Lane, he will meet a friend who will introduce him to the proprietor of a small coin shop, thus leading to J.P.'s career as a dealer of antique coins.

Immediately below that came another progression:

(⨍⅛ටʒ⍵) If J.P. turns right down Folken Lane, he will proceed to buy a loaf of bread that shall turn out to be exceedingly hard, causing J.P. to be in bad humour for several hours afterwards.

Leif paged through several more of these books before continuing his climb. They all detailed intricate cause and effect relationships, and each book focused on just one person. At first it was all very exciting – this idea of seeing someone's life unfold on the printed page – but it soon grew tiresome. Leif hoped for something more exciting. He stopped when he reached a section with names beginning with the letter "B." He stepped off the main ladder and tiptoed along a narrow ledge. He passed *Bidderbold*, then *Bijorge*, and then found himself at *Bilba, Sven*. The name after that was *Bimox, Jon*. But in between these two books was an empty space. It appeared as if once, perhaps not long ago, a book sat here.

"Bilblox's book," whispered Leif to himself. The long-shoreman's full name was "Paks Bilblox" and this is where his book ought to be. *Could it be? But where'd it go? Did the boy take it?* Impossible to know. Leif stood on the ladder for a long time, lost in thought, until finally he remembered that he had business to take care of and, reluctantly, he resumed climbing upward.

Leif continued his ascent until he came upon an opening that led into a cozy nook. The nook, as far as Leif could tell, was situated inside a large knot in the tree which had been hollowed out and turned into a small office of sorts. The room contained a desk, a fireplace, and a few book-shelves. The fireplace was lit with a strange, green flickering fire which created no smoke. There were no burning logs, briquettes, gas tubes, or anything at all that appeared to be fueling the fire. Above the desk hung a picture with a sturdy frame made of thick tree limbs. The frame was old and worn and, along one edge, it had two deep claw marks. The canvas itself was blank. "Huh?" said Leif to himself. "What kind of artwork...?"

Leif walked over to the desk and took the picture down from the wall. As soon as he did, a parcel wrapped in thick brown parchment fell out. Apparently, someone had hidden it there, tucking it away behind the back of the picture frame. Leif presumed that this was the thing that he was meant to burn. He studied the parcel closely. It felt light and brittle in his hands. The parchment was yellow and ancient looking. It appeared as if the whole thing might disintegrate into dust at any moment. Leif walked over to the strange green fire that was crackling in the fireplace. It was scorching hot. Leif took the package and held it over the flames. As he did this, he recalled Imad's warning: *Take what you find and burn it there. Don't open it or... or God help us all.*

Suddenly, Leif had a very strong hunch about what the package contained.

"I don't believe it," said Leif aloud. "He leads me right to it and then tells me not to look inside." Before he could second-guess himself, Leif ripped off the parchment covering the parcel. Inside was an old, leather-bound book and, on the front cover, in thick block letters were two words: ALFONSO PERPLEXON.

"Ah, give me a break!" said Leif angrily. "What am I supposed to do with this?" He sighed heavily. He started to open the book, then slammed it shut. "No I can't," he said. "I'll regret it, I know I will." Instead, he held the book up to the fire, allowing a green flame to blacken its cover. The pages started to turn a golden brown, the way slices of white bread do in a toaster. Then, suddenly, Leif pulled the book back into his arms and fanned out the embers that had started to form on its pages. His mind was racing with thoughts. *What if the book contained some vital information about where Alfonso was? What if his son was in danger? Perhaps the book could help Leif find his son – perhaps even rescue him? Could he really walk away from such information? But what about Imad's warning?* Imad knew what the book said. Presumably, Imad had written these books himself. Given that, wasn't it foolhardy to ignore Imad's advice – his warning?

Desperately, Leif yanked open the front cover of the book. The title page had the following inscription.

The Life & Times of
Alfonso H. Perplexon
A Concise Listing of Prophecies, Scenarios,
& Unusual Permutations

Like the other books in the library, the ensuing pages contained row after row of neatly written "what if" scenarios. The beginning was filled with scenarios Alfonso had already encountered.

(ɔïc⅛) If A.P. refuses to go to school on 7th of April, he will fall asleep at lunchtime and sleep-walk to school.

Leif nodded his head and couldn't help but smile. This was precisely what had happened.

(‡ℕ⊹☼⅞) If A.P. travels to the Boundary Waters for a canoe trip, on his fifth birthday, he shall have an ear infection.

This too had happened. "Amazing," muttered Leif.

Leif paused and realized he could read these for several hours and just delay the inevitable moment. He sighed deeply and flipped to the end of the book. The last page was filled with row after row of what-if scenarios, but it was different than the ones before. It appeared to be written hastily, and almost in panic. At the top was written:

Addendum
The Perplexons & the Shadow Tree

There was also a brief note:

> *Note Bene: If the cursed Tree is allowed to grow, there will be famine, the likes of which the world has never seen. Millions will die (between 7,865,234 – 44,324,210 or so says the Pen).*

"Hmm," said Leif. He kept reading.

> *If the Tree is planted, you will know, for the earth will shake with great tremors. If this happens, there are two scenarios in which it may be destroyed...*

"Great tremors?" said Leif. This made no sense, but he read on.

> *Scenario I. L.P. reunites with his son, M, and C.N.T at the obelisk. Together they set off for Dargora through the clouds. They arrive at the southernmost edge of the Petrified Forest where the three rivers converge, near the caves where the fog wolves live. From there, L.P., his son and M escort C.N.T. through the forest to ensure her safety. Where the forest ends, C.N.T. continues alone to Dargora. She recovers the Pen from its hiding place within the anatomical snuffbox. In broad daylight, she destroys the Shadow Tree. (✿ ‰ ⅛⅞)*

"L.P. must be me," said Leif to himself. At a glance, this scenario seemed favorable. He and Alfonso didn't have to go into Dargora and C.N.T. took care of destroying the Shadow Tree. Still, there were so many questions. What, for example, was the "anatomical snuffbox"? *And who in God's name was C.N.T?* There was nothing to do but keep reading...

Scenario II. *A Perplexon will rejoice with friends in the dark of the chasm. He will then destroy the Tree by himself. A Perplexon will succeed, but he will also die. (‡‰⅘⅄№⅞)*

"'A Perplexon' must be Alfonso," muttered Leif. He recoiled. His heart was pounding and his breath seemed to stick in his throat. He struggled to regain his composure. He began to process the significance of this what-if. The prophecy was clear, in the second scenario, Alfonso died. This meant that – at all costs – Leif could not let his son enter Dargora and attempt to destroy the tree. He needed to find Alfonso and quickly. But how? And where? The prophecy. The answer had to be in the prophecy. Leif quickly took another look at what was written. The first prophecy said that Leif would reunite with his son "here" and then showed the following picture...

The question was: What was this thing? And, more importantly, where was it? It appeared to be a tower of sorts, covered with ornate carvings. There was nothing in the background – no context or setting at all. But what about those carvings? Leif squinted closely at the drawing of the obelisk and saw that the following pattern was repeated again and again on the obelisk itself. It appeared to be a map of sorts. It showed a bunch of islands and rivers in the form of curlicues. In the center was a small white hole. Leif stared at it closely…

Clearly this pattern meant something, but what? He simply needed more time to solve this puzzle.

Leif took the small framed canvas with nothing on it and tucked it under his arm. He was taking this with him, though he couldn't say why. Then he took hold of Alfonso's book, and tore out the page listing "Scenario I" and "Scenario II." Finally, he took the book, kissed it gently with his lips, and tossed it into the fire.

CHAPTER FOURTEEN
TRICKS OF THE MIND

Bilblox lay face down in the snow, jaws clenched, eyes firmly shut. The coldness of the snow offered his only relief from the excruciating pain in his head; for Bilblox, it felt as if someone were slicing his brain in half, very slowly, with a red-hot knife that had been heated on the coals of a fire. Time ticked away slowly, imperceptibly – perhaps it was hours, perhaps it was days that passed – it was impossible to tell. Eventually, mercifully, the longshoreman fell into a very dark and prolonged sleep. When he finally rose from his slumber, Bilblox heard the sound of swords – and a great many of them – being drawn from their scabbards. He forced himself to pry open one of his eye. The light from the sun was blinding, but as the world around him came into focus, he saw that he was surrounded. There were four dozen soldiers, all dressed in leather armor adorned with feathers – the trademark garb of Dragoonya horsemen. Kiril was standing with them, looking remarkably at ease.

"Where did they come from?" groaned Bilblox.

"From an outpost just south of Dargora," replied Bilblox. "I got them while you were sleeping." Kiril reached down to his waist, unfastened his pouch, and dipped his fingers into the small bag. "Care for a pinch of ash, my friend?" asked Kiril. He drew close to Bilblox, squatted down on his haunches, and whispered soothingly, "Would you like to put the ash in your eyes – or shall I help you?"

"I should have killed you when I had the chance," whispered Bilblox.

"That's all behind us now," replied Kiril calmly, "Let us focus on the matter at hand. That's the sensible thing to do, isn't it?"

Bilblox grunted.

"What you are feeling now is the withdrawal from the green ash – and it will get much worse before it gets better," continued Kiril. "The pain is just beginning. You are still lucid – you can hear me – which means your mind has not yet begun to play its tricks. That will happen soon, very soon, and this is when men go mad. That is when you will beg me to end your misery. Trust me, my friend, you don't want to go down that road." Kiril then reached into the pouch and took out a generous dollop of the green powder. "Take it," said Kiril, "For your sake – not mine."

"No," whispered Bilblox.

"Just yesterday you were asking for it," said Kiril, "Why now the sudden change of heart?"

"I waited too long," said Bilblox hoarsely. "I should have… Alfonso… I should have…" But he didn't finish his sentence; instead, he passed out and his head fell heavily against the snow.

"Is he dead?" asked one of the Dragoonya horsemen.

"No," replied Kiril, "He is just in terrible pain."

"What shall we do with him?" asked another of the horsemen.

"Put him on a horse," said Kiril. "He's coming with us."

Bilblox felt as if he were falling and the sensation continued for hours. He kept falling through darkness, wondering at what moment his body would crumple upon impact with a hard surface. Perhaps this was the sensation of dying – to fall without end.

But then the falling stopped, seemingly without impact. He was lying face down in pebbly sand. Water covered him, and then retreated. The cries of grown men playing a game echoed in his ears. He couldn't decide whether he was underwater, still falling, or very much alive on a beach.

Bilblox lifted his head and then moved to a sitting position. He was on a beach near the water and several hundred feet away he saw a massive freighter lying on its side.

"Well I'll be," whispered Bilblox. "The *Nyetbezkov*." It was the place where he and Alfonso had first met, during a game of ballast. Alfonso had just begun learning how to become a Great Sleeper, and Bilblox had taken him under his wing.

Ropes dangled from the Russian ship and Bilblox could see longshoremen scurrying up and down. They were clearly playing ballast.

Bilblox smiled and then waved his hands. He tried to stand but somehow was unable to do so. He tried to yell towards them, but no sound came from his throat. A sudden itch erupted on the palm of his hand, and it quickly turned to pain.

Suddenly panicked, Bilblox thrashed around but was still unable to stand. He heard a low-pitched buzz that became louder and louder. Bilblox glanced out to see and saw the origin of the noise. It was a ten-story tidal wave about a mile from shore. It was heading straight towards them.

Bilblox screamed mutely. He opened his mouth again and again and tried to force out a sound – any sound. The tidal wave picked up the *Nyetbezkov* as easily as an egg shell and swept it towards Bilblox. At the last minute, with the wall of water almost on top of him, Bilblox was aware of a presence sitting calmly to his left. It was Judy, Alfonso's mother.

"Shall we leave?" she asked Bilblox. "World's End is much safer, and you still need to save Alfonso."

As he awoke, Bilblox could still hear the sound of the tidal wave in his ears. Soon it turned to cheering, just as his head-ache returned with great ferocity. Bilblox cracked open one eye and then the other; he found himself slumped over in the backseat of a small sled that was being drawn by a team of three white stallions. The only other occupant of the sled was a man, standing up proudly, clutching a small leather pouch in his right hand and pumping his left fist in the air triumphantly.

The man was Kiril.

Kiril glanced over at Bilblox, noticed that he was awake, and yelled over the roar of the crowd, "Hello there Bilblox, good to see you up, you have been out cold for almost two days." Then he added, "Quite a sight, isn't it?"

Bilblox took in his surroundings for the first time. He could still see quite well – so the power of the green ash was obviously quite long lasting – but his headache had returned and he knew that it would not go away unless he took the ash again. Bilblox looked around. The sled was making its way down a long snow-covered thoroughfare that was lined with tens of thousands of people who were all cheering raucously. Some of the people in the crowd were clearly Dragoonya soldiers, dressed in full battle gear, but the vast majority of them appeared to be wretched prisoners dressed in rags – filthy, half-starved, and wild-eyed. There were feeble old men, toothless old women, and even children, clamoring about on all fours, mouths hung wide open like mangy, famished dogs. Bilblox mustered his strength, sat up in his seat, and looked out at the people around him. They were not just cheering – they were screaming madly – and a few appeared to be foaming at the mouth.

"Who are all these people?" asked Bilblox hoarsely.

"Most of them are slaves," replied Kiril.

"Why are they cheering?"

"Because," replied Kiril, "This whole city has just been given new life."

Bilblox felt too weak to say anything or even contemplate a reply. Instead, he tried to get a sense for the "city" that was around him. There were no buildings to be seen. The only structures were a series of pillars that resembled massive bones; each was firmly anchored into the icy ground and disappeared into the cloud-filled sky.

"What is this place?" asked Bilblox finally.

"Dargora," replied Kiril.

"When did we get here?"

"Early this morning," replied Kiril. "We've been home for almost a full day and you've been out cold the entire time."

Kiril guided his sled for another mile or so, down a snow-covered road, lined with a series of tall, proud evergreen trees. On either side of the road, beneath the trees, were throngs of screaming slaves. Eventually, the sled arrived at a large, empty clearing, roughly the size of a small city park. The perimeter of this clearing was roped off and guarded by several hundred Dragoonya soldiers. In the center of the clearing was a large stage made of ice. On the stage stood a small muscular man who held a large bronze canister in his hands. Kiril eyed him appraisingly, then stepped down from his sled, and walked briskly over to the stage.

"Hello Konrad," said Kiril, as he greeted the man. "How are you my old friend?"

"Amazed," replied Konrad, his voice choked with emotion. "When your note arrived by the bird, I was.... well, stunned. You did it – *you did the impossible.*"

Kiril nodded proudly, pleased by the praise from his oldest and most trusted lieutenant.

"What about the girl?" asked Kiril. "Have you found her? Is she alive?"

"Not to worry," said Konrad. "I found her. She is fine and overjoyed to hear of your return."

"Good," said Kiril softly.

Just then a slender teenage boy, with sickly pale skin and two white eyes, strode onto the stage and embraced Kiril.

"You have done very well my son," said the boy.

"Thank you Nartam," replied Kiril, bowing his head before the person whom he had long considered both his king and his father. It was strange for Kiril to see Nartam this way – as a boy, really – but he tried to limit his reaction. No doubt it would all seem normal in time, thought Kiril. Nartam reached up and ran his finger across Kiril's face. "Your scar is gone," observed Nartam, "No doubt thanks to the green ash."

Kiril nodded. It was, of course, Nartam who had given him this scar as punishment for his failure to follow Leif Perplexon all the way to the gates of Jasber.

"I hope you haven't gotten greedy with that ash," said Nartam.

"Not at all," said Kiril.

"Hmm," said Nartam. He seemed unconvinced. "Well, in any case, let us accomplish at last what we have waited ages to do. You have done this. *You.* Today they cheer for you – not for me."

Kiril studied Nartam closely. He seemed proud, but did the pride mask a deeper jealousy? Kiril couldn't suppress his feelings of uneasiness.

"It is said that whoever plants the Shadow Tree is bound to it forever," said Nartam. "The planter and the tree are joined. Centuries ago, when Imad destroyed the Shadow Tree that Resže planted – Resže died with the tree. Resže wrote in his notes, *We are one.* So it will be once again."

Kiril understood what Nartam was telling him and what he now had to say.

"I insist that you have the honor of planting the tree," said Kiril.

"Are you completely certain, my son?" asked Nartam. "It was *you* who made this possible?"

Kiril looked his father in the eyes. *He's not really asking me,* thought Kiril. *He's telling me.*

"Of course," said Kiril. "The honor must be yours."

"My planting this tree will change everything," said Nartam rather cryptically. "You understand that, don't you?"

"I think so," said Kiril.

"I will still be king," said Nartam, "But I will also be the servant of this tree – just as the Great Sleepers of ages past were servants of the Founding Trees."

"Does that mean that I will also be a servant of the Tree?" asked Kiril.

"No my son," said Nartam. "You must *not* be. That is why I am telling you this. And, when we burn this tree, I forbid you from using any of its ash. *You must be the one man who always sees everything clearly.* Do you understand?"

Kiril nodded.

Meanwhile, back in the sled, Bilblox watched Kiril carefully. Bilblox was trying to grasp what was taking place – or what was about to take place. He saw the small, muscular man open the bronze canister and hand the teenage boy something about the size of a nut or perhaps... perhaps a seed. Then he saw Kiril offer his pouch of green ash to the teenage boy. It was at this moment that Bilblox realized that right here and now, on this stage of ice, the boy was about to plant the Shadow Tree.

This was the moment.

Bilblox lunged for the door of the sled, but his legs remained stubbornly in place. He looked down and, for the first time, noticed that his right ankle was manacled and chained to the sled. Bilblox thrashed about madly, trying to rid himself of the chain, but it was no use. And at last, as he finally grasped that he was trapped – and that he had failed, failed spectacularly – the haggard longshoreman looked up into the crowd, into the faces of countless screaming slaves and momentarily locked eyes with one slave in particular. She was a teenage girl with matted blonde hair and, as he saw her, his lips involuntarily formed a single word: Resuza.

CHAPTER FIFTEEN

SLAVES

Resuza blinked her eyes into the glare of the polar sun. Around her were thousands of excited, apprehensive slaves and quite a few armed Dragonya guards. All at once, the guards began to cheer, soon joined by the hand-picked slaves who enforced the Dragoonya commands. Soon, the crowd of slaves began to do the same, although their cheers were more like wild screams. Resuza knew better than to ask why everyone was cheering. If she had learned anything from her time in Dargora she knew this: when everyone around you did something, it was best to join in, and do so with more vigor than anyone else. And so she screamed as loudly as she could – screamed until her throat burned, her nostrils flared, and her jaw ached.

Resuza spotted Bilblox well before he noticed her. She watched in disbelief as a sled emerged from the distance carrying none other than Kiril and – sitting in the backseat of his sled, staring passively out at the crowd – was Bilblox. She rubbed her eyes, as if perhaps her vision was failing her, but what she'd seen appeared to be true. She gasped and then nudged Hill, who was standing next to her. Hill made no response, which worried Resuza.

Captivity had been hard on him, but in the past weeks, Hill had aged years. His face was drawn and thin, his skin was a sickly yellowish color, and his eyes had a sad, faraway look to them.

As the sled carrying Kiril and Bilblox sped past, Resuza nudged Hill again, ever so gently, and suddenly his eyes came alive.

"Is that...' he began.

"Yes," she said, "It's him."

"But how?" asked Hill. "Is Alfonso with him?"

"I have no idea." Resuza stared at Bilblox – the long-shoreman looked drugged. "I really hope not."

Hill made no reply. He watched as Kiril stepped out of the sled and left Bilblox sitting alone in the sled. Hill and Resuza watched as Kiril joined Nartam and another smaller man on stage. The smaller man handed Nartam a bronze canister and, moments later, Kiril handed Nartam a glass vial that sparkled in the sunlight. Nartam raised his hand high in the air and everyone who saw this simple gesture went silent; this silence rippled through the entire crowd until not a living soul uttered a solitary sound. "Oh no," whispered Hill. No one paid him any mind because his words were drowned out by the sound of the wind.

Nartam turned to Kiril and the two of them chatted for some time. Eventually, Nartam dropped down to one knee and knelt by a hole that had been dug into the ice. Then he placed something into the hole – it was impossible to see what exactly – but presumably it was a special seed. Then Kiril handed something to Nartam. It appeared to be a vial of liquid. Nartam held the vial with both hands and lifted it into the sunlight. The crowd began to murmur. Nartam opened the vial and poured the liquid contents into the hole. Immediately, four enormous Dragoonya soldiers began to shovel dirt into the hole. They worked furiously, in what appeared to be a panicked state.

Seconds later, the ground shook, exactly as it would after a distant earthquake. A thin black tentacle emerged from the ice. It resembled the charred leg of a giant octopus as it wiggled and squirmed upward, reaching for the sky. The tentacle grew quickly in length and width, and it began to undulate in the arctic air. A second and then a third and fourth tentacle emerged from the ground.

Hill drew close to Resuza and whispered into her ear, "Look at the evergreens." Resuza redirected her attention to a series of tall evergreen trees that lined the road that led up to the spot where the tree had been planed. The vibrant green coloring of the pine needles had disappeared and the needles were now a dull brown. "They're all dead," whispered Hill. Just then there was a gust of wind, the trees shook, and suddenly millions of dead pine needles fell downward – fell en masse – raining down on the slaves so thickly that for several seconds it was impossible to see the sky.

When the pine needles had all fallen, and visibility returned, Resuza and Hill saw that the tentacles had grown taller and were now at least ten feet long. They whipped around as if searching for something. Suddenly several of the tentacles grabbed one of the Dragoonya soldiers and thrust him high into the air. The guard began to scream. The tentacles started to slowly squeeze the soldier, and at the same time, the tentacles continued to grow and sprout new fingers. The guard continued to struggle but soon the tentacles enveloped him completely until it was no longer possible to see him at all. The tentacles proceeded to elongate, divide, and multiply and eventually they wound together forming the trunk of the tree – with the guard still inside.

The tree grew swiftly and turned even more repulsive. Its smooth bark glistened as if it were sweating from its own exertion. Soon the entire tree was nearly a hundred feet tall, with millions of intertwined branches that ended in sharp point, as if each individual branch was a dagger.

"It's the Shadow Tree," said Hill. "Everything will die – trees, grasses, animals, people – everything. Wherever its roots reach, death will follow."

"How could he?" asked Resuza.

"Who?"

"Bilblox," she replied, "He was in the sled."

Hill shook his head wearily. "I don't know. Maybe his blindness became too much for him."

"Get moving!" barked a voice in the distance. It was one of the Dragoonya soldiers. An order had obviously been given, and the soldiers began to corral the slaves back into the cave. All the slaves turned and began heading back toward the cave, except for one elderly woman who seemed to slip effortlessly between the small gaps in the crowd. With great dexterity, the old woman made her way against the flow of the crowd, toward Hill and Resuza. When the old woman was within earshot, she hissed and then grabbed Resuza's arm with a cold firm grip, pried open Resuza's fingers, and clasped her hand. "You look just like my pet," purred the woman, "Are you kin?"

Resuza recoiled from the woman. Her hands were ice-cold, her breath smelled of rotten fish, and she had no teeth.

"They took her from me," said the old woman.

"Took who?" asked Resuza, stepping backwards as she asked the question.

"My pet... she looked just like you," said the woman, "Only smaller and more frightened."

Suddenly, Resuza pulled the old woman close. "Are you talking about Naomi?" she demanded. "Have you seen her – have you?" The old woman appeared startled by Resuza's ferocity, but Resuza could not control herself; she had given up hope that Naomi might be alive.

"You're the sister, aren't you?" asked the old woman. "You're the one who left her to die."

"That's not true," protested Resuza.

"Oh yes, yes, yes it is," muttered the old woman, "My pet told me – told me everything. She doesn't want to see you ever again. She told me that many times before they took her."

"Took her where?"

But their conversation was interrupted by the great movement of the crowd. Someone shoved Resuza forward and, moments later, the old woman was drifting away in a gaggle of emaciated bodies.

"Where did they take her?" yelled Resuza.

The old woman's voice was not loud enough to carry over the crowd, but she heard Resuza's question, and instead of speaking she simply pointed skyward, gesturing up toward the giant bone-like pillars that stretched upwards from the slave quarters and then disappeared into the clouds.

Hill realized the old woman was no threat to Resuza, and took advantage of the situation to slip away. It would take a while for all the slaves to return to the massive cave that functioned as their work and living quarters. He had perhaps ten minutes before whistles would blow and force them back to work. In this time, Hill had something important to do or, more specifically, something to protect.

The Pen.

It was no longer safe in the barracks. The day before, one of the other slaves, a tall, thin man who slept next to him had seen him hiding the Pen in his shoe. "What's that?" the man asked. Hill denied having anything and tried to shoo the man away, but he persisted. "Give it to me or I will tell the guards," said the man. The man knew that, if he found anything valuable, he might be able to trade it for food. "I know you're hiding something," persisted the man. "Give it to me." Hill got out of bed and brushed passed him. The man hadn't followed, but Hill knew he wouldn't give up. This tall, thin man was starving. He was desperate. He would do whatever he had to do if it enhanced his chances of surviving.

Hill pushed his way through the crowd, squirming his way back into the slave quarters. He rubbed his hands against his shoulders as if to warm himself. Anyone observing him would see an old, weak man desperate to return to the warmth of the cave.

Hill entered the cave with the first group of slaves. Most lingered in the entrance, discussing what they had seen and reveling in their small taste of leisure time. Hill hugged the wall and walked towards his bunk bed. After a glance to confirm that he was alone, Hill continued to the end of the hallway. He looked around one last time, and ducked under the table that was nestled into the alcove. He pushed his hands against the dirt wall and it gave way easily. This was the entrance to their tunnel – the one that they had hoped would help them escape. They had filled it with a pile of dirt, just so it would go unnoticed. Hill climbed into the tunnel and crawled as quickly as he could.

It took Hill just two or three minutes to reach the storage depot. The floor of the depot was still piled with supplies. He and Resuza clung to the hope that they would find some way to escape. If that time came, they would need these supplies. There were still two main tunnels leading into the storage depot – the one heading back to the barracks and the other leading south toward the spot where Resuza had encountered the ice canyon. There was also now a third tunnel leading directly up to the surface. It didn't actually go all the way up. It stopped just shy of breaking through the ground above. Hill had dug this tunnel. He had done it in case they needed to make a quick escape. He and Resuza had come to call this tunnel their "emergency exit."

Hill climbed almost all the way to top of the emergency exit. There was still a thick slab of ice overhead, in-between him and the surface, and a murky beam of light filtered down through it. Just below this layer of ice, Hill groped around until he found a small nook in the ice. It was a perfectly-carved hiding spot for the Pen. Hill had the foresight to create this nook in the event that a day might come – like today – when he suddenly decided it was no longer safe to keep the Pen on him any longer. Hill withdrew the Pen and stared at it in the ambient light. Then a far-off echo of slaves' footsteps reminded him that he had little time. Hill set to work on the second part of his plan.

Hill used the Pen to burrow a very narrow hole, through the slab of ice overhead, to the surface above. He then withdrew a fork from his pocket and wedged it into the hole – just beneath the surface – so that the pointy tines of the fork would just barely be visible to someone walking up above. The landscape above ground was so uniform, and so blindingly bright and white, that no one would ever notice the small divot in the ground that was the mouth of their emergency exit. A person, if he was looking carefully, might notice the fork, but this was a chance that Hill was willing to take. He wanted to keep all of his options open. This way, no matter what happened – whether they were above or below ground – they'd still be able to find the Pen.

When he had finished with his work, Hill packed snow and ice around the fork to anchor it in position, and began his crawl back to the slave quarters. As he crawled back, Hill felt his heart pounding and his mind swam with worries and plans. But most of all, he thought about Bilblox. He hoped his friend's appearance meant that Alfonso was nearby. But the image of Bilblox's pale, sick face terrified him, and he dared not speculate what it meant about Alfonso's fate.

Chapter Sixteen
Hold Your Form

All around him, children were screaming – at least one hundred of them. It was deafeningly loud, but Alfonso struggled mightily to focus on his breathing; he sucked air in through his left nostril, held it, and exhaled through his right. He had to hold his form. He and Marta were now both young children – no more than seven years old – and whatever happened they could not allow themselves to morph again. That would be disastrous. Under normal circumstances, a mob of elementary-school-age children would hardly be cause for concern – let alone fear – but the current circumstances were anything but normal.

Presently, he and Marta were at the center of a mob. The children around them were howling like wild dogs. In truth, they looked more like animals than human beings. Their faces were caked with dirt and grime; their clothing, or what remained of it, was ripped and filthy; and they grunted more than they spoke. They stank of sweat and rotten food. They were massed in a great, writhing pack, where they were smashing into each other savagely. Something had happened to these children; they had either done something or witnessed something so terrible that they appeared to have lost their sanity.

Alfonso and Marta had morphed on the run – in the very last seconds before the mob converged upon them.

They had cut it close – too close – and Alfonso was fairly certain that two of the children had witnessed them morph. The children were twin girls – no more than four years old – and both had long, matted, black hair. The girls now stood on either side of Alfonso, pressing up against him.

"Stop!" yelled a lone voice.

All at once, the children went quiet and became perfectly still. Alfonso felt a surge of relief. *Breathe,* he told himself, *just breathe. Hold your form.*

At the edge of the pack, a solitary figure stood apart from the others. He was at least a head taller, and perhaps a few years older, than all of the other children. He had a broad forehead, a handsome Roman nose, and a strong chin, but there was something wrong with his eyes – they were slightly too close together. But it wasn't just that. A careful observer would notice that one of his eyes was blue and the other brown. The effect was subtle, but disturbing. The boy appeared to be in his early teens and, from the way that he carried himself, and from the way that the other children fell silent at his command, it was obvious that he was their leader.

"Where have the betrayers gone?" asked the teenage boy.

The children made no reply.

"They were just here," said the teenager impatiently, "I saw them with my own eyes – where are they?"

The children began to murmur, and from the sound of it, they were conversing in several different languages.

Marta leaned close to Alfonso and whispered into his ear: "Betrayers?"

"He's talking about us," replied Alfonso in a whisper. "We have to find a way out of here."

Alfonso looked around frantically. In the distance, perhaps a hundred yards away, was the obelisk. And here lay their sole cause for hope – a large, locked wooden door – at the base of the stone monument. It was an entrance leading directly into the stone tower. *If they could only get inside... but how?* The door was locked but, if Alfonso could somehow just get there, he felt reasonably confident that he could enter hypnogogia, reach through the solid door, and unlock it from the inside.

"Are you my father?" asked a slight, trembling voice. Alfonso looked over and saw that it belonged to one of the twin girls. She was speaking directly to him and it was clear that she expected an answer. "My father had a beard just like yours," said the girl. "Can you turn back into my father? Please?"

"Please take us away from here," said the other twin. She was slightly smaller than her sister and appeared more fragile. Indeed she seemed close to tears. "Turn back into Daddy and take us away from this place. Take us away from that awful boy."

Alfonso frowned. "I will try," he told them. "Just keep quiet."

"Enough!" shouted the teenage boy. The mob of children drew quiet instantly. "I will find the betrayers myself. I will hunt them down. Betrayers are not welcome here! It was betrayers who left us children here on our own – to die – but we won't let them forget what they did to us."

One of the twin girls, the bigger of the two, clutched Alfonso's hand and whispered: "I won't let him hurt you Daddy – I won't."

The other twin girl, the smaller of the two, began to cry.

"Everything will be okay," whispered Alfonso. "Please don't cry – not now."

But this only made the girl sob more loudly. The sound of her crying rang out across the silence and attracted the attention of the teenage boy. The boy eyed the girl sharply and then he seemed to notice Marta. *What had caught his attention?* Soon it became obvious: it was her clothing. When she and Alfonso had morphed, their bodies had changed, but their clothing had remained the exact same size; and so, despite the fact that they were now both young children, they were still wearing oversized adult clothing. Alonso had done his best to roll up the sleeves of his shirt and the legs of his pants, but Marta's clothing still hung off her body in a ridiculous fashion.

The teenage boy began walking toward them. As he approached, the children scrambled to clear a path for him. It had begun to rain and a fine mist filled the air. The boy smiled as he drew closer. His face was damp and his hair slick. His blue eye surveyed the scene – taking everything in – his other eye, the brown one, remained motionless, as if it were dead.

"Where did you get those clothes?" demanded the boy. He was addressing Marta; he apparently had not noticed Alfonso.

"I found them," replied Marta. Her voice was small, but defiant. Alfonso hoped she had the good sense not to pick a fight with the boy. But this was Marta after all – she was not easily bullied.

"Where?"

"On the ground," replied Marta.

"Liar!" screamed the boy.

The boy was close now – just a few feet away from Marta. Something bad was about to happen. Alfonso could feel it. Alfonso concentrated on his breathing – *in left nostril, hold, out right nostril...* But it was no use. He was distracted – both scared and angry all at once – and he could feel his body being tugged from the inside.

"Tell me the truth!" demanded the boy. "Tell me the truth and I won't punish you."

"I don't remember," said Marta. "Where did you get *your* clothing?"

The boy stepped forward and struck Marta hard across the face, causing her to topple backwards. There was an instant movement from the mob and, all at once, children were running for cover. The teenage boy snatched a rock up off the ground – a big hefty, hunk of stone – and raised it up over his head as if to clobber Marta.

"Don't do it!" pleaded one of the twins, the larger and bolder of the two. "She's a mommy – I saw her – she just changed into a kid's body!"

"Then she's a witch!" screamed the teenage boy. "Everyone pick up stones – we must stone the witch!" All of the children rushed to pick up stones. They looked more terrified than bloodthirsty. "On my command!" shouted the teenage boy.

"But maybe the witch knows where our parents are," said one of the children, a red-headed girl, the smallest of the group, who was no more than four years old. "I don't want to throw stones at her."

"You *must* do as I say," said the teenage boy. "Now everybody throw your stones on three – one, two…"

Marta screamed.

But the blow never came. Instead there was another shout – a deep, loud, authoritative shout: "No – don't you dare!" Everyone looked to see who had barked this command. They all saw a tall, powerfully-built man in his twenties. His eyes were piercing and deadly serious. "Drop that rock right now *little boy*," said the man. The teenage boy looked around nervously, as if to see what the other children were doing, and whether they might come to his aid. "They won't help you," said the man. "This is between you and me."

CHAPTER SEVENTEEN
GREAT TREMORS

L eif slowly climbed up the ladder that rose up the in-
terior wall of the tree. His mind was deeply troubled.
Most of all, he wanted to see Alfonso. He wanted to hug him
tight and promise that nothing bad would ever happen to
him again. But after reading the prophecies, he didn't know
if he could promise anything at all. He vowed over and over
to himself that his only goal was to make sure Alfonso lived.
That was it.

After several minutes of climbing, Leif ran out of breath.
It wasn't just the physical exertion or even his mild fear of
heights – it was a general sense of doom. Sweat dripped
from his chin and slowly soaked his hair. Finally, he reached
a trap door, which he pushed open. Warm sunlight shone
directly on Leif. It was near sunset and the sky was awash in
soft, golden light. *How long had he been inside this tree? Hours,
days, a week?* Leif basked in the light. After the unremitting
gloominess of the Sea of Clouds and the dark of Straszydlo
Forest, the warmth of the sun felt wonderful. Leif pulled
himself up onto a small observation perched at the very top
of the tree, which offered spectacular views of the surrounding landscape.

Unbroken forest stretched for miles and miles. In the
far distance, he thought he glimpsed the Sea of Clouds, and
in the other direction, Leif saw foothills rising to the jagged

High Peaks of the Ural Mountains. A slight buzzing noise interrupted his thoughts and Leif turned in the direction of the distant Sea of Clouds. He saw something he must have missed initially. Now he eyed it closely and, hard as he tried, Leif found it difficult to grasp what exactly he was staring at. It was a curious circular object that hovered just above the trees, less than a mile away. The vessel, if you could call it that, had a huge oval balloon with a small wooden cabin on top. The cabin had two masts, each jutting off the roof at forty-five degree angles, and holding sails that hung down like floppy elephant ears. At the back of the balloon was a spinning propeller. The underside of the balloon had two large fins that appeared to function as rudders. To call it awkward-looking would be an understatement, but one thing was pretty clear – Leif was staring at a flying ship.

Leif stared at the ship for several minutes, trying to decide what to make of it. The skin of the balloon was a dark gray, and it did have an ominous air to it, but the aircraft did not appear to have any guns or weapons. The design was unique, something that likely was conceived as a test model, and which was never mass produced.

After some debate, Leif decided that he should signal the ship in the hopes that whoever was flying it might help him – at the very least – get out of this forest. He knew he was taking a risk, but given the situation, it seemed like a risk worth taking. He began to wave his arms frantically and shout as loudly as he could. A minute or so later, a dark cloud appeared on the horizon. The cloud came from the north. It appeared to be a storm, a bad one, and it was moving quickly. Still, for it to cover the northern horizon so rapidly was unusual. Leif turned to go back down. The cloud made him uneasy, and he felt a sudden rush to return to the library.

Before he could climb down, however, he heard a deafeningly-loud WHOOOSH. All at once, every tree around him began to whip ferociously back and forth. The observation deck vibrated and began to come apart. Far below, Leif could hear the land groaning as the ground became gelatinous and waves rippled across the earth. The clumsy airship was caught by the wind and it hurdled topsy-turvy towards Leif. For a moment, Leif thought the airship might actually collide with the observation deck, but several hundred yards before reaching him, the airship went down into the treetops, where it finally was snagged by a thick tangle of tree branches.

Leif dropped to his stomach and held onto the observation deck with all his might. Branches of all sizes tore off trees and whirled around; one of them slammed into Leif's forehead, and then everything went black.

Leif never knew how long it was that he lay unconscious. When he finally came to, however, he felt something sharp pressing against his throat. He blinked his eyes in a daze, and when his vision finally returned, he saw that someone was towering over him and holding the point of a sword to his neck.

"Were you the one shouting and waving your arms?" the person asked in a low, almost conversational voice. "What the devil were you up to?"

Leif concentrated and tried to focus his blurry eyesight, enough at least to make out this person's features. She was tall with dark hair that shone almost as if wet. Her face was angular, with a sharp nose and chin, but was still quite pretty. Her eyes were a pale blue and she stared at Leif with a fierce gaze.

"Who are you?" Leif asked.

"In case you hadn't noticed, I am the one with the sword," said the woman. "So I'll be the one asking the questions." She withdrew her sword, enough so that Leif could breathe more easily, and took a small step backwards. However, something about the way she moved gave Leif the impression she wasn't well. Her motions were jerky, as if perhaps she had suffered multiple sprains.

"Sorry," said Leif. "It's just that... I'm stranded in these woods. In fact, I signaled you because I was hoping that you could give me a ride."

The woman snorted. "My ship is in a pretty bad way," she said. "I'm not sure it can fly and, even if it could, why should I help you?"

"Because I have to find my son," said Leif, and despite himself, his voice trembled with emotion. "I could really use some help."

The woman took another step back and let out a long, weary sigh. "What is your son's name?" asked the woman finally.

"Alfonso," replied Leif.

The woman arched her eyebrow, as if she were surprised, and yet doubtful. "Alfonso," she repeated slowly.

Leif nodded.

"I thought you looked familiar," said the woman finally.

"Huh?" said Leif.

"Never mind," replied the woman, and as she said this, she returned her sword to its scabbard and offered Leif a hand in order to help him to his feet.

"Who are you?" demanded Leif.

"It doesn't matter what my name is," she replied crisply.

"I am..." began Leif.

"I know who you are," said the woman.

Leif felt something wet on his hand and saw that he had blood on his palm. At first he assumed the blood was his, but then he realized it had come from the woman's hand.

"Are you all right?" asked Leif. "Are you injured?"

"I am fine," replied the woman dryly. "I was in a bit of a fight and I have a few wounds that aren't fully healed yet. But I'm fine. And if you don't mind, let's get going before the tremors start again."

"The tremors," said Leif, almost to himself. The word hammered away at his brain – *tremors* – and suddenly there could be no doubt; that's what he'd just felt. Leif recalled the words of the prophecy: *If the Tree is planted, you will know, for the earth will shake with great tremors.*

"I have to go," said Leif nervously. The woman did not bother to respond because she was already on the move – scampering from tree branch to tree branch – moving with great agility despite her wounds, heading back toward her flying ship.

Chapter Eighteen
Naomi

Resuza's younger sister, Naomi, was an unusually small girl for her age. She was almost ten years old, but she could easily be mistaken for a six-year old. Her bones were thin and delicate, her face long and slender, and when she moved in quick, darting movements, she resembled a greyhound. She was a thin girl, even in the best of times, but there was a wiry strength to her that was quite similar to her older sister. She projected a tense, keyed up manner, which was very much in evidence as she sat on her bed staring at the closed wooden door to her room.

BAM! BAM! BAM!

Someone was hammering on the other side of the door. Ordinarily, no one ever knocked – instead, they simply entered at will – after all, Naomi was a slave, and slaves were not allowed to have any privacy. Not that there was much for her to enjoy in the privacy of her room. The enclosure resembled a jail cell. The walls and floor were made of solid oak; there were no windows; and the door was a massive slab of timber reinforced with iron crossbars and bolts. The door was unlocked, Naomi could leave at will, but there was nowhere to go. Escape was an absurd notion because Dargora was surrounded by nothing but hundreds of miles of desolate, windswept fields of snow and ice. Of course, it could have been worse. Naomi could have been one of the common slaves who worked in the caves, boiling blubber and feeding coal into ovens. Fortunately, however, Naomi was a skilled slave who was given certain luxuries – like bread, heat and private sleeping quarters.

BAM! BAM! BAM!

For a moment the door began to give under the force of the pounding, but it cracked open just slightly, because Naomi had effectively locked herself in her room. She had taken a small cast-iron frying pan – which she had stolen from the kitchen – and wedged it carefully between the door and a divot in the stone floor. It worked like a charm and the door remained fixed in place. Naomi took some satisfaction in this. She was very good at fixing things and this handiness – this ability to repair a stove or true a wheel – is what had earned her a spot in the ranks of the skilled slaves. Naomi's satisfaction, however, was short lived because her plan was very short-sighted. She had locked herself in her room to keep *him* out, which had worked, but what now?

BAM! BAM! BAM!

He was Ure, a monstrous hulk of man. He was a *Goon-ya-radt*, a slave whose job it was to enforce the rules and, in so doing, to bully and terrify the others. Ure was excellent at his job. He could instill terror with a simple look. Ure's face was horribly damaged by frostbite – he had no nose and the skin around his eyes was purple and lumpy. Naomi knew that it was Ure who was on the other side of the door, pounding furiously; apparently, somehow he had learned that she had stolen the fish and, of course, the frying pan.

BAM! BAM! BAM!

Naomi had only stolen the fish out of desperation. In the last few days she had been more hungry than she had ever been in her life. There had never been very much in the way of food in Dargora – even for the skilled slaves like

Naomi – but now even that meager food was gone. Everyone now hoped to survive by ingesting the black ash from the Shadow Tree. So far, on pure instinct, Naomi had resisted taking any of the ash. The slaves who used the ash frightened her. Their eyes turned white, their hair and fingernails fell out, and they stopped speaking. Naomi was determined to avoid using the stuff for as long as she could.

Suddenly the door exploded open, the cast-iron pan skittered across the stone floor, and Ure stuck his grotesque head through the doorway. "Where did you get that pan?" barked Ure. "And it stinks of fish in here. You little thief! Why I ought to beat you for…"

"You'll do no such thing," interrupted another voice, which was, cool, calm, and yet utterly firm. The man who spoke these words entered the room. He was a tall fellow, with a wide brim hat, a strong face, a lantern jaw, and two entirely white eyes. The man turned toward Ure and said with scorn, "You have displeased me very much."

Ure bowed his head submissively, almost the way a stray dog might. "It will not happen again," said Ure, voice trembling. "I shall kiss the girl's feet if it pleases you – Lord Kiril."

Kiril backed Ure into a corner and grabbed him roughly around the neck with his hands. Ure could have tried to swipe his hand away, he could have screamed; but he didn't. Somehow, deep down, he understood that there was no escaping Kiril. And so Ure stood perfectly still as Kiril, ever so slowly, clasped his left hand around his throat. His grip was firm, so firm that Ure could just barely breathe, but what Ure felt more than anything else was the sharp points of Kiril's long fingernails scraping his skin.

"Your fingernails," wheezed Ure.

"Yes," said Kiril. "You must forgive me. You see, my health is unusually good as of late, and so my fingernails, which would usually be rather brittle, are as resilient and sharp as razor blades. I have found that they can cut most anything. Why just this morning I was cutting steak with them. Wonderful isn't it? I no longer dine with a knife."

"Please," gasped Ure.

"Now listen up, you hideous wretch," said Kiril, "If you ever touch this girl, or so much as look at her again, I shall see to it that you are skinned alive and fed to the Fog Wolves. Do you understand?"

Ure nodded and then scampered out of the room like a frightened dog. As soon as he was gone, Naomi walked over to Kiril and shook his hand seriously.

"Thank you," she said. "Although I was ready to dispatch him." She slyly withdrew a dagger she had hidden up her sleeve.

"I expected as much," said Kiril proudly.

"You were gone for a long time," said Naomi. "Why?"

"I did not intend that," said Kiril. Kiril looked down at her small, slender face and felt a surge of compassion. It was almost the same feeling that he had the very first time that he met her. He had come to know Naomi through her sister, Resuza. It was a peculiar arrangement. Kiril had met Resuza by chance. He was staying at a Dragoonya outpost, just outside of Barsh-yin-Binder, when he discovered Resuza – then, a filthy, wild-eyed slave girl. He caught her hiding some stolen potatoes in a secret stockpile of food that she kept in the hollowed-out root of a tree. The stockpile was filled with all manner of things – radishes, flour, sugar, knives, boots, a map, and a pocket watch. Resuza was terrified when Kiril discovered her. And rightly so. She was, no doubt, convinced that Kiril would beat her, or at least yell at her, but instead Kiril simply clucked his tongue and said, "I could use a clever girl like you." From that moment on, Resuza worked directly for Kiril, mainly spying for him – eavesdropping on conversations – reporting which Dragoonya officers were lazy, greedy, or disloyal. "I'll do whatever you ask of me," Resuza had told him, "So long as you try to find my sister and help her."

"Where is she?" Kiril had inquired.

"She is a slave," explained Resuza, "And I believe she is in Dargora."

"What is her name?"

"Naomi," explained Resuza. "And she looks just like me."

"I will do what I can," said Kiril.

And he had honored his promise. Kiril found Naomi working in one of the underground slave barracks in Dargora. She was frail and malnourished, but alive, thanks in large part to a toothless old woman who had cared for and watched over her with the fierce devotion of a grandmother. The old woman was half-mad – she called Naomi her "pet" – and she screamed hysterically when Kiril took Naomi away. Kiril fed Naomi bread with butter and bowl after bowl of hot milk with cardamom. She never gained much weight, but she quickly gained strength. Kiril found her curious and intelligent, and taught her the basics of self-defense. She was a natural, and so he taught her more. In time, he began to think of her as his apprentice. People were loyal to Kiril because they knew he was fair and just, as long as they served his interests. And Naomi did exactly that. She was his eyes and ears in the slave milieu of Dargora. More than a few times she had provided him with intelligence that proved extremely useful.

"I am glad you are in good health," said Kiril. "Are you all right?"

"Within reason," replied Naomi curtly. "You were gone for a long time, and your enemies became mine. It was difficult."

Kiril stared at her. Clearly, the girl had not been treated well. But the fact that she still stood before him was a testament to her strength and keen survival skills. It also emphasized the importance of his vision. She would be needed in the future, for a role that was as yet unclear. At that particular moment, Kiril vowed to help her. Someone like Naomi would prove useful many times over. And she would prove deadly as an enemy.

"I see that you have not taken the ash," said Kiril.

"No."

"Good," he replied. "You mustn't. I will give you all the food you need. All will be well. No harm will come to you. I promise." Kiril smiled as he said this, though all the while, he couldn't help recalling his vision, the one in which an arm – with the bloody crescent-shaped wound – reached out and tried to shove Naomi into an abyss.

"Thank you," said Naomi. "You promised many times to train me, so that I can fight and kill like you. Will you, now that you have returned?"

"Of course," replied Kiril. "Right now, however, I need your help."

"I'll do it," said Naomi. "What is it?"

"I am looking for your sister, Resuza, I need to find her," said Kiril.

"Why?" asked Naomi with a frown.

"She betrayed me," said Kiril. "But I am willing to forgive her so long as she gives me something that I want. The problem is she could be anywhere."

"What is it that you want?" asked Naomi.

"It is something that she has taken," said Kiril. "I believe she has a Pen, a very powerful Pen, and I must have it."

"Why?" asked Naomi.

"Because," said Kiril. "It could cause troubles for me – for *us*."

"I don't want to see her," said Naomi angrily, "You're not going to bring her here are you? I hate her. I don't want to see her – not now – not ever. Please don't bring her up here. Leave her down in the barracks forever. That's where she belongs."

"Down in the barracks," said Kiril with a start.

He seemed shaken. "What are you talking about?"

"You didn't know?"

"Know what?" demanded Kiril.

"I thought you must know – you know everything," said Naomi nervously. "Resuza is here in Dargora, working as slave, in one of the caves where they boil the blubber."

"Are you sure?" asked Kiril.

"Yes, positive," said Naomi. "I saw her a few months ago, on one of the parade days, when all the slaves were marched out."

"Did she see you?" asked Kiril.

"No, she didn't."

"I don't believe it," said Kiril, almost to himself. "What a stroke of luck."

Naomi smiled for the first time. It lifted her spirits to make Kiril happy, even if briefly.

"You must help me, my dear," said Kiril finally.

Naomi nodded.

"And you can start," said Kiril, "By writing a note."

Chapter Nineteen
The Obelisk

"You can't talk to me like that," the teenage boy replied. His words sounded tough, but his voice betrayed his fear. He stared at the powerfully-built man who was walking towards him with unmistakable menace. At that moment, it didn't seem to matter that he commanded so many children.

Alfonso Perplexon, the teenager who had morphed into this 20-something man, approached the boy in a manner he had seen played out in playgrounds all his life. Only this time, he wasn't the victim or the bystander. He was the bully. He knew exactly how to act: keep moving, keep talking, keep threatening. Push once, shift your weight, curl your hands into fists.

"I can talk to you however I want," Alfonso sneered. As he moved towards the boy, he raised his hand high above his head, ready to strike. The boy flinched and most importantly, the children surrounding them moved back.

"Don't hurt him!" one of the children cried out.

Alfonso laughed. "I'll do whatever I want, and you'll take it," he replied. "Do you know how easily I could make you bleed?"

He looked at the ground and saw Marta lying there. Her eyes were wide and surprised. She seemed as shocked as the children were. Alfonso approached her, picked her up, threw her over his shoulder, and walked to the door of the Tower. He put her down to investigate the door further.

It looked absolutely impregnable. The door itself was covered with rusted iron plates, and two spyholes were hammered shut from the inside. He threw his weight against the door. It didn't move an inch.

"You can't open it," said the teenager.

Alfonso turned around. The teenager had come up behind him and was standing just a few feet away. Behind him were the children. Their expressions had changed from fear into something different. Interest, perhaps. Or perhaps even a little confidence. The element of surprise was now gone, and they realized that they were unharmed. Alfonso knew he had to do something quickly.

He turned back to the door and examined the hinges. They too were made of metal, and looked secure despite their age.

"You can't open it," the teenager repeated. "We tried. You can't do it. You're not that strong." The first titters of laughter made their way through the children. Their hero – the teenage boy – was back. Alfonso had to make short work of this, or he and Marta would be in serious trouble.

Alfonso turned quickly and within five steps he was next to the boy. He pushed him so hard that the boy flew roughly to the ground.

"Insult me again and I'll use a knife," Alfonso roared. He then turned back to the door and focused on the problem at hand. Perhaps he could use hypnagogia to enter the keyhole, but he wasn't sure how it would work in this new state. Plus, going through a keyhole just didn't seem like the type of aggressive, muscular move he needed to make to win over these savage children.

His eyes traveled across the perimeter of the door, looking for anything that might indicate a way in. The closer he looked at the keyhole, the more he doubted he could use hypnagogia to get in that way. Something was covering it. Perhaps a piece of wood or metal, but there was no way of inserting a key into it. And it wasn't as if others had not tried. The weak sun lit up the area around the keyhole and highlighted a profusion of faint scratches.

He continued his close examination of the door. The bottom edge drew his attention. It was the only part of the door that was not covered with metal. About four inches of wood was exposed, starting where it touched the ground. This narrow band ran the width of the door. More importantly, a few areas in this band looked dark in contrast to the rest. Alfonso leaned down and poked inquiringly at the dark areas. They were soft. Alfonso was reminded of building tables and cabinets with Pappy back in World's End. They built most of the greenhouse storage by themselves. Rotting wood was always a concern for them, and he had become very good at identifying where it had appeared.

"You can't get through," repeated the teenager. "No matter how much you push me down, you still can't get through that door."

Alfonso whirled around and the teenager flinched. Instead of hurling himself at the boy, he smiled all-knowingly.

"Pay attention little boy, and you may learn a few things," he said.

Alfonso crouched down and poked again at the bottom of the door. He nodded as if satisfied and stood up. Alfonso paused, took a deep breath, and then kicked the bottom of the door as hard as he could. The blow landed squarely on the darkened, rotted area. He crouched down again to examine the effect. He nodded, and kicked that part of the door over and over. His last kick was so foreceful that he fell to the ground. Another titter of laughter spread among the children.

"Too bad," said the teenage boy. He took a step forward, as did the other children. They knew what would happen next, and they were looking forward to it.

Alfonso ignored them. He rose to his feet, approached the door again, and grabbed the metal edge at the bottom of the door that had been exposed by Alfonso's repeated kicking. With one mighty pull, he ripped the metal sheet and it began to lift away. Several pulls later, it was lying on the ground.

Alfonso walked quickly to the teenage boy and lifted him off the ground by his jacket.

"Do you still doubt me?" he hissed.

The teenage boy shook his head.

Alfonso let the boy fall back to the ground. He walked back to the door and kicked it again. This time the metal could not protect it. The door flung open, revealing a grim, dust-filled staircase. At long last, the obelisk would reveal its secrets.

CHAPTER TWENTY
THE LAST THREAT

The polar reaches of upper Asia are wide and long and empty of human life. Winds routinely reach hundreds of miles an hour, and in the darkest of the winter, to be outside for longer than a half-hour is to court a swift death. Everything is in short supply: food, vegetation, light, life.

And yet in this desolation, Nartam had created the last refuge of the Dragoonya. *Dargora*. The city was surrounded by a vast petrified forest and in the center of this forest was a great ice field where the city itself was situated. Everything in the city was white – either because it was made of snow, ice, or bleached bones – and the result was that, from a distance, the city was almost impossible to see under the bright glare of the sun. It was only truly visible at dawn and at dusk, when the light was soft, allowing the human eye to discern the subtleties in many various shades of white.

On most days, there was not much to see. The slaves all lived in barracks that were situated underground. The most dramatic feature of Dargora were several giant pillars. These pillars, which rose up from the earth and stretched into the clouds, often swayed and groaned in the wind as if they were still part of a living being. In addition, there were a few buildings scattered here and there, all made of ice. And then, of course, there was the Great Cave.

The Great Cave was the original location of Dargora. Hollowed out by the grinding of glaciers, the cave was spacious, protected from the wind, and surprisingly comfortable. Nartam had outfitted the place with an abundance of fur rugs and copper urns lit with brightly burning fires. Nartam even had a throne here, as well as several long rows of tables and chairs. And nowadays the Cave also had another benefit as well: it offered a perfect view of the newly-planted Shadow Tree, which sat just a hundred or so feet from the mouth of the Cave.

Nartam and Kiril were standing in the Great Cave, chatting quietly. Behind them, deeper within the cave, several dozen Dragoonya officers and noblemen were seated at tables. In years past, the Dragoonya leaders gathered here to feast – consuming great quantities of roasted pig, fried whale, grilled reindeer, and ice wine. Today, however, no food was being served. There were just bowls and bowls and bowls of black ash. The men seated at the table were not singing, or talking, or even whispering. They were all sitting motionless, simply staring off into the space. They almost looked like figures at a wax museum – life-like, but too still to be real. The men using the ash had all lost their hair and their fingernails but, other than this, they appeared quite healthy-looking. Occasionally, one of them would extend an arm, scoop up a pinch of black ash, and rub it into their eyes. This was the only sign that they were alive.

"Have you tried it?" asked Kiril.

"Yes of course," said Nartam. He was dressed in furs that were far too big for him. All of Nartam's clothing was too big for him these days. They had been designed for a full-grown man – not a sixteen year old boy – and the shirt sleeves and pant sleeves hung down from his limbs. "But unlike these greedy fiends," he said gesturing to his officers, "I have taken it gradually – a little more with each dose – and that is why I still have my hair, my nails, and my wits about me."

"That's sensible," said Kiril. "You are taking the proper dose, but these other fools have lost their senses and overdosed."

"It's true that they have become poor conversationalists," said Nartam, "But they are splendid fighters, and when ordered, they will fight with an inhuman ferocity, as if their lives and the lives of their loved ones hang on the outcome. I have been letting the men use it twice a day. Any more than that and they'd be worthless. One of them demanded more, and I had to put a sword to his throat in order to talk him down."

"I see," said Kiril. "Don't you worry that others will demand more as well? How do you keep them in line?"

"I planted the Shadow Tree," said Nartam with a smile. "And that makes me the Tree's father, and theirs. It is incredible to see, but they will do anything for me. Plus, I have you as a failsafe, just in case anything untoward happens. Isn't that so?"

"Of course," said Kiril.

Kiril glanced back at the cave opening. It was small, and from the outside no one could guess at the cathedral-like space of the Great Cave that existed just beyond the opening. But it was not the opening that Kiril was looking at. Just beyond it, in a bare patch of carefully swept ground, stood the Shadow Tree. Its smooth, oily bark reflected the many torches and candelabras that lit up the Great Cave. To one side of the tree, a giant bonfire raged. A few Dragoonya climbed carefully up and down the tree using a metal ladder. They sawed off limbs and tossed them into the fire. Each time they did so, the fire crackled and whined, as if afraid. And on the ground next to the fire was a mound of black ash, growing higher and higher with each burned limb. The tree itself didn't seem to mind. It was constantly in movement, its branches twisting like the restless legs of a centipede.

"Kiril, my dear son, you look troubled," said Nartam. "Pray tell me, why?"

"The black ash," said Kiril finally. "It presents certain… dangers."

"True," said Nartam thoughtfully, "But that is only because it is so powerful and, whoever controls this power, will control everything within his grasp."

"Perhaps," said Kiril, "But do you control this Tree – or does it control you?"

Nartam laughed.

"Why do you laugh?" asked Kiril.

"Because it makes no difference," said Nartam. "We are one now – the Tree and I."

Kiril made no reply, except a slight frown.

"I am unused to seeing you afraid," said Nartam.

"Perhaps a little fear would behoove us," replied Kiril.

"No," said Nartam, "Fear is what we must instill in others – not in ourselves. If we allowed it to fester, fear and self-doubt would be our undoing."

"If you say so, father."

"Come," said Nartam. "Why don't you have just a pinch of the black ash – it will ease your mind."

Kiril hesitated. Just several days before, Nartam had made it clear that Kiril should never touch the stuff. *So why was he offering it now?*

"Maybe some other time," replied Kiril politely.

"As you like," said Nartam. "You know," he said, taking a step closer to Kiril, "In the past I have been hard on you, I have wounded you, I know, but it was only to make you stronger. You understand that don't you?" There was genuine tenderness in his voice as he said this, which was exceedingly rare for Nartam. "I hope you do, my son."

Kiril rubbed his cheek, momentarily surprised that his scar had vanished. He wanted to say something more, perhaps something pleasant and friendly, but words escaped him.

Instead, he bowed low.

"I will need you in the coming days and weeks," said Nartam. His eyes grew wide and stared into the distance. It was a strange expression, and one that made Kiril uncomfortable.

"We shall have visitors soon," said Nartam ominously.

"Leif and his son?" inquired Kiril.

Nartam nodded. "Most likely they are on their way. Of course, the Founding Trees know what's happening – they understand, in their own way, that the roots of the Shadow Tree will kill them. The trees will struggle with each other and we, inevitably, will be pawns in their delicate game of chess."

Nartam smiled with a sudden excitement, and his eyes bored into Kiril's. "My son, it is a thrilling experience, to understand the Shadow Tree the way I do. *To be a part of it!* It is a wonderful, wonderful thing..."

Kiril cut him off. It was unnerving to listen to Nartam speak so passionately. His father had always been a coolly rational man, devoted only to the accomplishment of goals and ideas. "How will they attempt to destroy the Shadow Tree?"

"The same way that Imad did," replied Nartam. "By using the Foreseeing Pen."

"Daros," said Kiril. "I know where the Pen is." He watched Nartam's immediate interest blossom across his face. "I believe that it is *here* – in Dargora."

"Don't toy with me," said Nartam.

"I'm quite serious," said Kiril, "Alfonso had the Pen, but he gave it to the girl – the one whom we once employed – Resuza."

"You're sure?"

"Fairly certain," replied Kiril.

"Hmm," said Nartam. "Can you find her? I believe she has a sister, a girl named Naomi, if I recall, she was briefly your slave – isn't that so?"

Kiril was astonished; Nartam never forgot anything.

"Naomi is dead," said Kiril. The lie came to Kiril's lips so quickly that he never even had a chance to consider why exactly he'd said it or what trouble it might bring. Somehow he just sensed that it might be better for Naomi if everyone, including Nartam, thought she was dead. He did not want her becoming a pawn. "But don't worry," added Kiril quickly, "I believe I have already found Resuza. For the moment, I won't say more – just know that I hope to have the Pen for you within the coming days."

Nartam smiled. "My son, my son, you are indeed a-"

Just then, two of the Dragoonya seated at the long table stood up suddenly and looked about anxiously. Both men were bald. Their entirely-white eyes were bloodshot. In unison, they began clawing at their eyes, as if their retinas were burning, but because their fingers had no nails they did not scrape themselves too badly.

"Stop it!" barked Nartam irritably, "Before you succeed in gouging out your eyes."

Kiril shook his head and sighed. Grown men clawing at their eyes were the least of the problems that lay ahead, given the highly potent and addictive nature of the black ash, and it concerned Kiril that Nartam did not sense this. *You must be the one man who always sees everything clearly,*

Nartam had told him. *But what was he supposed to do about what he saw?*

"You haven't told me why you brought him," said Nartam, as he pointed over to a corner of the cave where a large man lay unconscious on the ground. It was Bilblox. He had been that way for hours, barely moving. He was going through withdrawal and Nartam knew that the longshoreman must be in a great deal of pain. "You must have a reason."

Kiril was ready for the question.

"I came across him on the shores of the Sea of Clouds," replied Kiril. "He was nearly dead and I left him there. Several hours later, I was struck by a thunderclap of images brought on by taking the Jasber Ash."

Nartam nodded. Kiril could tell that the Dragoonya leader was pleased.

"I know these dreams," said Nartam. "And Bilblox was in them?"

"Only in one," Kiril replied. "In that dream, you were falling into an abyss. He saved you."

Nartam stared blankly at Bilblox. "He saved me?"

"Yes," Kiril lied. He held his breath and cursed himself for the first lie about Naomi that then led to this second lie. It was a bad idea, but it was too late.

"Well," said Nartam, "If that is the case, then I want Bilblox at my side at all times."

"At all times... but why?" asked Kiril, with a trace of uneasiness in his voice. "If my dream tells the future, isn't it just a matter of letting fate run its course?"

"No, not at all," said Nartam. "The moment that you had this dream of yours, you acted upon what you saw – *you brought Bilblox here because of that dream* – and when you did that, you altered the course of fate. It may still happen exactly as you foresaw in your dream, but it may not. In any case, I don't want to take any chances, so I insist on keeping Bilblox nearby so he is there whenever I may need him."

Kiril nodded, but said nothing. Suddenly he had a problem that he had not anticipated. He had lied to Nartam, but because of this lie Nartam now wanted Bilblox at his side at all times, which meant that Bilblox might not be there to save Naomi at the crucial moment. Kiril had made a mistake and he saw no immediate way to undo it.

"You are truly skilled," Nartam said. "To turn a man like Bilblox into a slave takes unparalleled skill. He is a wonderful gift to me."

"Thank you," said Kiril. He bowed deeply. "You taught me everything, father."

CHAPTER TWENTY-ONE
CLIMBING THE BONE

After the planting of the Shadow Tree, the tension in the slave quarters grew steadily. You could see it on the faces of the slaves, as they wondered what would happen to them. Wild rumors circulated that the slaves would be fed one by one to the Tree. Even the guards appeared uneasy. Hill and Resuza had additional worries as well – namely, Bilblox and Naomi. Bilblox had looked pale and close to death as he sat in the back of the sled. *What had happened to him and why was he sitting in Kiril's sled?* His mysterious arrival now presented yet another complication. If they were able to escape, wouldn't they need to rescue Bilblox too?

And what about Naomi?

After her encounter with the old woman, who had called Naomi "her pet," Resuza constantly searched the slave quarters for her. But the old woman seemed to have disappeared. The slave quarters were enormous, holding thousands upon thousands of slaves, but they weren't impossibly large. It didn't seem possible that this old woman could just melt away. And yet she had.

For both Resuza and Hill, their lives in the slave quarters now seemed to drag on with excruciating slowness, as they waited for something to happen.

And then it did.

One evening, after a long day of toil, Resuza had muttered goodnight to Hill and fallen into bed. A sudden crinkling noise interrupted her quick descent into sleep. She slammed open her eyes, but saw no one. Eventually, she reached underneath her pillow and pulled out a note. There was a very faint light emanating from dying fires of a distant coal oven and, in this murky glow, Resuza read the note:

> Tomorrow night, at midnight, the main door will be unlocked. I've bribed the guard. Climb the yellow pillar to the north of the slave quarters. I'll meet you at the top. Bring _everything_ and do not linger. They're coming for you. - Fonzia

"Fonzia" was the nickname that Resuza had once called her little sister, Naomi. The two girls used it only when they were playing in the woods. It was a secret name. No one else could possibly know about it. This note had many implications, but the most profound of them appeared to be confirmation that Naomi was alive.

As she sat on her bed with the note lying limply in her hand, Resuza could still recall their parting with startling clarity. It happened early one summer morning in the small town of Tulov where she, her sister, and her parents lived. The entire family was still asleep when the slavers rode into town on their horses. The horsemen had torches and they set fire to all of the homes. Her parents ran out of the house to fight the flame and, when they did, the horseman had killed them. Cut them down with swords. Resuza and Naomi hid in the house for as long as they could, coughing on the smoke, until they were finally forced out into the street. In the chaos, no one saw them emerge.

"Come on," Resuza had yelled, "We've got to run for the river!" Naomi, however, stood in place, frozen like a statue, staring at the bodies of their dead parents. "Come on!" begged Resuza, tearfully, "We must go before they see us!" Naomi wouldn't budge. Resuza tried to drag her, but Naomi pushed her away. Just then, a horseman spotted them. They were out of time. Resuza turned and ran as fast as she could, darting in and out of the smoke, zigzagging her way down to the river, where she hid among the reeds. She had simply followed her instincts and ran for her life. There was nothing else she could have done; at least that's what she told herself again, and again, and again, to assuage her own guilt. The guilt had festered over the years like a wound, especially because she had, eventually, concluded that her sister must be dead.

Incredible as it seemed, however, the reality was that Naomi was alive and had actually been watching over her. It could, of course, be a trick. This could be Kiril or Nartam toying with her. But why would they bother? After all, Resuza and Hill were slaves – captives – there was no need to trick or trap them; they were already trapped. In any case, heeding the advice on the note – and escaping – seemed like the only sensible thing to do.

The following evening, at exactly midnight, Hill and Resuza made a run for it. Instead of relying on the uncertainty of a bribed guard, they used their escape tunnel and emerged into the snow directly above the slave quarters on a fiercely cold polar night. For the better part of a half-hour, they crept across the snow, heading north, until they found the one pillar that appeared to have a slight – very slight – yellow tint to it. Then they started climbing, which was relatively easy to do, because the pillar had many holes and crevices to grab hold of. It became increasingly obvious to them that they were climbing a vertical column of human and animal bones – jaws, clavicles, femurs, arms, rib cages, skulls – which had all been fused together into one single column.

As they went higher and higher, just one thought kept fluttering its way across the synapses of Resuza's brain: *Don't look down!* As she climbed upward, she struggled to stay focused, concentrating on each and every crevice that she used to hoist herself upwards; and yet, despite herself, she involuntarily stole a quick glance downward. What she saw was dizzying enough to make her want to vomit. She and Hill were far above the ground, perched precariously on a narrow stone ledge. They were so high up that only a hundred feet above them was the first layer of impenetrable clouds.

From this perch, they could see all of Dargora, including the hideous Shadow Tree, which was growing at an astounding pace. Within a few days time it had grown to a height of over two hundred feet and, despite the fact that a small army of Dragoonya soldiers was working around the clock burning the tree's limbs and collecting its ash, the tree was still growing steadily in size. The other thing that was apparent from this height was that every tree, shrub, plant, and patch of moss within eyesight was now dead. Dargora had never been an especially green place, but there was a modest collection of vegetation here and there – especially in the north of the city where there were a few hot springs – and now all of this was brown, wilted, finished. The roots of the Shadow Tree had spread a ripple of death in every direction.

"Do you think we're climbing the correct pillar?" asked Resuza finally.

Hill shrugged wearily.

"Where do you suppose it leads?"

"No idea," replied Hill. "I'm too exhausted to think properly."

Hill and Resuza surveyed the landscape below. Resuza looked again at the Tree.

"What do you suppose my sister meant when she wrote, *They're coming for you?*" asked Resuza finally.

"I've been asking myself the same question," replied Hill. He ran his fingers through his long beard and picked out a few pieces of ice that had formed. "It's curious because we have no value to them. We don't know where Alfonso is, I couldn't find my way back to Somnos if I had to, and I am too weary to do much work. They must want something else."

"The Pen?"

Hill nodded.

"Do you have it with you?" asked Resuza.

Hill stared at her blankly, and then rubbed his hands together, but said nothing; apparently, he did not intend to answer her question.

"Do you?" she pressed.

"No," said Hill finally.

"The note said to bring everything with us," said Resuza.

"I know," said Hill cryptically. "That's why I chose not to bring it with us."

Resuza rolled her eyes. Without saying any more, she stood up and began to climb. Hill watched as she climbed easily. He sighed and started up after her.

Soon they arrived at the layer of clouds and began to climb through it. It was eerie to be stuck in a thick, white-gray mist, but they welcomed the respite from the constant wind. They climbed without speaking and lost track of time. Hill's mind shut off and he became a machine, taking one careful step after another. Then Resuza uttered a low cry that woke him up.

Hill looked up towards Resuza. It was hard to see her even though she was only several feet away, but her body appeared to be glowing white.

"What is it?" he shouted. "Are you OK?"

She didn't reply and Hill furiously continued climbing until he was directly beneath her. He looked up and saw what had caused her to yell out.

They had emerged above the cloud layer, and the moon bathed them in a milky glow. Directly above them, stuck like a marshmallow on a stick, sat an old wooden ship. As they looked around, they could see other ships suspended on the many pillars that jutted up towards the night sky. They were all different, but most were quite large and big enough to cross the ocean with hundreds of passengers.

It looked as if the Dragoonya had taken several dozen antique warships – the sorts that pirates and old sea captains like Horatio Nelson once sailed – and hoisted them up onto the tops of these massive pillars made of bone. The ships were now homes, the strange equivalent of tree houses, in which the Dragoonya lived. The clouds hovered just beneath many of these ships, which gave the illusion that there was an entire armada of ghost ships floating gently on the clouds. Many of the ships had windows, which were brightly lit, and others even had decorative flags and sails fluttering in the wind. Most ships were connected by a series of swinging rope bridges. All in all, the ships comprised a strangely beautiful city that appeared to rest on the clouds. Hill and Resuza stared at the sight, gaping in awe.

For several minutes they remained motionless, spell-bound. But then the wind picked up again, and they looked up to measure their progress. Their destination, a large warship connected by rope bridges to several other ships, looked to be a short climb away.

"Do you think your sister will be waiting for us?" Hill asked.

"I hope so," Resuza replied. As she said this, she couldn't help feeling nervous about the upcoming encounter. It had been so many years. Resuza had tried to protect her during that time. After the Dragoonya had captured Naomi, Resuza followed them all the way to the gates of Dargora, pushing herself to the brink of death before finally turning back. Later on, when she was working for Kiril, Resuza had made Kiril promise to take care of Naomi. Resuza had been Kiril's loyal servant until, during the battle of Somnos, she defected and switched sides in order to help Alfonso. She simply couldn't stand the thought of betraying Alfonso who had been such a loyal friend to her. It was only later, in the hours after the battle, that she began to wonder about her sister. What had become of Naomi? What would Kiril do with her? Would he kill her?

Once again she had abandoned her sister. Resuza had always intended to return to Dargora and set her sister free, but it hadn't worked out that way; in fact, now it was Naomi who was helping Resuza make a break for freedom.

"Come on," said Hill. "We're almost there."

Resuza nodded and began to climb. She went faster now, and Hill did the same. In no time at all, they were at the intersection of the pillar and the ship's hull. Outlined in the hull they saw a rectangular door. It had no knobs or levers and no obvious way to enter.

Resuza looked at Hill. "What should I do?" she asked.

Hill shrugged his shoulders. "Push?"

Resuza tentatively pushed on the door. Although the wood had warped and made the door tight, it soon opened. Resuza listened, hoping to hear her sister's voice, but she heard only the wind.

"Naomi?" she whispered loudly.

There was no answer.

"It could be a trap," she said.

"I know," replied Hill. They both stared into the dark opening, trying to find any reassuring sign at all.

Resuza sighed.

"Well, we can't wait here forever," she announced. "Let's go." With that, Resuza and then Hill climbed into the pitch-black hull of the ship.

Chapter Twenty-Two

Kolo

Inside the uppermost floor of the obelisk there was an observatory, equipped with shiny brass telescopes, giant wall-maps, old dog-eared atlases, several desks stacked with papers, a few leather chairs, numerous old rugs, and six perfectly round skylights that allowed crisscrossing beams of sunlight, each swirling with dust, to illuminate the entire space. The ceiling was covered with a vast canopy of gauzy spider webs. Clearly, no one had been here for a very long time.

At first glance the observatory appeared to be a celestial lookout, a place to watch the stars, but a closer examination proved that it was truly a watchtower meant to monitor the movement of passing travelers on the forests and plains below. Indeed, there was an entire library of books, organized by date, with careful notations on which armies, merchants, and lonely travelers had passed through here.

Currently, the observatory was packed with roughly one hundred children – and Alfonso and Marta – both of whom had taken the form of adults in their twenties. Among the children was the teenage boy who had once been their leader. Now, instead of giving orders and issuing threats, he sat quietly, seemingly awed and intimidated by his surroundings. Several hours before, when Alfonso had ordered the boy to drop his rock, the boy had caved. Immediately after that, he had become a meek figure – shoulders slouched, head down, face pouting – like a child who had been severely scolded by his teacher. The transformation was dramatic. At first, Marta had insisted on tying him up.

"It's not necessary," said Alfonso cooly.

"Why not?" asked Marta. "He tried to kill me!"

"He won't bother anyone now," said Alfonso confidently. As he said this he looked the boy directly in the eyes. "He is just a coward – a scared boy playing bully – nothing more. Trust me, I know the type, you can find them in any schoolyard."

Marta frowned. She didn't trust the boy, but she went along with it. As the children settled down in the observatory, Marta asked them questions. "How long have you been without your parents?" she asked one of the children, a small sallow-faced girl with clumpy brown hair.

"They took mama away to be a slave when my sister and I were three or maybe four years old," replied the girl.

"Who did?" asked Marta.

"The feathered horsemen," replied the girl.

"She means the Dragoonya," interjected the boy who had once been the leader. He looked about uneasily, unsure of himself. "They didn't bother with us because we were too small to do their work."

"Instead we had to do *his* work," said the girl with the clumpy hair as she pointed accusingly at the boy.

The boy said nothing in his own defense, he simply looked away.

"What's your name?" Marta asked the little girl.

"Basia," replied the girl.

"Everything will be okay now," said Marta and, as she said this, she reached out and clasped the girl's hand. Basia smiled and her eyes filled with tears. Their conversation was interrupted by several of the smaller children who had begun to cry.

"They're hungry," explained Basia. "We haven't eaten in a very long time."

"There's food here," said Marta. "I saw a room filled with provisions several floors below."

"What kind of food?" asked Basia hopefully.

"I'm not sure," said Marta, "But come with me and we can have a look."

"That's a good idea," said Alfonso.

Marta stood up, gestured for the others to follow, and then headed toward the stairs. The other children followed eagerly. Marta currently had the physical appearance of an adult – in reality, of course, she was not even ten years old – but the other children deferred to her because of her calm and confidence. It seemed miraculous to Alfonso that, just a few hours previously, these same children had been chasing Marta with the aim of killing her.

"Do you need help?" asked Alfonso.

"No, I'll be okay," replied Marta as she took Basia by the hand and disappeared down the stairs. The other children followed en masse. The teenage boy stood up, as if to follow them, but Alfonso shook his head. "Not you," said Alfonso. "You stay here with me."

The boy sighed heavily, as if in protest, but he did as he was told. For several minutes neither of them spoke. "What is this place?" asked Alfonso finally. "Do you have any idea?"

"It's an old Czuczke watchtower," said the boy.

"Czuczke?" inquired Alfonso.

"Yes," said boy, "They were traders and hunters and they set up these watchtowers along their trading routes. At least, that's what my brothers told me, before they were taken…"

The boy frowned and then grew quiet, as if he were angry at himself for revealing so much of his own story.

Alfonso studied the boy closely. He was filthy. He had food stuck in his teeth, months of dirt packed under his fingernails, and a dark coating of dust, sweat, and grime covering his face. It was hard to tell exactly how old he was. He had the look of a boy who was large for his age – perhaps a ten year old who was big enough to pass for fourteen. But he wasn't dumb. Alfonso felt certain of this.

"What's your name?" asked Alfonso.

"What does it matter?" asked the boy angrily.

"If we're going to talk, it helps to know each other's names," said Alfonso. "Mine's Alfonso."

"Okay, fine – mine's Kolo," said the boy grudgingly. "So tell me, Alfonso, what are you going to do with me?"

"Well one thing is for certain," said Alfonso. "I'm not leaving you here with these kids. Your days as king are over."

Kolo shrugged, as if he didn't care.

"What happened to your brothers?" asked Alfonso.

"What does it matter to you?" asked Kolo.

"Just answer the question," said Alfonso.

"Slavers took them," said Kolo sourly.

"Took them where?"

"To their city," Kolo replied. "The one they call 'Dargora'."

This got Alfonso's attention.

"Why didn't they take you?" asked Alfonso.

Kolo said nothing.

"I asked you a question," said Alfonso.

"I begged them to take me too," said Kolo finally. His face contorted in pain, as if recalling this memory dredged up some deep bitterness in him. "I tried following the convoy, but the guards threw stones at me. I followed anyway, at

a distance. I wasn't the only one. A bunch of us kids did this
– a gang of us – we didn't know what else to do."

"Then what happened?" asked Alfonso.

"I – we – followed them for a long time, until we came to
a junction with three rivers."

"How long did you follow them for?" asked Alfonso.

"I don't know, a long time – until we were nearly dead,"
said Kolo. "We tried to make it through the stone forest, but
couldn't."

A stone forest. This was it, Alfonso thought. The petrified
forest that Resuza talked about...

"Why not?" asked Alfonso.

"Because of the fog wolves," explained Kolo. "They come
out each night and roam the forest. We hid from them for a
while, but they found us." The boy shuddered suddenly, as
if chilled. "I was the only one of our group to make it back."

"And since then you've been ruling over these kids and
trying to kill strangers by throwing stones at them?" asked
Alfonso pointedly.

"I'm not going to lie to you," said Kolo. "I have done
some bad things since then – really bad things – but *you*
would have done the same things if you were me. Sometimes
that's the only way to stay alive."

Chapter Twenty-Three
Flying North

Leif Perplexon was good at fixing things, especially while asleep. He always had been. Ever since he was a teenager, he had shown a great knack for repairing virtually anything with moving parts – bicycles, lawnmowers, chainsaws, mopeds, fans, tractors, fancy exercise machines – it didn't matter what the thing was, if it was broken, you just gave Leif a wrench and a hammer, and his sleeping-self would do the rest. He was just like his brother Hill in that respect. These skills often came in handy, and this was certainly the case in the tree canopy of Straszydlo Forest. When he finally made it across the canopy of tree branches in pursuit of the mysterious woman who claimed to know Alfonso, it only took him about fifteen minutes to assess the problem with her flying machine.

The right and left ailerons were damaged.

Ailerons are the hinged flaps near the tip of the wing that allow the plane to roll to the left or roll to the right. This flying contraption didn't have wings, but it had two fins that essentially functioned in the same way. Leif saw that the hinges were busted as were the cables that connected the ailerons to the pilot's steering mechanism. This particular flying machine was most definitely not an airplane. It looked more like a flying donut. Its large oval-shaped balloon was filled with some sort of gas that had the same effect as helium, thus lifting the machine off the ground. There was also a propeller in back. Below the balloon was a small cabin equipped with chairs upholstered with velvet, leather couches, a table, two or three oil paintings, a large bearskin rug, and a small potbelly stove. It was, without a doubt, the oddest vehicle that Leif had ever laid eyes on.

At present, both Leif and the woman were perched on a branch inspecting the right aileron.

"Where'd you get this contraption?" asked Leif.

The woman ignored the question. "Can you fix it?" she asked.

"It shouldn't be too hard," said Leif confidently. And he was confident. In the flying cabin, there were tools and enough odds and ends that would function as spare parts. "If you can get us off this tree branch, we should be okay."

"I'll get us off the branch," replied the woman. Then, without uttering another word, she took out her sword and began hacking away at the branches and vines that were currently wrapped around the body of the aircraft.

"I'll join you in a sec," said Leif, "But first I have to do something."

"What?" demanded the woman.

"You'll see," explained Leif. "I need to get something I left behind." He had no intention of revealing too much to this strange person. And for the time being, she needed him.

It took Leif the better part of two hours to find a rope and a pulley and make a harness. He was just getting ready to depart when the woman tapped his shoulder and handed him a loaded crossbow. It was a small compact weapon, which was already loaded with a sharp metal bolt. "Take this," she said. "You may need it." Leif thanked her and then began lowering himself to the ground with the use of his rope and pulley. The closer he got to the ground, the more uneasy he became. The sun had set and the forest was totally dark; it was impossible to see even the faintest trace of a shape; nonetheless, Leif could hear movement below him. Branches were snapping and, at one point, it sounded like bark was being peeled off a tree. When he was about fifteen feet above the ground, Leif whistled loudly. He heard a howl and then a great scampering of feet. Leif let himself drop down another few feet and whistled again. There was a great, WHOOOSH, and something slammed against Leif's chest. Leif felt damp fur and a wet tongue. He closed his arms.

It was Korgu.

For a moment Leif felt something tug on his foot, but before the thing could take hold, Leif shot it with his crossbow. There was a horrible scream. Frantically, Leif began using the pulley to hoist himself and Korgu upwards as quickly as he could. Leif was tired and it took a long time, but once they were more than ten feet off the ground, he relaxed and pulled at a measured pace.

The woman said nothing when Leif arrived with Korgu, the giant wolf. She simply nodded, and they both set to work on the repairs. It was night, and Leif nodded off to sleep with tools in his hands. His sleeping self immediately set to work. The woman seemed nonplussed by this strange sight of someone working while asleep. In fact, within an hour or so she had started to sleep-work as well.

They labored through much of the night. At dawn, the flying machine was more or less fixed. Leif had hammered the dented ailerons back into shape and had mended the steering cables as best he could. The thing wouldn't fly like new, not even close, but it should work. The woman, despite her injuries, had worked all night hacking away the branches and vines.

"Let's go," she yelled.

Leif scrambled into the vessel. The woman took a seat at the front of the cabin, flicked a couple of switches, and then said, "Hold on." Seconds later, there was a loud groan and the entire ship lurched forward. They appeared to be stuck, then the ship lurched again, and suddenly they were floating upwards. Leif felt a surge of relief and excitement all at once. The woman said nothing. She simply guided the aircraft back up into the sky. She steered by using two rudders, which she operated with her left and right hands. The ship flew surprisingly well. The cloud cover was thick and, initially, it was difficult for Leif to make out anything on the ground.

"Where are you headed?" asked Leif. He was anxious to find Alfonso and, if possible, sooner rather than later.

"To the same place as you," the woman replied matter-of-factly.

"Oh?" said Leif.

"Have a look," said the woman, pointing downward with an index figure. Leif glanced in the direction in which she was pointing. The clouds were slowly clearing and he was able to see glimpses of the ground. He soon found himself staring at a vast forest of what appeared to be evergreens, only all the trees, for as far as the eye could see, were dead. There was no trace of a forest fire, which is the only thing that could have done this. It was as if the trees had, en masse, simply decided to shed all their pine needles.

"It hasn't reached Straszydlo Forest yet, or perhaps Straszydlo is somehow immune, but the rest of the world is going to hell – and quickly," said the woman.

"The Shadow Tree?" inquired Leif.

"Yes," said the woman. "It must have been planted a few days ago."

"How quickly does it grow?"

"Not sure," said the woman. "Truth is, I don't know much about it. When I was growing up in Somnos we used to sing a nursery rhyme about it – *Let me tell you of a dark shadow tree and the world's end* – but it was just a story to scare kids."

"You're Dormian?" inquired Leif.

The woman nodded.

"And that's where you met Alfonso – in Somnos?"

The woman nodded again.

"So," said Leif with a sigh of frustration, "Would you mind telling me what you're doing, flying around, by yourself, in this crazy balloon?"

"Looking for Alfonso," replied the woman, "And perhaps the Shadow Tree as well."

"And what exactly is your plan?" asked Leif. "I mean, once you found this tree, what were you going to do?"

"Still working on that," said the woman, and she flashed the briefest of smiles.

"Fair enough," said Leif, also smiling for a moment.

"How about you?" asked the woman. "What were you doing on top of a tree in the middle of Straszydlo Forest?"

"Looking for a ride," said Leif.

"Fair enough," replied the woman, again smiling briefly.

In the corner of the cabin, beneath the table, Korgu was fast asleep and snoring. For some reason, the sight relaxed Leif. How could the wolf possibly sleep in these bizarre circumstances? It was wondrous. Leif took a deep breath and looked around, examining the cabin a bit more closely. The couches, the chair, and the table were all very finely made, as if taken from the parlor of a wealthy family. The oil paintings on the wall were all of fish, which seemed very odd to Leif. There was a cabinet with silver cutlery and fine china plates. In the far corner of the cabin, there was a small framed certificate, which Leif had somehow failed to notice before. It read:

Hammerson Brothers Zeppelins – London, England.
Flying Fishing Vessel. Prototype SFS 2A.
Built for the Lord and Lady Groh.
Equipped for use on inland seas, modified
for rooftop landings.

This plainly made no sense.

Leif glanced out the window and, for a moment, saw something gray and pointy sticking through the clouds. He glanced around the ship, spotted a small pair of binoculars, grabbed them, and used them to survey the ground below. "Hey," shouted Leif excitedly, "What is that over there? Bring us in closer." The woman agreed, but when they got closer, what Leif saw turned out to be just an outcropping of rocks on the top of a mountain.

"What were you hoping to find?" asked the woman.

"Nothing," replied Leif dejectedly.

"Well, there is some pretty good shepherd's pie in the icebox," said the woman. "Help yourself."

"Shepherd's pie?" said Leif incredulously. "Where the heck did you get that."

"It's a long story," replied the woman.

Leif ate his meal and stared out the window in a daze. Dead trees and shrubs for as far as he could see. It was a total wasteland. All of Asia and perhaps Europe also would soon look like this. And yet right now all he could focus on was stuffing his face with the shepherd's pie and savoring the taste of chicken. When he was done eating, he suddenly felt extraordinarily tired. He moved himself over to the couch with the intention of lying down for a few minutes – just to rest. He awoke several hours later to the sound of the woman's voice.

"You better come have a look at this," said the woman, from the front of the cabin.

"How long was I asleep for?" asked Leif.

"A while," she replied. "Quick, you should see this." Leif hustled over to where she was standing. The woman was pointing down at the ground, at a narrow road, which was filled with people; they were swarming like ants, all heading in the same direction. "They must be refugees," said the woman. "They are probably fleeing the droughts that the Shadow Tree is causing."

Leif made no reply because he wasn't looking at the road. He was looking off into a bank of clouds. He grabbed the binoculars to take a closer look. Something else had caught his attention. He was looking at a blanket of clouds which was pierced in a dozen places by pointy mountain peaks.

"What?" asked the woman. "What is it?"

"I think I recognize those clouds," said Leif.

"What?" said the woman. "Recognize them from where?"

"From a drawing..." said Leif, mainly to himself. "The carvings..." Leif reached into his pocket and pulled out the page with the drawing of the obelisk. He studied the pattern that was carved into the obelisk again. Suddenly it all snapped into perfect focus. Those weren't islands and rivers – they were clouds! And each of those curlicues represented places where the mountain peaks were jutting out of the clouds. "Look here," demanded Leif, pointing at the drawing. "This pattern is actually a map – can you take us to the spot in the center where the hole is."

"I don't see what you are talking about," said the woman.

"Look closely," said Leif excitedly. "The pattern on the drawing of the obelisk with the curlicues mirrors the way those mountains poke through the clouds."

"Yes, I see it!" said the woman. "Where did you get this?"

"Never mind, I will explain later," said Leif. "Can you just take us to the spot where the hole is?"

"I think so," said the woman. She began navigating the ship and consulting the drawing. Several minutes passed. Leif grew more and more excited. "Do you see something poking through those clouds over there?" asked Leif. "Right where the hole is on the map?"

The woman squinted her eyes. "Yes," she said finally. "It looks like another mountain top."

"No," said Leif. "It's too tall and slender. Get us closer!"

Leif squinted at the clouds, rubbed his eyes, and squinted again. Unless his eyes were deceiving him, he felt fairly certain that he was staring at the top of a pointy tower – an obelisk.

"There is a man standing at the top of that thing," said the woman. "Do you see him?"

Leif squinted. The woman steered the aircraft closer yet. Leif now felt certain that he was staring at the top of the very same obelisk depicted in the prophecy. There was a narrow terrace on top and, sure enough, a man was standing there. The man appeared to be in his early twenties. He looked, well... he looked an awful lot like Leif.

Leif frantically struggled to open one of the windows in the cabin. It screeched open. Leif stuck his head out. The aircraft was now just a hundred feet or so from the top of the obelisk. "Hello!" shouted Leif as loud as he could. The man on the terrace waved back excitedly. He appeared happy. Overjoyed. "I'm looking for my son," screamed Leif. "I'm looking for Alfonso Perplexon." It was a stupid thing to say. Leif had no reason to believe that the man even spoke English.

Moments later, however, the man called back and yelled a long solitary word: "DAD!"

CHAPTER TWENTY-FOUR
TIME TO TALK

K iril could not sleep, which surprised him because he had always slept well, despite the many terrible things he had seen and done. While on the hunt or during battle, he could go several days with only bits of sleep here and there – and, of course, he often slept while marching or fighting, as all Dormians did – but what he treasured most were the rare times when he could sleep and simply sway in a hammock or sit in a chair and whittle with his knife. That was the greatest of all luxuries.

Tonight, however, was a different story. He had insomnia. The instant he lay in bed, his mind kicked into overdrive, thinking about Nartam. He replayed the events that had led to him telling one lie, and then another, and concluded that these lies would inevitably multiply. It was the nature of lying – with each successive invention, it becomes easier and easier to keep going. Nevertheless, Kiril believed it was right to have lied. *What choice did he have?* His bigger concern was the Shadow Tree. He could barely bring himself to look at it. And the way that Nartam talked about the tree, as if it were an extension of himself – it was very unsettling.

Eventually, after several hours of restless turning, Kiril gave up, dressed quickly and climbed to the deck of the massive man-of-war that served as Dragoonya headquarters and the living chambers for Nartam and his most trusted aides. There were several guards on the deck, but all of them appeared comatose, lost in a dream world created by the black ash. Kiril walked up to one of the guards and examined him closely. His eyelids were covered with ash. Kiril snapped his fingers in front of the man's face and he didn't so much as bat an eyelid. In the old days, the Dragoonya always used the ash in moderation because there was so little of it; now they had such an abundance of it, that even common guards were overdosing on the stuff – and while on duty! Kiril strode away from the gathering of lights in the forecastle and to the quarterdeck where Nartam lived.

He had to talk to him now, thought Kiril. *If it wasn't already too late.*

Kiril wasn't exactly sure how he was going to say it, but he knew that he had to speak frankly about the Tree. Kiril had seen the stockpiles of ash that his men had gathered. There was enough ash there, if used wisely, to last them a very long time. The tree had served its usefulness. Kiril was glad of that. Indeed, he had risked his own life many times so that the tree could be planted, but it had become a liability – worse than a liability it had become an insidious presence that was starting to affect the minds of his men and of Nartam himself.

Kiril was relieved to see that the guard stationed in front of Nartam's door was awake and alert.

"Where is Nartam?" demanded Kiril.

"Down in the Great Cave," said the guard. "Shall I send someone down with a message?"

"No," said Kiril, "I'll go myself."

Twenty minutes later, Kiril was on the ground, trudging through the snow, making his way to the Great Cave. It was so cold out that the snowflakes on the ground had turned into dry crystals that swirled like sand beneath his feet. He walked as quickly as he could, face tucked into his jacket, eyes trained on the ground. Eventually, he looked up. The cold stung his eyes. *And there it was.* In between Kiril and the mouth of the Cave stood the Shadow Tree. The trunk of the tree was enormously thick – equivalent to that of a Great Sequoia – which seemed inconceivable, given that the tree had only been planted days ago. Its trunk was badly disfigured – studded with the stubs of old limbs that had been cut off and burned. The uppermost branches of the tree squirmed and wiggled like thousands of skeletal fingers that, all at once, had come to life and were grasping for something to grip.

Two guards stood at the base of the tree. It was impossible to tell if they were alert and doing their jobs or whether they too had taken the ash and lost their senses. "Hey there!" yelled Kiril as he approached the men. Neither of them responded or even budged an inch. As he drew nearer, Kiril could see that their eye sockets were dark with the stain of ash. "Wake up!" screamed Kiril. "You are supposed to be…"

Kiril never finished the sentence, because the two men both drew their swords at once and charged him. Kiril was so caught off guard, so totally shocked, that he barely had time to draw his own sword before the two men were upon him. The first guard lunged at Kiril wildly and Kiril parried his attack and deftly stepped out of the way so that the man crashed to the earth and nearly impaled himself with his own sword. The second guard was more cautious. He circled around Kiril and waited for his companion to get back on his feet.

"Drop your swords *now*," growled Kiril, "Or I shall kill you both."

The men said nothing. They seemed incapable of speech. One of them stared at him with dull, deadened eyes and the other was foaming at the mouth like a rabid dog. A long few seconds passed and then they both attacked Kiril at once. The guard who was closer, the one who was foaming at the mouth, lunged at him recklessly. Kiril turned sideward, swung his own sword with blazing speed, and cleanly took off the man's head. Kiril barely had time to fend off the other man's attack. He brought up his sword to block the guard's thrust. There was a great clang of steel meeting steel. Kiril feinted left, then spun right, and slashed the man across his side. The guard howled in pain, dropped his sword, and fell to the ground.

Then there was silence. The only sound was the wind whistling through the branches of the Shadow Tree. Kiril looked up at the tree and then backed away as quickly as he could. His heart was pounding in his chest. He had never felt so frightened in his life.

"What has happened?" yelled a frantic voice. Kiril looked up. It was Nartam. He was standing in the Mouth of the Great Cave and he too looked terrified. "Is everything okay?"

"Yes," said Kiril wearily. "Fine."

"Oh what a relief!" yelled Nartam. Kiril walked toward him. Kiril was amazed to see that tears were streaming down Nartam's cheeks. "Thank heavens," said Nartam with the worried voice of a father. "I feared something had happened to the Tree."

Chapter Twenty-Five
An Unlikely Guide

As his airship hovered alongside the obelisk, Leif didn't know what to say. Leif was now just twenty feet or so from the terrace where the man was standing – the man who had called him *dad*. Leif could see him clearly. It was uncanny. The man was the spitting image of Leif. "Dad," yelled the man again, "It's me Alfonso!" Leif stared at the man uncomprehendingly. The man nodded, and his face took on a look of fierce concentration. The man looked as if he were about to pass a kidney stone. Then something miraculous happened. The man changed forms – shrinking in height by almost a foot – and then Leif found himself staring at a teenage boy who was, quite plainly, his son.

"As I live and breathe!" gasped Leif.

"Hold on," yelled the woman, who was still steering the aircraft. She was far too busy working the ships' controls to notice what had just happened. "I'm going to bring us as close as I can get." She swung the ship around and docked it alongside the obelisk's terrace and, as she did so, Leif opened the side door. Immediately, Korgu leapt to the opening and sniffed the air. For the last hour, the wolf had been on a state of high alert, and her whole body trembled with expectation.

Alfonso smiled at Korgu, climbed over the railing of the terrace, leapt through the door of the cabin, and followed his momentum right into the open embrace of his father's arms. Leif nuzzled his nose into his son's hair and smelled his familiar scent. It was his son – by God, there was no doubt about it!

Finally, reluctantly, Leif let his son go. Alfonso glanced around the cabin and then locked eyes with the woman. He recognized her at once.

"Colonel Treeknot?" said Alfonso, in disbelief.

The woman nodded.

"But how?" asked Alfonso.

"It's a long story," explained the woman. "Kiril left me for dead in the Fault Roads, but I managed to escape and make it all the way to the Lighthouse. I will tell you the whole story. It was just by chance that I..."

"Wait a minute," interrupted Leif. "What did you just call her?"

"Colonel Treeknot," said Alfonso.

"What's your first name?" demanded Leif, almost shouting at the woman.

"Why does it matter?" asked Colonel Treeknot.

"It means everything!" said Leif breathlessly. "What is your first name?"

"Nathalia," she replied finally.

"I don't believe it," said Leif quietly, almost to himself. "You are C.N.T."

Several floors below, Marta and the children discovered an enormous stash of food. There were rows of giant wooden crates filled with rice, flour, sugar, salt, dried mushrooms, and dark brown biscuits. There were large vats of olive oil and huge casks of wine. And there were countless shelves stacked with jars of pickles, jams and preserves. The children from the village, who had been living on the brink of starvation for as long as most of them could remember, were now gorging themselves. Marta tried to stop them, warning them that they would get sick, but it was a lost cause; and so eventually she gave up and joined the meal.

After the feast, everyone headed back upstairs to the observatory, and Marta was flabbergasted to find Alfonso speaking with two adults – a man and a woman – who appeared to have materialized out of nowhere. "Who are *they?*" asked Marta.

"This is my dad," explained Alfonso happily. "And this is Colonel Nathalia Treeknot."

"Where did they come from?" asked Marta, still in a state of shock.

"We came by airship," explained Nathalia. She went on to relate a few of the details of their journey. As she spoke, Alfonso was – at the very same time – trying to tell his dad everything that had happened to him since they had been separated in Jasber. For the time being, Leif said little about his own adventures; he didn't want to overwhelm his son and, besides, he was mainly concerned with Alfonso's well being and how exactly his son now magically seemed able to change forms, shifting at will from a teenager into a fully-grown man.

"It's the green ash from Jasber," explained Alfonso. "Ever since I got it into my eyes I have been able to morph my body like that. I'm just like Marta now. She calls us 'agelings.'"

"Agelings," said Leif uneasily. He was frowning. It was a strange concept, brought on by a substance that Leif did not understand but feared completely. He had heard of the Jasber Ash, and he wanted his son to have nothing to do with it. Unfortunately, it appeared as if this ageing complication wouldn't be going away. And to make matters stranger, Alfonso's eyes had become very pale, almost white. It made him look possessed.

"It's all right," said Alfonso reassuringly. "I feel good."

"And what about *you*?" asked Alfonso.

As he said this, Nathalia and Marta abruptly stopped talking and an awkward silence followed.

"I think I should probably answer that question first," said Nathalia. Nathalia paused and looked around. The children all around them looked exhausted. Most of the children had dropped to the floor and were either sitting quietly or were already asleep on one of the observatory's old dusty carpets. "Let's go over here," she said, motioning to a far corner of the observatory where there was a desk, a few chairs, and a large bookshelf stacked with maps. "This way we won't disturb the kids."

Alfonso, Leif, and Marta followed her over toward the desk. Nathalia took a seat in one of the chairs. "So," said Nathalia, "I realize I have some explaining to do." As she said this, she was trembling slightly. Her forehead was covered with sweat and she looked as if she might have a fever. Leif looked at her with concern.

"Are you okay?" asked Leif.

"I'm fine," said Nathalia.

"Are you sure?" asked Marta.

"I have a few wounds," explained Nathalia. "I may have an infection and that explains the fever. But I'm fine. Truly I am."

"What happened to you?" asked Alfonso.

Nathalia sighed, settled into her seat, and proceeded to tell her story. She explained how her uncle, Josephus, lured her down to the Fault Roads by lying – insisting that he had permission from the Grand Vizier to escort Kiril all the way to Jasber. "He seemed so confident," recalled Nathalia bitterly. "By the time we reached the Hub, I knew we had a serious problem." As she recalled it, Josephus' plan quickly fell apart at the Hub when they were attacked by an army of monstrous creatures – known as zwodszay – who succeeded in killing all of Nathalia's knights. Kiril, Nathalia, and Josephus passed through the Jasber Gate but, shortly thereafter, Kiril escaped and left her and her uncle for dead. After that, a gang of zwodszay attacked repeatedly and, in the chaos, Nathalia and Josephus were separated. "It took me almost three weeks to claw my way out of those Fault Roads – eating bugs, drinking from stagnant puddles, and inching my way along those cliffs," said Nathalia grimly. "After that, I managed to row to the lighthouse where I found Misty and Clink and they nursed me back to health."

"And the flying ship?" asked Leif.

"It belongs to Clink," replied Nathalia. "It came with the lighthouse. I guess the previous owner used the ship to fish, or to fly from the lighthouse back to shore, or something like that – I'm not really sure – but I told Clink that I would use it to try to fly back to Somnos. Then I got caught in that storm and I ended up tangled up in the trees, which is where..."

"Where you met me," finished Leif.

"Yes," said Nathalia.

"Okay," said Alfonso, nodding his head slowly, trying to grasp everything that had just been said. "But wait a minute. Dad, why were you up in the treetops?"

"If you can believe it," said Leif, "I had just finished visiting a library."

"Library?" said Alfonso. "What?"

And so then it was Leif's turn to tell his story. He told them everything, yet when it came to reading Alfonso's prophecy, he hesitated. *How much should he tell his son? Was it wise to say anything at all? Should he lie?*

"What is it?" asked Marta, sensing his uneasiness.

"Yeah what'd you find there?" asked Alfonso.

"Nothing," said Leif, as he shifted in his chair uncomfortably.

"Come on dad," said Alfonso.

"Yeah," said Marta, "We're not kids anymore – were age-lings – I'm old enough to get a tattoo – we can handle it."

Leif bit his lip.

"Alfonso, I found your prophecy," said Leif finally.

"And?" asked Alfonso.

"I didn't read the whole thing, but I read part of it – here, I brought it with me." Leif handed his son the piece of paper with the two scenarios in which the Shadow Tree could be destroyed. Alfonso studied it carefully. Marta and Nathalia read it over his shoulder.

"So I have to destroy the Shadow Tree," said Nathalia finally. She seemed stunned, but beneath her surprise was a trace of pride.

"Yes," said Leif.

"How do you know the prophecy is accurate?" asked Alfonso.

"So far it's been spot on," said Leif. "It said that I would reunite with you, someone named, 'M,' and someone named 'C.N.T.' right here at this obelisk – and that's exactly what happened. I believe it. And I believe that Nathalia can do what needs to be done."

Nathalia coughed, wiped her brow of sweat, and nod-ded her head.

"You don't look well," said Alfonso, looking at Nathalia. "You really think you're up for this?"

"Yes," said Nathalia. "I'll be fine."

"Hmm," said Alfonso, as if he weren't totally convinced. "It just seems strange doesn't it?"

"How so," said Leif – as coolly as he could.

"Well," said Alfonso, "I mean, don't you feel it, dad?"

"Feel what?" asked Leif. Leif did his best to look confused, but in truth, he knew exactly what his son was talking about. He'd been feeling it since the shipwreck and perhaps even before that.

"You know," said Alfonso. "The pull, like gravity or something, just tugging on you constantly."

"What are you getting at?" asked Leif. There was just a trace of irritation in his voice. *Take it easy old man*, he thought to himself. *Play it cool.*

"My point is that I feel the pull of the Shadow Tree all the time – even in my sleep," said Alfonso. "I mean, here we are, two Great Sleepers, being pulled toward Dargora and yet it's Nathalia who is meant to destroy the Shadow Tree?"

Leif nodded, but said nothing.

"I doesn't seem right," said Alfonso. "I don't buy it."

"There's nothing to buy or not to buy," said Leif irritably. "Nathalia will take care of this."

"But what if she can't do it?" asked Alfonso. His voice was somber. "That means..."

"No!" shouted Leif. He hadn't intended to yell, but he had. A few of the children stirred. Leif changed his tone, speaking more quietly, but firmly. "Absolutely not," said Leif. "I'm your father and I am telling you, there is no way in hell that I am going to allow you anywhere near that tree. Forget it! I've lost seven bloody years of my life on this quest, you were nearly killed in that fire in Jasber, and now you've become some kind of... ageing. How much can they expect of us? We've done enough. So I don't want to hear another word about it – understand?"

Leif stared at his son and what he saw was unnerving because Alfonso was – in physical appearance, at least – a grown man. Leif had to remind himself that Alfonso was really only fifteen years old. And yet, in the last several months Alfonso had clearly been through so much, Leif suspected that his son was no longer the boy he'd once been. Leif also realized that he'd messed up – he'd gone about this business all wrong – speaking to Alfonso like this in front of all these people. He wanted to take it back – say something to fix the situation – but what?

"You've been away a long time," said Alfonso finally, breaking the silence. His tone was cold. "I don't think you know the first thing about me."

While the children slept, Alfonso, Leif, Nathalia, and Marta gathered around the desk and examined a large map of the region, which they had found in one of the desks. The map was old. The date in the corner indicated that it was made in 1849 by a mapmaker from the city of Gdansk on the Baltic Sea. They all scrutinized the map, searching for a place where three rivers converged because, as the prophecy noted, this is where they would need to drop off Nathalia so she could fulfill her destiny. For the time being, at least, that was the plan. They read and then reread the directions offered in the prophecy: *They arrive at the southernmost edge of the Petrified Forest where the three rivers converge, near the caves where the fog wolves live.* Yet there were no markings on the map pointing to a Petrified Forest, and unfortunately, there were numerous places where three rivers converged.

"This is useless," Nathalia said. "We'll never find it on a map. Dargora didn't stay a mystery for all this time for no reason. It's hidden well."

"I can take you where you need to go," said a voice. They all turned around. It was Kolo – the teenage boy who had once lorded over the children. "I know the route the slavers take toward Dargora – I almost wish I didn't, but I remember every horrible mile of it."

"How?" demaded Nathalia.

"I followed my brothers when they were taken," explained Kolo. "I made it all the way to the caves where the fog wolves live." Kolo then recounted the details of his journey, telling Leif, Nathalia, and Marta what he had already told Alfonso earlier. Then he added: "I can show you where the path through the Petrified Forest begins. After that, you're on your own. I won't go in there again. There's something wrong with the trees... they're only half dead."

"I presume you aren't doing this for free," said Nathalia. "What do you want in return?"

"Your air ship," said the boy. It was a bold request, and the boy made it unapologetically.

Nathalia chortled, half-amused, half-shocked.

Marta was shaking her head. "Forget it," she said. "I don't trust you for a second."

The boy smiled. "Then try to find this place by yourself," he countered. "You may not trust me, but I know the way." The others said nothing. "Just let me know what you decide," said the boy, with a half-smile. "I'm ready to help."

The boy walked away quickly.

Alfonso stood rock-still.

"No," said Marta. "Absolutely not."

Chapter Twenty-Six
The Lucky Rabbit

Bilblox had never slept so deeply in his life. When he finally woke up, he found himself walking up a driveway to a cottage set amidst trees and flowering bushes. Vines covered the walls and the smell of baking bread emanated from the chimney.

As he stepped on a frayed but clean welcome mat, the door opened. It was Judy Perplexon, Alfonso's mother. Bilblox smiled nervously. The last time they had spoken he had made a promise to protect her son. And now he had no idea where he was.

Instead of inviting him in, Judy closed the door behind her and they walked slowly together down the driveway. Bilblox felt light-headed. A dull ache came from the palm of his hand, and he wondered when he had injured it.

"The lake is unusually cold for this time of year," Judy said in a conversational tone. "But the kids still go swimming. They won't be stopped by a little cold. Shall we take a look?"

Bilblox nodded but said nothing.

"You needn't worry about finding Alfonso," she said in the same easy manner. "He'll find you. You two have an extraordinary friendship, and I hope it continues for many decades to come."

"It will," said Bilblox. "You can trust me on that."

"I don't doubt you," replied Judy. "But I wonder whether this can happen after the Shadow Tree." She stared into the distance.

Bilblox's dream abruptly shifted from the driveway to the pristine shoreline of Lake Witekkon. He followed Judy's gaze and before his eyes, watched the lake transform from a sparkling body of water to a fetid swamp bubbling with noxious gases. One by one, teenagers the same age as Alfonso ran into the swamp thinking that it was still the lake. Seconds after entering the water, they began screaming again and again. Their bodies began to shudder until they fell motionless into the oily black water.

Bilblox ran to save them but just when he arrived at the shoreline, it changed again. It was now an absolute wasteland of dust and sullen desert. A line of people waited patiently for what appeared to be a pinch of black powder. Their bodies looked misshapen, as if their bones had been repeatedly broken and reset badly. Bilblox tried to yell but still could not. Judy stood next to him. Bilblox was suddenly afraid and refused to turn to look at her. He did not want a glimpse of how she looked after taking the black powder.

"I'm so tired," said Judy in a monotone. "These poor, poor children."

"My poor, poor child," said a raspy voice. "My poor child."

Bilblox immediately became aware of two things. The first was that this voice did not belong to Judy; the second was that he had a pounding headache. The pain in his head was his cue that he was back in reality. Slowly, he half-opened one of his eyes and saw that he was lying on a soft bed wrapped in red velvet blankets. He was sweating profusely and the blankets and the bed sheets were soaking wet. A constant shiver wracked his body. Bilblox rubbed his eyes, forced them open, and looked around. The daylight was so painful – like a squirt of lemon juice in the eyes – and he winced and groaned as he forced himself to keep his eyes open.

"My poor, poor child," said the raspy voice again. "Everything will be okay, you are just experiencing withdrawal."

Bilblox turned his head to see who it was that was speaking to him in this manner. It was a teenage boy with a square-shaped jaw, and a small mouth, and two white eyes. The boy was now running his hands through Bilblox's hair, as if to comfort him, but the effect only intensified Bilblox's pounding headache.

"Where am I?" muttered Bilblox.

"In my bedroom," said the teenager. "I watched over you while you slept – you poor, little rabbit – to make sure you were okay."

"Who are you?" asked Bilblox groggily.

"My dear, dear, dear Bilblox, do you not recognize me?" asked the boy. "We met in Barsh-yin-Binder several years ago."

"We did?"

"Yes," said the boy, "And then again in the roots beneath the Founding Tree in Somnos."

Bilblox blinked and then forced himself to focus on the boy's face.

"Nartam?" asked Bilblox in disbelief.

"Yes indeed," replied the boy as he continued to run his fingers through Bilblox's hair. "I am much younger than when you saw me last."

"My head," groaned Bilblox.

Nartam leaned forward, bringing his lips to Bilblox's ears, and whispered, "What you need is a pinch of ash – black ash."

Bilblox wanted to say yes. The thought of having another nightmare was unbearable. And then there were the headaches. They were killing him. And yet, he couldn't let himself.

"No…" said Bilblox firmly and as he said this, he sat up in the bed and stared Nartam in the eyes. "I don't want it."

There was a knock on the door. Bilblox glanced around anxiously, looking for the door and, as he did, he took in his surroundings for the first time. He appeared to be inside a ship, in a spacious room with very little furniture other than a mound of pillows on which he now lay. There were a number of windows, whose views were all obscured by clouds. There was another knock on the door.

"Come in," beckoned Nartam. A narrow wooden door swung open and there, in the doorway, stood Kiril.

"How is he?" asked Kiril.

"Ask him yourself," replied Nartam.

"How are you feeling?" asked Kiril.

"I'm not taking your stinking ash," replied Bilblox angrily. "And first chance, I get, I'm bustin' outta here."

"No," said Nartam smoothly. "I'd prefer you stay by my side – it appears that I will have some use for you – you are my lucky rabbit."

Bilblox was staring at Kiril and, as Nartam spoke, for a fraction of a second, Kiril grimaced – as if he were somehow unhappy with this arrangement.

"If you don't mind," said Kiril, "I would like to borrow Bilblox for a moment."

"Why?" asked Nartam pointedly. "I don't think that's wise. I'd rather he stay here."

"I need him to help me," said Kiril very deliberately, as if he didn't want to go into any further detail in front of Bilblox. "It involves the matter we discussed."

"I see," said Nartam. He stared at Kiril as if trying to decide on a issue of great importance.

"But you musn't take too long. The final confrontation is imminent. He'll be here soon – on the full moon – in this very room…" His voice trailed away like the last chords of a song. After a few seconds of awkward silence, he turned back to Kiril with a manic smile. "The symmetry is excellent. You know that he and I are essentially the same age."

"Yes, I know," said Kiril.

"I want you to get a battalion of your best men – put Konrad in charge of them – and have them patrol the south-ernmost perimeter, near the trench."

Kiril nodded but shot Nartam a warning look to say nothing further. They both looked at Bilblox, who lay motionless on the bed, apparently still suffering from with-drawal. In fact, Bilblox was watching the two men closely through nearly closed eyes. He had always been an astute observer of human behavior. Although he had very little formal education, and had only read a few books in his life, he knew people – their expressions, ticks and hesita-tions. This skill had made him an excellent player of any game of chance, and on more than one occasion, it had saved his life.

One thing was quite apparent to Bilblox – it appeared that both Kiril and Nartam believed Alfonso was coming to Dargora. That was the only conclusion which could fit Nartam's words – *a final confrontation* with someone who was *essentially the same age*. It had to be Alfonso. *Was he really com-ing? What made Nartam so certain?* And there was something else that Bilblox had noticed as well. For some reason both Kiril and Nartam wanted Bilblox's company. Bilblox could think of no reason why this would be the case, but he felt certain that it was true.

Kiril walked over to Bilblox's bed and shook him gently. Several seconds, Bilblox moaned, stretched and with apparent effort, lifted his head.

"Come on," said Kiril.

"Where to?" asked Bilblox skeptically.

"We have to meet some people," said Kiril, "Some old friends of yours."

Bilblox studied Kiril's face. Kiril seemed uneasy. *He's scared I'll say 'no,'* thought Bilblox. *He's afraid that I'll tell Nartam I want to stay here and that Nartam will agree.* The conversation between Kiril and Nartam had kindled a spark of hope in Bilblox. *For some reason, both of them need me,* thought Bilblox.

There was a chance here, an opportunity to be seized and exploited – if only Bilblox could figure out *how.*

CHAPTER TWENTY-SEVEN
THE TERMS OF THE DEAL

Bilblox rose to his feet slowly, struggled to gain his balance, and followed Kiril out of the room – never looking back or stopping to bid Nartam goodbye. He followed Kiril out into the hallway. The hallway was long and narrow, with many doorways, much like the hallway in the hull of a large ship. The wooden walls seemed to creak and the hallway itself seemed to be swaying slightly. Kiril walked at a brisk pace. Bilblox decided not to say anything or to ask questions while they were still within earshot of Nartam. At the end of the hallway, Kiril pushed his way through a doorway and out onto an open-air deck. Bilblox followed. The view was breathtaking. They were on the deck of an old wooden ship that appeared to be suspended in the sky. For the moment, at least, the clouds had cleared and there was a spectacular view to be had. Bilblox could see the icy ground below, the slave barracks, and the Shadow Tree with its wiggling branches; beyond this he could see a landscape covered with millions of trees made entirely of stone and he knew that this must be the legendary Petrified Forest that surrounded Dargora.

Kiril continued walking. There were other ships nearby, just like this one, and they were connected by a series of swinging rope bridges. All of them sat on giant pillars that rose up from the ground below. A stiff wind was blowing.

Kiril proceeded across one of these rope bridges, moving quickly, never once glancing downward at the ground below. Bilblox steadied himself and hurried to keep up. They crossed two more bridges until they reached the deck of a small ship.

"Where are ya takin' me?" asked Bilblox, panting for breath. He felt incredibly weak.

"There is something you need to do for me," said Kiril, as they continued across the deck of the ship.

"Why should I help you?" said Bilblox, hurrying to stay with him.

"It's not me you'll be helping," said Kiril, "It's *her.*" Kiril stopped walking and pointed at a thin girl, with delicate features, dressed in a simple black cloak. Bilblox hadn't noticed her at first, because she was sitting between two large coils of rope, but now he stared at her unabashedly.

"Resuza?" inquired Bilblox hesitantly.

"No," said Kiril, "It's her sister – Naomi."

"Her sister… you gotta be kiddin' me," said Bilblox. "You want me to help her – how?"

"You're going to save her life," said Kiril matter-of-factly.

"That's all?" replied Bilblox. "Anything else while I'm at it?"

"Only you can do it," said Kiril, his tone conveyed his seriousness.

Bilblox stared at Kiril and then at the girl. She remained silent, but it was apparent that she was quite scared. "And why do you care about this girl so much?"

"I just do," Kiril replied.

"And that's why you brought me with you – instead of leaving me to die?" asked Bilblox.

Kiril nodded.

"Does Nartam know about this?" asked Bilblox.

179

Kiril hesitated, pursed his lips, and said, "No."

Bilblox whistled, then despite himself, he laughed. It felt good to laugh, for a moment he forgot about his headache. "Kiril old boy, you're in a jam, ain't ya?"

Kiril ignored the question. "Will you help me or not?"

"Why should I?"

"Come now," said Kiril. "We both know why you'll help her. You will help her because she is an innocent girl and because she is Resuza's sister."

"Is that right?" said Bilblox. "And tell me, what's gonna happen to you when you don't bring me back to Nartam nice and quick like you promised you would?"

"Let me worry about that," replied Kiril.

Bilblox looked at Kiril thoughtfully. "There's something else you ain't telling me about," said Bilblox finally. "You're a good liar, but ya ain't that good – ya better come clean."

Kiril nodded and gestured for Bilblox to follow him. "Naomi," said Kiril, "Stand guard here."

Naomi nodded.

Kiril searched the deck of the ship carefully, as if studying the planks of wood, and eventually he found a small handle and yanked on it. A trapdoor sprang open, revealing a steep set of stairs. The two men descended the stairs and emerged into a large empty room, perhaps intended for storage, which was dimly lit with a few lanterns. Kiril walked over to the far corner of the room and, with his finger, pointed at a small hole in the wall. It was apparent that he wanted Bilblox to look through the hole and, somewhat reluctantly, Bilblox did so. At first, it was difficult for Bilblox to see anything, but slowly he was able to make out two figures sleeping on the floor. It took him a moment, but then he recognized them – one was Hill and the other was Resuza.

Kiril tapped Bilblox on the shoulder and motioned for him to follow him silently. Kiril led the way back onto the deck above, where Naomi was waiting for them. Kiril walked over to Naomi and nodded.

Bilblox stared at Naomi closely. She clearly was taking instructions from Kiril.

"Hill and Resuza are perfectly fine," explained Kiril. "I even left some food for them. They're just sleeping now."

"What do you want from me?" asked Bilblox. The long-shoreman was stony-faced; it would have been impossible for anyone to discern what he was thinking.

"Hill and Resuza have something that I need – a Pen," said Kiril finally.

"So why don't you just take it from them?" asked Bilblox.

"Because they don't have the Pen with them," said Kiril.

"How do you know?

"The food I left put them to sleep – and I searched them," explained Kiril. "There is no Pen, which doesn't entirely surprise me. Hill isn't a fool. He must have hidden it."

"And you want me to help you get that Pen?" asked Bilblox.

Kiril nodded.

"You want me to betray them," said Bilblox angrily.

"Come on," said Kiril. "Look at yourself. You've taken the ash again, you followed me willingly all the way back to Dargora, and you've been staying with Nartam in his quarters. It's a little late to be worrying about betrayal now, isn't it?"

Bilblox ignored this. "What's so important about this Pen anyway?" asked Bilblox.

Kiril made no immediate reply. He stood motionless, as if lost in thought, as if debating how much he ought to say. For a very brief moment, Kiril flicked his eyes off into the distance. Bilblox followed Kiril's gaze and saw that was look-ing at – the Shadow Tree.

"The Pen can cut down the tree – can't it?" asked Bilblox.

Kiril said nothing.

Bilblox's eyes widened suddenly as if he just realized something startling. "No don't tell me," said Bilblox. "You would actually..."

"No," said Kiril. "Not really – not right *now* at least. But there may come a time..."

"But why?" demanded Bilblox. "After everything that you did to grow it?"

"Because," said Kiril. "We've gotten what we wanted. We already have enough ash to last us a century. And I suspect that once the Shadow Tree has been destroyed, the ash will be safe to take, but until then..."

"Come on – you're telling me you'd really do it?" asked Bilblox. "I don't believe it."

"I'm the only one who could," said Kiril coolly. "Think about it – I'm the only one who could get close enough to do the job."

"You don't have the guts," said Bilblox. "Besides, what about Nartam? You've turned on him now? Is that what you're tellin' me? I ain't fallin for that. I've heard you mut-ter his name – *Daros* – father."

"*NO*," Kiril urgently replied. "Not at all. Believe it or not, I'm doing precisely what he told me to do."

"Which is what exactly?"

"Be the one man who always sees everything clearly," said Kiril in a whisper, almost to himself.

"So tell me," said Bilblox. "What are ya gonna do for me, if I get it for you?"

Kiril nodded his head, approvingly, as if he hoped Bilblox would ask – after all, the mere asking of such a question sug-gested that Bilblox was at least considering the deal.

"If you get me the Pen," said Kiril, "I'll get you out of Dargora – along with Hill and Resuza."

Bilblox said nothing.

"And," said Kiril, "I'll cure you – I'll give you an herb potion I've used in the past to cure the withdrawal. Your headaches will disappear. You'll even be able to see a little."

"One more thing," said Kiril, "If you're thinking about escaping on your own with the Pen, and double-crossing me, then forget it," said Kiril, "I plan to have you followed and watched at every step of the way. I'll have Konrad out there with some six hundred men. And don't forget where you are – in the middle of nowhere. The only way out of here is with my help. Better men than you have tried to escape, and all have died in the wilderness. No one escapes here. Just remember that."

"What about Naomi?" asked Bilblox. "What happens to her?"

"She goes with you," replied Kiril. "She will be well protected."

Bilblox looked at Kiril and then at Naomi. She didn't seem to need protection. More likely she was Kiril's eyes and ears. Still, it was difficult to think of another way out. After a pause of several seconds, Bilblox looked again at Kiril and nodded. "I'm a fool to take your deal," said Bilblox, "but I'll do it. But look at me now. I'm weak and barely able to stand up. You need to give me that potion, so I can think clearly."

"I suspected as much," replied Kiril. He handed a small vial from inside his jacket to Bilblox.

"Drink it in one gulp. You'll be fine for a while. And when our deal is complete, you'll get as much as you want, as well as the instructions to make it on your own."

Bilblox nodded and took the vial. He had no doubt that he was following Kiril's plans to the letter.

CHAPTER TWENTY-EIGHT
IMAD'S CLUE

The flying ship departed the obelisk at dawn. All of the children gathered on the stone terrace at the top of the obelisk in order to wave goodbye – all of them except Kolo, who was in the ship, at the helm, standing alongside Nathalia. Nathalia had made it clear to him that, no matter what happened, he was never to leave her side. As for the ship, she told him that if and when they were done with it, which might not be for some time, then he could have it. "But I want you where I can see you," she told him coldly. "And if you cross me, boy, I will hunt you down." Kolo nodded and looked sufficiently scared. As the ship pulled away and began ascending upward, into the clouds, the aircraft rattled slightly.

Marta, who was exhausted, lay dozing on one of the couches. Meanwhile, Leif and Alfonso sat in one of the leather-upholstered chairs, nestling their feet into the plush bearskin rugs. "Well," said Leif with a shrug, "If you have to fly to Dargora, you might as well do it in style." Ever since their argument back in the obelisk, Leif had been trying very hard to be as cheerful as possible. It was clear that Leif felt badly about what he'd said – or at least how he'd said it – but he hadn't yet apologized. This really irked Alfonso and he had barely looked his father in the eyes since then.

Leif got up and began building a small fire in the ship's potbelly stove. Once it had lit, he put a kettle of water on top it in order to brew some tea.

"You want some tea?" asked Leif.

Alfonso nodded his head absent-mindedly. His thoughts were still on the prophecy from Imad's library. He didn't usually put any faith in this kind of stuff. In fact, he had little patience for people who wasted their time fussing over tarot cards, palm reading, and Chinese fortune cookies. But this was different. These were the words of the Foreseeing Pen. And his dad was right. So far, the Pen had predicted their unlikely rendezvous at the obelisk with pinpoint accuracy. This meant either he or Nathalia would have to destroy the Shadow Tree. Alfonso looked up at Nathalia. She was navigating the ship expertly, but even from the way that she was sitting in the pilot's chair – slumped against the back of it, almost like a limp doll – it was clear that she wasn't in good health.

"Here," said Leif. "Have a look at this." Leif tossed something into his son's lap. Alfonso saw that it was a blank canvas, with the frame made of tree limbs. "This is the thing that Imad asked me to take from his library." Alfonso studied it for several minutes, staring at it contemplatively. "What do you make of it?" asked Leif. "You've always been good with puzzles – better than me anyhow."

"Not sure," said Alfonso, who was grateful for the distraction. "What did Imad say about this thing?"

"Not much," said Leif. "Just that I shouldn't worry about it because I wasn't in the proper frame of mind – or something like that."

"Frame of mind," repeated Alfonso.

"Yeah," said Leif. "What do you make of the thing?"

"I think I ought to rip it apart," said Alfonso thought-fully. He then proceeded to tear it apart, pulling off each of the wooden pieces that made up the frame.

"What are you doing?" asked Leif uneasily.

"Not sure," said Alfonso. He quickly broke the wooden frame down into four separate pieces, one from each side, and then he began to play with them – placing the various ends together – as if he were somehow trying to reconnect them. Leif was shaking his head, getting ready to reprimand his son, when he heard a very audible *click*. Alfonso had succeeded in connecting two of the pieces so that they formed a single, vertical shaft. Moments later there was a second click – and then a third. Alfonso soon connected all four pieces so that they formed a single column or shaft. At the top of the shaft, there was a small round hole, perhaps half-an-inch in diameter. The other end of the shaft was wider around the base and, when Alfonso placed this end on the floor, the entire shaft stood up on its own.

Alfonso picked the stick up again and studied the base of it. "Whoa, what's this?" he exclaimed. He began using his fingers to twist the base of it, as if he were trying to unscrew a lid. "It looks like there's a small cap here that twists off," said Alfonso, his face strained with effort. "Yup... it's moving."

"Careful," cautioned Leif.

"There!" said Alfonso triumphantly, as he pulled off the small cap and held it triumphantly in the air. "It came off." Alfonso studied the stick again. "Hey check this out." He and Leif took a close look. Built into the base of the stick, beneath where the cap had once been, was a strange-looking compass of sorts. There were no markings for directions, just a hand which – for the time being – was pointing north. The hand looked as if it were made of small roots from a tree. It looked like this:

"Where do you suppose it's pointing?" asked Alfonso.

"Not sure," said Leif.

Alfonso placed the stick down, so that its wide base was on the floor, allowing the stick to stand up, on its own, vertically.

"Looks like a walking stick," said Leif.

"Or a tree trunk," said Alfonso.

Leif took a second look. There was no doubt about it now. The stick looked just like the trunk of a tree. In the middle of the trunk there was a small knot in the wood and, just above this, was a gash that looked a bit like a claw mark.

"My goodness," said Leif. "That gash – just above the knot – that must be where we're meant to…"

"Cut the thing down," said Alfonso. "Strange, huh? I never would have thought to cut the tree in the middle of the trunk like that."

For a brief moment, Alfonso and Leif smiled at each other.

"Me neither," said Leif. "I better show this to Nathalia so she knows what to do when…"

"Dad," said Alfonso.

"What?"

"Do you really think she's the one to do it?" asked Alfonso.

Leif sighed heavily and then pursed his lips, as if he were considering carefully how to answer this question. "I don't honestly know Alfonso," he replied. "But she has to try."

"Fine, but what if she fails?" said Alfonso. "Then what?"

"Then we'll figure something out," said Leif.

"That's not an answer," said Alfonso.

"What do you want me to say?" asked Leif, a flash of anger in his voice. "You want me to say, 'Yes, by all means, go ahead – destroy the tree and kill yourself.' Is that want you want? Because I'm not going to say that."

Alfonso took a deep breath and kept his calm. His father had been under so much strain these last few years. Alfonso had to go easy on him; and yet, in the same instant, Alfonso recalled his dream in which the roots from the Shadow Tree had destroyed World's End. And he remembered his father's words at the end of the dream: *I thought we'd be safe here... I should have known – it was all written out so clearly.*

"The tree must be destroyed," said Alfonso. His voice was eerily calm. "You see that don't you?"

"Yes," said his father, "I do."

"Someone has to do it," pressed Alfonso. "We can't just walk away from this."

"Yes, yes, of course," said Leif. "And we won't."

Alfonso frowned.

"What?"

"I don't believe you," said Alfonso.

Chapter Twenty-Nine
A Bad Omen

The airship flew steadily north and, as it did, the weather worsened. The wind grew in strength and the air ship shook violently. The turbulence was so severe that Nathalia had to keep them hovering just one hundred feet or so off the ground – just in case they suddenly had to make an emergency landing. The air also grew steadily colder but, fortunately, Marta found a stash of fur coats tucked away in a storage compartment at the back of the ship. There were seven or eight coats, all made of soft fur, and everyone was soon wearing them and happily so. Kolo played the role of the navigator dutifully, helping Nathalia steer a course northward deep into the Yamalia Peninsula. Using a map, a compass, and a pair of binoculars from the ship, Kolo routed them along a series of rivers, which is the same way he claimed to have gone when he followed the slavers who captured his brothers, though it was still unclear whether Kolo was telling the truth about his previous trip.

The only real drama occurred when Alfonso took a brief nap. The cabin in the ship was quite cozy – with the couches, the rugs, and the fire crackling in the potbelly stove – and Alfonso couldn't help but doze off for a few minutes. He awoke, to the sound of screaming. Alfonso opened his eyes and found himself lying on top of Kolo with a knife to the boy's throat. There was blood on the knife. Kolo's eyes were bulging in terror. Marta was screaming; Nathalia was shouting; and Leif was talking sternly to his son. "Drop the knife Alfonso!" ordered Leif. "Drop it right now, son."

Alfonso dropped the knife and sprang to his feet. His hands were shaking violently. He stared at Kolo in horror. For a terrifying moment, he wondered whether he had cut the boy's throat. But he hadn't. It was just a superficial cut. Kolo, however, was nearly hysterical.

"He cut me!" screamed Kolo. "He cut me!"

"Everything is okay," said Nathalia calmly. "It's just a nick. Alfonso was in some kind of sleeping trance. He is not trying to kill you."

"I'll kill him if he comes near me again!" screamed Kolo. "I mean it – I'll kill him!"

"No you won't," said Nathalia firmly. "Now come to the front of the ship and stand next to me. I'll make sure nothing bad happens to you. I promise. Come on now." Kolo rubbed his neck, assuring himself that it was just a scrape, and then scurried to the front of the ship and stood so close to Nathalia that he appeared to be standing on her toes.

Alfonso was still shaking.

"Are you all right?" asked Leif.

Alfonso nodded.

"What the devil was that about?" asked Leif.

"I have no idea," said Alfonso hoarsely. "I was asleep when I did it."

"I know why," said Marta.

Both Leif and Alfonso looked at her.

"Great Sleepers always do things in their sleep for a reason," she said.

"But I was trying to kill him," said Alfonso, his face still ashen.

"And you would have," said Marta, "If we hadn't woken you up."

"What are you saying?" asked Alfonso hotly. He was obviously badly shaken. "Are you saying that I should have killed him?"

"I'm saying you should have listened to me," said Marta. "We never should have taken him along."

"That's enough!" shouted Nathalia. "We made a decision and now we have to live with it. Now everyone is going to sit down and be quiet. Understand?"

Everyone nodded and returned to their seats. The rest of the journey, to everyone's relief, was uneventful. Kolo stayed close to Nathalia, though he was constantly looking over his shoulder to see where Alfonso was situated. Alfonso drank tea and resolved not to sleep under any circumstances. By sundown they could all see a place, far in the distance, where three rivers converged. Just beyond that, there appeared to be a field of boulders, but it was impossible to see farther with any clarity. Nathalia used the ship's binoculars and saw that the boulders were all tall, slender and identical in shape. This was promising. She brought the ship as close to the ground as she could, just above the treetops of a vast pine forest, in which every single tree was dead.

Alfonso was staring so intently at the ground below that he barely noticed that Marta was standing right beside him. "That's what I saw," she whispered into his ear.

"What are you talking about?" he whispered back.

"When I had my vision earlier – you know, back in the field, by the obelisk – I had a vision like this," said Marta. "It was summer, but everything was dead."

"How far into the future are we talking?" asked Alfonso.

"A long time," said Marta.

"How do you know?"

"Because of the mountains," she replied. "They had changed. The peaks were worn down. They had eroded. That takes a very long time – at least I think it does – centuries, probably longer. You understand what I'm trying to say, right?"

"If the Shadow Tree grows, the damage… it'll be lasting."

Marta nodded.

"Alfonso," she whispered. "I overheard what you said to your dad."

"You did?"

Marta nodded.

"It's not his fault," said Alfonso. "He just doesn't want anything bad to happen to me, but I don't think he gets what's coming – not really."

"But I do," said Marta. "That's why I didn't go back to Jasber. Even though I want to see my family so badly, I've seen what's coming. And, if it comes to it, I'll help you do what you have to. I will."

"You don't sound like any nine-year-old girl I've ever met," whispered Alfonso.

"You're starting to get it, aren't you?" she replied. "I'm not nine any more than you are fifteen. None of that matters any more. We're nine, and fifteen, and thirty-six, and ninety-eight all at once. We're agelings. And there are only two of us, so we better stick together."

Alfonso nodded. He reached into his pocket and took out the small piece of paper in which the two scenarios of Imad's prophecy were written. For some reason, Alfonso had kept the paper, instead of returning it to his father. He re-read Imad's word for the umpteenth time.

"Do you believe it?" asked Marta.

"I don't know," replied Alfonso.

A few minutes later, the airship crossed over a small clearing in the woods, and Nathalia glanced down and saw a number of shadowy figures dashing in and out of the woods. "There's something down there," she muttered, almost to herself. No one spoke as Nathalia navigated them the last few miles. Kolo made gestures with his hands, but said nothing. By the time they neared the spot where the rivers actually converged, the sun was down and it was pitch black. The only lights were two flickers of red in the middle distance.

"That's a small Dragoonya fort," whispered Kolo.

"You didn't mention that," growled Nathalia.

Kolo said nothing.

Nathalia eased the ship downward and landed in a ravine near the fort. Everyone took a sigh of relief as the airship gently came to a rest in the snow.

"This is the wrong place!" said Kolo. "I'll take you to the right place."

"I think we've had enough of your advice for one day," Nathalia replied.

"We should probably keep going and cross the forest through the air," said Alfonso. "Don't you think?"

"We'll never make it," replied Nathalia, "The wind is way too strong. Besides, we're almost out of fuel."

"What does the ship run on?" asked Alfonso.

"Kerosene,'" said Nathalia.

"Do you think they might have any kerosene in the fort?" asked Alfonso.

"Could be," said Leif. "But it seems awfully risky. We can't just go and knock on the door and ask for it."

"Why don't we at least have a look," said Nathalia. As she said this, she stood up and headed over to the door of the airship. "We can climb up to the top of the ravine and observe from afar – see if we can spot anything."

"I'll do it," said Leif.

"That's not necessary," said Nathalia.

"I know," said Leif. "But..."

"I'll be okay," said Nathalia.

Leif started to object again – he didn't want anything happening to Nathalia – but by the time he opened his mouth, she was out the door. The others sat there, barely daring to breathe. Every sound from the outside seemed to magnify and echo through the thin walls of the airship. Every so often, they heard a distant howl. It started low and then ended in a terrifying high pitch. Alfonso had heard wolves back in World's End, Minnesota, but these noises were different. His skin crawled from the sound, and from the looks of the others, it was a common effect.

About a half hour later, Nathalia crept back into the airship, and closed the door behind her. She was smiling.

"The fort is poorly guarded," she said. "There are only two guards on duty."

"Let's just avoid the fort completely and go into the forest," said Leif.

Nathalia shook her head. "They got a bunch of lamps on the outside of that fort and they look like kerosene lamps to me," she said. "If we can get some of that kerosene we'll be golden. But it'll be tricky. We'd need an elegant way of doing it." She looked around.

"I have an idea," said Marta.

CHAPTER THIRTY
A TENDER REUNION

Resuza woke up slowly, groggily, like an animal waking from hibernation. The delicious warmth of the ship was so unlike the dampness of the slave quarters that it had made her and Hill almost delirious. *How long had they been in this darkened room?* It was hard to tell. Several hours at least, but then several thoughts wandered into Resuza's tired mind and forced her to wake up. *Where was Naomi? Why wasn't she here? Was it her sister who had provided the soft blankets and food they had found?* It couldn't have been anyone else.

Resuza sat up and stretched. Hill began to stir and finally, he sat up as well.

"Naomi still isn't here," he remarked as he rubbed his eyes.

Resuza shook her head.

"Strange," said Hill.

"Do you think something's wrong?" Resuza asked.

Hill shrugged. "Who knows?" he said, stifling a yawn. His thoughts were still too muddled to think properly. It had been ages since he had slept so well. "Can you pass that bread? I'm ravenous. We haven't had food this good in months, maybe years."

Resuza smiled. "The last time it was this good was back at the lighthouse," said Resuza. "Remember that mutton stew and spiced caramel they had for desert?" As she said this, almost involuntarily, she thought of Alfonso. She remembered sitting with him, in his bedroom in the lighthouse, sipping hot cocoa as the waves crashed below. And she remembered kissing him, ever so briefly. That was months ago and, strange as it was to say, that was her last good memory. The thought both cheered her and depressed her all at once. And now where was Alfonso? No idea. What were the chances that he was even alive? No, she told herself, she mustn't think that.

"I think of that meal at the lighthouse just about every day," said Hill with a sigh. "But this food is a reminder. If we can get out of here, we'll be eating like that again."

"If we make it out of here, what's our destination?" Resuza asked.

"Back to the Sea of Clouds," Hill quickly replied. "We need to find Alfonso."

With a rising excitement, they began to discuss how they might go about searching for Alfonso. They were so engrossed in their conversation that the telltale sigh of a door opening escaped their attention. It was only when a floorboard uttered a creak that they realized someone had entered their small room. A match flared in the darkness and moved towards a fat candle. The candle wick lit and threw a dull light over several feet. Just behind the candle, her hair flickering in the light, stood a young, thin girl with a nervous expression on her face. Her hands clutched the candle but her fingers were in constant motion.

Resuza stood up and took a step forward. Time seemed to slow down. She had dreamed of this moment for so many years and now that it was actually happening, she felt distant from it, as if she was floating above her body and looking down on the scene.

"Naomi?"

The hands stopped moving and the candle slowly moved up towards the face. Resuza took another step forward and as she did so, Naomi's face came into the light. Resuza stood there, immobile. When she had last seen Naomi, her younger sister had just begun to speak in complete sentences. She was just a toddler. And now she stood in front of Resuza, nearly the same height, with hair that hung straight and long like Resuza.

Naomi looked at Resuza, and smiled. It was a nervous, reluctant smile, but it was a smile nonetheless, and it lit up Resuza's heart like a beacon in the darkness. Resuza covered the distance between them, opened her arms and with a sob she flung them around Naomi's shoulders.

"It's you, it's really you," she whispered into her neck.

"Yes," replied Naomi, taking a tender step backwards. "It is really me."

"Are you okay?" asked Resuza, stifling a sob. "Tell me you're okay. I haven't stopped thinking about you since the day…"

"Since the day that I was abandoned," finished Naomi. There was a slight edge in her voice. "Yes, I haven't stopped thinking about you either."

"Naomi," said Resuza, her voice was ragged with emotion, "We've both been through an awful lot and I am so, so sorry that I left you and I will make it up to you – you will see – I will be there for you now, I promise, I really do."

These words obviously affected Naomi. Her face tensed up and it looked as if she were about to cry. However, she made no reply, nor did she move to hug Reuza. The two sisters stood in darkness, silently – close but not touching. There was both everything and nothing to say.

Hill was only half paying attention to any of this. He was on full alert and listened for other noises that might indicate that Naomi did not come alone. At first he sensed nothing, but then he heard something that made his heart sink. There was someone else in the room and whoever it was had just shifted their weight from one foot to another right by the entrance.

He stood up noiselessly and leaned over towards Resuza. He patted her lightly on the shoulder, but she did not respond. She appeared to be in a trance, staring at her long-lost sister.

"We're ready," Resuza said finally. "We'll go wherever you take us, all that matters is that we stick together."

"Good," said Naomi, she too was still struggling to control her emotions. "That's good."

"Wait a minute," interrupted Hill loudly. Naomi was startled.

"Wait for what?" asked Resuza somewhat annoyed.

"There's someone else in this room," Hill said. "You there – by the doorway – who are you?"

Another match flared near the doorway and a suddenly visible hand lit a candle. "After all we've been through, don't ya think I should get a tender reunion?"

Bilblox stood at the doorway and smiled at the three of them.

"Bilblox!" Resuza yelled. "You're here – you're alive!" She ran to him and flung her arms around his thick neck. "But how?"

"It's a very long story," said Bilblox slowly, carefully, as if he were choosing his words with great care. "And I wouldn't be here if it weren't for Naomi and the fact that the Dragoonya have taken such a liking to her." As he said this, Bilblox looked at Naomi intensely – almost glaring at her – daring her to contradict him.

"We saw you on a sled with Kiril," said Resuza. "To tell you the truth, you looked almost dead. How did you get out of all that?" She stared into his eyes as if trying to read his mind. Then she noticed something else had changed too. "And your eyes are different. Can you *see?*"

Bilblox nodded. "I've had quite a few changes," he started. He looked at the floor. "I'm sorry – it's too long of a story and we don't have time for it now. We gotta get out of here – and quickly."

For several seconds, nobody moved. Hill sensed something was wrong, but he didn't know what to do. Bilblox was one of his most trusted friends and he had saved Alfonso's life many times over. On their original voyage to Somnos, when Hill had questioned Bilblox's loyalty, Alfonso correctly defended him. Still, despite all this history, something felt wrong. Hill glanced at Naomi. The young girl appeared outwardly calm, but she wouldn't look him in the eyes.

"Are you ready?" Bilblox said. "We gotta go." He stared at Hill intently and raised his eyebrows to the door. Hill began to say something, but Bilblox shook his head, as if to say: *Not here – not now.* Hill was confused and more than a little nervous. Was it possible that someone was eavesdropping on this conversation? Was there a subtext here? Was there something that Bilblox was not saying – some unsaid message that Hill was missing? Or was it a trap? Was it possible that Bilblox had betrayed them – perhaps for some ash – after all, how was it that Bilblox could see again? And what about Naomi? She would never betray her own sister, would she?

"Let's go – now." Bilblox repeated.

Hill nodded. He had many questions, but clearly, answers would not be given or found standing in this small room.

"We have nothing of value," he said in a clear, direct voice – just in case others were listening. "We just want to leave."

"I know," said Bilblox. He walked to Hill and gave him a strong hug. Just as he was about to let go, he drew close to Hill's ear.

"Be strong, my old friend," he whispered. "Have faith."

Bilblox turned and walked out the door, followed by Resuza. Naomi followed behind, and Hill was the last one out of the room. Before he left, he glanced back at the tiny room that had been so comfortable. He had a sinking suspicion that it would be a long time before he would find similar surroundings. At last, he turned and followed the others. It was pitch dark, and as they walked up the stairs, the creak of the wood sounded like gunshots in the cold air. Hill's heart pounded as if at any moment he expected the shouts of Dragoonya soldiers. *It's coming, the ambush is coming,* Hill kept telling himself. But it never came.

They made it onto the deck of the ship. It was so dark that they could barely see each other even though they were only feet apart. The wind howled and tore at their exposed faces. Although it made sense for them to escape under the cover of darkness, Hill was nonetheless amazed that he and Resuza had slept as long as they did. It felt like only a few hours, but clearly, they had slept the entire day after arriving at the ship the night before.

They continued along a wooden deck, exposed to the night sky, until they came to a rope bridge that swung in the breeze. It was impossible to see where the bridge led because it disappeared into a bank of fog. Naomi paused for only a second before climbing onto the rope bridge, which was swinging in the wind.

"Where does this lead?" Hill whispered. He remembered seeing other ships connected to each other, but he had no idea in what direction they were headed. He turned to Bilblox with a concerned look.

"Don't worry," replied Bilblox, who was still behind him. "Everything will be fine. Naomi knows these ships inside and out."

"Can we trust her?" Hill asked.

Bilblox paused. "You can trust me," he replied.

CHAPTER THIRTY-ONE
THE FORT

Osoba was not a young man, almost sixty years old, but he had never felt better. Like the other Dragoonya soldiers at the Fog Wolves' Fort, for the last week he had been on a steady diet of nothing but black ash – no meat, no bread, no ale, not even any water – just the ash from the newly grown tree. Each night, the captain gave them their rations and the soldiers took turns rubbing the fine, black ash into their eyes. The effect was immediate and miraculous. Within a day, Osoba felt incredible; the arthritis was gone from his joints, the cough vanished from his lungs, and the cold brittle feeling that resided deep in his bones had vanished.

Osoba had to admit there were some drawbacks. His eyes had turned a rather sickly white, much of his hair had fallen out, and his fingernails were gone, making it slightly uncomfortable to grip his sword. And his mind felt curiously dull, as if in hibernation. It was probably just a short-term side affect. The soldiers also seemed quick to anger. Already, there had been three or four fights at the fort, and in one of these brawls, a soldier had died. But this was always what happened whenever a very coveted commodity was in short demand – whether it was gold, food, or black ash. It couldn't be helped.

Tonight he and another guard, Uzależniona, were charged with manning the gate to the fort. Lately, the night shift was much better than the day shift. Ever since the new tree had been planted, and its roots had ravaged the land, people had begun to show up at the fort – refugees, entire villages of people on the brink of starvation – but they only came during the daylight hours. At night, they retreated back to the other side of the river, back into the dead pine forest. They were too frightened to stick around at night, because that's when the clouds rolled in and the fog wolves came out to prowl for food. So the nights tended to be quiet. And this is why Osoba was startled when he saw a lone figure emerge in the distance, walking slowly through the snow toward the fort.

"Do you see that?" asked Osoba.

"Yes," said Uzależniona, who already had a crossbow out and was aiming it directly at the approaching figure. "It looks like an old woman."

Osoba squinted into the distance. The snow was swirling and it was difficult to see, but Uzależniona appeared to be right, it was an old woman. And she was carrying something. Something small.

"She has a baby," said Osoba.

"What in holy hell is she doing out at this time of night?" asked Uzależniona. "She must be out of her mind."

"Turn around!" yelled Osoba. "We're not taking slaves tonight."

The old woman either didn't hear Osoba, didn't understand him, or simply didn't care. She continued marching forward and she was moving more quickly now. It almost appeared as if she were running. It was bizarre to see an elderly woman moving so quickly with a baby in tow.

"Halt!" screamed Osoba at the top of his lungs.

The woman broke into a run, charging the gate in a dead sprint. For a moment, Osoba and Uzależniona were too stunned to react. The woman was now a dazzling blur of motion. Uzależniona aimed his crossbow and started to squeeze the trigger. But before he could fire, the woman hurled the baby up into the air, and then dove into a somersault role. Half-horrified and half-stunned, Osoba gawked at the sight of an infant flying through the air. Then something totally astonishing happened; midway through the air, the infant changed forms, literally morphing into a nearly full-sized man. This newly-formed man landed on the ground gracefully, just a few feet from where Osoba was standing, and then kicked him in the head so quickly and so ferociously that Osoba flew backwards and was unconscious by the time that his body hit the ground with a heavy thud.

After kicking the Dragoonya guard in the head, Alfonso spun around quickly to make sure that Marta was okay. She was fine. In fact, she was standing over the body of the other Dragoonya guard, the one who had shot at her; he too was now slumped on the ground, knocked unconscious. Marta had the man's crossbow in her hand.

"Do you know how to use this thing?" asked Marta.

"Sure," said Alfonso. He took the crossbow, aimed it, put his finger on the trigger, and indicated that this is what you squeezed to fire the weapon. "Can you do that?"

Marta nodded somberly, and Alfonso remembered, that despite her appearance, which was still that of an elderly woman, she had only been alive for nine years – almost all of which she had spent sitting in a chair on a remote island.

"Be careful with it," said Alfonso, as he handed it back to her.

"Don't talk that way to me," said Marta, "I'm old enough to be your grandmother." Marta smiled and her face was a leathery contortion of a thousand wrinkles. The old lady's face then morphed slightly, becoming even more shriveled and wrinkly, as if she had aged five more years in the span of three seconds.

"Cut it out," said Alfonso, "You know I hate it when you do that."

"Come on," said Marta teasingly, "Lighten up."

"Yeah sure," said Alfonso with a smile, "But please grow back some teeth – you're freaking me out grandma."

Marta closed her eyes and morphed again into the form of a woman in her mid twenties – tall, lean, and very athletic. She was quite pretty and it was bizarre to Alfonso that the little girl, the pretty twenty-something, and the old woman were all Marta.

"Come on," said Alfonso, "Let's see if we can find any kerosene."

Alfonso and Marta worked quickly to tie up and gag the guards. Then Alfonso grabbed a set of keys from one of the guards, and after fumbling with them for a while, used the keys to unlock the back door to the fort, which was a massive slab of steel on a set on three rusty hinges.

The doors creaked open slowly. They paused for a second to listen, and continued through the gate into a huge room with stone floors, high vaulted ceilings, and a hearth with a large crackling fire. Along the perimeter of the room there were a series of jail cells, each of which was occupied by twenty or so prisoners. The prisoners were well-clothed, most of them were men dressed in furs, but their faces were so gaunt and desperate-looking it was soon apparent that they had not eaten in some time. Most of the prisoners were asleep, though a few stared hopefully at Marta and Alfonso.

One of the prisoners, a short man with an enormous beard, stood up, walked over to the door of his cell, and opened it; amazingly, the cell was unlocked. The man whispered eagerly, "Have you come to take us to Dargora?"

"No," said Alfonso. "We're not Dragoonya, we're just..." Alfonso hesitated, uncertain of what to say.

"Visitors," said Marta, finishing his sentence.

"What kind of visitors?" asked the bearded man skeptically.

"The kind who don't need to answer questions from prisoners," said Marta as she raised her crossbow at the man.

Alfonso had to suppress a smile; he was impressed. You didn't mess with Marta.

"Oh," said the man with the beard. He sighed dejectedly, walked over to the fire, warmed his hands for a moment, and then returned to his cell. "No disrespect intended," said the man. "I just fear we will all starve if we do not get there soon."

"What's the difference?" asked another man in the same cell, whose face was hidden in the shadows. "They will work us to death soon after we arrive."

"No," said the bearded man, "No one dies in Dargora any longer. Now that they have the ash."

The man whose face was hidden in shadows snorted, but made no reply.

"Why are you here?" asked Alfonso. "If you want to go to Dargora, what are you waiting for?"

"You can't just cross the Petrified Forest on your own," said the bearded man with a nervous laugh.

"Why not?" asked Alfonso.

"You'll drown in the snow drifts," said the man with the beard. "Either that or-"

"Or what?" said the man, whose face was hidden in shadows.

"Or the fog wolves will find you," said the bearded man gravely. "They run through the forest every night to get their meat."

Marta and Alfonso exchanged glances.

"I don't get it," said Marta, "Are you slaves then?"

"Not yet," said the bearded man. "We hope to be."

"Hope to be?" inquired Alfonso.

"Yes," said the man whose face was hidden in the shadows, "I have been asking myself the same question. For years we ran from the Dragoonya whenever they came on their raids, trying to capture us, and now we come begging to be taken. Ironic isn't it?"

"What choice do we have?" asked the bearded man. "Everything within a thousand miles of this place is dead."

"Including our wives and children," said the man whose face was hidden in the shadows.

No one spoke after that.

Alfonso and Marta searched the premises further, and saw no sign of guards. It was a sign of how things had so quickly changed. In one corner of the main hall, they found a steep, spiral staircase that led to the smaller second floor.

"What's upstairs?" asked Alfonso.

"Don't know," said the man with the beard. "I haven't been up there."

"We're looking for kerosene," said Alfonso. "Is there any up there?"

The man with the beard shrugged.

"Come on," said Alfonso. "Let's have a look."

Marta shook her head.

"Come on," insisted Alfonso. "We'll be quick."

Marta sighed and together they quietly climbed the staircase, pausing frequently to listen for any noise. It was quiet. Eventually, they reached a wooden door. Marta turned the doorknob and the door suddenly swung heavily towards them. As it did so, something heavy that had been leaning against the door fell onto them. Marta gasped and shrugged the weight off. It appeared to be the body of a large man. Alfonso ducked and stared mutely as the man tumbled down several steps until coming to rest. The man – dressed in the uniform of the Dragoonya – was dead, and had likely been so for several hours. Daggers stuck out of his back like thorns and around his neck were several long chains of gold and inset diamonds.

"We should leave," whispered Alfonso.

Marta nodded.

And yet neither one turned to go down the stairs. The doorway had opened into a small banquet hall lit dimly with a few candles. Marta took a step into the banquet hall, and felt Alfonso slide into the hall just behind her. It was so quiet that it seemed to be empty, until they saw about two dozen Dragoonya soldiers lying flat on their backs around a grand fireplace that contained only embers.

Suddenly, something moved directly to Marta's left. It was a skeletally-thin looking man with sickly, sallow skin. He grabbed Marta by the throat. The hand couldn't quite clench her throat because it was twitching spastically – as if zapped by electricity. The man's hand continued to twitch until, in one especially violent spasm, all five fingernails popped off, like windows on a cheaply-made toy car. The soldier released Marta's throat to look at his hand. In a nervous gesture, he ran his hand across his scalp, pulling out a huge clump of hair that peeled off as easily as Velcro. He cleared his throat, moved his tongue around his mouth, and spit out several horribly decayed, yellowish orange teeth.

"That's a rather nasty habit," whispered Marta as she crunched up her nose. "Would you mind not doing that again?" Then she hit the man hard in the stomach. The man crumpled, dropping down to his knees. Marta had knocked the wind out of him and he was both stunned and gasping for breath. He was also staring at Alfonso. "We have... been... expecting you," gasped the man. His lips were so horribly chapped that when he smiled, blood formed at the corners of his mouth. "Yes, yes... Lord Nartam... said you would... be coming." The man reached out his hand quickly, but Alfonso struck first, punching the man squarely in the chest, causing him to fly backwards. Two more men, who were lying nearby, had also woken up and were now scrambling to their feet. Then both men fell to the ground. Alfonso spun around and saw Marta holding the crossbow.

"I told you this was a bad idea," said Marta with a trace of irritation in her voice. "But, no – the Great Sleeper always has to have his way."

A number of soldiers, who had been lying inert on the floor, were now also scrambling to their feet.

"Run!" yelled Alfonso.

Marta sighed, as if she were more annoyed than scared, and then said: "Yup, that sounds like a good idea."

Marta and Alfonso turned and ran down the stairs, with the yells and screams of the ash-fed Dragoonya right behind them.

When they arrived at the main hall, the would-be slaves clamored out of their cells. The bearded man was the first among them. "Good heavens," he said. "What's going on?"

"Good news," shouted Marta. "We've spoken with the Dragoonya and twenty of you fellows will be given the chance to be slaves – the first twenty to reach the top of the stairs."

"I knew it!" shouted the bearded man. A tide of prisoners surged forward and began pressing up the stairs. The prisoners ran towards the group of Dragoonya who were just beginning to exit the stairwell. In the angry melee that ensued, Marta and Alfonso dashed out of the fort and headed back to the airship.

As they ran, Alfonso couldn't help but suppress a grin. "It really is a good thing we're not getting married!" yelled Alfonso.

"Why not?" yelled Marta.

"Because you'd destroy me!" said Alfonso. "You're a wrecking ball!"

"Aw, come on now!" yelled Marta. "I'm just a nine-year-old pipsqueak, right? Besides, don't be so happy. We didn't find any kerosene back there and I think we just made those guys really, really mad."

Chapter Thirty-Two
The Way Down

Hill and Naomi had been hiding in the small utility closet for almost two hours now. The old wooden floor was cold and the air smelled of kerosene and damp rotting rope. The room was dark, except for a faint glow of light emanating from the space in-between the floor and the bottom of the door. Hill sat, legs folded up against his chest, and stared at Naomi – studying her face, trying to discern what he saw in her eyes. When he had asked Bilblox whether they could trust her, Bilblox had replied simply, "You can trust me." *But what about her?* Hill wanted to believe that everything would be okay, but his intuition told him something was amiss.

"They've been gone a while," said Naomi. She sounded worried.

"I am sure they're just waiting for the right moment," said Hill as reassuringly as he could. "In a situation like ours, the natural tendency is to rush and to panic – but that's exactly what'll get us caught. We just have to be patient."

Truth be told, Hill didn't know what was taking Bilblox and Resuza so long. They had left over two hours ago with the aim of finding a safe way down to the ground below. Naomi had told them that the Dragoonya used a primitive system of elevators, in which old rowboats were hoisted up and down via a system of ropes, pulleys, and counterweights.

The elevators were self-operated. According to Naomi, you simply got into one of these rowboats and operated an old-fashioned winch to lower yourself down to the ground. The challenge for them, of course, was to do this without being seen by anyone. Naomi suggested that they hide somewhere – that somewhere ended up being the utility closet – and then wait for a quiet moment, when no one was watching, in which they could make their descent unnoticed. Bilblox said he'd be the lookout and Resuza quickly volunteered to go with him. This was smart, thought Hill, just so they made absolutely sure that Bilblox wasn't leading them into a trap. You could never be too careful.

"Tell me about the town where you and Resuza grew up," said Hill in a whisper.

"Why?" asked Naomi somewhat standoffishly.

"Because I'm curious," said Hill kindly. "And because sitting here in the silence isn't all that much fun, wouldn't you agree?"

"I don't really remember much," said Naomi reluctantly.

"What do you remember?"

Naomi sighed deeply. "I remember that I lived in a round little hut – we called them *gers* – I don't know what you would call them," she said finally. "It was my parents, me, and Resuza. Dad herded reindeer. Mom, well, mainly she stayed with us."

"Your mother," said Hill, "What was her name?"

Naomi paused. The questioned seemed to rattle her. She became flustered for a moment and then her eyes grew moist. She struggled to regain her composure and then she uttered her mother's name. "Yolanda," said Naomi. "Her name was Yolanda."

"You were close?"

"Yes," said Naomi. "We had a good life until they came…"

"The Dragoonya?"

Naomi nodded.

"How old were you?" asked Hill.

"I don't know," said Naomi. "I couldn't even say – not more than four years old I would guess. I can remember it though. I wish I didn't, but I do. They burned the town with their torches. Sometimes I can still smell the scent of the rooftops burning. And I remember mom and dad lying in the street. I was too scared to move. That's when Resuza left me."

Hill said nothing for a moment or two.

"That must have been very hard on you," said Hill finally.

"It was," said Naomi, so softly that Hill could barely hear her. "I'll never forget standing there all alone, by myself, staring at mom and dad in the street. I kept calling out for Resuza, but she never came."

"She's here now," said Hill hopefully.

"Yes," said Naomi wearily. "I know."

There was a very long silence.

"Please don't blame her," said Hill finally.

"I don't," said Naomi. She pursed her lips and smiled slightly as she said this, but something about her smile made Hill very uneasy. *Why is she lying?* Hill again felt a feeling of foreboding. It was obvious that Naomi was bitter, but was she so bitter that she would betray her own sister? Resuza would never even consider such a possibility, but Hill had to.

"Naomi," said Hill, as tenderly as he could, "Resuza has been looking for you ever since that day. She spent her whole life trying to find you. I can't image how hard it has been for you, and I have no idea what's going through your head, but you mustn't let your own hurt and pain lead you to do something that you will regret. Resuza is your sister – you're joined by the bond of blood. You have to help her."

"That's why I am here," said Naomi slowly as if in a trance.

"I think we both know why you're here," ventured Hill. "But it's never too late to change your mind."

Hill paused after he said this, waiting and hoping that she would get angry and proclaim her innocence – but she made no reply.

Just then the door to the closet swung open and Bilblox stuck his head in. "The coast is clear," said Bilblox excitedly. "We gotta go now – come on."

Hill and Naomi followed Bilblox along the main deck of a small ship that looked as if once, long ago, it might have been a fishing vessel. When they came to the mainmast there was a small boat, known as a cockboat, rigged with ropes and pulleys and pressed into service as an elevator. Bilblox walked right past it.

"Wait," called Naomi, "Where are you…"

Bilblox turned and gave her a fierce look, indicating that she should shut her mouth right this instant. Bilblox continued until he came to the pointy front of the ship, known as the bowsprit, and peered over the edge.

"What now?" asked Hill.

"Have a look," said Bilblox.

Hill and Naomi peered over the edge. There was a small rope ladder that dangled downward and dropped into another cockboat, this was one significantly smaller than the first, but also equipped with ropes and pulleys. Unlike the first cockboat, however, this boat was not rigged to drop straight down like an elevator; instead, it was attached to a long rope that made its way down to the ground – not vertically – but at a forty-five-degree angle, so that the boat would slant its way downward the way a gondola slopes down the side of a mountain. Resuza was already waiting for them in the cockboat.

"It's too small," said Naomi.

"No it's not," said Bilblox. "It'll work – get in."

"This wasn't the plan," said Naomi.

"The plan is whatever I say it is," snapped Bilblox. "Now get inside."

Hill watched the two of them arguing. *What was going on here?* For a moment it looked as if Naomi was going to refuse to go with them, but finally she sighed, and scurried down the ladder into the cockboat. Hill and Bilblox followed.

"How does this thing work?" asked Hill.

"This thing here is the arm," said Resuza pointing to a metal pole that shot up from the center of the cockboat like a mast. "It has wheels on top that run along the top of the main rope allowing the boat to descend like a cable car." Hill nodded. "And you control your speed using this winch," explained Resuza, as she pointed to a large wooden cylinder at the stern of the cockboat which was coiled with rope. "You just unlock the winch and the boat will slide down the line."

"Let's go," said Bilblox as he stepped down into the boat. He had two very large packs on his shoulder.

"What's in there?" asked Resuza.

"Some supplies that I found," he replied. "We're gonna need 'em." Resuza nodded, moved to the stern of the boat, and pulled a small rusting lever on the side of the winch. The entire boat jolted and then began to slide down the rope toward the ground below. The boat operated like an open-air cable car. Everything was going quite well until everyone heard a sudden pop, which sounded like metal snapping under pressure. Suddenly the cockboat began to build speed. Rope whizzed out of the winch at a dizzying speed as they shot down toward the ground below.

"You should have listened to me!" Naomi shouted. Bilblox did not reply. He knew they were going too fast, but he had no interest in having an argument – especially right now, when they were hurtling towards the frozen tundra with absolutely no way of slowing down. Hill, Resuza, and Naomi gripped onto the gunnels of the cockboat in stunned silence. "We'll be fine," Bilblox shouted above the howling of the wind. "Just hold on tight. The snow will cushion our impact."

"This wasn't the plan!" Naomi shouted.

At that moment, the wooden basket hit the ground and the sides shattered. Pieces of wood flew off into the distance and the occupants all tumbled heavily to the ground. Tiny particles of snow rose into the air around them and seemed to hover there, like instant fog.

CHAPTER THIRTY-THREE
SEAL THE SHIP

As soon as he heard shouting from the fort, Leif sprang to his feet in a fit of panic. Korgu reacted even quicker. The wolf sprang through a small open window and started running towards the fort. Leif followed seconds later, and Nathalia – with Kolo in tow – followed on his heels. As they ran towards the fort, two teenagers burst out of it and began running towards them. Momentarily confused, Leif and the others quickly realized they were Marta and Alfonso.

Korgu narrowed the distance to them quickly, and greeted them with a wagging tail. They all came together on the wind and snow swept plains in front of the fort.

"What happened?" demanded Leif.

"Going to the fort wasn't the best idea after all," said Marta. "And we didn't make any friends."

"We have to leave for the forest now," gasped Alfonso. "The Dragoonya in the fort are after us. We have to leave now!"

They all started running back to the ship together.

"It's dark!" yelled Kolo, as he ran. "We can't enter the forest. I won't! Go, and leave me with the airship." He paused to gasp for air, as he struggled to keep up with the others. "I've kept my end of the bargain."

"Be quiet," said Nathalia.

"But we had a deal!" Kolo protested.

"We still do," said Nathalia. "You'll get it, once we're done using it."

As they continued running back towards the ship, they heard more shouting; it sounded as if it were coming from the roof of the fort. It was the Dragoonya, who had spotted them and were quickly closing in. Korgu turned and raced directly towards the Dragoonya. They wavered at the sight of this monstrous wolf coming towards them. Clearly, they were also spooked by the presence of wolves. Korgu leapt onto the closest Dragoonya soldier, who screamed in terror. That was enough. The rest of the Dragoonya bolted back to the fort. By the time Alfonso and the others had returned to the airship, Korgu had caught up with them.

"Good pup!" yelled Leif. They soon got into the airship. Nathalia began working the controls and the airship lifted into the sky.

"Where to?" asked Leif.

"Dargora," said Nathalia. "I'll try to get us as far as I can, but we don't have much fuel left." A blast of wind rattled the ship. Nathalia struggled to hold a steady course. Below them they could see the Dragoonya fort. A group of men were running around on the roof of the fort, but it was impossible to see what they were up to. As they drew closer to the stone forest, the ship began to pitch and yaw erratically. Everyone looked at Nathalia, who was visibly struggling to maneuver the ship.

"Don't know what's happening," she muttered. "It's some sort of wind surge that's getting stronger as we near the forest." That was an understatement. Wind began pounding the aircraft, shaking it violently. Leif held on to the couch, which, thankfully, was nailed to the floor. Kolo clung to a chair and screamed. Nathalia braced herself in her seat and worked the levers that controlled the ship.

Just then a monstrous gust of wind slammed into the ship causing it to plummet downward. Another came moments later, and it felt like a giant hand had slapped the side of the aircraft. Parts of the ship that had been tied down were knocked loose.

Suddenly, the ship lurched again,

"Turn us around!" screamed Kolo. He was trying to wrestle the ship's controls away from Nathalia. His eyes were ablaze with panic. "We'll never make it!" Nathalia was trying to hold him at bay with one arm and steer the ship with the other; but it wasn't working and the ship quickly went into a nosedive.

Alfonso, Leif, and Marta watched on helplessly. The ship was now spiraling downward and the g-force had pinned them to their seats. Suddenly, the petrified forest came into full view. Directly in front of them was a vast field of stone pillars. The pillars were massively thick, and hundreds of feet high. It almost looked as if someone had ripped the ceiling off the biggest temple in the world and now all that remained were the giant support columns – millions of them. Many of these trees, perhaps as many as a third of them, had a canopy of branches at the top, which looked like intricate spider webs made of stone. The ground of the forest, rather curiously, was not visible because it was shrouded in a heavy blanket of fog.

The ship screamed downward, riding a rollicking down-draft of wind, shooting in-between two massive stone pillars and into the Petrified Forest. Nathalia finally managed to free herself of Kolo's grip by kicking him in the stomach. Kolo fell to his knees and began to vomit. Nathalia regained control of the ship momentarily, slalomed around several pillars, and managed to navigate the ship back out of the forest. For a moment, it looked as if she might even avoid crashing, but then the wind took hold of the vessel again and slammed it down into a huge bank of powdery snow. There was an explosion of snow spraying everywhere and then, as the ship skidded along the ground, the snow crashed through the front windshield of the ship and poured into the cabin. Nathalia was knocked to the floor. For a moment she lay deathly still, then, gingerly, she stood up.

"Is everyone okay?" she asked.

Kolo sat huddled in a corner, staring vacantly at the wall. Leif was massaging his head and appeared bruised, but very much alive. He had a gash on his forehead that was bleeding, but not excessively so. Alfonso and Marta slowly got up as well, but looked to be in no worse shape than Leif.

Leif went outside and struggled to get his bearings. They were currently situated just inside the Petrified Forest amidst the first, neat row of giant stone pillars rising up into the sky. About a hundred feet further in, a blanket of fog obscured what lay beyond. It appeared to be around seven feet tall, and it covered the entire forest floor like a vast gauzy blanket, which undulated with the wind. To his right, Leif saw a great sprawling open field of snow stretching back to the Dragoonya Fort.

Leif turned to Nathalia and asked, "Any chance this ship can still fly?"

She looked doubtful. "Hard to say," she eventually replied.

"Well we should…" began Leif, but he was interrupted by the sound of a lone distant howl – a piercing, mournful cry – the kind of awful noise that sucks the wind from your lungs. Leif, Nathalia, Alfonso, and Marta looked up. The lone howl lingered in the air, ringing in their ears even after the sound itself had died. Then came a chorus of howls. These weren't the calls of coyotes or wolves. They started off deeper, rich with base – almost like the growl of a tiger – and gradually became sharper and more horribly shrill. They all looked at Korgu. She was intently alert, every hair on end. But she also seemed a bit scared, which was the most frightening of all. Korgu was *never* scared.

"What in God's name is that?" asked Leif.

"The fog wolves," said a voice from behind them. It was Kolo. He was still huddled in the corner and the vacant look was still very much in his eyes. "They're running from their caves and into the forest – that's what they do at night."

"We need to seal the ship," said Alfonso.

No one needed any more convincing than this. They began to seal any and all possible entryways. The ship's doors, both the one in front and the one in back, were intact. Nathalia closed both doors and locked them. Marta pulled up a loose floorboard and used it to block off the ship's largest window. Meanwhile, Leif and Alfonso ripped the couch from the floor, carried it to the cockpit, and pushed it into the gaping hole where the front windshield once was. Luckily, it was a decent fit, and with a few good kicks, the couch was wedged in very tightly. Because of the crash, much of the ship was actually buried in the snow, leaving them fairly well protected.

Then they sat still for a quarter of an hour. The minutes ticked by with excruciating slowness. It was very quiet in the ship. The snow was a good insulator and it effectively muffled any and all sounds from the outside world.

Chapter Thirty-Four
Into the Fog Tunnel

"I don't hear anything," said Alfonso finally.

"You usually can't hear the fog wolves," replied Kolo, in a dry monotone.

"So how will we know when it's safe to go out?" asked Marta. "Or should we just send you outside?"

Kolo smiled sourly, the first sign of any expression or emotion that he'd shown since the crash. "You won't know when it's safe," he said tightly.

"Tell us," said Leif quietly. "A while back you told us there was something wrong with the trees in the Petrified Forest – that they were dead, but not quite dead. What did you mean by that?"

"They're dead because they're made of stone," said Kolo, "But they're not completely dead, because you can hear them."

"Hear them how?" asked Leif.

Kolo grimaced. "I only entered once," he explained. "It was when I first tried to follow the slavers. The fog was so thick, I couldn't see the trees, but I could hear them in my head, you know... talking to me."

"What were they saying?" asked Nathalia skeptically.

"They kept saying, *"Don't touch us, boy, don't touch us."*"

No one spoke after this. Everyone seemed to be deep in thought, mulling over what Kolo had just said. Several more minutes passed until Korgu started to whine. She seemed nothing like the frightened wolf from before. Instead, she seemed ready to run around. She went up to Leif and licked his hand, as if she wanted to play.

"Korgu wouldn't behave this way if the fog wolves were still around," said Leif.

"I'm going outside to look around," said Nathalia. She walked to the rear exit, slid the bolt that unlocked the door, and stuck out her head. It was eerily silent. Korgu slid around her, and bounded out of the ship. She immediately ran toward the fog and disappeared within. She emerged a minute or two later and let out a sharp, playful growl.

"She wants us to get going," said Leif.

"Then let's do it – we probably don't have much time before the fog wolves return, and if there's anyone I want on my side against them, it's Korgu," said Nathalia. She jumped out of the airship and headed towards the fog bank. Everyone else followed quickly behind. Korgu took a winding route to enter the fog bank and once inside, it continued to veer in inexplicable ways. The fog was so thick that it was impossible to see more than a foot in any direction. Eventually they entered a tunnel that cut through the fog. The ground in this fog tunnel was well-beaten, revealing a path made by others – namely, the fog wolves. The animals apparently knew, either by instinct or by memory, the way through the snow, because the snow beneath the path was very firm and easy to tread upon.

The fog was cool and wispy to the touch but so opaque that it seemed strange it didn't have more substance. As they trudged quietly through the tunnel, Marta ran her fingers through the whiteness. It disappeared where she touched it. The tunnel was likely made by the very act of walking through the fog – nothing more than that.

They walked quickly – at times breaking into a run – for a long time. No one had any idea where they were, and all hoped Korgu knew what she was doing. It seemed foolish to suddenly pin their hopes of finding Dargora on a wolf, but she had come through for them in so many ways that it seemed strange *not* to do so.

Alfonso found himself in the back of the group, right behind Kolo. He wondered how that had happened – Kolo should not have been with them. But in the confusion of the crash and their sudden dive into the Petrified Forest, no one had stopped and ordered Kolo back. And for some reason, Kolo had decided to join them. Perhaps it was simply a matter of self-protection. He didn't want to be by himself in a badly broken airship. Alfonso hoped this was the case, and that Kolo did not have any other plans.

As he ran, Alfonso remembered the picture frame from Imad's library – the one that could be assembled into a stick – and he pulled out the piece of the stick which had the strange-looking compass embedded in its base. He glanced quickly to see where, exactly, the compass' hand was pointing. It was pointing straight ahead, down the tunnel. Then, as Alfonso continued to run, the hand of the compass turned to the right; moments later, the tunnel turned to the right. This happened again and again. It was as if the compass knew exactly which way the tunnel led and where they were supposed to go.

"What are you looking at?" asked Leif at one point, as he circled back to check on his son.

"The compass," said Alfonso. "It's like it knows exactly where I'm supposed to go."

"You mean where *Nathalia* is supposed to go," said Leif. "You better give it to her soon. She's the one going to Dargora."

"I will," said Alfonso, but he simply continued on his way with the device in hand.

They continued running for as long as they could, following the fog tunnel as it wound its way through the forest. There was no way to judge how far they had gone or see which way they were going because the fog surrounded them on all sides. Occasionally, they came upon pieces of bones lying across the path, all of which were meticulously picked clean.

Alfonso thought back to his conversation with the prisoner in the Dragoonya fort who told him that the wolves entered the forest for meat; presumably, these bones were the remnants of whatever meat the wolves had eaten. Alfonso wondered where the meat came from. *Was it possible that the wolves traveled all the way to Dargora to get it?* No way to know. It seemed possible, however, because despite the twists and turns that they had taken, they appeared to be headed steadily north.

They kept going for what seemed like hours. The path itself was very narrow and, in places, slippery. On one occasion, Marta slipped and actually toppled over through the wall of the fog tunnel. Instantly, and with great speed, she began to sink into a powdery drift of snow. By the time that Leif reached out and clasped her hand, which was just a matter of seconds later, Marta's head was submerged. Leif hauled her back onto the path. Marta appeared more dazed than frightened, too exhausted to betray much emotion. They all stopped for a second and caught their breath.

"Where is that dog leading us?" asked Kolo.

No one answered. Korgu had circled back when she realized they had stopped. She sat patiently a few feet away, her tongue out and her sides heaving with exertion.

"How long do we have before the wolves come?" Marta asked.

"Probably not very long," said Kolo, "They move very quickly – much quicker than us."

"Can they climb?" asked Alfonso.

Kolo shrugged.

At that moment, Korgu sprang to her feet and looked intently up the tunnel. She advanced a few feet, and then retreated. She growled quietly, and then louder. Within seconds, the growls had become defeaning. She began to run back and forth in front of them, as if trying to protect them on as many sides as possible.

They were all thinking the same thing, but only Marta spoke.

"They're coming," she whispered.

CHAPTER THIRTY-FIVE
ONE LAST THING

Hill tried in vain to stand up but his body wouldn't respond to orders from his brain; and then his vision began to dim – as if night were falling. He was suddenly very cold and he felt snow pressing down on him at every angle. *I am buried*, he thought to himself. Hill stopped struggling and focused only on one goal: keep breathing. He lay motionless for what seemed like a long time, and only when he felt ready, did he start moving his fingers and toes. They worked. He began trying to move his arms when, all of a sudden, he felt someone or something grab hold of his legs and pull him upward. Snow cascaded off his body.

"There you are!" boomed a loud voice.

It was Bilblox.

"We didn't know what happened to ya!" Bilblox bent down and grabbed Hill's outstretched hands. With one easy movement, he lifted Hill to a standing position. Hill stood there motionless, amazed that he was standing on firm ground. And most importantly, nothing appeared to be broken. Hill glanced around quickly, but all he could see were snowdrifts and, in the distance, the pillars of Dargora.

"Where is everyone?" Hill asked wearily. Clumps of snow still clung to his eyebrows, cheeks and beard. Bilblox shrugged his head over to his left. Standing huddled together were Naomi and Resuza. Hill walked over to them.

"Everything okay?" he asked.

"I guess," said Naomi. She was clearly still shocked by their hard landing.

"I told ya!" said Bilblox. "I told ya it'd be fine. I knew if we took the other elevator-boat we'd land smack in the middle of downtown Dargora – and what a mess that'd be!"

"You were right," said Resuza. "But where are we?"

"Beyond the edge of Dargora," replied Naomi. "Not far from the Petrified Forest." As she said this, she turned and pointed at a curtain of massive trees, all made entirely of stone, about a mile away. The stone branches glistened with ice. The woods were both surreal and eerie. It looked as if someone had taken a primeval forest, turned it into stone, and then sprayed it with liquid ice. Cyclones of snow swirled in-between the tree trunks. Long shadows darkened the forest floor. The whole place was deathly still because, even when the wind howled fiercely, not even the smallest branch on the smallest tree moved by so much as an inch.

"You can go in there," she said ominously, "But the trees will see you."

"See us?" said Resuza.

"Yes," replied Naomi, "And so will the Fog Wolves."

No one spoke for a moment.

"So what's the plan?" asked Hill uneasily.

"Ask him," said Naomi, gesturing toward Bilblox.

Bilblox seemed lost in thought, as if he were struggling with a difficult choice and couldn't quite make up his mind.

"We cross the forest," said Bilblox finally. "We've made it through worse places than this. We've got plenty of supplies. We'll make it."

"What about the trench?" asked Naomi.

"The trench?" inquired Resuza.

"Yes," said Naomi. "There's a giant trench that surrounds the city. It's impossible to cross, except at one heavily guarded bridge. You can't see it until you've nearly fallen in, but it's between us and the forest."

"Delightful," said Hill wearily.

"I've got rope and a grappling hook," said Bilblox confidently. "We'll be fine. Let's go." He turned in the direction of the forest.

"Not yet," said Hill.

"What is it?" asked Bilblox. He seemed annoyed.

"I've got to go back for something," said Hill. "One last thing."

"It's too late for that," said Bilblox, "Come on, we gotta go."

"No," said Hill stubbornly, "Impossible."

"Are you sure you remember where it is?" asked Resuza. Hill nodded.

"What is it?" demanded Bilblox.

"Something we've had for a long time," said Hill cryptically. "I'm not leaving without it."

"Fine," said Bilblox with a heavy sigh, "But let's be quick about this."

"There's no *us*," said Hill resolutely. "I'm going alone." He refused to make any eye contact, and instead stared into the distance.

"How long will you need?" asked Bilblox.

"Give me two hours," said Hill. "If I am not back after that – go on without me."

Hill walked for a half-hour, which then dragged into a full hour. His pace gradually slowed. The impact from the hard landing had caught up to him and his body protested with every step. The cold settled into his bones and he soon lost feeling in his toes and fingers. Still he trudged onward. At last he stopped in an area of rock, snow and ice. The snow gathered in little eddies behind rocks, and the ice was blue and treacherous underfoot. In the near distance, he could see a door down to the slave quarters. It boggled his mind that he would ever, purposefully come back here, but here he was.

Hill approached a large boulder, about twenty feet in height. Aside from two pillars in the distance, this boulder was the only landmark of note in the area. Once he reached the boulder, Hill bent over and began to examine the ground. He did this for several minutes, shivering as he worked, until suddenly he saw what he was looking for – a gleaming, silver fork. Hill dropped to his hands and knees and began pawing at the snow. He dug downward through the snow until he hit a chunk of ice about the size of a soccer ball.

"Need help moving that?"

Hill looked up.

It was Bilblox.

"I thought I told you to stay put," said Hill.

"I never was good at taking orders," said Bilblox with a smile.

Hill frowned.

"Watchya diggin' for?" asked Bilblox.

"None of your business," said Hill.

"That's where you're wrong," said Bilblox. "All of our crummy lives are wrapped up in *that Pen*."

Hill looked stunned.

"W-w-w-what makes you so sure it's a Pen under there?" stammered Hill.

Bilblox reached down with one hand and picked up the hunk of ice; then, with the other hand, fished out a shiny silver Pen. He studied the Pen carefully turning it back and forth in his giant hands.

"You knew all along didn't you?" asked Hill. "You knew I'd hidden it and I wouldn't leave Dargora without it. But *how?*"

"Kiril," replied Bilblox.

"He knows we have it?"

Bilblox nodded.

"For crying out loud!" said Hill angrily. "Enough playing games! Why didn't you come clean with me?"

"How about *you?*" asked Bilblox. "You're the one who said you'd just be gone two hours and that, if you weren't back, we should go on without you. What was that all about? We both know you had no intention of comin' back, did ya? Ain't that right, buddy?"

"That tree," said Hill shakily. "We have to cut it down."

"Hill, listen to me, I have a plan," said Bilblox. There was urgency and a trace of desperation in his voice. "You've got to trust me!"

"You keep saying that," fumed Hill, "But you've given me no reason to do so!"

"Man, oh man," said Bilblox with a rather sad smile, "You've known me all these years Hill old boy and you still don't really know me at all – do ya? Remember during the trip to Somnos, when the avalanche almost killed us? You were ready to drop me like a hot potato. Only Alfonso trusted me. And that turned out pretty well, didn't it?"

Hill frowned.

"OK," he said. "I'll trust you. What's this plan of yours?"

"It's still a bit of a work in progress," admitted Bilblox.

"Go on," said Hill.

"Well, it starts with you lettin' me keep the Pen."

"Forget it," said Hill.

"What are you thinkin'?" asked Bilblox. "You're just gonna stroll towards the Shadow Tree all by your lonesome and destroy it? Have you seen all those people guardin' it? If not, I'll clue you in. The whole Dragoonya army is crazy with that stuff, and the Shadow Tree is doin' somethin' to them, controllin' them. You'll die way before you get close to it."

Hill said nothing but held out his hand. "Give me the Pen back."

Bilblox looked down at the Pen, which was still nestled in his beefy palm.

"What happens when you press the emerald button?" he asked.

"Try for yourself," replied Hill with a shrug. "Hold it down for a few seconds."

Bilblox pressed the button and held it down. Seconds later, a green light shone from the tip of the Pen and the three dimensional image of the skeleton's hand appeared.

"Holy smokes!" said Bilblox. "That's quite a trick."

"I've been trying to figure out what it means," said Hill.

"Ain't ya ever done studied magic tricks?" asked Bilblox with a laugh. "I thought you were into that kinda stuff."

"What are you talking about?" asked Hill.

"Have a look," said Bilblox, as he tilted the Pen so Hill could have a better look at the glowing three-dimensional image of the hand. Once again, Hill studied the skeletal hand with the numbers etched on and in-between the fingers.

"It's the old coin spinning trick," said Bilblox.

"Huh?"

"It must be the oldest trick in the book," said Bilblox. "That and Three Card Monty is the bread and butter of any decent swindler. As a kid, on the docks of Fort Krasnik, you know how many suckers gave me coins that twirled between my fingers before dissapearin'?"

"I don't follow," said Hill.

"The fingers and the slots between the fingers are all numbered," explained Bilblox. "Like the slot in-between the middle finger and the ring finger – we call that slot 'twenty-three' for short, 'cause it's in-between fingers two and three. You follow? That's the slot where most coin tricks start. The numbers are how you keep track of the moves you need to make in a given trick when you're spinnin' coins."

"Spinning coins?" said Hill quizzically.

"Or Pens," said Bilblox. Hill nodded his head slowly. "I'm not exactly sure what the circle is about," added Bilblox, "Probably a variation in a particular trick – like the coin has to end up there or somethin'."

"I'll take the Pen now," said Hill.

"Sure," replied Bilblox. He pressed the emerald button again and the glowing three-dimensional image disappeared. Then, in one amazingly fluid motion, he rolled the Pen onto his fingers and made it dance across his fingertips in a blur of motion. For a brief moment the Pen disappeared – Hill gasped – and then the Pen reappeared. As soon as it did, Hill snatched it away and stuffed it back into the coat of his pocket.

Bilblox smiled, looked upward at the sky, and studied the moon thoughtfully. It was almost full.

"Hill old boy," said Bilblox.

"Yes?"

"At some point, I do believe I'm gonna need that Pen back."

"Why?"

"You'll see," replied Bilblox.

Chapter Thirty-Six
The Knothole

"Come on," said Alfonso. "We have to find a tree to climb – that's our only chance." He broke into a sprint, charging down the path – deeper into the Petrified Forest – toward the wolves. The others followed him unquestioningly. After three or four minutes of running they came to a clearing. Here the tunnel of fog, through which they had all been running, opened up into a bigger space, about the size of a tennis court. The snow here was all firmly packed and was solid to walk upon; it was also covered with thousands of bones. There were bones of all sizes. Some were small enough to have come from rodents; others were much larger. Mixed into the debris were a few human skulls. Apparently, this is where the fog wolves dined on their victims.

In the center of this clearing, was the base of an enormous tree, whose trunk continued upward through the ceiling of fog above. Alfonso led the way through the graveyard of bones and over to the base of the tree. Even though the tree was made entirely of stone, and resembled a pillar from afar, it looked quite different up close. The tree's exterior had a rough surface – with many furrows, cracks, and crevices – which very much resembled bark. The tree also had a series of small, stone bumps, each the size of a doorknob, which formed a pattern that spiraled its way up and around the base of the tree almost the way a string of Christmas lights would.

The surface of the tree, with all of its bumps and cracks, made it readily apparent that the tree could be easily climbed. Although they had never seen her climb a tree, Korgu bounded up, jumping from one crack to the next until she paused on the lowest limb. She growled at them to follow her. Without saying a word, Marta and Alfonso both simultaneously reached out to touch the tree.

"No," hissed Kolo, "Not a good idea."

"We don't have a choice," said Marta.

"They won't like it," said Kolo, almost in a whimper.

Marta was startled to see the boy, who had so recently been such a bully and a tyrant, now reduced to a sniveling child. *Why was he so spooked? What had he seen in this forest?* The whole thing was unsettling.

"You can stay here if you like," said Nathalia. "But we'll take our chances climbing." With that, Nathalia began climbing up the side of the tree with great agility. Alfonso and Marta followed closely behind her. Leif waited for a moment with Kolo; he couldn't help but feel a small measure of sympathy for the boy. It was hard to explain why. On some level, Leif knew that Kolo had seen or witnessed something terrible – perhaps many things – and that this experience had taken a toll on him, twisted him even. The thought of this weighed on Leif. "We've got to go," said Leif kindly, "Come on Kolo."

"No," said Kolo resolutely. "If the trees don't get me, your son will."

"It's going to be okay," Leif said as calmly as he could. "Alfonso will not harm you, I promise. Now come, follow me." Leif turned to the tree and began to climb it, gesturing for Kolo to follow. He was just a little ways up the tree, when the wolves drew near. There was a great clattering sound, as if all the bones on the floor of the clearing were trembling. Kolo turned to Leif, his face stricken with terror.

"Come on!" screamed Leif.

Kolo shook his head. For a moment, it looked as if he would simply stand there and let the wolves devour him, but instead he scrambled across the clearing and dove head-first into the fog. And then he was gone – vanished – enveloped by the fog.

Leif was out of time. The only thing to do now was climb. He clamored upwards as quickly as he could. Leif proved an able climber and soon reached the ceiling of fog, which they pushed through, and continued upward. The fog was damp and cold and it made the climbing more treacherous so everyone went slowly. Visibility was nil. Leif climbed for many long minutes, and it seemed clear that in this part of the forest, the fog was especially thick. Eventually he caught up with the others. Someone asked where Kolo was. Leif shook his head grimly and explained, "He wouldn't come."

They were all still in the thick of the fog, struggling upwards, when the wolves returned en masse. Everyone heard them all at once because the animals made quite a ruckus. There was no growling or howling or anything like that. The only sound from below was the sickening snapping and crunching of bones. The wolves were feeding. Then, at last, there came a cry; but it was not that of a wolf, but of a person. Someone below was shrieking and they all knew it was Kolo. High above, in the fog, clinging to the tree, everyone pressed their faces to the stone bark and gritted their teeth.

"May God have mercy on him," said Leif softly.

They continued upward and, just a few minutes later, broke through the fog and emerged into the clear, crisp air of night. There was a half moon in the distance that offered a fairly good light. Alfonso reached into his coat and took out a small pair of binoculars – the ones he had found in the airship. What he saw was breathtaking. All around, as far as he could see, were the stone shafts of the other trees, emerging from the fog and stretching up into the sky. Those trees with branches on top looked spectacular in the moonlight – somewhat skeletal like ordinary deciduous trees in winter – but their long delicate limbs were more silver in color, almost iridescent, shimmering and ghost-like in the moonlight. Alfonso noticed that all of the trees had the same curious pattern of bumps, resembling door knobs, which spiraled up their trunks. There was, however, no time to dwell on such matters. From down below, Alfonso could still hear the frenzy of the wolves mashing their food. The only sensible thing to do right now was to keep climbing until, perhaps, with a little luck, they could find a ledge or perch on which to rest.

They climbed for another ten minutes or so before coming upon the giant knothole. Alfonso had, of course, seen knotholes in ordinary trees – hollow spaces in the side of a tree where a branch had decayed and fallen off – but he had never seen one like this. The knothole was a great dimple in the side of the tree, so large, that it almost resembled a cave, the depths of which were shrouded in dark shadows. Alfonso clamored into the space, sighed exhaustedly, and slumped to the ground. The others soon arrived as well and, together, they all collapsed. They were so exhausted, they could barely move – even to unclench their aching fingers. No one spoke. Everyone simply pondered their predicament, trying to think of a way out. Far below, they could hear the sounds of the wolves still gorging themselves.

The wind began to pick up and everyone made their way inside the knothole – everyone but Korgu, who remained perched on the ledge. She refused even to look inside, and kept stretching a paw to see if there was some other place to go. She made no sound at all, which was very unusual. The innermost hollow of the knothole was both dark and surprisingly warm. The air was moist and smelled oddly boggy, ripe with the scent of decay. The ground here was softer, more like clay than hard stone. It was a relief to be in a sheltered place and yet there was something spooky about being inside the tree.

"Alfonso," said Marta, with a glimmer of hope in her voice, "Can't you climb the fog – you know, like you did in Jasber – when you rescued my parents from the roof of their house?"

"Yeah, I have been thinking the same thing," said Alfonso. "I'm pretty confident that I could make it all the way to Dargora."

"By yourself?" asked Nathalia.

Alfonso nodded.

"Forget it," said Leif. "That's not an option."

A tense silence ensued.

"Has anyone brought food?" asked Marta finally. "I'm famished and I've always fancied having a picnic inside a giant stone tree."

"We have some food," replied Leif, who was eager to change the subject. He reached into his backpack and pulled out a round, wooden container of tough biscuits, known as hardtack, which he had brought with him from the flying ship. As he was passing the container to Marta, the container slipped through her hands, fell to the floor, and wobbled deeper into the knothole. It eventually toppled over and came to a rest in one of the shadows. Marta chided herself and sighed. She wasn't eager to venture any deeper into the knothole, but her hunger got the best of her. Slowly, she tiptoed after the container of food. What happened next everyone present would remember for the rest of their lives. The stone wall at the back of the knothole split open in the middle, with the upper half of the wall folding upward and the lower half dropping downward – opening much the way an eyelid would – revealing a gelatinous, quivering, ten-foot-high, bloodshot orb. Marta stared at the thing for a moment before grasping that it was, in fact, a giant eyeball. This wasn't a knothole, she realized, it was an eye socket.

"Uh, ah-," stammered Marta. She was too terror-struck to scream. The others looked over towards the strange noises she was making. Leif reacted first. He lunged for Marta to pull her back. They all scramblied out of the knothole. Korgu, who was in a frantic state, was now trying to get inside to see what was going on. In the chaos, Leif tripped over Korgu and lurched forward, slamming into Nathalia. Everyone struggled to regain their balance, desperately reaching out to grasp something – anything at all – but for Nathalia there was nothing to grab and she stumbled backwards. For a moment, it looked as if Nathalia might steady herself, but her momentum was too strong and, instead, she pitched backwards off the ledge.

What no one saw at the time was that, at the very moment that the giant eyeball opened, the stone tree instantly transformed itself; indeed, all of the many doorknob-like bumps on the tree's stone bark slid outward and formed a series of curved steps that wrapped upward around the trunk of the tree like a magnificent spiral staircase. After free falling downward for a hundred feet or so, Nathalia landed with a sickening thump on one of these steps. Korgu simply seemed to vanish.

Alfonso was the first to see where Nathalia landed. He raced down the steps as quickly as he could, practically leaping the entire way. As soon as he reached her, he knew that she was gravely injured. Her body lay in a crumpled mass and her breathing was quick and shallow.

"I'm going to pick you up," Alfonso told Nathalia. "We'll go back up. Don't worry. Everything is fine."

She smiled slowly. "That's what I would have said," she whispered. "No, I can tell. It's too late... too late for all that."

"I won't leave you."

"Yes... yes you will," she wheezed.

Alfonso heard a pattering of steps from below. Something was coming up the stairs. He turned to see what it was. It was Korgu. Apparently, she had landed a flight or two below with no obvious injury. But now the wolf was growling and yelping loudly. Alfonso's heart sank. He knew what it meant. Sure enough, a few seconds later, he heard a series of high-pitched growls and yips. The fog wolves were coming up the stairs. There wasn't much time. No wonder it was impossible to survive in the forest by climbing the trees. The trees were alive, and when they wished to, they allowed the fog wolves to climb up and grab anyone who was hiding in their branches. It was a perfectly symbiotic relationship, and in this case, it meant that the fog wolves were probably less than a minute away. There was no time – for anything.

"I'm so sorry," gasped Nathalia. "So sorry, so sorry..." Her eyelids fluttered for a moment and then her eyes went lifeless. Alfonso felt her pulse.

She was gone.

The first wolf appeared on the steps just below them. It was perfectly white, down to its claws. Only its nose and eyes were another color – jet black. In another context, the wolf would have been considered beautiful. It looked at Alfonso, Nathalia and then Korgu with great interest. Alfonso became momentarily hopeful. Perhaps a miracle would happen and the wolves wouldn't attack. This hope was dashed seconds later when the wolf sprang towards Alfonso. In the blink of an eye, the wolf had covered the ten feet separating them and had slashed its fangs into Alfonso's shoulder.

Alfonso screamed and fell to one side, his legs coming up to protect his core. Korgu launched into the wolf and tore open its neck. The mortally-wounded wolf clung to Korgu and the two of them began tumbling down the stairs. Korgu was much bigger than her foe and the fight was over quickly. The fog wolf's bloody body fell down several more steps, directly in front of the main pack. At least twenty of them seemed to be crowding the stairs, and only Korgu prevented them from rushing Alfonso. Korgu let out a tremendous howl, and lunged towards them. The wolf pack was confused by the death of their leader, and retreated. Korgu continued to chase them down the steps.

By this point, Alfonso was standing, and realized that Korgu had bought them a few precious minutes, but not much more. He pushed Nathalia over to the side of the stairs, in a vain hope that her body would be protected. Then he spun around and began sprinting back up the stairs. At the knothole, he told Leif and Marta about the situation – that Nathalia was dead, and Korgu had bought them a little time before the fog wolves came back. Father and son locked eyes. Nothing was said, but they both knew how dire the situation had just become. Marta stood on the steps with her crossbow pointed downward.

"We'll have to use hypnogogia to climb across the fog," said Alfonso hurriedly. "My dad and I will carry you, Marta. We'll have to go slowly, but we can still make it to Dargora."

"No!" said Leif. Then he struggled to regain his calm. "Son, you have to listen to me," said Leif. "You can't step foot in Dargora."

"It's too late for that now dad," said Alfonso. "You must see that. Nathalia is dead. She can't fulfill the prophecy."

"Please," said Leif. He took a step toward his son. Alfonso turned and locked eyes with Marta. She knew implicitly what he was asking. From below, they could hear the sound of the fog wolves coming. Leif took another step toward Alfonso and extended his arm. Alfonso spun around so that he was facing the foggy abyss and crouched as if he were preparing to dive off the tree. Leif grabbed at Alfonso's coat, but Alfonso roughly broke his father's hold. He sprang off the ledge, headfirst, and plummeted down into the fog below. As he fell, he relaxed his mind and let himself slip into hypnogogia. Meanwhile, up above, Leif leaned over the edge and screamed for his son. He did not turn back or even respond.

The howling of the wolves was loud now – the beasts were almost upon them.

"Get up!" screamed Leif. "There may still be time to catch Alfonso!"

Marta stood up, for once playing the role of the obedient nine-year-old. She had seen this moment coming and had always been unsure of how she would act. If Alfonso went to Dargora, he would die. But if Leif prevented him from going, the world around her would die. It was an impossible choice. In the end, she couldn't make up her mind, and so she did nothing – which made her feel wretched.

Leif grabbed her by the hand, holding her as tightly as he could, and yanked her off the steps. Leif and Marta soared downward, hand in hand, like a pair of cliff divers. As the wind rushed through his hair, and roared in his ears, time seemed to slow down for Leif and his mind raced backward in time. He recalled having a similar feeling, of the cold wind blowing in his face, on the day that Alfonso was born. At the time, he was riding his motorcycle to the hospital with Judy, pregnant and very much in labor, riding alongside him in a sidecar. Leif remembered other things about that day as well. He remembered wearing the bright blue scrubs that the hospital staff had given him and he recalled holding a scrawny, kicking Alfonso in his arms. He remembered how small Alfonso's fingers were and how downy soft his hair was. He even recalled the smell of the Lysol that the hospital janitors used to clean the linoleum floors. Then, like that, he was back in the present moment – free falling.

The last image that Leif saw before entering hypnogogia was of his son, almost a quarter mile in the distance, running across the top of the fog. The moon lit up the sky in hues of silvery light. Alfonso was moving so quickly and with such grace. Leif knew that he had to keep his son in sight. Alfonso had the compass – which was leading him directly to the Shadow Tree – and therefore he knew where he was going. Leif did not. Leif did, however, know what his son planned to do. Leif also knew – with every fiber of his being – that no matter the cost, he would stop him.

CHAPTER THIRTY-SEVEN
A STRANGE DISAPPEARANCE

Hill and Bilblox quickly returned to Naomi and Resuza. The girls had hunkered down in a makeshift snow cave and were well camouflaged. Despite knowing the exact location where they parted company, it still took Hill and Bilblox several minutes to come upon them. But even then, they only found them when Naomi let out a cry and abruptly stood up.

As they approached, it became clear that Naomi had been crying. Resuza had as well.

"What happened?" Hill asked.

"Nothing," Naomi quickly replied. "And that's the problem. Nothing ever happened for years and years and years."

Hill looked at Resuza. Her face was white and looked cold. She shook her head, warning Hill not to pursue this conversation any further.

"Enough," Bilblox interjected. "I don't care what's goin' on. We gotta get some shelter. We'll die out here in the next few hours if we don't find some place away from the wind."

He turned to Naomi. "You know a place nearby, don't you?"

Naomi stared questioningly into Bilbox's eyes, as if she was unclear what he meant.

"Yes," she finally replied. "I know of a place. It's very protected and we'll be safe there."

"Do we have to cross the moat?" Hill asked.

Naomi shook her head. "It's on this side. We can't attempt a crossing today. Not enough time."

"Let's go," replied Bilblox.

Naomi turned right and began blazing a path that ran parallel to the Petrified Forest and directly into the wind. Bilblox followed immediately behind, as did Resuza. Hill, on the hand, held back at first. Something about this scene felt wrong to him. There were conversations going on that he didn't understand. They were conducted in glances and nods, and he had no idea what was about to happen. All his instincts, however, told him to beware.

And yet, what choice did he have? Bilblox was right – to stay exposed to the weather meant death. Hill made his choice. He pressed a hand against his coat pocket to confirm the Pen was still there, and he ran to catch up to the other three. As he ran, he thought of Bilblox again and wondered what had happened while Bilblox was in Dragoonya captivity. Truth be told, he had the same question about Naomi.

They pressed onward for what seemed like a very long time. The sun wavered just above the polar horizon for a half-hour, and then quickly retreated. Darkness fell upon the arctic and quickly grew deeper. And worst of all, the wind grew in ferocity as Hill, Bilblox, Resuza and Naomi trudged onward. To Resuza, it felt like they had been walking for days. Her body ached from head to toe. And eyelashes felt so heavy; this was due to a build-up of ice that covered each individual strand, but the effort it would take to wipe off the ice seemed too much, and so Resuza kept walking, barely able to see, hoping for relief.

Naomi led the way steadily, as if she knew exactly where she was going. Bilblox and Resuza followed closely behind, while Hill brought up the rear. It was difficult to tell how much time had passed when Naomi stopped at the base of what appeared to be a small cliff. Above them, the exposed rock swirled with snow. Neither Hill, Resuza nor Bilblox could see anything resembling a cave. "What now?" shouted Bilblox. Naomi kept walking towards the cliff face; at the last minute, she turned sideways and then disappeared into the rock. Resuza started after her immediately, realizing that her sister had found a narrow passageway in the cliff. It was so narrow that it was impossible to enter by walking forward. The only way to enter was by turning and walking sideways. Resuza entered the passageway and caught only a glimpse of Naomi about ten feet in front of her.

Just outside, Hill looked at Bilblox.

"It looks like they're going straight into the cliff," said Hill. "No offense, but you should probably go first. Just in case you can't make it and you need someone to pull you out."

Bilblox nodded.

"Listen," said Bilblox, "About the Pen…"

"Not now," said Hill. "Get inside first."

Bilblox shrugged, walked over to the opening, turned sideways, sucked in his stomach and pushed his way into the narrow passage. It was a tight fit, but he knew he'd make it as long as it didn't get any narrower. Hill followed Bilblox through the passageway. Hill had always been somewhat claustrophobic – and this was almost unbearable for him. Hill's chest seized up and he tried to stop thinking that about the stone walls pushing against his body from both sides. Sweat appeared on his face and gathered along his scalp. By the time the passageway ended and he stumbled into the large cave, Hill was breathing heavily. He sunk to his knees to gather himself.

Resuza ran to his side. "Are you OK?"

Hill nodded, but it took several minutes before he could say anything. In that time, he sat on the cold stone floor and took in his surroundings. The cave was large and stretched for hundreds of feet in every direction. The ceiling was relatively low compared to the width and length of the cave. It was perhaps thirty feet tall and covered in a sheen of thick ice. The supplies that Bilblox had with him apparently included a number of candles, because the others had already lit half a dozen of them and placed them in a wide circle. The flickering light reflected off the ice-covered ceiling and walls and caused the cave to look brighter than Hill thought possible.

Naomi grinned. "There's no heat, but it will work for the next few hours," she said. "It's pretty, isn't it?"

Resuza nodded. "You did great," she said with a smile.

It took several minutes for everyone to settle down on the floor comfortably. Bilblox dug into his bag of supplies and handed out several heavy fur cloaks. They were all exhausted and lay on the floor of the cave in silence. Hill vowed not to fall asleep and as his eyes grew heavy, he told himself he would just rest for a moment; but soon he fell into a heavy sleep. He awoke some time later with a start. He lay in place, listening, before moving or talking. A vague premonition unsettled him and he sat up. The candles still burned, but they were almost out, and the light had retreated to a small circle around their group.

A crack, like someone stepping on thin ice, echoed in the distance. Hill reached into his shirt pocket for his Pen. *It was there.* He lay there motionless for several more minutes, but heard nothing. One by one, the candles began to burn out. Hill sat up.

There was another crack.

Hill took the Pen out of his pocket and unscrewed it. Then, as quickly as he could, he grabbed the last candle, which was still flickering weakly, and placed the upper chamber of the Pen over the candle. A flame leapt from the candle into the barrel of the Pen and, like that, the Pen was lit like a small burner on a gas stove. Hill screwed the Pen back together. It was armed. Hill looked around nervously. Resuza and Naomi were still lying on the ground asleep. Bilblox, however, was sitting up and staring at him with a curious look on his face.

"Hill," whispered Bilblox.

"Yes?" whispered Hill.

"There is one thing you must always remember about me," said Bilblox. "I am always loyal to my true friends. Please remember that." Hill furrowed his eyebrows, in a look of confusion. Then Bilblox whistled – a loud piercing whistle that echoed through the cave. Moments later, Hill heard the sound of several bodies charging through the darkness, rushing toward him.

Betrayal.

Hill didn't hesitate. He whipped out the Pen and pressed the emerald embedded on the top of the device. Hill pressed as hard as he could. There was a loud click. A second later, a raging blast of fire exploded from the tip of the Pen and surged across the cave. Yellow and red flames exploded like fireworks. Hill shielded his eyes and half-expected to be burned to a crisp. Suddenly men were screaming, a putrid burning smell filled the air, and the entire cave was illuminated in a brilliant light. Small fires were burning everywhere. Several men were rolling on the ground, trying to extinguish the flames that covered them. Bilblox, Naomi, and Resuza were on their feet shouting at one another. A large number of Dragoonya soldiers, perhaps fifty in number, surrounded them. Most were armed with crossbows and Cossack cavalry rifles. Hill prepared to use the Pen again, and had almost pressed the button, when he heard a familiar voice call out..."

"Don't!"

Hill looked – it was Kiril. He stepped forward slowly, making no sudden moves.

"I have another two hundred men outside," said Kiril. "You can't fight your way out of this cave. Please be sensible."

Hill looked at Bilblox for a quick moment. His face was a mask, but he thought he detected the tint of shame on the longshoreman's face.

"Give me the Pen," said Kiril calmly.

Hill did nothing.

"We don't have time for games," said Kiril. "I'll count to three."

Again Hill looked at Bilblox. He was mouthing something. Hill couldn't quite make out the words. Meanwhile, Kiril had begun his count.

"One," said Kiril.

Hill looked at Kiril.

"Two," said Kiril.

Hill looked back at Bilblox and this time he could make out what Bilblox was saying: *Give me the Pen.*

"Three," said Kiril.

Hill spun quickly and tossed the Pen in a high arc towards Bilblox. Several Dragoonya soldiers lunged forward just as the Pen landed in Bilblox's outstretched hand. Bilblox moved his fingers quickly and the Pen began to whirl, spinning and flickering in a mesmerizing dance across his fingertips. Bilblox moved the Pen so quickly through his fingers that it took everyone several seconds to realize the Pen had vanished into thin air.

Chapter Thirty-Eight
The Chase

Alfonso sprinted for hours and hours across the thick, billowy layer of fog that covered the Petrified Forest. He didn't dare look down at his legs, for fear of losing confidence in them. He began to feel short of breath, then nauseous, and finally he lost his concentration and slipped out of hypnogogia for a moment; as he did, he felt himself drop downward, the way an airplane does when it hits a patch of rough air. *Focus!* He had to maintain his focus and stay in hypnogogia. He regained his concentration briefly and then again felt himself slipping. He needed to get down to the ground right away. Cold, damp winds blasted his face. He felt as if he were at the base of a waterfall, struggling to stay afloat as a torrent of icy water beat him down. He was falling now – all he could do was try and check his momentum – as he plummeted downward and ultimately crashed into a bank of snow.

Alfonso clawed his way to the surface, gasping for air, and finally collapsed in a fit of exhaustion. He took a while to catch his breath. Oddly, he felt warm, as if he were lying in front of a roaring fire. It was the realization that he might soon freeze to death that finally spurred him to sit up. He shivered violently and looked around. Although still night, the reflected light of the stars through the fog bank was enough to make the area visible. It was a moonscape, devoid of anything living. Far off in the distance, behind him, Alfonso could see a shadowy curtain or wall cutting across the horizon. This was almost certainly the Petrified Forest. In front of him, he saw only rolling dunes of snow and outcroppings of bare rock that glittered with ice. He saw nothing resembling even a shack, much less the mythical city of the Dragoonya.

What he did see – the thing that finally motivated him to get moving – was a silhouette in the distance, far off to his right. It was like a shadow moving within a shadow. He would've missed it completely, except for a certain part of his exhausted mind that told him to look carefully at the Forest. That, and the sense that the silhouette was familiar. Perhaps it was the connection that all Great Sleepers felt for each other. Or perhaps it was nothing more complicated than the instinct that allows children to sense when their parents are near. It was his dad – and he wasn't alone. There was a second figure just behind him, darting in and out of view. He wondered if this was Marta, but knew he didn't want to stick around and find out. It was time to leave.

By the time the horizon had begun to lighten, Alfonso had fallen into a walking stupor. The landscape appeared unchanged and Alfonso forced himself to dismiss the possibility that, somehow, he had gone in a circle. Alfonso began to feel a creeping sense of doom. He thought back to the fights he had with his father. Of course it made sense that his dad wanted to stop him, but couldn't he understand that there was more at stake? Why couldn't his father see what would happen if this tree took hold? Obviously this wasn't an easy choice, but the truth of the matter was that this wasn't a choice at all. Alfonso really had no say in the matter. In fact, he felt as if he were being pulled forward by the Shadow Tree, at least this is how he felt at first; but with time, he came to understand that he wasn't being pulled as much as he was being pushed. It was as if an invisible hand was exerting pressure on the small of his back. And he knew deep down it was the Founding Tree of Somnos – the tree he had planted, *his* tree – goading him forward, coaxing him to do the deed, pushing him to his own death.

Part of Alfonso felt bitter. There was no doubt about it. Why him? Why was he forced to shoulder this burden? Hadn't he and his father already given enough? And yet, at the same time, Alfonso knew this was also the voice of the selfish coward who lives deep within each of us. This was the voice that had to be squelched. He forced himself to think of Hill, Lars, and all the other Dormians he had met. They were a part of him, and to ignore the threat of the Shadow Tree was to say that those lives weren't worth saving. There were times when Alfonso hated everything Dormian and, all the while, part of him nurtured a dream that perhaps he'd go back to Somnos and live out his life there, alongside *his* tree, the one that now seemed intent on killing him. No matter how upset he became, he never blamed the Founding Tree, because at long last he had come to understand that he and the tree were one. The tree was not a foreign entity forcing him to do something he didn't want to do; the tree was part of him and it was merely urging him to do what he knew was right. If his Dad did catch up to him, he'd explain all this in a way he wasn't able to before. He would make him see.

The thought that really gave Alfonso pause, however, was Resuza. He had no idea where she was, though he suspected that she was in Dargora, in search of her sister. Of course, part of his motivation to destroy the Shadow Tree, was to help her – to save her – yet even if he succeeded he would never see her again. This thought depressed him. On one of the times that he had used his powers as an ageling, and had morphed from being a teenager to being an adult, he had stumbled across a peculiar memory – a series of images, really, that flickered across his mind like scenes from an old-fashioned picture show. He saw two little children and a woman in her mid-thirties, sitting at the end of a dock, at the edge of a lake in the mountains. The woman was smiling and splashing the children. It took Alfonso a moment to recognize her, but he came to understand that the woman was Resuza, and that the children were *theirs*. He had seen a glimpse of their life together. It existed in the future – or some permutation of the future that might occur if he lived. He had not encountered the memory again. It was lost, like a dog-eared snapshot in a huge bin of photos. The curious thing – the thing that really unnerved him – was that the nearer he drew to Dargora, the faster the memories of his life slipped away. It was becoming harder for him to morph, because the memories were vanishing, like bits of debris spiraling down the drain.

Alfonso took a deep breath and tried to quell the panic he suddenly felt. Dargora. Where was it? He was running out of time. He thought back to his conversations with Resuza about Dargora. Resuza had attempted to find the city, years ago, in the hopes of rescuing her sister. Resuza had recounted meeting a hermit woman who had spoken of a petrified forest and a city of bones that lay within. She had been wrong, of course. Dargora wasn't inside the petrified forest, unless Alfonso had somehow missed it. But perhaps her information wasn't all wrong. She had spoken of a city so well hidden that it was only visible for a brief moment during twilight. And Resuza had confirmed this – she had actually seen Dargora. He remembered her words: *"For a minute or two it flickered into sight—a vast city made of rocks the color of dry, bleached bones. "*

Alfonso looked up and noticed that the daylight was already beginning to fade. This far north, the day consisted only of a few hours. In fact, the sun had never appeared behind the thick veil of clouds, but he could tell from the way the clouds glowed near the horizon that the sun was already retreating. Night was coming and he felt weak. His head was throbbing and he felt hot all over. Alfonso suspected that he was running a fever. He was spent. He looked behind him. He couldn't see anything. Maybe he had, at the very least, succeeded in losing his father. He needed rest desperately. He dropped to his knees and collapsed on a bank of snow. He had to close his eyes – just for a moment.

Sleep came swiftly.

He awoke a short while later and was alarmed to see the possessions from his backpack had been taken out and placed neatly in a row in front of him. Had someone been here? Impossible. There were no tracks in the snow. He must have done this in his sleep. There was some extra clothing, a knife, several antique Pens he had kept as souvenirs from Bilblox's airship, an old passport picture of his dad, and the small engraved box he had found in the cavern underneath the Three Sphinxes in Egypt. A sudden charge went through Alfonso as he withdrew the rosewood box. He had forgotten about that – forgotten that there was one door he hadn't entered. His thoughts were interrupted by the sound of a voice.

"Alfonso!" called the voice. "Please, for God's sake, if you can hear me, show yourself. Please. I'm begging you."

Words formed on Alfonso's lips, but he could not utter them. He contemplated standing up, but he was too tired. Instead, he sat cross-legged in the snow, held the rosewood box in his hands and focused as before on the thousands of minute indentations engraved across the box. He slipped into hypnogogia and concentrated. Once again he saw that some of the indentations were octagons and some were nonagons and – when he blocked out the octagons – the nonagons clearly formed a doorway complete with a handle. Seconds later, Alfonso found himself back in the windowless room that was Imad's antechamber. It was the same as he remembered it, down to the cool marble floors and smooth wood-paneled walls. The only difference was that instead of the original three doors, only one door remained. He walked to the door and examined it. It was made of rough wooden planks, like the other two, and it also featured a bronze doorknob engraved with the image of an ocean wave.

Alfonso took a step back and looked around the room. At first glance, it had seemed empty except for the door, but now he realized the same narrow desk was sitting partially hidden in a dark part of the room. He walked over to the desk and as before, a sheet of parchment paper lay on the top.

My dear Alfonso:

You have done well. Enter the last doorway, use its knowledge, and let us be rid of this heavy burden forever. I most seriously assure you that the Shadow Tree will not stop. It must feed, and like a malignant cancer it will eventually consume the world. I regret most sorrowfully the heavy responsibility that is yours.

Your loyal and eternal servant,

Imad

Alfonso walked quickly to the door, took a deep breath and opened it. He faced an absolute darkness but deep within, he could hear a whistling, followed by the sound of water crashing. He stepped into the darkness and fell for what seemed at least a minute. During this time, he became aware of a mix of water, ice and snow droplets surrounding him. Gradually, this mixture began to form into the shape of a wave. It withdrew, formed, and then rushed towards him. At the last instant before hitting him, the multi-form wave abruptly disintegrated, withdrew, and started the process again. This happened over and over until one particular wave actually hit him, at which point Alfonso's entire body snapped straight.

Alfonso became aware of leaving hypnogogia. He opened his eyes and gradually realized he was lying on the ground, face up, staring at the cloud-covered polar night sky. The rosewood box sat in an outstretched hand, and a light snow fell. Alfonso lay there motionless and gazed at the snowflakes landing on his parka. For a moment, he thought he had died. His body felt stiff and brittle and slowly he realized that he had morphed into a very old man, who was perhaps ninety-five or one hundred years old. Alfonso's thoughts were muddled. His breathing was shallow and his heart had momentarily stopped beating. He suddenly understood that his ageing body had taken on the form of a man near death. Just then, Alfonso heard sobbing, and the choked cry of a man. "My child," sobbed the man. "My only child." Alfonso knew without looking that the cries were his father's.

"My child... my dear boy..."

He thinks I'm dead, thought Alfonso.

The wind gusted wickedly, blowing a mound of powdery snow over Alfonso's body. He was soon covered from head to toe, consumed by the snowy landscape that surrounded him.

CHAPTER THIRTY-NINE
FATHER & SON

Nartam stood by the large window in his room, which had once been the captain's quarters of the ship. He looked down on the world below in a daze. Strong winds were gusting from the south, howling across the Petrified Forest, pushing the clouds northward and swirling them about like wisps of milk in a freshly-stirred cup of tea. When he tired of looking out the window, Nartam paced back and forth across the creaking wooden floor of his room. There was no furniture – no bed, or sofa, or table, or chairs – just a large vacant space. This was because Nartam was restless. He could no longer lie down, or sit still, or even stand in one place for more than a few seconds before his limbs began to twitch – slightly at first and then violently. If he forced himself to stay still, his muscles would go into spasms. Twice he had lost control of his arm and punched his fist through a wall made of solid oak.

There was only one explanation for his restlessness, of course, and that was the black ash from the Shadow Tree. Nartam had taken too much of it lately. But this was understandable, he reasoned, because he had to test the outer limits of what the ash could do. Lately, he had been conducting little experiments. Just the day before, he had taken a dagger – so sharp that a man could use it to shave – and used the blade to slice off the index finger on his left hand. Truth be told, it didn't hurt all that much because one curious side-effect of the black ash was that it seemed to deaden the nerves in the limbs. A man using the black ash could hold his hand in a roaring fire for ten seconds without flinching. In any case, Nartam had taken the severed finger, dipped it in the black ash, and then pressed it back onto the flesh of his bloody hand. The veins in his finger had wriggled about, like thin translucent worms; then the bones began to fuse; and finally, a fresh layer of skin grew in a matter of seconds. Within five minutes he had regained full use of the index.

Nartam was stronger than he had ever been in his entire life – this much was clear.

As he paced back and forth, Nartam's thoughts remained fixed on Alfonso. Most likely he would arrive on the new moon, as the Shadow Tree predicted. Nartam's dreams had been filled with images of the full moon illuminating the night sky. This had to be what it meant. The boy was coming. Nartam was certain of it. The Founding Trees would send him – and his father, Leif, as well – pushing them northward like pawns. This thought made Nartam smile. In Dormia, Great Sleepers were always hailed as heroes – even saviors and martyrs – but the truth was they merely did the bidding of the Founding Trees. Once or twice, Nartam had wondered if the same was now true of the Shadow Tree – whether it secretly exerted more control over him than he cared to admit. In any case, most Great Sleepers gradually came to realize that they were really servants, one might even say, slaves. Leif had realized it during his long captivity in Jasber – and soon Alfonso would as well.

Nartam was summoned from his thoughts by a knocking at the door.

"Come in," he beckoned.

The door swung open and Kiril entered. His second in command looked preoccupied. And why was he avoiding eye contact? Nartam stared at Kiril. He had survived for so long because of a well-cultivated paranoia, and this sense was telling him to beware.

Nartam shook his head. Impossible. Kiril was not like others. He was his son.

"Hello Kiril, my son," said Nartam in a soft voice.

"Hello father," replied Kiril. "You summoned me?"

"Yes," said Kiril, "Come have a word."

Kiril walked across the room, but stopped several feet short of Nartam, as if not wanting to draw too near.

"You do not have the Foreseeing Pen." Nartam's tone was flat and neutral. It was a statement, not a question.

Kiril nodded.

"What happened?" asked Nartam.

"We captured Hill and Resuza," replied Kiril matter-of-factly. "They had the Pen. I saw it with my own eyes – and then it disappeared."

"Disappeared?" replied Nartam. "What the devil are you talking about?"

"I don't... I'm not exactly sure," said Kiril. "But I will find it."

"Where is Bilblox?" demanded Nartam.

"I have him," said Kiril. "I will return him to you at once."

Nartam nodded. "Good. He is important."

He turned away from Kiril and looked out the window at the Shadow Tree below.

"So the Pen just...disappeared," said Nartam softly. "That's most unfortunate." He turned slowly to look at Kiril. "Or convenient, depending on how you look at it."

"Convenient?" asked Kiril, a trace of surprise in his voice.

"Come now my dear, dear child," said Nartam softly, almost in a purr. "What do you take me for? We both know perfectly well what that Pen can do and how powerful it is. So if you tell me that you almost had it, and then it mysteriously disappeared, don't place yourself above suspicion. Don't forget, I am your father. I know you better than you know yourself. And I love you – even if you have deceived me. You know that, don't you?"

"Are you suggesting I am hiding it from you?" asked Kiril. His face reddened.

"Don't be too hard on yourself," said Nartam. As he said this, he took out his hand and tenderly stroked Kiril's face. "You wouldn't be the first son to betray his father. I am no fool. And neither are you. In fact, what I always admired most about you, my son, is that you never allowed anyone or anything to become dear to you. That is what makes a man strong. And that is what kept you safe... until now."

"The girl," said Kiril slowly. "Naomi."

"Yes," said Nartam. Nartam drew closer and whispered into Kiril's ear: "You were wise to hide her."

Kiril said nothing. His feet were rooted to the ground as if made of stone.

"But you were very foolish to lie to me and think you could get away with it," said Nartam.

Blood drained from Kiril's face.

"What kind of monster do you take me for?" said Nartam with a sad shake of his head, as if he were reading Kiril's thoughts. "Am I the sort who murders children? I beg you to recall that it was the Dormians who cast you – as a child – into the snow to die and it was I who saved you."

"What do you want from me?" asked Kiril.

"Bring me Bilblox," whispered Nartam. Suddenly all the tenderness was gone from his voice. "*Now.*"

Kiril nodded, spun around, and left the room. He ran back toward his quarters, cursing himself for his stupidity.

He was not his usual self. He had let the Pen slip through his fingers, and now Nartam was manipulating him. He owed Nartam everything, but he never let anyone manipulate him. That was Kiril's talent but somehow his talent was failing him.

When he made it back to his quarters, as expected, Kiril found the door broken down and the place ransacked. His possessions were all in disarray. Drawers were open and tables overturned. A great wooden wardrobe in the far corner of the room had been knocked over and all of Kiril's clothing was strewn across the floor – robes, coats, pants, shirts, scattered about. He had instructed Naomi to stay and hide, but she was gone.

Staring at all of this clothing strewn across the floor, Kiril realized that he was quite cold. Looking for something warm and dry, he found a pair of wool pants and a heavy winter kimono. Kiril hadn't laid eyes on the kimono for ages. He had gotten it centuries ago, in the mid 1600s, while exploring the coast of Japan with a Portuguese merchant vessel. At the time, Kiril was looking for a Great Sleeper, whom he never found, but along the way he had befriended a Japanese woman – he could no longer remember her name, but he could still picture her face. The woman had given him the kimono. The kimono was too big, too long in both the torso and the sleeves, but it was warm and light. He remembered wearing it during a particularly deadly but victorious battle. Good. It would restore his confidence for what was to come.

After dressing, Kiril paced back and forth rapidly, considering his next steps. Naomi was gone and Nartam had taken her – but where? Dargora was vast – she could be in any one of a thousand places. Looking for her would take far more time than he had. Kiril looked around his quarters again, this time, taking his time. The door to his quarters was broken down. Naomi had locked herself inside, as Kiril had instructed her to do. The door itself was massive, made of heavy teak, and reinforced with a latticework of steel ribs. It would have taken a while to knock down a door of this size and strength. That meant that Naomi had time before Nartam's guards seized her. He had taught his young apprentice to think quickly, and to always leave a way out. Had she learned his lesson?

Kiril walked to the small alcove where Naomi slept. The bed was made. Several heavy blankets, each one made of rabbits' fur, were folded neatly at the far end of the bed. The pillow was perfectly fluffed. Everything was as it should be. Naomi was meticulous with her things – much like Kiril. Slowly, without even fully realizing it at first, Kiril became aware of a faint whistling sound. The window directly above Naomi's bed was slightly ajar – just an inch or two. This was odd. Naomi, being a thin girl, was always lamenting how cold it was. She never opened windows, not even a crack.

Kiril leaned towards the window and opened it further. Frigid air roared in, but Kiril did not flinch. He leaned out the window. The clouds had cleared and below him Kiril could see Dragoonya burning freshly-cut limbs from the Shadow Tree. He glanced carefully around and paid special attention to a narrow ledge directly below the window. A faint image, almost imperceptible, had been traced in the snow that accumulated on the ledge. It was the outline of a large hand.

Kiril examined it closely. The hand was much larger than his, and lying where the palm would be was a tiny nub of lead. It was a Pencil tip. His mind raced and then, quite suddenly, he knew. He'd only met one man with a hand that large: Bilblox. Naomi was trying to tell him something. She was such a clever girl. The answer had to be right here. He knew it. The Pencil tip. What did it mean? What was Naomi trying to tell him? What had she seen? She had been standing very close to Biblox, back in the cave, when he made the Pen disappear. She had seen something – but what?

Chapter Forty

The Trench

H ill and Resuza sat huddled at the bottom of an icy canyon. When they looked up, all they could see was a narrow slice of the sky because, on either side of them, walls of sheer ice rose upward. The sides of this canyon were studded with small notches and outcroppings and, from these notches, hung icicles – gigantic, gleaming, slabs of ice that likely weighed several tons each. If one of these missiles fell, it could easily crush a car or even a small house; and every so often, as powerful gusts of wind blasted through the canyon, an icicle would break free and explode on the floor of the canyon. When this happened, enormous shards of ice would rip through the air with enough force to decapitate a horse. Such was life at the bottom of the giant trench that circled Dargora and protected the city like a castle moat. It was a dismal setting and, quite plainly, this was the place where Hill and Resuza were expected to die.

After being captured, Kiril and his men marched them across the snow until they reached the precipice of the trench. Here was an old rope ladder, staked into the ground, and draped over the edge and down into the trench below. "Go on," Kiril had told them, "Climb down." Several soldiers held crossbows and old rifles, which they pointed menacingly at Hill and Resuza. Hill nodded somberly. He seemed to understand that this was a death sentence. Resuza stood frozen in place, apparently in a state of shock. One of the soldiers, who appeared to be a halfwit, was staring at Resuza and gnawing on his own lip with great relish – as if it were a very tasty morsel of food.

"Come on my dear," said Hill softly, "We better do as he says."

Together they descended the rope ladder, deeper and deeper into the trench. Once or twice, as they descended, they paused when they heard the sound of icicles falling and shattering on the ground below. When they finally reached the floor of the trench, they both stared at the rope ladder dangling loose against the ice wall. Someone whistled from far above them, and the ladder rose quickly. It snagged on a piece of ice, sending down pieces of rope and shards of ice. The Dragoonya were obviously impatient to leave. They pulled harder on the ladder and it broke in two, with the lower half falling to their feet. The sound of the rope hitting the ice echoed with an awful finality.

"Bilblox betrayed us," said Resuza dully, as if she were only half conscious.

"It would appear so," said Hill.

"And Naomi," said Resuza. There were tears in her eyes. "It was a trap all along."

"We don't know that," said Hill.

"It's my own fault," said Resuza softly. "I never should have left her in the first place. But it all happened so fast! And I tried to find her. I did. And I spent all that time with the Dragoonya in Barsh-yin-Binder, trying to get back to her. I even double-crossed you and Alfonso on the way to Somnos. It was all for her...."

She sat down on the ice and buried her head in her hands. Her body shook with deep sobs. It was an awful sound, one Hill hadn't heard from Resuza. She had always been the optimist, but suddenly she sounded broken.

He sat down and put his arms around her. She sobbed even louder.

"We're going to die," whispered Resuza. "But worst of all, I'll die knowing that my sister hates me so much that she has done this to me..."

Hill said nothing except hugged her tighter. As he sat there holding Resuza, his mind passed quickly over the last months of captivity to a happier time back in Somnos. He closed his eyes and thought of the house he had helped design, the waterfall out back, and the lush grounds that made it a tropical paradise in the middle of the Ural Mountains. But most of all he thought of his wife Nance. After a certain point in his early 40s, Hill had given up on the idea that he would ever find someone. He was content enough living in Chicago and repairing antique watches. There was no reason to keep searching, so he had stopped.

However, his sleeping-self had other plans. It tapped into the deep awareness that binds Dormians to the Founding Tree, and started the process of bringing the Dormian Bloom to Somnos. And even though his path had led him here, to his current situation, marooned in a polar crevasse, he wouldn't take it back for a second. He had found his native land, and he had contributed to making it better. He had saved it and while doing so, he had saved himself. He had met the love of his life, and even if fate would not allow him any more time in her company, no one could take away those blissful years together in Somnos. Hill smiled through cracked and broken lips. A profound tiredness had settled onto his shoulders, and he was unsure of whether he'd be able to shake it off. Perhaps this was the end.

He sighed. *Not yet,* he thought. *Not yet.* He looked at Resuza. She was silent, nearly catatonic, and her clothes were covered in shimmering snow crystals, making her look like a statue chiseled from ice. Hill stood up and rummaged through the supply pack Bilblox had given him. He removed a small pocket knife, gathered up the remnants of the rope ladder and with the knife in hand, began cutting off slender strands of twine. Once this was done, he tied these strands together so that they formed a single line. Next he took off his coat and used his knife to cut out a piece of cloth from the lining of his coat. He cut the cloth very, very carefully, and paused on many occasions – as if to contemplate the exact shape of the material that he was cutting. He also cut out a small hole in the upper portion of the cloth. When this was done, he took out two wooden rods, which were built into the frame of his backpack, and fastened them to the piece of cloth using small bits of string.

"What are you doing?" asked Resuza finally. Her voice sounded distant, as if all of the months of strain had changed the way she spoke.

"Trying one last trick," said Hill with a faint smile. "And hoping for a bit of luck."

Chapter Forty-One
The Distress Beacon

Alfonso's heart was barely pumping blood. It would have taken a highly skilled doctor with a stethoscope to hear his faint beating. It was bitter cold and Alfonso's skin was a grayish-blue. His lips had turned almost black and his body looked so stiff that anyone would conclude rigor mortis had set in. Alfonso's brain just barely sensed the wind whistling far above and the snow softly falling across his body. Alfonso willed himself to stay like this. He needed his father to think this, so that he would give up, turn around, and let Alfonso do what he had to do.

Leif wept over Alfonso's body for almost an hour. Marta sat by his side, stony faced. *Did she know?* Impossible to say. Finally, she persuaded Leif that they needed to build a snow shelter if they wanted to survive the cold. Marta built the shelter and, after some time, she convinced him to come inside.

Once Leif entered the snow shelter, Alfonso set his mind to morphing. He pictured the scene inside the burning armory and imagined the scent of the smoldering timbers. He willed himself back into that moment, back to that point in his life, back to being fifteen years old. Anybody looking at Alfonso morph back into life would have witnessed an unforgettable scene. Tiny ribbons of color wormed their way from Alfonso's heart, through his circulatory system, into the far reaches of his body. These arteries then fed frozen veins to restart the entire body. His color changed from a dirty white to a slight pink and then back to normal. His lips lost some of their black color, but not all, and they remained cracked and sore. Alfonso was happy not to have a mirror – he felt terrible and he figured he looked even worse – but he was fifteen again.

Alfonso rose to his feet. The wind blew loudly and there was no chance that his dad would have heard him getting up. Alfonso briefly felt an urge to run to his dad, to ease the incredible pain he would be feeling, and to tackle the destruction of the Shadow Tree together. Alfonso even took two steps in the direction of the cave before stopping.

No. He couldn't take that chance. The Shadow Tree was his burden, and he had to face it. Alfonso stood in the darkness for a few minutes more. He was feeling better, enough to tolerate eating a handful of dried fruit and to drink some water. That done, he stood quietly for a moment.

He was alone, surrounded by hundreds – perhaps thousands – of miles of the most inhospitable terrain on earth; and yet, even in these most dire of circumstances, there was so much to admire: the delicate build-up of snowflakes on his boots, the shrill yet melodic rush of wind across the snowdrifts, and even the absolute stillness that occurred whenever the wind died down. Alfonso checked the strange-looking compass from Imad's library. The hand was pointing northeast. This was something new. For most of his journey the compass had been pointing due north. Why the sudden change? He shrugged. Northeast it would be.

His thoughts drifted back to Imad's antechamber and the final door. Again he pictured the waves. He knew exactly what he had to do. It was all so perfectly laid out it was as if Imad had planned it all – or, at the very least, foreseen it all. Alfonso shouldered his backpack and with some effort entered hypnogogia. He locked his concentration on a single snowflake. The snowflake seemed to slow down, as if in slow motion. Alfonso watched it flutter, watched it rotate slowly on it axis. Then, slowly, Alfonso expanded his realm of concentration, allowing himself to become aware of other snowflakes around him. He tried to imagine these snowflakes as tiny tiles or pieces that he could manipulate and, sure enough, the snowflakes seemed to respond to the power of his will. The bits of snow jostled and shoved each other, like huskies getting ready to pull a sled. Gradually, they took on a strange momentum, and began to move together in a rhythmic fashion. Snow from nearby drifts joined this nucleus, and the particles grew into a massive body that unfurled like a great ripple in a small pond.

Then a wave formed. It was a curious wave – it simply curled and undulated as if it were about to crash, but it never did. When it had grown to a height of about twenty feet, Alfonso climbed tiredly to the top. To his surprise, the footing was surprisingly firm, even though the wave itself felt rather mushy.

He rode the wave of snow slowly at first, but then as his confidence grew, so did his speed. The wind bit at his cheeks, and Alfonso shivered. He had been outside and exposed to the elements for over twenty-four hours – he was utterly exhausted – but he couldn't help smiling. He was surfing on a wave of snow that was rolling northeast across the landscape faster than the speed of a car. It was exhilarating. By this point, the pitch-black sky had begun to lighten and what passed for dawn in this bitterly cold world was near. Alfonso slowed down and turned his focus to the world around him. If there was any time to discover the true location of Dargora, it would be now. Due north, the horizon lightened even more, and all across that section of the sky, a diffuse light began to spread.

As Alfonso admired the majesty of this polar sunrise, the clouds in that direction cleared momentarily. He gasped. In the far horizon, above the clouds, he clearly saw several ships that appeared to be flying through the air. They were old vessels from the 19th century, with tall masts and tatters of rigging like strands of hair. The largest had several decks stacked on top of each other, each one larger than the one beneath. Even from the long distance, Alfonso could tell they were being maintained. Each shimmered in the morning light as if freshly painted. Alfonso wondered if he was hallucinating from a polar sickness – perhaps it was a strange type of blindness. But then he saw that each ship was not actually flying. Instead, each sat at the top of a pole, some of which were curved slightly, like tusks.

Dargora. He took a deep breath. He was close.

Alfonso felt sick in the pit of his stomach. At first he assumed it was just exhaustion coupled with nerves. Then he felt himself slipping out of hypnogogia involuntarily. The wave of snow dissipated beneath him and he crumpled to the ground. Exhausted, he staggered onward. He was so tired he nearly tripped over several large rocks that lay half-buried in the snow. Several feet beyond this, he suddenly noticed the precipice of a great chasm. The chasm was very deep and it went for miles in either direction like a great trench or perhaps even a moat. It formed a perfect defense – just the thing to stop an advancing army.

His heart sank. There was no way in his condition that he'd be able to cross it. He looked in both directions, hoping there was a bridge he might cross. Just then, something in the sky caught his attention. It looked like a large bird, but he realized it was something manmade – a piece of cloth, perhaps. He walked towards it. It seemed completely out of place, but it was hard to avoid the conclusion that this was a kite on a string, and the string descended into the trench below.

Obviously it could be a trap, but that didn't appear likely. The Dragoonya were not the type to spend their leisure time flying kites, or even to imagine that a kite could be used to lure someone closer. No, something else was going on. Alfonso walked along the edge of the trench until he came to the spot where the string was descending downward. He reached out over the precipice, grabbed hold of the string, and began hauling in the kite. Moments later he was holding the thing in his hands. He studied it closely.

Something about the shape of the kite looked familiar. At first glance it resembled the head of a bird with a hole for an eye. No, that wasn't it. Alfonso studied it further, and suddenly smiled from ear to ear. He recognized the shape. It was a near perfect rendering of the State of Minnesota and the hole at the top was in the exact location of his hometown, World's End. Only one man in the entire world would make such a whacky, goofy distress beacon. Then he recalled the words in "Scenario II" of Imad's prophecy: "*A Perplexon will rejoice with friends in the dark of the chasm.*"

"Uncle Hill!" Alfonso screamed into the bottom of the trench.

No response.

"Uncle Hill!" he screamed again.

Silence.

He looked again at the kite and realized there was no way it could be anything but his Uncle Hill. He shivered and walked back to the rocks buried in the snow. He opened his backpack. There were two coils of rope. He took out one of the coils, wrapped it carefully around the largest rock, and threw the loose end over the edge. Moments later, he began rappelling downward.

CHAPTER FORTY-TWO
OLD FRIENDS

Blackness. Not even the slightest trace of light. Bilblox could hear the wind howling, but that was the only information he could gather from the outside world. Bilblox let out a long, heavy sigh. Once again, he was locked up. There were heavy iron handcuffs around his wrists and manacles around his legs.

Bilblox had been in prison several times before. He'd been jailed in Fort Krasnik for brawling, and of course he had been imprisoned in Somnos after it was discovered that he'd burned a leaf from the Dormian Bloom; but this was different. When the door to his cell closed this time, the click of the lock had been louder and more menacing than he remembered.

He stared into the darkness for so long that he couldn't tell whether he was awake or asleep. It all became one long, rolling wave of semi-consciousness. His dreams were scattered and empty, just scenes of devastation. It felt like watching a silent movie that flickered on for only seconds at a time. He closed and opened his eyes but nothing changed.

And then abruptly, it did change. He opened his eyes from a fitful sleep and saw a glow of light coming from the far corner of his cell. The glow emanated from a lantern; and sitting next to the lantern, with his back propped up against the wall, was Kiril. Bilblox blinked his eyes. He was amazed to see Kiril and equally amazed that his eyesight was still working even though it had been quite some time since he'd taken the green ash. Kiril had given him the potion so nonchalantly that he figured it wouldn't last very long.

"I thought you could do with a bit of light," said Kiril thoughtfully.

"Yes," said Bilblox slowly, blinking his eyes as he struggled to adjust to the light. Bilblox sat up and, as he did, he rubbed his temples. Kiril handed Bilblox a flask of potion and Bilblox took it eagerly. However, before he brought it to his lips, he looked at Kiril suspiciously.

"Go ahead, drink it." said Kiril casually, "It's the same thing I gave you before. I promise." He smiled. "Your suspicion is comforting – it shows how much you and I have in common."

Bilblox studied him for a second, and then lifted the flask to his lips. He drank deeply.

"You're wrong," said Bilblox, once he finished. "We ain't got nothin' in common."

"Listen…" persisted Kiril.

"Naw," said Bilblox with a violent shake of his head. "Spare me the whole bit where you tell me that we are both black sheep who been vilified, but really we're a bunch of swell guys who gotta band together and we're in this thing together. That's not your way. You got no interest in helpin' me or anyone else but yourself."

"Normally I would agree with you," admitted Kiril. He shifted his body, trying to find a more comfortable position, as he leaned against the stone wall. "But not today."

"No?" said Bilblox doubtfully. "So why are you here?"

"Unofficially," said Kiril. "I'm here to ask you again – *where is the Pen?*"

"I ain't got a clue," said Bilblox.

"Don't be a fool!" said Kiril. "Have you seen what that Tree is doing? It's not too late for us to do something about it."

"*Us?*" said Bilblox with a snort.

"Do you have it?" persisted Kiril.

"I ain't got it," said Bilbox. "How many times do I have to tell you? You can question me and beat me all you like, but you won't squeeze blood from this turnip."

The two men sat in silence for a long minute or so.

"So," said Bilblox finally, "Why are you here – officially?"

"Nartam asked me to get you," said Kiril.

"That seems easy enough," said Bilblox. "So why do you look so bent out of shape?"

"He's holding Naomi as a hostage," replied Kiril flatly. "And I doubt he'll return her until he has his Pen."

"As a hostage?" said Bilblox. "What the heck happened between you and Nartam anyway? You two used to be as thick as thieves, other than the occasional fight in which he'd cut your face with a knife. Is that what this is all about?"

Kiril said nothing.

A sudden look of understanding dawned on Bilblox's face. "It's the Shadow Tree ain't it?" he asked. "Of course it is. That's why ya wanted the Pen in the first place. Ironic ain't it? You gave up two years of your life for that Tree and it's given you nothing but grief. It almost makes me feel sorry for you. Almost."

Kiril made no reply.

"So tell me *why* Nartam wants to see me?" asked Bilblox.

"He says he wants you by his side," replied Kiril.

"By his side?" said Bilblox quizzically. "Ha, that's a good one, but I don't buy it. Tell me something else, Kiril, buddy – why is it that Nartam has taken such a keen interest in me lately. Why was he callin' me his lucky rabbit's foot before – what was all that about? That guy looks crazier than usual."

"You really want to know?"

Bilblox nodded.

"He thinks you're going to save his life," replied Kiril.

Bilblox half-choked in a snort of laughter. "Why on earth would he think that?"

"Because I told him so," explained Kiril angrily. "I told him that I had a vision in which you save him. You see, I needed an excuse to keep you around, so you could..."

"Be your pawn," finished Bilblox.

"No," said Kiril, "I brought you here to help Naomi."

"I never took you for the sentimental sort," replied Bilblox.

"I'm not," said Kiril.

Kiril rose to his feet and walked over to where Bilblox was standing. He then reached into his pocket and took out a large brass ring that jangled with skeleton keys. Kiril searched until he found the key he wanted and then knelt down, and used the key to unlock the manacles on Bilblox's feet. Kiril then walked back across the cell and used another key to open the door. "You're free to go," said Kiril. "I have to leave the handcuffs on until we reach Nartam's quarters – as Nartam requested."

Kiril led the way out of the jail cell and walked down a long hallway and up a narrow set of stairs. The wooden floorboards creaked beneath their feet and, every minute or so, the entire ship shuddered as icy gusts of wind slammed against its sides. They continued onward until they came to the door leading into Nartam's chambers.

Bilblox raised up his wrists, indicating that he wanted Kiril to unlock his handcuffs.

"What's your plan?" whispered Kiril.

"It doesn't concern you," replied Bilblox.

Kiril leaned in close to Bilblox's ear.

"Listen to me," he said. "I'll be blunt, because I know that's the only way you'll understand me. I am the *only* person that stands between you and a life of blind obedience to your new master Nartam…"

"Spare me the whole song and dance," interjected Bilblox. "I don't want to hear it."

Kiril pushed Bilblox forward and while doing so, reached into his pocket for the key to unlock Bilblox's handcuffs. The sleeve of his kimono got in the way and he roughly flung it back. At that moment, he felt a sharp bite on his wrist as if he has just been stung by a hornet. He looked down at his hand and saw it was covered in blood. Kiril quickly pulled back the sleeve and saw that something sharp and metallic – a tiny blade – was sticking out of the sleeve of the shirt. Kiril often stitched small knives and vials of poison into his clothing – so that if he were ever in dire circumstance he could kill his enemies. Apparently, when he had rolled up the sleeve, the blade had cut his wrist. It was a peculiar, crescent-shaped wound.

Kiril froze.

"What happened?' hissed Bilblox.

Kiril stared at the wound on his wrist. This was, without a doubt, the wound in his vision. It was *his* arm. And, apparently, it was *his* hand that would push Naomi into the abyss.

Just then, the door to Nartam's chamber swung open and there, standing in the doorway, was Nartam.

CHAPTER FORTY-THREE
REUNION IN ICE

It took ten minutes until Alfonso's feet touched the bottom of the trench. The area was deathly quiet, and he paused before turning around to look. He was afraid of what he might find.

When he surveyed the scene, he saw them immediately – two figures, huddled together, cowering beneath a small ledge of ice. It was Hill and Resuza. They looked terrible, near death. Hill's face was a clammy white and his beard was thickly matted with ice and dirt. Scratches ran across Resuza's neck and hands and her fingers looked almost bluish. Their eyes were closed. Alfonso rushed over to them and shook them. He was terrified that they had frozen to death, but then they opened their eyes slowly and Alfonso's heart surged with joy. Hill began mumbling and Resuza threw her arms around him, refusing to let go. Alfonso could feel her terribly thin shoulders and arms and he had to conceal his horror. He knew he mustn't show how shocked he was.

"You saw the kite," whispered Hill. "Thank heavens. I had a…a feeling you would be nearby. They forced us down a rope ladder, and they meant for us to die here."

Resuza stared close into Alfonso's eyes.

"It's been so long," she whispered.

Alfonso nodded. "Since before Jasber, even before the razor hedges."

"So much has happened," replied Resuza. "I don't know where to begin."

"Not now," replied Alfonso. "We have to leave this place."

Resuza nodded, and put her hands on Alfonso's cheeks. She drew him close, and very deliberately, kissed him on the cheek.

The slightest trace of a smile appeared on her face. "You're a sight for cold eyes," she said in that playful, teasing way that Alfonso fondly remembered.

"So are you," replied Alfonso. He stared back at her and wanted this moment to continue on and on, but he couldn't ignore that Resuza's body was trembling nonstop. They had to leave. Hill was now shivering violently and Alfonso took off his fur parka – the one he had taken from the airship – and placed it on Hill's shoulders. Hill smiled gratefully. Now he had to get them out of here. Under other circumstances, he would have simply eased his way into hypnogogia, and particle-climbed out of the chasm – carrying Hill and Resuza with him. But he knew this wasn't an option. He knew intuitively, deep in his core, that hypnogogia was done and to try was to court death.

"I think I can get us out of here," said Alfonso. "It's a little unusual, so you mustn't be too shocked."

"Okay," said Resuza tentatively.

Hill nodded.

Alfonso sat on the ice-covered ground and closed his eyes. He concentrated, breathing in four seconds through his left nostril, then breathing out through his right nostril. This continued for another minute or so. Once again, he began searching his mind for memories. There seemed to be so few left. He saw the same image of himself in the snow, as a teenager, three or four times. There were almost no memories of him as an adult. Then, for a fraction of second, he caught a glimpse of himself chopping wood. He was a young man, in his early twenties perhaps.

Gasps from Hill and Resuza told him he hit the mark. He opened his eyes and looked down at his hands. They were strong, calloused hands.

"What in blazes is going on?" Hill approached him with a look of great concern.

"Don't worry," smiled Alfonso. "This is something that happened to me in Jasber. I've become an ageling."

"Your eyes," said Resuza. "They're paler than I remember. Almost white."

"That's one of the side effects," said Alfonso. "Now watch."

Grabbing the other coil of rope, he began climbing the wall that Hill and Resuza had been forced to descend. It took him only ten minutes to get to the top of the chasm. Once he had made it to the top, he tied the end of the rope into a loop, which could serve as a harness. He then tossed the rope down into the crevasse below. "I'm going to pull you up – one at a time!" he yelled down. "Just sit in the harness!"

It took Alfonso roughly thirty minutes to hoist Resuza up out of the trench. It was harder with Hill. Even in his emaciated state, Hill weighed a lot. Alfonso and Resuza worked furiously to pull Hill upward and, after nearly an hour of back-breaking work, they succeeded.

"What now?" asked Resuza.

"We need somewhere to rest for a bit," said Hill. "And ideally we need some food as well."

Alfonso nodded his head thoughtfully.

"What's your plan?" asked Resuza.

"I need to go to Dargora," said Alfonso. "To the Shadow Tree."

"What?" said Resuza. "Why?"

Alfonso hesitated. He was uncertain of how much to tell them. Best to keep it simple.

"I know how to destroy it," said Alfonso. Then he picked up his walking stick – the one with Imad's compass embedded in it – and held it up so they could see. "This thing here will help me do the job," said Alfonso. "I just need to get close enough to use it."

"Where did you get that stick?" asked Hill curiously.

"Actually my dad gave it to me," said Alfonso.

"Leif!" exclaimed Hill. "He's alive! Where is he?"

"He's coming... I mean I think he is," stammered Alfonso. *How much should he say? What could he say?* Hill looked electrified with excitement. "We came here together to destroy the tree, but we had a bad time crossing the Petrified Forest. We were attacked by a pack of wolves and we got separated."

"Did you look for him?" asked Hill.

"Kind of," replied Alfonso uneasily. "But, the thing is, I think my best chance of meeting up with him is at the tree itself – that's where he was headed – and knowing dad, he'll find it."

"Hmm," said Hill. He didn't seem entirely satisfied.

"It's a very long story – and we don't have much time," said Alfonso. "Please, if you can, just show me how to get there – to the tree."

"It's not so easy," said Hill wearily. "It is a good distance from here and, besides, there will be Dragoonya soldiers everywhere."

Alfonso sighed.

"I have an idea," said Resuza. "In fact, I have the perfect solution."

"Huh?" said Hill. Then slowly a look of realization spread across his face. "Are you sure about that?" asked Hill.

"Positive," said Resuza.

CHAPTER FORTY-FOUR
LOVE AND LIES

Resuza led the way and, after several hours of walking, they came upon a giant rock that resembled an oversized egg. Resuza then began to search around frantically, until she found a small hole in the snow. She kicked at the hole and it opened up, forming the entrance to a tunnel or passageway of sorts. This was her escape tunnel – the one that she had made with the Pen. She quickly led them down into the long, dark passageway that wound its way all the way back to their storage depot and the slave quarters beyond. Compared to the frigid cold, the tunnel that Resuza had carved out during her experiments with the Foreseeing Pen was warm and cozy. As they walked, Hill peppered his nephew with questions. *How had he become an ageling? What had happened to Marta? Where was Leif? Where had Leif found the walking stick with the compass – the one that he believed would destroy the Shadow Tree?* Alfonso answered some of these questions – and he assured his uncle, repeatedly, that Leif was okay – but he refused to discuss anything about the Shadow Tree.

"Uncle Hill, I know this is very hard to accept," said Alfonso, "But there are some things that I just can't explain right now. I love you, and I am so happy to see you, but you just have to believe me when I say, *I know what I'm doing — and I have to do it on my own terms.* Okay?"

Hill frowned, but said nothing.

"There's something you're not telling me about your father," said Hill. He seemed angrier than Alfonso had ever seen him. "And it's wrong. Leif is my brother. I deserve to know the truth!"

Alfonso nodded. He knew that his uncle was right.

"Are you going to level with me or not?" demanded Hill.

"There was a prophecy," said Alfonso finally. "It's a long story, but dad found it in Imad's library – and this prophecy, it said that I had to destroy the Shadow Tree. Dad didn't want me doing that because he was worried about what would happen to me. We had a fight and I... I ran away..." Alfonso sighed. He felt better. It wasn't the whole truth, but it was most of it.

"I see," said Hill. "And you believe this prophecy?"

"Yes," said Alfonso. "Everything it said, including how I would meet you guys – it all came true."

No one spoke for a while. Resuza led them all the way to the storage depot and, as she did, she tried to break the tension by chatting – recalling how she used the Pen to create the tunnel. When they reached the depot, they were all overjoyed to see all the supplies were still there. They feasted on biscuits and cider in silence. Afterwards, Hill said that he was in dire need of some rest and that he wanted to take a cat nap. "Wake me up if I start doing anything funny in my sleep," he told them. They promised him that they would. "And don't you dare try to sneak off," added Hill. Alfonso nodded. Hill fell asleep almost immediately and, meanwhile, Alfonso and Resuza tried to make themselves comfortable.

Alfonso wished there was more light so that he could see Resuza's face properly. He could feel the charged atmosphere and he wanted nothing more than to see her smile.

He had known her for a long time, but since they last met their interactions now were somehow different. Perhaps it was because of the memories that he had seen – the one from the future, where Resuza was playing with the children on the dock at the edge of the lake. *Their children. Their children who would never be.* Alfonso couldn't help but shiver.

"What's wrong?" asked Resuza. "You look like you just saw a ghost."

"Nothing," said Alfonso.

"Why have you become so secretive?"

Alfonso shrugged.

"What aren't you telling us?"

Suddenly he had an overwhelming desire to tell her absolutely everything – about his father believing that he had died, the prophecy, the tree, and his visions of the future. He needed to get this off his chest. He needed to tell *her*.

"Resuza…" he said seriously.

"Yes?"

"Do you remember that room in the lighthouse?" he asked. "That was an awfully nice place. In fact, I think that's just about the last good memory that I have."

"You were going to tell me something else," she said.

He nodded.

"Something bad?" she asked.

He nodded.

"Something bad that's going to happen?"

He paused and nodded again.

"To you?"

He shivered.

"Can we talk about something else?" he asked, almost pleadingly. "Please."

To his great relief, she asked no more questions. Instead, she leaned over and gave Alfonso a kiss on the lips. It was long and lingering, and Alfonso felt as if he was floating. Eventually she stopped and leaned back to look at him through the murky light.

"Don't get any ideas," she said with a smile. "That was just to say thank you for saving us."

Alfonso could imagine a more collected version of himself saying something meaningful yet lighthearted, but that would take more energy and experience than he had. Instead, he just smiled at her. It felt like the happiest moment in his life. Alfonso knew that he ought to get going – he had a job to do, one last job – but he couldn't make himself go. Not just yet.

After the kiss, they both relaxed, as if something had been resolved between them. They each talked about what had happened to them since that fateful parting just outside the razor hedges, though neither one was completely truthful. Resuza skated quickly over her last encounter with Naomi. It was just too painful to imagine that she had found her sister only to discover that Naomi had betrayed them. And Alfonso discussed Leif, but never mentioned the terrible moment just outside the Petrified Forest, when Leif thought he had come upon the frozen body of his son.

Eventually, Hill woke up and – famished as they were – they all ate again. Alfonso also shared what remained in his backpack: several handfuls of dried fruit, which Hill and Resuza devoured. In between bites, Alfonso thought over Resuza's story, especially about the events leading to the disappearance of the Foreseeing Pen.

"So in the cave, the Pen just disappeared when Bilblox was holding it?" asked Alfonso.

"Yes," said Resuza. "Just like that."

"And where is Bilblox now?"

"We can't be sure," said Hill. "But if I had to bet, I'd say he is on Nartam's ship. That's where they had kept him before." Hill paused and asked if he could change the subject. He wanted to hear about his brother.

"He's alive," said Alfonso.

It was hard to see Hill's reaction. Eventually, he whispered in a choked voice, "After all these years. Leif. Is he well?"

Alfonso nodded. He couldn't bring himself to speak. It broke his heart to be less than truthful with his uncle about such an important matter.

Hill's voice, suddenly stronger after hearing about Leif, returned. "So what now?" he asked.

"I need the Pen," said Alfonso. "And I'm assuming if I find it, I'll find Bilblox. Which ship is Nartam's?"

"We can lead you to it," replied Resuza. "It's the biggest one up there."

Knowing the response, Alfonso still hesitated before he said, "I'm going alone."

"No way!" replied Resuza. Her voice was much too loud and they all sat there for a few seconds silently fearing that perhaps, somehow, they had been overheard. "You can't," she continued in a whisper. "What could possibly possess you to say that?"

"I want nothing more than for you and Hill to come with me," said Alfonso. "But it's too risky. The prophecy says nothing about me destroying the Shadow Tree with help. I have to do it myself, alone. Trust me, I'd rather not. I'd really, really rather not. But if we've come this far, I don't want to do anything to mess things up."

"You're too wrapped up in this prophecy," said Hill. "You need to trust yourself and your instincts. What do they tell you?"

"Not very much," admitted Alfonso. "That's why I'm relying on the prophecy." He paused. "I guess the only thing I know for sure is that I have to find Bilblox. He will know where the Pen is. That much I feel pretty certain about."

"You've been right before about Bilblox," said Hill. "Maybe you're right again."

"I have to go," said Alfonso.

"He should use the emergency exit," said Hill. "Show him the way."

Resuza stood up and gestured up the tunnel that led directly to the surface above. No one spoke. Alfonso grabbed for their hands, squeezed them once, and his eyes filled with tears. He wanted to say goodbye, but he was afraid his voice would betray him. Instead, he let go of their hands and rushed away.

Chapter Forty-Five
A Most Welcome Ally

Kiril's most trusted aide stood atop a large snow bank, binoculars pressed to his face, scouring the horizon for any signs of life. He was standing a mile due south of the ice moat that ringed Dargora and separated it from the surrounding area. Slowly and methodically, he scanned the edge of the Petrified Forest. Once he saw something move, but it was only a fog wolf dragging some kind of carcass back into the forest. Konrad thought it highly unlikely that anyone would be able to cross the Petrified Forest, alone and on foot, but he kept looking nonetheless. Kiril had told him to be on the lookout for a grown man in his late thirties or a teenage boy. "Leif or Alfonso will come to destroy the tree," Kiril had told him. "Probably both. Be ready for them."

Konrad had taken his best men, a battalion of two hundred soldiers known as the "Forlorn Hope." Konrad had trained the battalion himself. He borrowed their name from Dutch fighters known as the "Verloren Hoop," who were famous for making the most daring assaults and charging into battle fearlessly even when casualties were bound to be high. Konrad was among the Dragoonya elite who had lived for many centuries by using the ash to extend his life. On and off during this time, he worked as a mercenary and he had fought with everyone from Attila the Hun to Peter the Great. Konrad knew how to train soldiers and the "Forlorn

Hope" were the best fighters he had ever seen. As a rite of passage, these men burned their own flesh with fire in order to deaden the nerves and make themselves more impervious to pain. Konrad was very fond of them.

During the Battle of Somnos, it was the Forlorn Hope who led the charge through the breach in the city's walls and, when the rest of the Dragoonya army broke into a full retreat, it was these same men who held their ground, cutting down waves of Dormians in the counter-attack. They only retreated when Konrad ordered them to and they did so reluctantly. "If we'd had another battalion of those men," Nartam told him afterwards, "We would have prevailed."

For the moment, the Forlorn Hope were the only soldiers in the Dragoonya army not allowed to use any of the black ash. "The ash is perfect for the rabble – it makes them ferocious yet compliant – but I need you and your men to have your wits about you," Kiril had told Konrad. "If you catch them with the ash, put them to the sword. They will get their share, once we've assessed the proper amount to give. We won't have them being guinea pigs."

Konrad had assured him this wouldn't be a problem. And it wasn't. His men proved perfectly disciplined and obedient. They were also sharp-eyed and several hours into their watch, they spotted two solitary figures in the distance, heading toward Dargora on foot.

"Are you sure it's only two people?" asked Konrad.

"Yes," replied his lookout. "And one of them is waving his arms – as if he wants to be seen."

Leif Perplexon waded through knee-high snow, waved his arms frantically and shouted as loudly as he could. "I'm right here!" he screamed at the top of his lungs. "Come on! I thought you were fierce soldiers!"

"What are you doing?" asked Marta. "Are you crazy?"

"No," said Leif, "Just desperate."

"They're going to capture us," said Marta.

"That's the idea," said Leif.

It had taken Leif some time to come to the realization that Alfonso *might* be alive. Initially, when he and Marta emerged from the makeshift snow cave, he was ready to turn to caring for Alfonso's body, and preparing both of them for the long voyage home. But when he couldn't find his body after hours of searching, a kindle of hope lit up inside him. "He must be alive," Leif told Marta. "He must have turned into a younger person and just walked away."

"Then where are his tracks?" asked Marta skeptically.

It was true – there were no tracks of any kind in the snow.

"I don't know," said Leif, "But we have to look for him. We have to press on for Dargora."

"If you are set on going, I'll come with you," said Marta. "I owe you that much."

"Marta," said Leif sternly, "If you try to stop me…"

"Don't worry I won't," said Marta. "Besides, I doubt anyone could stop you."

And so they pressed on – together. The problem was, without Imad's compass, and without any trail to follow, they had no idea where they were going. And so they wandered aimlessly for hours on end. Leif grew frustrated and then desperate. By the time he saw the soldiers in the distance, he was willing to take a risk, and a big one at that.

It took several minutes for the group of Dragoonya soldiers to make their way over the snow and ice covered ground – even with the help of dogs and sleds. When they finally arrived, they formed a tight circle around Leif. The soldiers carried a mix of rifles and crossbows. They wore armor made of black leather and silver feathers. Many of their faces were blackened and blistered with gruesome burns. None of them spoke. Finally one of them stepped forward. He was short, but muscular. He wore no hat, despite the cold, and his raven-black hair was plastered to his skull and encrusted with ice.

"My name is Konrad," said the man. "And I presume you are Leif."

Leif nodded.

"We have been expecting you," said Konrad. "But I never imagined that you would give yourself up."

"Me neither," said Leif.

"I will say this just once," said Konrad. "Don't try anything unwise. My men here are not the gentle sort, if you take my meaning."

Leif and Marta both looked about nervously. They were surrounded by at least fifty men who looked as if they would be only too happy to kill them. "All I want to do is give you a message," said Leif. Konrad raised his eyebrow, unconvinced. "I swear it," said Leif.

"Then speak," said Konrad.

"My son Alfonso is, at this very minute, heading for your Shadow Tree with the aim of destroying it," said Leif. "He managed to trick me into thinking that he was dead. He knew it would be a suicide mission and he's got it in his head that he is going to do this alone."

"He won't succeed," said Konrad. "We have several hundred men guarding the base of the tree. No one can harm the Shadow Tree because it does not wish to be destroyed."

Konrad's quiet confidence rattled Leif, and he wondered for a second whether he was doing the right thing.

The Shadow Tree sounded even worse than he imagined. Still, he continued.

"Those men won't do you any good," replied Leif. "The tree can only be cut down at a place where it has a gash in its bark, just above a small knot, which is situated halfway up the tree's trunk. Alfonso will float right over your soldiers' heads and destroy the tree before they even know what's happened."

"Float?" asked Konrad skeptically.

Leif nodded his head, then closed his eyes, and for a full ten seconds he levitated off the ground. "Yes," said Leif as he returned to the ground, "Just like that."

It was Konrad's turn to be flustered. He turned to one of his officers and conferred with him quietly. Eventually, Konrad returned his attention to Leif.

"How do you know all of this?" asked Konrad.

"Trust me," replied Leif, "I am a Great Sleeper, I know."

"But it doesn't make sense," said Konrad. "Why would you betray your own son?"

Leif paused and took a deep breath. He knew that everything depended on how he answered this question. "I spent almost a year carrying a Dormian Bloom halfway across the globe and delivering it to Jasber," he explained. "As reward for a job well done, I spent several more years in solitary confinement as their prisoner. Now my son, my one and only child, has to set off on a suicide mission at the bidding of the Founding Trees. There is only so much loss that any man can take. I have given enough. I will not give up my son. Can you understand that?"

There was a long silence.

"I can," said Konrad finally. He turned and gave several hand signals to his men. Seconds later, the soldiers were quickly mounting their sleds. "So you'll help me stop Alfonso, if I spare his life?" asked Konrad. "Is that it?"

"Yes," said Leif, "But I insist on being the one who stops Alfonso."

Konrad's head tilted slightly. It was hard to tell whether he was agreeing to Leif's demand or simply listening.

"What about the girl?" asked Konrad, pointing to Marta. Marta had morphed back to the form of her true age, nine years old.

"She comes with me," said Leif. "No other explanation is necessary."

Konrad stared at Leif. After a few seconds, he nodded.

"Get on the sled," he ordered.

"Where are we going?" asked Leif.

"To the Shadow Tree," replied Konrad. "Where else?"

CHAPTER FORTY-SIX
A PERPLEXON

Alfonso walked for roughly half an hour before he rounded the top of a tall snow bank. From this perch, he caught his first glimpse of the Shadow Tree in the distance. Something he could only describe as lightning flashed inside of him. He closed his eyes and in his mind he saw the oily, bumpy branches of the Tree turning towards him.

It knew he was coming.

Alfonso took a deep breath. He looked up to the night sky, and saw the twinkling lights of the ships hanging in the air like kites. He continued his careful trek towards the Tree. It was puzzling that he saw no one around. Where were all the guards he assumed would be swarming Dargora? Soon enough, he had his answer – or at least a partial answer. As he crested another small bluff of snow, the Shadow Tree came into full view. Around the base of the Tree was a huge mob of soldiers – at least a thousand of them – and they moved in an undulating, serpent-like motion. It resembled a dance, although no dance had ever filled Alfonso with such dread.

High above them, in the upper canopy of the tree, soldiers with torches were lighting branches on fire. The trunk of the tree never caught fire; it seemed impervious to flames. The branches, however, were another story; they squirmed and wiggled, as if they didn't want to be set ablaze, but once they caught fire they burned like firecracker fuses – sizzling, smoking, and disintegrating quickly. Then a cascade of black ash would fall down to the ground below and the men would momentarily stop their dance and fight ferociously, trampling one another in order to get their ash. All in all, it was a horrifying sight.

What now?

Alfonso studied the trunk of the tree closely. He could see the knot with the gash above it – just like on his stick that he had assembled, using the wooden sides of the blank picture frame. This had to be the tree's weak point. Although he had a sudden urge to fling himself at the Shadow Tree – to be done with this tension once and for all – he forced himself to sink to the ground. He watched the terrifying parade of soldiers, and the ash falling to the ground. He looked up and saw that a light mist of clouds had parted, revealing a moon that flung shadows across the flying ships. Just above the Shadow Tree was the largest of the ships, a man-of-war from the 1700s lit up from end to end with red pinpricks of light. It was Nartam's ship – he was sure of it.

Meanwhile, back in the tunnel, Hill and Resuza waited irritably in the gloom of the storage depot cave. Hill consoled himself with the realization that now at least he was warm – thanks to the fur overcoat that Alfonso had lent him. Hill burrowed his hands into the coat's pockets and, as he did this, he felt a crumpled piece of paper with the tips of his fingers. Hill pulled out the wad of paper, unfolded it, and read it. It was a curious document with two headings labeled "Scenario I" and "Scenario II." The first scenario was hard to follow; it described someone named "C.N.T." crossing the Petrified Forest, infiltrating Dargora, and destroying the Shadow Tree. This had to be the prophecy that Alfonso had spoken of! Although he read the first one with great interest, it was the second scenario that grabbed Hill's attention:

Scenario II. A Perplexon will rejoice with friends in the dark of the chasm. He will then destroy the Tree by himself. A Perplexon will succeed, but he will also die. (‡‰ᴬ⁄ₛ┴№⅞)

Hill felt his chest tighten as he realized what his nephew intended to do. *The boy has set off on a suicide mission*, Hill thought to himself with great alarm. *He believes this is the only way to destroy the tree.* Then another thought dawned on Hill: *Perhaps this is the only way to destroy the Tree.* After all, this shred of a prophecy had already correctly predicted that Alfonso would reunite with "old friends" in the "dark of the chasm." It had predicted their reunion at the bottom of the trench. Hill forced himself to read the note over and over. Then something else occurred to him – another thought all together – and he gasped.

"What is it?" asked Resuza. "What's wrong?"

"Alfonso," said Hill, his face stricken with panic.

"What about him?"

"He's made a terrible mistake," said Hill. "He has misunderstood the prophecy..."

"Hill?" Resuza was suddenly concerned. He wasn't making any sense.

"Let's go," announced Hill. "We don't have much time."

CHAPTER FORTY-SEVEN
A HELPING HAND

"Come in my friends," said Nartam as he opened the door. "This is a most welcome visit."

Bilblox studied Nartam carefully. He looked so young – no more than sixteen years old – there were pimples on his face, the faintest trace of a moustache, and he stood barely five and half feet tall. He was a fraction of Bilblox's size. It seemed absurd to be afraid of this boy and, for a second, Bilblox wondered what would happen if he smashed Nartam with one of his massive fists. But something told him that defeating Nartam couldn't possibly be as simple as this.

"Shall we have a spot of tea?" Nartam asked as he gestured toward a small table at the far end of the room, on top of which rested two burning candles, several porcelain cups, and a tall copper samovar, steaming with the scent of mint and cardamom. There was also a gold urn, filled with a heaping pile of iridescent black ash, which gleamed and twinkled in the flickering light.

"Why not?" said Bilblox with a shrug. "Some tea might do me good."

Kiril nodded, but said nothing. He looked quite pale, visibly shaken, but there was no time for Bilblox to ask him what was wrong.

"Have you seen a ghost?" asked Nartam playfully. "You're not yourself, Kiril. You need a rest?"

Kiril nodded and then shrugged, as if it was nothing to be concerned about.

"You fellows have been on quite the adventure together – haven't you?" asked Nartam cheerily as he poured himself a cup of tea. "And it is so heartening to see that you have become fast friends. Long journeys will change a man's perspective on many things, wouldn't you agree, Kiril?"

"When you two were gallivanting about," continued Nartam, "I was making a trip of my own – a little walk in the woods, you might say."

Nartam smiled again and led the way across the room. It was very dark in the room. Three small lamps cast a murky glow across his spacious but empty quarters. Bilblox noticed that there was hardly any furniture at all in the room other than a large wooden chest in the far corner of the room. The walls were barren except for several long brass handrails that were bolted to wooden window frames – these rails were, no doubt, vestiges of the days when this ship sailed the seas and sailors needed something to grasp in stormy weather. Nartam continued over to the table where the tea was brewing and gestured for them each to take a cup.

Bilblox reached for a cup, but suddenly Nartam grabbed the longshoreman's wrist and said, "No, no, no this won't do."

Bilblox stood still, uncertain of how to react.

"Kiril, be a good chap and give me the keys to these handcuffs," said Nartam. "Bilblox here is my guest, my lucky totem, and I simply won't have him sipping tea in my quarters with both of his hands cuffed like a common criminal."

Again Kiril nodded. He reached into his pocket, pulled out a set of keys, found the proper key, and handed it to Nartam.

"Much obliged," said Nartam. He then knelt down on one knee and used the key to unlock the handcuff on Bilblox's left wrist. Bilblox let out a small, barely audibly sigh of relief. Nartam took a little longer with the second handcuff. He seemed to be fumbling with the key and yanking the handcuffs back and forth; then suddenly, after it was too late to act, Bilblox saw what Nartam had done. He had *not* unfastened the second handcuff, but left it as it was – firmly locked around Bilblox's right wrist – and, instead, he had fastened the opened handcuff to the brass handrail that was bolted into the wall. Bilblox was now, in effect, chained to the wall.

"What gives?" demanded Bilblox.

"Sorry old chap," said Nartam as he rose to his feet and took a step back, "But I can't have you running off on me, now can I?"

"I ain't gonna be able to save your life if ya got me chained up like a dog," said Bilblox, trying to keep his tone as light as possible. "Right?"

Instead of immediately responding, Nartam turned to look at Kiril. His trusted deputy stood paralyzed, unsure of what to do. Nartam turned back to Bilblox and smiled.

"Oh come now," he said. "We both know perfectly well that you are not going to save my life. Who do you take me for? It was just a bunch of rubbish Kiril made up so that I would keep you around. The prophecy was quite clear, you are going to save the girl's life – or at least try to. Isn't that so?"

As he said this, Nartam pointed out a glass door, just ten feet away, that led out on to a small, open-air balcony. At first neither Bilblox nor Kiril saw what he was pointing toward – all they could see was blackness – but then, all at once, they saw the outline of a figure standing, in the darkness, on the other side of the glass door. The figure was standing on the balcony, huddled in a fur coat. Nartam picked up a lantern, which hung from a hook on the wall, and carried it over the glass door so they could all get a better view. Moments later, Naomi's face became visible.

"I believe this is the spot where someone is destined to give her a shove – isn't that so Kiril?" asked Nartam.

Kiril stared out at the balcony and had a strong feeling of déjà vu. There was Naomi, dressed in furs, standing on a snowy platform, on the edge of a ship. It was exactly like his vision. This had to be the spot where.... Where *he* – Kiril – pushed her into the abyss. *But how? And why? And could this fate be altered?*

Kiril took a step toward the door, instinctively wanting to do something, but then Nartam raised a finger and said, "I am sure that you are eager to speak with her, though is it really wise to go near her – given what the prophecy says?"

Kiril froze. "The prophecy?" It was the first time that he had spoken and, as he did so, he seemed hesitant and a bit confused. "What I had was a vision and…"

"That's not what I am talking about, my son," interrupted Nartam. "I am talking about a prophecy – a prophecy from Imad's library, which told me the story of Bilblox's life – all that *has* happened and all that *may* happen to our beloved longshoreman."

"Yeah right," said Bilblox with a snort. "The story of my whole life. That's a good one. And what about your life? I'm guessin' you read your own future as well? You know everything that's gonna happen – is that it?"

"No, not my life," replied Nartam calmly. "Imad, clever chap that he was, knew the trouble that might happen if I got hold of my own prophecy and so he had the foresight to remove it from his little library. But I assure you, I know most everything about your life, Master Bilblox. Of course, some things are left to chance, and can play out in a number of different ways, but other things are fairly certain. Would you like to hear about the manner in which you will die? It's at sea, in a shipwreck, fitting for a longshoreman, no?"

"That's rich," said Bilblox, but there was a hint of uneasiness in his voice. He sensed that something terrible was about to happen and that he needed to get himself free as quickly as he could. He jerked his right arm and shoulder violently, in the hopes of pulling the brass rail out of the wall, but the rail barely budged and he only succeeded in tearing the skin on his wrist.

"Let the girl inside," said Kiril as calmly as he could. "Whatever it is that you want I can help you get – I can give to you – but there is no reason to make the girl suffer."

"You speak as if you are in control," replied Nartam as he walked across the room toward the wooden chest. "Or perhaps you think I am in control. Neither is accurate. All of this has been ordained many thousands of years ago. It is what Imad wrote in his prophecies."

"Imad's prophecies – but how?" asked Kiril. "You found them?"

"Yes, yes – quite right," said Nartam calmly, with the cool air of a school teacher. As he spoke, he opened the wooden chest, and took out a gleaming metal battleaxe. Bilblox thought he was seeing things, but it looked as if the hand holding the battleaxe grew thicker, as if responding to the weight of the weapon and of the prospects for an imminent fight.

Nartam smiled again, in that strange, ash-induced way which made his face look plastic.

"While you chaps were gallivanting around, having your fun in the wilderness, I made a trip of my own to Straszydlo

Forest. You see, it has long been known that Imad hid his prophecies near to where he hid his sphere. Of course, no one knew where his sphere was hidden, until Alfonso found it in Straszydlo Forest. I suppose I owe a debt of gratitude to Alfonso. In any case, I simply retraced Alfonso's footsteps, did some poking around in the woods, and eventually found my way into Imad's library. That's where I read about Bilblox and how he would hide the Foreseeing Pen in his anatomical snuff box."

"Anatomical snuff box?" said Kiril.

The wind gusted outside. Naomi made her presence known by pounding on the door. It appeared to be locked from the inside with a bolt.

"Kiril, my son, go ahead and open the door," said Nartam politely. He was now walking back across the room with the battleaxe in hand. "It's time."

Kiril didn't move.

"Or perhaps you want to ask your friend Bilblox for a hand," said Nartam, as he continued toward them, casually raising the battleaxe up over his shoulder, as if preparing to strike someone or something with it. "As it so happens, I too was going to ask Bilblox for a hand."

Suddenly it all clicked in Kiril's mind – he understood what Naomi had tried to tell him with her drawing in the snow and he grasped, with sudden horror, at what Nartam was about to do.

CHAPTER FORTY-EIGHT
ANSWERING THE CALL

A lfonso couldn't believe it, but he appeared to be staring at an elevator. It was descending downward through the fog via a series of ropes and pulleys. Alfonso had watched the egg-shaped object rise and descend twice from the ship that he suspected contained Nartam's quarters. Each time the elevator reached the ground, it let out more Dragoonya soldiers. They seemed to be leaving Nartam's ship; very few went up.

As it neared the ground, Alfonso began his approach. The wind and snow had caused him great suffering, but at the moment it was welcome. He walked in a wide circle towards the elevator so that the soldiers disembarking would have their backs to him. The oval landed and the doors opened, disgorging a dozen Dragoonya soldiers. As he expected, no one was waiting to board. Alfonso rapidly began to close the distance to the oval. When he was several feet away, the elevator's circular door began to close, and Alfonso had to dive through the doorway in order to make it. As he struggled to his feet, the elevator began its ascent. Alfonso's sigh of relief was cut short when he realized he wasn't alone.

At the other end of the oval elevator was a barrel-chested man with enormously thick arms. He had a bald head, a toothless mouth, and a shockingly red face, as if he had spent time too close to a fire. The skin around his eyes was stained black with traces of ash. The man was sitting on the floor, slumped against the wall. His teeth were chattering and he was foaming at the mouth, but he did not appear to notice Alfonso. The doors shut and the elevator began moving upward. Alfonso tried to stand perfectly still. There was a small window nearby and he glanced out of it. He saw the Shadow Tree; but what caught his attention was the mob at the base of it. The number of soldiers around the tree had doubled. There were now at least two thousand soldiers, all doing their dance – running, jumping, pushing, clawing, and convulsing forward in a counter-clockwise motion. Just half-an hour ago, there had only been half that number. It was startling. And there were more coming. In every direction, as far as he could see, little specs of figures were converging on the tree. It was as if the tree was calling for help and its devotees were answering the call.

Alfonso stared at the tree below, transfixed, until he felt the elevator begin to slow. He glanced around the cabin quickly, looking for a place to hide. There was none. The only thing that he found was a pile of thick overcoats, laying on one of the elevator's benches. The man with the barrel chest remained comatose. Alfonso rushed over to the pile and looked for a coat that would fit. At last he found something that was close enough. The overcoat was lined with fur and had an enormous hood that could cover his entire head. The coat smelled putrid – a mix of sweat and vomit. Still, it didn't matter. Alfonso knew it was a temporary disguise, and with any luck, it would do the trick.

Moments later, the door opened. Alfonso did not wait to see who would enter. Instead, he lunged through the door with an air of being in a terrible hurry. He wore the overcoat and the hood covered his head and face. He stepped outside onto a platform built on the deck of a Dragoonya ship and came face to face with a pack of Dragoonya soldiers waiting to board. The soldiers didn't pay him any attention. They simply pushed him out of the way, rushed for the elevator's door, and crammed into the cabin. When it became clear that there wasn't room for all of them in the elevator, they began to fight. *They've all gone mad*, thought Alfonso. *And they're headed for the tree.*

The deck of the ship was strangely empty and the door leading down into the living quarters was ajar. Far below he could hear the muffled sound of shouting. Something was wrong. Alfonso was unarmed, but a thought occurred to him, and he quickly assembled the wooden stick with the compass embedded in its base. The wood appeared solid and strong – it would do for the moment. He grasped his weapon and walked cautiously down a curved staircase.

On the icy ground far below, a convoy of dogsleds raced toward the Shadow Tree. The sleds were less than half a mile from their destination and, as they approached, soldiers cleared the way. At the head of this convoy was Konrad, snapping his whip, goading his dogs, and screaming for soldiers on foot to clear a path or be shot. The soldiers on foot were all gravitating toward the Shadow Tree. They were drunk on the black ash to the point of being almost mindless, but even in this state, they were able to register that these men on sleds were the Forlorn Hope and they were not to be crossed.

Leif and Marta sat on the back of Konrad's sled, horrified at the scene. The soldiers on foot – the ones now scampering out of their way – did not resemble soldiers at all. Their arms and legs moved spastically, like men having fits of epilepsy. Many of them wore no hats or helmets and their heads and faces were bulbs of gleaming flesh – they had no hair, no eyebrows, no eyelashes and no beards. Many appeared to have no teeth or fingernails either. Quite a few of them were walking with their eyes closed, clutching the shoulders of those around them. They moved together – not like individual people – but like a single organism that reacts, moves, and thinks as one. Even the strange noises that they made, a mix of grunting and growling, seemed to be synchronized. In the middle-distance the Shadow Tree loomed, its uppermost branches wriggling and crackling as they broke their sheaths of ice.

Leif was terrified, not only at what he saw, but at the prospect that this madness would spread. Is this the fate that awaited the rest of the world? Yes, at last he saw, this would be the price of him saving his son's life. It was an awful realization to behold.

Eventually, the convoy reached a point where it could get no closer to the Tree. As fearsome as it was, the Forlorn Hope regiment only had a few hundred men, and they were greatly outnumbered by the thousands of soldiers who were converging on the Shadow Tree. Konrad saw this and he whistled for his men to stop. He took out a pair of binoculars and, with great care, studied the tree and then scanned the sky.

"I don't see him," said Konrad.

"He'll be here soon," said Leif. "I'm sure of it."

Near the base of the Shadow Tree itself, the soldiers were so numerous, and their chests were pressed together so tightly that many of them found it difficult to move or even breathe. At the very base of the tree, however, there was a clearing where only the biggest, fiercest, and most berserk soldiers dared go. These soldiers pushed, kicked, punched, elbowed, embraced, bit, and choked one another in a frenzied melee that resembled a cross between an insane celebration and a fight to the death.

Hill and Resuza stood at the very edge of this madness. They wore heavy fur coats, which they had found in the snow, cast off by soldiers who – in their ash-induced euphoria – were too far gone to realize that they were quickly succumbing to frostbite. It had taken every bit of strength for Hill and Resuza to fight their way to the base of the tree and, now they paused to assess their next steps. Resuza wasn't sure of Hill's ultimate intention, but it seemed clear that he was determined to climb the Shadow Tree. And she was determined to go with him. She had quite enough of being sidelined.

The distance between them and the trunk of the tree was only twenty feet. The men brawling in this space were monsters – they could easily rip both of them from limb to limb – but they were so enraptured that they could hardly be called observant. Resuza sensed an opportunity, but they would have to be very fast.

She grabbed Hill by the hand and motioned for him to crouch down with her.

"Keep your eyes down," she yelled into Hill's ear. He nodded. Although there was no black ash in the air at that moment, it was only a matter of time. Resuza watched and waited. Inside the clearing, just a few feet away, a giant of a man was jumping up and down on the chest of another man who, himself, was consumed in wild fits of laughter. After taking a kick to the head, the laughing man reached up with both hands, and pulled the giant down on top of him. The two of them, sandwiched together, began to roll around on the ground. Instinctively, those around them stepped back. An opening formed.

Resuza darted forward, half-pulling a slower Hill. Both of them leapt over the two giants rolling on the ground, crouched again to avoid a slow-moving but powerful fist, and fell heavily onto a fat, oily root that extended from the base of the tree. The berserk Dragoonya saw nothing. Resuza frantically motioned Hill up the wet, rutted bark. She helped push him up the first several feet. A hand grabbed a thick strand of her blonde hair. In one smooth motion, Resuza grabbed a dagger holstered across her arm, and cut off the hair that had been grabbed. She fell back against the Shadow Tree, turned to grab hold of the sinewy bark, and began climbing upwards as quickly as she could.

CHAPTER FORTY-NINE
PATRICIDE

Kiril curled his hands into fists so tightly that they turned a blotchy white. He watched in a daze as Nartam approached Bilblox. The longshoreman remained helpless with his left hand chained to the wall and Kiril finally understood what was about to happen. He realized now why Naomi had placed the Pencil-tip in the snow, within the crude drawing of Bilblox's hand. Somehow, and Kiril could not begin to fathom *how*, but Bilblox was hiding the Pen *within his own hand!*

"Stop!" yelled Bilblox. "Don't do it!"

Nartam did not hesitate at all. Instead he picked up his pace, and swung the battleaxe in a wide arc so that it whizzed through the air toward Bilblox's left wrist. At the last possible second, Bilblox jerked his hand upward. The blade of the axe clanged loudly against the metal of Bilblox's handcuff and bounced away. Bilblox yelled in pain. His wrist was severely bruised, but still intact. Nartam tried to hold onto the battleaxe, but its momentum caused it to ricochet wildly through the room.

Kiril eyed the battleaxe and then looked over at Naomi. She was making her way along a narrow ledge alongside the exterior of the ship, clearly heading for the window that had been smashed in. She was climbing over a series of jagged slabs of glass, which stood vertical, like shark fins. If she slipped, she could easily cut herself deeply and sever a major vein or artery. Kiril could help Naomi or Bilblox – but not both – and, given the prophecy, it was not even clear that he should rush to help Naomi. However, there was no time to think all these matters through. He could only rely on his centuries-old instincts. Kiril made a split-second decision and rushed toward Naomi. Using the tip of his boot, he kicked away the glass, and then opened up his arms. Naomi needed no more encouragement and she leapt through the open window into Kiril's arms. She was safe. It wasn't supposed to happen like this – and yet it had.

Meanwhile, in the time that all of this had transpired, Nartam had retrieved the battleaxe and was once again threatening to attack Bilblox. He was presently lifting the battleaxe over his head, preparing to strike. Bilblox dropped to his haunches, and as Nartam began to swing, Bilblox exploded upwards and succeeded – at least partially – in ripping the brass rail from the wall. His effort was too late, however, and as the blade of the battleaxe came downward it missed Bilblox's wrist but still managed to cut deeply into his forearm. Bilblox's only response was a deep moan.

"Wait!" yelled Kiril.

"Stay out of this!" yelled Nartam.

Nartam raised his battleaxe again, bringing it all the way back over and behind his head, but before he could bring it down, Bilblox kicked desperately and swept Nartam's legs out from under him. Nartam toppled backwards and, once again the battleaxe clattered to the ground close to Bilblox. Bilblox grabbed the axe and, with a quick chop, broke the chain on his handcuffs. In the blink of an eye, however, Nartam was back on his feet. Bilblox lunged at him, axe in hand, but Nartam deftly stepped out the way and used Bilblox's own momentum to push him forward. Bilblox tried to regain his balance, but his forward momentum was too strong. He exploded through the glass door and onto the balcony where only minutes before Naomi had been stranded.

It was really more of an observation deck than a balcony; there were no chairs or even a guard rail to enclose the space. Wisps of clouds blew past. Bilblox lay face down in a pile of glass. Blood was trickling out of his body in a quick stream. Nartam ran over to Bilblox's prone body and raised the axe above Bilblox's neck. Kiril ran over as well. There was no way out for either of them. Bilblox needed to buy some time.

"Bilblox," said Kiril sternly. "Give us the Pen."

"Have you lost your appetite for fun?" asked Nartam. "I think it would be far more memorable to simply chop of the fellow's hand – don't you?"

"No wait," gasped Bilblox. "I'll give you the Pen."

The wind on the balcony was blowing fiercely and Bilblox wasn't sure if Nartam even heard him.

"Then do it," ordered Nartam. He put his foot on Bilblox's chest.

"Give it to him," Kiril shouted at Bilblox. "And be quick about it."

Bilblox turned his blood-streaked face to one side and awkwardly maneuvered his two hands together. He used the thumb and the index finger on his left hand to probe and then to squeeze his right hand just beneath the base of the thumb. What happened next was so astounding, Nartam and Kiril couldn't help but gasp. The skin on Bilblox's hand began to bulge as if something jagged were trying to break its way out. Moments later, a silver point broke through the skin – without causing so much as a drop of blood to spill. Bilbox grabbed the point and, very carefully, pulled a silver

Pen out of his hand. As soon as the Pen was out, the skin on Bilblox's hand sealed itself again, leaving no trace of where it had opened – not even a small scar.

"Where? How did…" asked Nartam.

"The instructions were inside the Pen," gasped Bilblox. "It's all yours." He snapped his wrist, flicking the Pen across the balcony. It came to a rest lodged in the accumulated snow, just inches from the far edge. Nartam lunged for the Pen. With his incredible agility, he seemed to appear next to the Pen instantly. He held it up to the moonlight, as if transfixed, and studied it.

Kiril took a step toward Nartam, but Nartam saw this and held out his hand.

"Stay where you are!" he warned. "I want you to back off this balcony slowly, I'm not taking any chances."

Kiril was considering his next move, when he felt an angry presence next to him. It was Naomi, and she was staring with hatred at Nartam. He knew enough about her that she had an angry streak that clouded her judgment. If they ever made it out of this situation alive, she'd have to work on this. But for the time being, he could use it to his advantage. In fact, he suddenly understood exactly what he was destined to do.

"No one will bother you or your Pen," Kiril said soothingly. "But Bilblox is in terrible shape. Naomi, quickly, check on him. He needs pressure to stanch the bleeding."

This seemed to reassure Nartam and he turned back to looking at the Pen. What happened next was a moment that Kiril would play over and over in his mind for many years to come. As Naomi scampered toward Bilblox, Kiril shoved her roughly, causing her to stumble forward and to trip over Bilblox's prone body. By the time that Nartam saw what was happening it was too late for him to do anything. Naomi collided roughly into Nartam. Nartam lost his balance. His arms pinwheeled wildly and he lost his grasp on the Pen. It flew away from him with such force it almost seemed to be alive. Nartam roared. He fell backwards off the balcony and disappeared into the snow-filled air.

Although Nartam had taken the force of Naomi's fall, her momentum still took her over the edge. She tried to hold on but lost her grip. Bilblox saw this and lunged forwarded to save her – extending a massive hand and grabbing her by the leg. He then pulled Naomi backward with a ferocious yank. Naomi crumpled to the floor of the observation deck, sobbing. Kiril witnessed all of this impassively.

Naomi got up teetering and crawled over the broken glass towards Kiril. She was sobbing, but hatred shown in her eyes.

"Why did you do that?" she cried. "You shoved me... shoved me almost off... off the edge. ...I could have died."

"Yes," said Kiril softly, "I am afraid that's true."

"I thought you would protect me," she sobbed. "I thought you loved me."

"I did love you," said Kiril as he peered over the abyss into which Nartam had fallen. "And, for a time, I loved that man too."

For a long moment, there was no sound but that of the howling wind.

"I knew you'd come," said Bilblox finally. "I knew it."

For a moment, Kiril thought that Bilblox was talking to him, but it quickly became evident that Bilblox was looking past him – over his shoulder – toward someone else. Kiril spun around and there, standing in the doorway that led out onto the deck was Alfonso.

CHAPTER FIFTY
THE SHADOW TREE

Hill and Resuza quickly climbed up the Shadow Tree. It was one of the easier trees to climb, even though their hands and arms were soon covered with the oily sap it was excreting. The bark itself was quite rough and bumpy. It was also warm enough that an inch-thick fog clung to the bark. Hill had wanted to climb the Tree because he knew it was the one place Alfonso was sure to go. It also gave them a high vantage point to see what was about to unfold.

"What now?" asked Resuza.

"Wait and watch," said Hill, panting for breath. "And look for Alfonso."

There was a crash overhead and a large burning branch tumbled downward, spraying them with embers and ash. The branch missed them narrowly. They both looked away and used their arms to shield their eyes.

"That was close," said Resuza.

"Those fools up above us are burning branches," said Hill.

"Let me have a look," she told Hill. "I'll climb just a little ways and see if any of them are climbing down toward us."

Hill hesitated.

"It'll be more dangerous if they surprise us," said Resuza.

Hill nodded.

Resuza disappeared into the branches above. Hill walked further out along one of the major limbs. He went as far as he dared before it became too narrow. The branches were incredibly resistant to weight, as if made of steel, allowing Hill to sit down and survey the surrounding area while only a foot away from the tip of the branch. He could see nearly all of Dargora: the low slung slave and support buildings on the ground, the spindly pillars that reached up to the sky, and the ships that appeared to be floating through the air.

Hill shuddered from the cold, and lay flat against the branch in order to get some of the Tree's heat. He tried to think about what would happen next, and tried unsuccessfully to extract the piece of paper containing the prophecy from his jacket. No matter. He had committed it to memory: *A Perplexon will rejoice with friends in the dark of the chasm. He will then destroy the Tree by himself. A Perplexon will succeed, but he will also die.*

It was during this moment that something caught Hill's attention. A speck was descending from the largest floating ship, and was heading towards the Shadow Tree. The speck grew quickly until Hill could tell it was a wooden gondola swinging from a tarnished, charcoal-colored hot air balloon. It was a very strange sight. But what really caught Hill's attention was the person standing in the gondola and pointing towards the tree. It was Kiril and, standing next to him, was none other than Alfonso.

Alfonso had been reluctant to follow Kiril, but he had no other choice. Alfonso needed to get to the Shadow Tree as quickly as possible – in order to destroy it – and Kiril insisted that this was precisely what he wanted to do as well. Kiril also had a means of transport, a hot-air balloon, and this sealed the deal. So far the Dragoonya leader had delivered as promised. With Naomi's help, Kiril had expertly bandaged the most severe of Bilblox's wounds, and led them all down a series of staircases until they came to a large wooden platform that jutted out into the air. Tied up next to the edge was a large wooden gondola tied to a hot air balloon. They quickly boarded. Naomi and Bilblox lay on the floor while Kiril and Alfonso stood. Kiril expertly fired up the burners, untied the mooring ropes and minutes later, they were descending through the clouds and floating directly toward the Shadow Tree. By manipulating the burners and assessing the wind currents, the balloon descended on course.

The polar sunrise had begun and the bright orange orb that was the sun rose up from the horizon. Kiril grabbed his binocoulars and studied the ground below. At one point, he took a small mirror out from a pocket in his inner coat, and began fanning it back and fourth in a rhythmic fashion – so that it was reflecting the sunlight in a peculiar manner. He did this for several minutes and then from down below he was rewarded with a response, which came in the form of another flashing light. Apparently, someone on the ground also had a mirror and was responding.

Alfonso watched Kiril carefully.

"Don't bother," said Naomi. "It's a code that Kiril uses to send messages. I've been trying to figure it out for months." She said this with a certain amount of pride, even though she clearly wasn't privy to the communication.

"I guess he don't trust you either," whispered Bilblox.

"He doesn't trust anyone," said Naomi tightly.

"Here," said a voice from behind them. It was Bilblox. Bilblox unclenched a fist and, in his hand, was the Pen. He handed it to Alfonso.

"I knew you'd have it," said Alfonso. "It seems to find you."

Alfonso studied the Pen for a moment, rolling it back and forth in his hand, and then he nodded his head. In his other hand, he held a wooden stick. Alfonso spun the stick, so that the skinnier end was pointing upward, and used his finger to probe a small hole that was burrowed into the tip of the stick. He then inserted the Pen into the hole. It fit perfectly, as Alfonso suspected it would. There was a click and, instantly, the entire stick began to emit a faint silvery glow – the color of moonlight.

Bilblox, Kiril, and Naomi watched on in amazement.

"I figured you'd know what to do with it," said Bilblox finally.

All the while, they drew ever closer to the Shadow Tree. Individual branches came into focus. They were gnarled and twisted and the uppermost branches appeared to be moving – not the way that a tree's canopy sways in the wind – but the way a terrified animal struggles when trapped. Alfonso stared at it with an awful familiarity. This was the tree he had foreseen in the Hub, during their trek through the Fault Roads.

"Can you set me down on one of those big branches at the top?" he asked.

Kiril nodded.

"Then what?" asked Bilblox. Overcome by curiosity, he and Naomi were standing as well and looking down at the Shadow Tree. "We just leave you there? And what happens when all the soldiers have seen what you done? They'll tear you apart. No, that ain't much of a plan. Forget it. Let me come with you."

"Bilblox," said Alfonso firmly. "You've got to trust me."

Bilblox grimaced, but said nothing.

"It's time," said Kiril, "Are you ready?"

CHAPTER FIFTY-ONE
IN THE BRANCHES

When Alfonso landed on the Shadow Tree, the tree itself shivered violently; and then, as if in response, a
groundswell of angry cries resonated from the Dragoonya
soldiers encircling the tree below. They all lunged for the
tree at once and began climbing it, pushing and shoving
each other to get ahead. It was as if every single person who
had taken the ash was now heeding the tree's call in a great
rush to save it. Those already in the tree – the leaf cutters –
immediately stopped their work and began heading towards
Alfonso. From every direction they converged on the spot
where Alfonso was currently standing.

Alfonso climbed quickly, stopping on a few occasions
to hide from the leaf cutters, and within a few minutes he
had arrived at his final destination – the spot on the tree
where there was a large, gaping gash on the trunk. He held
his stick, whose end was affixed with the Pen, almost like a
bayonet. All he needed to do was plunge the weapon into
the tree and the tree would die. If it was this simple, why did
it have to be him? Alfonso had no idea.

"I'll never understand why people don't just act." This
conversational voice came from just behind Alfonso. He
whirled around and stared uncomprehendingly at a sixteen-
year-old of small stature with a cruel face. The teenage boy
was standing on the same branch as Alfonso only feet away.

"Did you think I was gone for good?" he asked, with a half smile. "Oh goodness, that would have been convenient I suppose. How precious. Such wishful thinking will always get you in trouble, Alfonso, don't you know that?"

"Nartam," replied Alfonso.

"Good to see you my dear, dear boy," said Nartam. "Now please step aside before I slice open your guts and let you bleed to death."

Alfonso felt the weight of the stick in his hands. He slouched his shoulders in apparent defeat and let the stick dangle loosely in his hands.

"How did you get here?" Alfonso asked.

"Well, at first I fell," said Nartam. "It was rather dreadful falling all that way and breaking my neck and my spine as well. But I am not so easily killed. The ash really is marvelous in that way. It makes me nearly immortal. So then I got on my feet and climbed. Care to hear more details?"

Alfonso could hear a great commotion both above him and below him. There were people in the tree – scores of them – and they were converging on him.

"Details?" asked Alfonso as calmly as he could.

"Ah, yes," said Nartam, "The details are always..."

At that moment, Alfonso concentrated to make his move – a twirling jump towards the gash, weapon extended. But before he even moved a foot, Nartam had tackled and pummeled him onto the branch with such ferocity that Alfonso's very breath choked within his throat.

"No, no, no my lovely child," said Nartam in the same conversational tone. "You'll have to do much, much better than that."

Nartam picked up the stick and held it up to take advantage of the first rays of morning light. At that moment, a sharp rock whistled towards his head and struck his left eye.

Nartam howled, dropped the stick and put his hand to his eye. It came away bloody. Alfonso took advantage of the situation to escape from being underneath Nartam's foot. He stood up, picked up the stick and with all the force he could muster, thrust it – with the pointy tip of the Pen acting like a spearhead – deep into Nartam's belly. It lodged there like an oversized arrow. The Dragoonya leader grunted in pain and fell to his knees.

Who had thrown the rock?

Alfonso looked up.

Resuza.

"Hurry!" she yelled.

Alfonso had never been so happy to see anyone in his entire life.

Resuza jumped down next to Alfonso and the two of them faced Nartam. The Dragoonya leader was looking down at the stick protruding from his belly. It looked like a fatal wound although oddly, he was smiling.

"Do not fret," he grunted. "All is well." Nartam grabbed the stick and held it tightly. He closed his eyes, focused, and the stick blew apart. Shards flew everywhere and the Pen, which had formed the tip of the stick, fell down through the branches and vanished below. Nartam's left eye and his gruesome stomach wound rapidly healed.

"No!" yelled Alfonso and flung himself at Nartam. Instead of avoiding Alfonso, Nartam gladly welcomed the blow. It seemed to have no effect. Nartam quickly counter-punched and Alfonso flew backwards, slamming into Resuza, and together they toppled off the branch and into the air below.

The wind pounded their faces as they plummeted downward. Alfonso clung to Resuza tight and tried to force himself into hypnogogia one last time. He focused of the pulsing sound of the wind in his ears. He relaxed his mind, he felt hypnogogia within his grasp, like a brightly-lit doorway at the end of a dark hallway. But he couldn't do it. He tried again, and again, and again. Time slowed down. He lost sense of where he was. The presence of Resuza was the only reason Alfonso kept struggling. He had not saved the world, but at least he could save her. He managed to enter hypnogogia for a second or so at a time and, on each occasion, he managed to slow their fall. As they neared the ground, Alfonso succumbed to his wounds and fell into unconsciousness. He and Resuza crashed into a powdery snow drift.

Resuza was the first to open her eyes. She discovered that she was lying on her side next to an old man with paper thin skin stretched tightly across his face and long strands of white hair that dotted his cheeks and chin. For that moment, everything seemed quiet. Resuza felt as if she was alone in the world, even though she heard soldiers approaching.

"Alfonso?" she whispered.

The old man cringed at the sound of Resuza's voice.

"I tried," he whispered. "I tried."

Chapter Fifty-Two
The Watch Repairman

Hill wondered why no one had noticed him. Then he realized that for once, being overlooked was an advantage. Apparently, neither Nartam, nor the Shadow Tree, nor anyone else could possibly imagine that an untalented, untrained Dormian could pose a threat. And yet, Hill had always been good in a pinch. His sleeping self was primitive but effective. If he could repair an incredibly complicated watch, how difficult could it be to repair a stick? And perhaps most importantly, he understood the prophecy properly; and it seemed he was the only one who did.

Hill climbed the tree slowly, taking his time. He had witnessed the fight between Alfonso and Nartam – it had occurred within earshot, in the branches overhead. He knew what had happened and he knew what he had to do. He was looking for one item in particular. It had fallen away during the fight, and Hill was reasonably sure it was lying somewhere nearby, caught by the thick web of gnarled branches. He looked methodically, and took advantage of a cloud-free sunrise. He climbed deliberately, stopping every few seconds to look in each and every crevice. He took his time and kept his calm.

And there it was.

The Foreseeing Pen was lying just where Hill had suspected it might be, in the branch just below where Alfonso and Nartam had been fighting. Hill walked carefully out along the branch until he picked up the Pen. After all these months of worrying to keep it safe, it was back again in his possession, and it would remain that way until the end. He carefully placed the Pen back in his pocket and continued to search.

Within a few minutes, he had gathered all the main pieces of Alfonso's weapon – the Foreseeing Pen and broken shards from the wooden stick. He sat down cross-legged on the branch where the fight had occurred, and laid all the pieces out in front of him. This time, it was easy to fall asleep. Hill felt strangely calm, and the warmth from the branch helped as well. Within a minute, Hill's eyes had closed and his hands immediately reached towards the items in front of him. And then the old watch repairer set to work.

Alfonso lay on his back, staring up at the tree. He and Resuza had landed a good distance from the actual base of the tree, but he could still see the higher branches. There were shouts coming from nearby. Feet were pounding the snowy ground. There wasn't much time left. Alfonso summoned all of his strength and sat up. Resuza, who was by his side, helped him.

"Uncle Hill," he gasped.

"Where?" asked Resuza.

"Look."

Together they looked and saw, halfway up the tree, the unmistakable figure of Hill with a long stick in his hand. "No," whispered Alfonso. "It won't work. It has to be..." Again he considered the words of the prophecy: *A Perplexon will succeed, but he will also die.*

A Perplexon. Meaning, Alfonso Perplexon.

A sudden realization came to him. The "A" wasn't an initial that stood for Alfonso. It was a figure of speech, as in a member of the Perplexon family – any Perplexon – even Hill.

Nartam stood on the ground, at the base of the tree, looking up its trunk. Something was wrong. He could feel it. His heart was pounding, his breathing was shallow, and despite the cold he was sweating. Moments later he felt his muscles go into spasms. It took all of his concentration to quell the spastic convulsions in his body. Then, once again, the tree began to shiver. It made no sense. *What had he missed?* Nartam looked up and, to his utter amazement, he saw someone on the branch he had just left. He stared closer.

"No!" Nartam roared.

Seconds later, the Dragoonya leader was racing back up the Shadow Tree at an astounding speed.

CHAPTER FIFTY-THREE
REUNITED

L eif stood next to Marta and waited anxiously. His feet were in chains, but his hands were free, and presently he was using them to hold a pair of binoculars up to his face. Marta stood next to him, unshackled; apparently, the Dragoonya did not see her as a threat, probably because she was now in the form of a girl. Leif was presently using the binoculars, searching the tree, frantically looking for his son, but what he saw instead was haggard middle-aged man that looked vaguely like himself. Was that Alfonso? After all, he was an ageling, perhaps he had morphed again. Somehow, however, Leif knew this wasn't his son. It was just instinct, but he would know his own son – at any age. Then slowly a thought formed in his head. At first it seemed impossible, but then he felt increasingly certain. He was staring at his older brother.

"Hill," whispered Leif. "My brother – he's alive!" Leif could see the Foreseeing Pen glint in the morning sun. Leif shook his head. "What is he doing?"

As if in response, Hill smiled. He seemed to be looking directly at Leif from across the distance. Leif knew that his brother couldn't actually see him, but for a moment it was as if he and Hill locked eyes – two brothers who hadn't seen each other in decades, and had each feared that the other was dead. *Was it possible that Hill saw him?* Leif screamed his brother's name. But it was too far away for Hill to hear Leif shouting and, even if he had, it would have had no effect. Hill was focused on one thing only. Hill was now holding a stick high over his head. Something shiny, which was attached to the end of the stick, gleamed in the morning light. It was the Pen. It had to be the Pen.

As he continued to watch the scene unfold through his binoculars, Leif noticed something moving up the tree – a teenage boy moving quickly, bearing down on Hill. Leif recalled hearing the Dragoonya soldiers talk about their king, a man named Nartam, who lived in the form of a boy. This had to be him. Nartam was almost upon him, when Hill took the stick and thrust it powerfully into the knothole on the side of the Shadow Tree.

Zig zagging lines – like cracks in a sheet of glass – formed across the surface of the knothole. The bark of the tree began to shatter into shards and the shards exploded outward like millions of pieces of shrapnel. Streaks of light seemed to surge up through the core of trunk; steam hissed through the bark; and those climbing the tree began to shriek horribly. The effect was terrible. Even the battle-hardened Forlorn Hope dropped to their knees. The ground shook so powerfully that those standing were thrown off their feet. Leif embraced Marta and together they dropped to the ground.

High up above in what remained of the tree, Nartam inhaled sharply – it was the last breath of a life that had spanned many centuries. And then the explosion came. The Shadow Tree and all those who ingested its ash – those who were clinging to its branches like babies cling to their mother – everyone disappeared in a blinding flash of white light. The sheer power of the Shadow Tree's explosion sent a shock wave through the land. The pillars holding up the

Dragoonya ships swayed and then toppled. The giant sailing vessels slammed into the frozen ground and shattered into splinters. The Shadow Tree consumed itself in a plume of wind, light and heat. The hoards of Dragoonya soldiers who had become addicted to the ash charged into the inferno like moths drawn to a flame. An invisible wave of explosive power rippled through the landscape, tore off the roof of the slave quarters and toppled many of the stone trees in the Petrified Forest. For hundreds and thousands of miles, the ground shook and everything alive was thrown roughly to the ground.

"Look!" shouted Marta. She was back on her feet. Leif struggled to stand up and, almost immediately, he saw what Marta was pointing at. Seconds later, Marta was running and screaming a name. *Alfonso! Alfonso! Alfonso!* Marta churned through the snow, her lungs bursting from the effort. She ran toward two figures lying in the snow. One was Alfonso and the other was Resuza. All around them snow had begun to fall, thicker and whiter than anyone could imagine. It was as if the earth itself wanted to scrub away any last trace of the Shadow Tree.

Alfonso lay flat on the ground in the form of a very old man. Marta and Resuza were both crouching over him. Marta put her head to his chest. His breathing was slow and ragged; and for several seconds, it stopped altogether. Marta heard footsteps behind her. She glanced backward briefly and saw a small gathering of people. Kiril, Konrad, Leif, Bilblox, and Naomi stood and watched silently. And there were soldiers too – the members of the Forlorn Hope – all of whom stood at the ready. Marta ignored them all and, instead, leaned down close to Alfonso's ear. She grabbed his hands. "Breathe," she whispered. "Like I taught you. Breathe in and out – focus on every second and then move on to the next one."

Alfonso did not move.

"Remember the armory in Jasber," said Marta. "Feel the heat, smell the smoke, put yourself back there." Tears streamed down her face. He still wasn't breathing and his lips started to turn blue. "You're fifteen years old," she whispered. "Fifteen years old." Slowly, his chest began to rise and fall again.

CHAPTER FIFTY-FOUR

ESCAPE

The convoy of sleds raced across the polar plain, continuing for several hours through a stark landscape of snow and ice, and everyone seemed to cherish the quiet and the solitude of the ride. Kiril's sled led the way. He rode with Konrad and Naomi. Behind them was another sled with Bilblox and Marta. Then there was a third sled carrying Leif, Alfonso, and Resuza. Behind them were dozens of others, manned by the members of the Forlorn Hope.

In his sled, Leif held his son tightly as Resuza steered the sled. Alfonso clutched his father's coat and briefly closed his eyes. Alfonso's thoughts drifted, inevitably, back to the Shadow Tree. Again and again he pictured his Uncle Hill, perched in the ghastly Tree, taking one last look around before he struck his blow. Hill must have known that he wasn't going to survive. Alfonso wondered whether, in those last moments, his uncle was fearful or calm. The memory was still so raw Alfonso couldn't stand to dwell on it, and yet he did – indeed he felt he had to and so he forced himself to recall every painful detail. After some time, Alfonso began to sob. He was thinking of Nance, and the emptiness that would invade the rest of her life. She and Hill had been so happy together, and it had only lasted for a few precious years. Finally, when he felt about as low as he ever had in his entire life, another memory of Hill sprang into his mind rather spontaneously. Alfonso recalled seeing his uncle, on his motorcycle, speeding up the icy driveway to their home in World's End, Minnesota. Hill had been fast asleep and muttering to himself. The image made Alfonso smile.

As he held his son, Leif was also thinking about Hill. Oddly, though, he was not despondent like Alfonso, who had known Hill much better than he had. Leif had spent so many years assuming he would never see his brother again; and, when he was held captive in the cabin near Jasber, Leif believed he would spend his entire life away from everybody that he loved. And yet here he was, with his son, headed home. This was Hill's doing; this was Hill's gift; and, more than anything else, Leif was grateful.

Eventually the convoy reached the edge of the Petrified Forest. The stone trees, many of which were coated with ice, stood ramrod straight – as forlorn and still as gravestones. Kiril brought his sled to a stop and a deep silence washed over the entire convoy. It was as if the Petrified Forest, in its vastness and its absence of life, was absorbing and squelching every conceivable sound.

"What now?" asked Leif finally, his voice shattering the silence.

"What now – *for you?*" asked Kiril.

"Yes," said Leif. "Where do we go from here?"

"You cross the forest here," explained Kiril. "I will give you a map that shows the route. It is the shortest and easiest crossing, by far. As long as you stay on the path and move quickly, you'll be fine. The fog wolves will not bother you if you enter with purpose and direction. Once you leave the forest, you simply head due south for ten days or so and eventually you'll hit the rail line that goes between the towns of Bovanenkovo and Obskaya. There is a train that runs along those tracks every few days taking workers out to the natural gas fields. If you can flag down the train, you'll be okay."

Kiril handed a map to Leif and then gestured toward a nearby sled. "There are rifles, food, and other provisions on that sled," said Kiril. "Take it."

Leif eyed the long convoy of other sleds, many of which contained huge, ash-colored burlap sacks. Leif wondered if they were filled with black ash from the Shadow Tree. The soldiers on the sleds were silent and stony faced, offering no clues.

"What about you?" asked Leif, skeptically. "Why aren't you coming with us?"

"We're going to take another crossing – farther to the west," said Kiril. "We're headed to a port on Baydaratskaya Bay and from there north into Kara Sea." He allowed the tiniest of smiles to curl across his lips.

"What's in the Kara Sea?" asked a small voice. It was Naomi. "What's out there?"

"Nothing of any interest. Only some very desolate lands, mostly ice-covered," said Kiril with a smile. "It's no place for you."

"So this is it?" asked Naomi.

Kiril nodded. With that, he snapped his whip and his sled dogs took off. Everyone watched the convoy head west, across the polar plain, until they vanished into the horizon. The wind began to kick up. Naomi walked over to where Resuza was standing. The two sisters stood together silently. Eventually, Resuza put her arm around Naomi's shoulder. Naomi didn't resist and Resuza felt grateful – it was a start.

EPILOGUE

It took several weeks for them to finally return to the place
they said they'd all meet up again: the Dlugosz lighthouse
on the Sea of Clouds. Misty and Clink had seen them from
a long way off, and by the time that Alfonso and his companions dragged their makeshift-rafts onto the rocky shore
and walked inside, an incredible feast had been laid out.
Braised lamb garnished with tarragon and mint, a thick beef
bourguignon stew, several different types of salt-encrusted
fish, and an entire banquet table groaning from end to end
with sweet pastries, puddings and pies. Second-Floor-Man
had enlisted the help of First-Floor-Man to create this excep-
tional feast. Long-held rules were broken, and aged cheeses
and wines were brought up from hidden storehouses. They
ate for three days straight and slept for two days after that.

They would have continued on feasting and sleeping,
but the lighthouse was only one step in the return journey.
It had become home for Misty and Clink, but the others
had homes of their own to return to. First off, however, they
had to tell Nance about Hill. After a long discussion, it was
decided that Misty would take one of the lighthouse's two
remaining airships and travel back to Somnos to tell Nance.
Leif and Alfonso would head back to World's End where
Judy was waiting for them. Marta explained that she would
take the chain and Pendant, which the Abbot had given her,

and burn them – thus summoning the monks who would fetch her and take her back to Jasber. Bilblox would, of course, head home to Fort Krasnik and – for the time being at least – Resuza and Naomi would go with him. "The good news is that I'm richer than a king," Bilblox told the sisters. "I got a giant house that could use some feminine touches. You're both welcome to stay with me as long as you'd like – or until you think of some place you'd rather be."

The evening before they all left the lighthouse, Leif and Alfonso wrote separate letters to Nance, talking about Hill and what he had meant to them. They both promised they'd visit Somnos someday. Afterwards, Leif then went to bed, but Alfonso had one more thing to do. Just like the first time many months ago, when they had first arrived at the lighthouse, Alfonso snuck over to Resuza's room. She was awake and waiting for him. They hardly spoke and, instead, sat together and listened to the sound of the waves crashing below.

A tear ran down Resuza's cheek.

"I don't know if we'll see each other ever again," she said.

"I do," said Alfonso.

"What secrets are you keeping from me?" asked Resuza, wiping away her tear and smiling.

"Whenever I morph, I have these memories – but they're memories from the life I haven't yet lived," he explained.

"You mean like visions of the future?"

"Kind of," he replied.

"And?"

"I'll be seeing you again," said Alfonso with a wink. "Quite a bit of you I think."

Resuza smiled and squeezed his hand.

Leif and Alfonso walked side by side along an empty gravel road. It was mid-afternoon, and the springtime sun was strong enough that both felt comfortable without coats. The road was narrow and bordered on both sides by a mature pine forest. Birds chirped and called to each other from the treetops, providing a cheerful soundtrack to their journey.

Father and son walked along in a comfortable silence. They looked tired but relaxed, as if they were coming home after running a marathon. In a sense, this was spot-on.

This was especially true for Leif, who had unexpectedly vanished from World's End, Minnesota a decade ago. He had been forced to obey the strict orders of the Founding Tree of Jasber, and then once successful, he had been forced by the Jasberians to stay in a lonely cottage to live out the rest of his days. And finally he and Alfonso had heeded the call to destroy the Shadow Tree. Now at last, all that needed doing was done – or so it seemed. Or perhaps the only force stronger than the pull of a Founding Tree was the protective bond between Great Sleepers from the same family. Whatever the reason, Leif and Alfonso were now walking together, tired but happy, along this beautiful forest road.

"Will you stay a teenager?" asked Leif finally. "I'm mean, you're free to do what you like – but, I guess what I am asking is, can you control your body so that you look your true age?" Leif sighed heavily, as if the question had been weighing on him, and the mere act of asking it was a relief.

"Yes," said Alfonso with a smile. "I think I can – thanks to Marta."

"I'm glad," said Leif, with a somber nod of his head. "People might react strangely, you know, if they saw you morphing – that's all."

"I know," said Alfonso with a smile. "But listen, dad, you don't have to worry about me. I'm going to be fine. You never give me enough credit."

"That's not true," said Leif. "You're a remarkable young man and, the truth is, you're stronger than I am in many ways. It's hard being a parent, Alfonso, you'll see some day, you just worry all of the time. And you've already been through so much, I just want it all to be over. I want everything to be right for you – that's all."

"I know dad," said Alfonso, as he put his arm around his father and squeezed his shoulder. "I know."

Leif smiled, but said nothing.

"Look!" said Alfonso.

Leif followed Alfonso's gaze, and saw in the distance a slender gate barring the road.

Leif smiled. "At last."

They quickened their pace and within a few minutes had arrived at the gate. Next to it was a modest blue-and-brown sign that said "U.S. – Canada Border. Please present yourself to the nearest manned border crossing."

"It's a new sign," Leif remarked. "Very nice."

He veered into the woods, followed closely by Alfonso. Without discussing it, they knew their destination by heart, as if it was imprinted in their veins. It was a moss-covered bluff, a little alcove surrounded by old growth forest that provided a wide-lens view of their little part of the world. They had been coming there – he and Alfonso – ever since Alfonso was several months old and strong enough to hold his head up without support. It was their place to watch the world cycle through its seasons, in snow and rain, in the morning and at night.

Alfonso lagged behind and by the time he had reached the bluff, Leif was already there, staring at the landscape before him. The terrain was unbroken boreal forest, tall pine and birch trees. Directly below lay the four-hundred acre Lake Witekkon – a marvel of glacier scrubbed pristine water. And on the other side of the lake sat the cluster of houses that made up World's End, Minnesota.

Leif staggered backwards. Alfonso quickly grabbed and steadied him.

"Dad – you OK?" he asked.

Leif said nothing, but then he slowly nodded.

"I'm fine," he replied, his voice choking. Leif had thought about this scene – on his favorite bluff overlooking Lake Witekkon – for so many years it seemed impossible to imagine that he was now actually here, instead of just dreaming. He stood by himself and looked at Alfonso.

"I'm not dreaming," he said.

"No," replied Alfonso softly. "You're not – and neither am I."

They stood there silently for several minutes, and listened to the wind blow through the trees. During all those years away from World's End, the memory of this exact place had sustained him. This place, and his family.

They walked along the forest road as it wound its way down to Lake Witekkon. Leif looked at his watch, but realized it had stopped working several weeks ago.

"When we spoke to your mother, she knew we were coming home today? I'm not confused, am I?"

Alfonso smiled. "No – this is the day."

They had called Judy once they had arrived in North America, despite their fears that the revelation that Leif was alive, and coming home with Alfonso, would be too much of a sudden shock. It was better to call, they reasoned, then showing up unannounced in World's End. Leif said he wouldn't allow her to spend one more moment believing that her husband

and son were dead. He called her one afternoon, just before they were about to leave. What he said to her, and how she replied, were secrets that Leif would carry with him and treasure to the end of his days. Alfonso remembered back to the last conversation he had with his mother, when he was in the Twin Otter headed for Somnos. He hoped she had forgiven him, but he had no idea what to expect. Only his Dad had spoken with her. Of course, Judy had offered to pick the two of them up at the bus stop – at a lonely crossroads a few miles back – but Leif had been adamant that he wanted to walk the last leg of the trip, on his own two feet, just him and his son.

They neared the shoreline of Lake Witekkon, in an area of ore-streaked boulders and resilient pine trees that had wound their roots around them. A deep baying call sounded from the forest and seconds later, an enormous wolf bounded out and ran to the lake. The wolf ignored Leif and Alfonso, jumped in, and began happily paddling around in the icy waters.

It was Korgu, their companion over many hard months. When they had left the lighthouse on the Sea of Clouds, Alfonso was steeling himself to say goodbye to the wolf, but Bilblox surprised him yet again.

"You're the closest thing I ever had to a true brother," Bilblox had said as he picked up Alfonso in a massive hug. "By givin' you Korgu, I'm ensurin' that you stay safe. She's the protective sort, and when she's with you I breathe easy. That's the honest truth."

And so Korgu joined them on the Canadian Express train that began in the arctic foothills near Fort Krasnik and passed across the boreal shield forest. She was in her element here, in the remote woods of the Canadian-U.S. border. The forests filled with her calls, usually answered by the many gray wolves that roamed the area.

By the time they reached the driveway that led to their cottage, the sun had risen to its highest point in the sky and had just begun its slow journey to the west. Butterflies and bees picked their way through the many wildflowers that lined the driveway, and hearty grasshoppers contemplated their next jump while holding onto swaying cattails. Alfonso's legs and arms felt like rubber, as if they couldn't decide between stopping and sprinting. He vowed to remember every split-second of what was about to occur.

They both paused in the driveway as the cottage came into view. Leif sternly told himself to get a grip. It would do no one any good for him to start blubbering at this moment. Up ahead, a door slammed.

Judy appeared at the top of the driveway. She stared at both of them with wide eyes. Her arms trembled, then her legs. Her shoulders dropped suddenly, and she fell to the ground. This broke the spell. Leif and Alfonso dashed up the driveway, with Korgu right behind them. Father and son helped Judy sit up and then all three hugged each other fiercely as they sat on the driveway. They cried and cried, faces against each other so that their tears ran together to moisten the dust of the driveway. No words were spoken – none were needed.

"Come on inside," said Judy finally. "Supper is waiting."